Applause for the Crime of Fashion Mysteries

"Skewers Washington with style." (bestselling author Elaine Viets)
"Devilishly funny... Lacey is intelligent, insightful and spunky... thoroughly likable." (*The Sun,* Bremerton, WA)
"Laced with wicked wit." (SouthCoastToday.com)
"Byerrum spins a mystery out of (very luxurious) whole cloth with the best of them." (Chick Lit Books)
"Fun and witty... with a great female sleuth." (Fresh Fiction)
"A load of stylish fun." (Scripps Howard News Service)

Veiled Revenge
"Former D.C. reporter Byerrum continues to highlight the city she obviously loves and reveals the true power of good fashion. An intriguing plot, fun but never too insane characters, and a likable and admirable heroine all combine to create a charming and well-crafted mystery." (Kings River Life Magazine)
"Ellen Byerrum's Crimes of Fashion series is always well-written, entertaining, and stylish. This one has lots of personal drama, appearances by many favorite series characters, and fashion tips for weddings." (More Than a Review)
"Like fine wine that gets better with age, *Veiled Revenge* is the best book yet in this fabulous series and I can't wait to see where Lacey and her fashion-sense take us." (Dru's Book Musings)

Death on Heels
"Terrific... a fabulous Crime of Fashion Mystery." (Genre Go Round Reviews)
"Such a fun story... I loved the touch that Lacey was a reporter trying to track down a murderer, but could always be counted on for her fashion-forward thinking as well... If you haven't yet picked up a Lacey Smithsonian novel, I suggest you do!" (Chick Lit+)
"[A] fast-paced, fun story... Lacey is a character that I instantly fell in love with." (Turning the Pages)

Shot Through Velvet
"First-rate... a serious look at the decline of the U.S. textile and newspaper industries provides much food for thought." (*Publishers Weekly,* starred review)
"Great fun, with lots of interesting tidbits about the history of the U.S. fashion industry." (*Suspense Magazine)*
"A thoughtful mystery with an energetic, very likable heroine that will attract new readers to this established series." (The Mystery Reader)

D1572199

Armed and Glamorous

"Whether readers are fashion divas or hopelessly fashion-challenged, there's a lot to like about being *Armed and Glamorous.*" (BookPleasures.com)

"Fans will relish *Armed and Glamorous*, a cozy starring a fashionable trench coat, essential killer heels, and designer whipping pearls." (*Midwest Book Review*)

Grave Apparel

"A truly intriguing mystery." (Armchair Reader)

"Fun and enjoyable... Lacey's a likeable, sassy, and savvy heroine, and the Washington, D.C., setting is a plus." (The Romance Readers Connection)

"Wonderful." (Gumshoe)

Raiders of the Lost Corset

"A hilarious crime caper... Readers will find themselves laughing out loud... Ellen Byerrum has a hit series on her hands." (The Best Reviews)

"I love this series. Lacey is such a wonderful character... The plot has many twists and turns to keep you turning the pages to discover the truth. I highly recommend this book and series." (Spinetingler Magazine)

"Wow. A simplistic word but one that describes this book perfectly. I loved it! I could not put it down!... Lacey is a scream and she's not nearly as wild and funny as some of her friends... I loved everything about the book from the characters to the plot to the fast-paced and witty writing." (Roundtable Reviews)

Hostile Makeover (also a Lifetime Movie)

"Byerrum pulls another superlative Crime of Fashion out of her vintage cloche." (Chick Lit Books)

"The read is as smooth as fine-grade cashmere." (*Publishers Weekly*)

"Totally delightful... a fun and witty read." (Fresh Fiction)

Designer Knockoff

"Clever wordplay, snappy patter, and intriguing clues make this politics-meets-high-fashion whodunit a cut above the ordinary." (*Romantic Times*)

"A very talented writer with an offbeat sense of humor." (The Best Reviews)

Killer Hair (also a Lifetime Movie)

"Peppered with girlfriends you'd love to have, romance you can't resist, and Beltway insider insights you've got to read... adds a crazy twist to the concept of 'capital murder.'" (Sarah Strohmeyer, Agatha Award-winner)

"A sharp murder plot, entertaining fashion commentary, and gutsy characters." (Nancy J. Cohen, author of the Bad Hair Day mysteries)

Lethal Black Dress

A CRIME OF FASHION MYSTERY

Ellen Byerrum

Lethal Black Dress Press

Published by Lethal Black Dress Press

Follow Ellen Byerrum online at
www.ellenbyerrum.com

Books by Ellen Byerrum

The Crime of Fashion Mysteries
Killer Hair
Designer Knockoff
Hostile Makeover
Raiders of the Lost Corset
Grave Apparel
Armed and Glamorous
Shot Through Velvet
Death on Heels
Veiled Revenge
Lethal Black Dress

The Bresette Twins Series
The Children Didn't See Anything

Plays by Ellen Byerrum, writing as Eliot Byerrum
(published by Samuel French, Inc.)
A Christmas Cactus
Gumshoe Rendezvous

ACKNOWLEDGMENTS

People sometimes offer writers ideas they think we should write about. My standard answer is, "Thanks, but I have so many ideas of my own, I'll never get to them all. So why don't you write that one yourself?"

But in the case of *Lethal Black Dress,* my brother James Byerrum gave me a great suggestion which I was happy to make my own. That's the wonderful thing about family: You can swap trade secrets. Thank you, Jim. I also bothered my sister Diane Byerrum Yeoman, former chemistry major, with endless questions in her fields of expertise. Thank you, Diane.

I've been fortunate to attend three White House Correspondents' Dinners, and I've always thought: What a fabulous location for a mystery! How could one possibly arrange a murder at the most secure, well-guarded and glitziest event in the Nation's Capital? This was my chance to do just that. My thanks to my charming news sources who were my escorts at this uniquely D.C. extravaganza.

Working as a print reporter in Washington, D.C., I frequently observed the television media in action. Certain elements in this book are drawn from that experience. For additional insights into the broadcast field, I am indebted to journalists Dinah Zeiger and John Henrehan. I'm also grateful to my friend Lloyd Rose, Washington theatrical eminence, for inspiration and trusted theatrical guidance.

As always, if any errors of fact are to be found in these pages, please consider them all *fiction.*

Many thanks to all my Sisters in Crime, in particular, Beth Wasson and Cathy Pickens. Your support has meant the world to me, particularly on this book! I am so grateful. My books wouldn't happen without friends and fellow mystery writers, especially the invaluable Rosemary Stevens, who has always listened to me sympathetically and offered sound advice. My humble thanks.

I am indebted to artist Craig White, whose elegant cover illustration for this book carries on the smart, sassy look he created for the series, and that my readers and I love.

And lastly, to my husband Bob Williams. I simply wouldn't have been able to make it to the finish line on *Lethal Black Dress* without his encouragement and moral support, not to mention his editing, proofreading, and other technical expertise (and affordable rates).

Chapter 1

IT WAS A SEA OF BLACK. A seething, humming hive of thousands of Washingtonians, wearing their idea of formal evening dress. Against this surging mass of black-tie uniformity, one woman alone took a stand for—*color.*

Is this a convention of funeral directors? Or the press's biggest black-tie bash of the year? Lacey Smithsonian wondered with a sigh. *Black, the obvious choice. Black, the safe choice. Black, the inevitable choice, in every direction. At least there will be no funeral tonight,* she consoled herself.

They wore black. Lacey wore blue, the color of optimism. She, at least, was not guilty of dressing in the dark.

The evening might supply plenty of crimes of fashion to write about, but no actual crimes of violence. Everyone would go home safely tonight. Lacey couldn't always make that claim when she covered the fashion beat for *The Eye Street Observer,* but the White House Correspondents' Dinner was surely the most securely guarded event in Washington, D.C. After all, the President of the United States would be in attendance, along with the Secret Service and practically every metal detector in the Nation's Capital.

In the meantime, style scribe Lacey Smithsonian was taking mental notes on the evening wear of the Fourth Estate. Even though she wasn't there on assignment, she could always use more fashion faux pas for her Crimes of Fashion and Fashion Bites columns. As cameras flashed all around her in the hope she might be a celebrity, she turned and smiled. *Be a celebrity—or just look like one!*

The legendary White House Correspondent's Dinner was always held on the first Saturday in May at the Washington Hilton in Dupont Circle. Springtime in the Capital City was generally pleasant, with mild temperatures, but tonight was windswept, rain-soaked, and chilly.

Outside in the downpour, protesters against "the liberal media bias" were splashing around on street corners, the inflammatory messages on their signs dissolving in the mist. They may also have been angry because they were not invited inside the Hilton, where their journalistic adversaries were warm and comfy.

At the Connecticut Avenue lobby entrance, people were brushing rain off their black clothes and shaking water off black umbrellas. The attendees looked damp and frazzled, a little less polished than when they'd left home in their black limos and Lincoln Town Cars.

Lacey had anticipated this evening for a long time. A select few reporters at *The Eye* were allowed to attend the Correspondent's Dinner every year as a reward for excelling at their beats, and this year, Lacey was among them. She was curious to see how her fellow reporters would dress to the nines. Turned out, they didn't. *Maybe to the sixes and sevens.* The Washington media might be fearless in reporting the news, but they tended to be timid in their attire. Most of the outfits that crossed Lacey's path were, sad to say, merely boring. The completely wrongheaded outfits were far more fun to watch.

As usual, the Prematurely Serious ruled. In the most serious city in the nation, caring about what you wore and how you presented yourself to the world was considered a non-serious pursuit. Nowhere in the world were journalists more self-consciously serious, and it showed that night.

Reporters: the know-it-alls who don't know what to wear.

"So whatcha think about all these swells?" Detective Broadway Lamont rumbled at her elbow.

"Swells isn't the word I'd choose." She stifled a laugh. "Though swelled heads might do."

"Got that right. Positive epidemic of swollen egos in this city. Not like you and me."

The homicide detective at her side was her "source date" for the evening. The White House Correspondents' Dinner was full of odd couples: reporters and their sources. The longstanding rule for this event was that members of the White House press corps brought a news source, of either sex. *Or no sex at all.* Even though the media were not supposed to reward their sources, or expect rewards for their work, everyone knew attending the Correspondents' Dinner was one of the biggest rewards in Washington journalism. For the heavy hitters in the media, any random newsworthy celebrity of the moment would do for a date, the splashier or trashier the better. Some years it might be a Kim "Trashian" Kardashian. *Anything to raise eyebrows.* To their credit, *The Eye*'s reporters didn't have the clout to draw any tarnished movie or reality TV stars. They were stuck with real sources.

Lacey and Lamont wandered through the crowd, through the security checkpoints (where all the guards seemed to be Lamont's buddies), and down the escalators to the lower level where the pre-dinner cocktail parties were held, eyes peeled for notable or quotable guests. She would have loved to have her fiancé Vic Donovan at her side, but he wasn't exactly a "news source." Detective Broadway Lamont, on the other hand, was the most interesting and consistently helpful "official" source she had. He told her once that despite being black and being named Broadway, he did not sing or dance. He could, however, intimidate everyone in his path. Especially when he put his head down and glared, like a bull right before it charged. He also looked very impressive in evening wear. And sometimes a kilt, too, Lacey remembered.

In general, Lamont was not a fan of reporters. But he and Lacey had forged a cordial working relationship over several murders. He investigated them. She wrote about their fashion angles, and occasionally managed to make her own unique investigative contributions.

"Fashion clues," she called them. Lamont called it her "high-heeled hoodoo" and "fashion voodoo." He claimed to find her ability amusing, when he acknowledged it existed.

"So what do you think of that?" He indicated a tiny, ancient woman with a cloud of white hair. "The old dame? Looks like she knocked over a jewelry store? Ain't that one of your Crimes of Fashion?"

Lacey followed his gaze. He'd focused on Pepper Valencia, reigning grand dame of the Capitol press corps. The elderly lady was in a floor-length black velvet gown with a high neck and long sleeves. Over it, she wore what appeared to be the entire contents of a vein of turquoise—huge turquoise and silver bracelets, long turquoise earrings, a thick belt of silver and turquoise, and a heavy squash blossom necklace. It was a mystery how Pepper could stand up straight and carry the load. Yet she was erect as a flagpole and seemed to be having a wonderful time.

"Her?" Lacey said. "Oh, *her*. Oh no. She gets a pass."

"A pass? What for? She's got a rock for every wrinkle."

"And a year for every rock. She's nearly ninety and Pepper Valencia didn't get to be the elder stateswoman of the Washington press corps by being a shy wallflower."

"Convince me." Lamont didn't look impressed.

"Pepper's survived decades of Presidents and Congresses. She makes no excuses. She tells it like it is and she wears whatever she pleases. But it works. See how she stands out in this crowd, even though she's all of five-foot-nothing? She is rocking all that turquoise as if she owned the mine. I think she's fabulous."

"Fabulous, huh?"

"Yes. Besides, I don't pick on tough little old ladies. They scare me."

He chuckled, but his attention span was short. His head was already swiveling in the direction of an extremely tight purple dress trying to make its way down the corridor. Barely contained inside the grape-colored sheath was one of this year's hot television actresses and most of her ample curves. Her dress was inappropriately short and loud, and her white blond hair was an apparent homage to Marilyn Monroe, though that's where the resemblance ended.

Lacey observed that the curse of Lycra did not afflict only the stars. It exerted its evil stranglehold even on the posteriors of the press. Many Fourth Estate females were wearing dresses that were long, black, and stretched as tight as a coat of paint. It was only the occasional rebel that provided a welcome shock of color in this somber and ill-dressed crowd, like bits of brightly wrapped candy among the licorice.

Some of the "candy," however, was well past its sell-by date, Lacey decided, eyeing an out-of-date floral number with puffy sleeves and a full skirt, perhaps once a prom gown or a bridesmaid dress. Its occupant was out to prove that, indeed, she could rock that frock again, despite the fact she should not—and certainly not to the Correspondents' Dinner.

The men, of course, wore black tuxedos, most of them rented and many of them ill-fitted. They grumbled about procuring the requisite black tie attire for the dinner, while at the same time admiring their spiffed-up reflections in every shiny surface.

Lacey's escort, Broadway Lamont, appeared at his most distinguished, in a black shawl collar tuxedo, crisp white shirt, and traditional black bow tie and cummerbund. It fit him perfectly, a major tailoring accomplishment on his massive frame.

"Snappy tux, Broadway," she remarked to the big man at her side.

"I own it, too," Lamont rumbled with a grin. "Try renting a tux in my size some time. You're looking pretty snappy tonight yourself."

"I'll take that as a compliment."

"You don't look like someone died, at least." He had noticed the monochrome color palette too. "That one of your fancy, schmancy, vintagey things?"

"Yes, it is. Fancy *and* schmancy."

Lacey always followed a different fashion drummer. She had chosen color, and her most treasured vintage gown. Heads turned when Lacey strolled by in her Gloria Adams original. The shimmering blue flattered her pale skin and enhanced her blue-green eyes.

The dress was new, yet old: timeless, a recent recreation of a vintage design. The designer, Gloria Adams, who disappeared during World War II, was an old friend of Lacey's Great-aunt Mimi. Lacey found a packet of letters and the Adams pattern in Mimi's trunk, filled with vintage materials and patterns and partially sewn outfits. The finished gown flirted with the limits of the infamous Rule L-85, the US government clothing regulations instituted during the war to save fabric for the troops. But the design and the delight were in the details.

Gloria never saw the dress made, but she had specified silk in Morning Glory Blue, the color of those early-morning blossoms. A small sample of blue fabric was found attached to the pattern. Lacey's friends located a matching silk and shepherded the dress into reality for another event. The bodice was low but not scandalous, and it featured a sparkling beaded midriff with a pattern of shooting stars. The designer original fit Lacey like a glove, as if it had been intended for her all along. A hug from a different era, it was a big beautiful fantasy of a dress. When she slipped it on before the dinner, she had forgotten how beautiful it looked. She silently thanked both women, Gloria and her aunt, as if they were guardian angels. Lacey took the dress and the silk as gifts from a time, and a woman, long past.

Despite her excitement at simply being there, Lacey felt a hazy, oppressive atmosphere in the crowded Hilton. Perhaps it was due to the one-hundred-percent rain outside, and the ninety-percent humidity inside. The cocktail parties were held inside small suites, each with two doors, one to the inside hallway, and the other leading to the patio outdoors. That patio should have been full of partygoers as well, but the torrents of rain kept them inside. Tonight, the only people outside, hugging the walls to keep out of the spray, were the smokers. If the rain didn't keep Lacey inside, the pollution surely would.

A lot of women's hair was exploding into frizz in the humidity. Lacey's honey-blond Rita Hayworth waves were firmly under control, thanks to a tanker-truck portion of "product." But the oppressive feeling lingered.

"Uh oh, here comes trouble." Detective Lamont barely lifted his chin in the direction of the intruder. "Courtney Wallace. Channel One News. Glossy piece of pretty poison. You know her?"

Lacey's eyes followed his chin. "I thought she was too deeply disgraced to cover an event like this. I wonder who her latest victim is."

They both stared at the chirpy blond broadcast news reporter sashaying her way across the room. Although calling Courtney Wallace a *reporter* was too kind, Lacey thought. Wallace was a prepackaged TV personality on Channel One (their slogan: "One For All"). She had large green eyes, a wide mouth with gleaming Chiclet teeth and chiseled features. Her golden hair was long, thick, and wavy. She was the girl next door gone rogue, wielding a microphone like a cudgel.

Wallace's claim to fame was that she had won an Emmy for some now-forgotten, hidden-camera "gotcha" story. Forgotten, that is, by everyone except Courtney, who mentioned it at the drop of a hat. People ducked out of her way and dodged her microphone. The yellow-haired talking head had already made an enemy of Broadway Lamont, capturing an off-the-record comment with a hidden microphone and then misquoting him out of context.

Yet here she was, covering the dinner with live updates and a cameraman. No doubt hoping for a soupçon of scandal.

Infamous for poaching other reporters' stories, Courtney had also been treading on Lacey's fashion turf. Her ongoing video feature on "Vintage Through the Decades" was a direct steal from Smithsonian's Crime of Fashion columns. For the past week, Courtney had been reporting nightly on local shops where Washingtonians could inject some creativity into their wardrobes with great vintage pieces and looks.

During each short segment, she showed off a vintage outfit of her own: Courtney sporting a classic sweater set from the Thirties, Courtney shimmying in a "lampshade" dress from the Fifties. This accomplished two goals: producing a story and promoting herself. But from what Lacey had seen, she showed no real understanding of her outfits or their context, or that the clothes people wore revealed a multitude of stories, attitudes, and histories. Courtney Wallace was just playing dress-up for the camera.

She set Lacey's teeth on edge.

Lamont's height gave him a better view. "Don't look now, but I think she's headed this way. Looks like someone poked her with a cattle prod."

Courtney veered from left to right and back again, searching for prey. A congressman spotted her and ducked out the door to the patio. He obviously preferred the rain and polluters to an impromptu interview.

"Let's get out of range," Lacey said. It was easier said than done. She and Lamont were stuck in one of the many pre-dinner cocktail parties in the tiny reception suites, a labyrinth of congested spaces. There was barely room to turn around. Before Lacey could escape, a microphone was thrust in her face.

She wouldn't dare, Lacey thought, but Courtney did dare. There was a strange gleam in her eyes.

"Well, Lacey Smithsonian! And Detective Broadway Lamont! I'm sure there's a story here," she said into her handheld microphone. A clip-on might have spoiled the bodice of her black gown. "The two of you! Together! Say hello to our viewers on Channel One!"

Lamont glowered at her and she took a step back. Wallace turned smoothly to his companion.

"Lacey Smithsonian, style maven for *The Eye*." Courtney advanced on her. She towered over Lacey in her sky-high heels. "Talk to me about your dress. It's obviously a vintage piece. Do tell our viewers all about it!"

"No. Not on camera, and not for the record." Lacey backed away from her, not just because Courtney was in her face, but because her perfume was so strong. It was overpowering and sickly-sweetish, and Lacey thought she detected a whiff of garlic, though that seemed unlikely. *What reporter,* she thought, *even a bad one, would load up on garlic to get up in people's faces with a microphone?*

"It will just take a second, Lacey." Courtney's voice was sing-songy. Her cameraman was edging in close. "After all, you're Washington's most famous vintage fashion expert, right?"

Lacey covered the microphone with her freshly manicured hand. "I've already written extensively about this Gloria Adams original in *The Eye Street Observer*. And no means no."

Courtney showed a lot of teeth in an approximation of a smile. "I'm sure most people didn't see your little story. You haven't won an Emmy, have you?"

"Do you expect to win an Emmy for fashion reporting? I must change careers immediately."

"You can joke, but my viewers will have a chance to see that fabulous dress of yours on Channel One News, One For All. No one reads newspapers anymore."

"That's too bad, because there's so much that can't be explained in a ten-second news bite," Lacey said. "Or is it five seconds now, for the attention-span impaired?"

"You'd be surprised at how long a few seconds can be."

Not at the moment. The cameraman readied his lens. Lacey caught his eye. She shook her head. He froze. Lacey switched tactics. She suspected Courtney would much rather talk about herself anyway.

"Courtney, why don't you tell me about your own vintage dress? Forties, right?"

"My dress?" Wallace gestured to the stunning black gown she wore and smiled, as if for an audience of Emmy judges. "Fabulous, isn't it? It's early twentieth century. This snazzy number will be the culmination of my series on vintage fashion. Perhaps you've seen my features on Channel One?" A flash of green lining showed through the gown's artistic cutouts as she gave a half spin for the camera. They looked like symbols from the suits in a deck of cards, hearts, diamonds, clubs, and spades.

"Perhaps. But I wouldn't have to see it. I've already written the stories you cribbed your series from." *Do not get into a snark fight with this shark,* she warned herself.

"But I'm the one on TV. I'm just demonstrating that some styles are timeless and can go anywhere. Like this lovely black satin dress. And yours." Courtney gestured to the cameraman to continue, but Lacey froze him with another Look.

"Your dress is a great find, Courtney. Really beautiful. However, I don't want to be on camera. I'm a print reporter, not a broadcast, ah, personality."

Wallace's expression changed. Her eyes narrowed. Her lips pressed together in a tight line. "All right. Don't cooperate. You don't own vintage and you don't own fashion. And just remember, Lacey Smithsonian, ideas are not copyrightable." She spat the words.

"That makes it all right to copy me? As if you had ideas in the first place?"

"If you don't want to go on camera, I still have footage of your dress for the background. I don't need your help and don't expect any from me."

Meow. Lacey smiled back at her. "Have a nice evening, Courtney."

The woman spun away with a flounce. "Come on, Eric. I see that actress from that awful movie, what's her name again? Move your butt!"

Eric the cameraman seemed to be used to this treatment. "What actress? What movie? Did she take her clothes off?" He winked at Lacey and shouldered his camera.

They went in search of the elusive actress from the bad movie. This dinner might be in honor of the Fourth Estate, but the celebrity guests would be a bigger draw on the eleven o'clock news. Lacey and Lamont watched them go, Courtney Wallace in a flurry of anger and a rustle of silk and satin in green and black.

"You mean you media types aren't all the best of friends?" Lamont muttered. "Never would have guessed."

"Nobody likes a story thief," Lacey said. "I'm just glad she's on the least-watched channel."

"Didn't think you cared about the fashion beat." He lifted two glasses of champagne from the tray of a passing waiter and handed her one. "You complain about it enough. You actually worry that Wallace woman's been riding your coattails?"

"I do complain about my beat, it sucks sometimes, but it's mine. And as far as I'm concerned, Courtney Wallace can kiss my coattails." She saluted him with the champagne flute. "Besides, you got it right the first time: A piece of pretty poison."

Chapter 2

L ACEY CAST A BACKWARDS GLANCE and caught the whole silhouette of Courtney's stunning dress. She paused. Something about that inky black gown struck her as very familiar. What was it?

The details were clearly vintage, but there was more to it than that. It was classic, even, Lacey realized, iconic. The light bulb went on. It looked like a copy of the gown worn in the famous "Madame X" portrait by John Singer Sargent. But the so-called Madame X, the woman in the portrait, looked nothing like this brash, blond, twenty-first-century newswoman. The portrait's model was a striking brunette, pictured with her hair pulled up and off her face. Her profile was haughty and sharp and she had eerily white skin, like a corpse. The stunning dress and the scandalous portrait had been nothing but bad luck for her.

"I know that dress," Lacey said under her breath.

"Did you say you *know* that dress?" Lamont was nonplussed. "Excuse me, of *course* you know that dress. Say what?"

"Madame X. Wallace's dress is a duplicate. Almost. There are a few changes, like the lining and the cut-outs. But it's so close, it must be a deliberate copy."

"Madame who? This more of that clothing voodoo you're always throwing out?"

Lacey shrugged. "Madame X. And I'm just observing. I'm talking about a famous painting by John Singer Sargent."

The original Madame X gown incorporated velvet and satin with a tightly corseted waist. It featured a deep plunging neckline and thin jeweled straps. The original painting was shocking when it was first displayed in 1884. Courtney's vintage copy did not look as old as the Sargent portrait, and her jeweled straps featured costume jewelry stones. In fact, Lacey realized, it might be a genuine vintage copy from the Forties. Every decade's style took cues from earlier periods. Both dresses, in fact, looked oddly modern, though Wallace's version was less alarming than the original.

Lacey silently marked the difference between the frocks. Courtney's designer had taken artistic liberties with the skirt, where the small open cut-out designs revealed a lining of emerald green. And the skirt was hiked up on one hip with a rosette to reveal a flash of leg. The effect rendered the skirt slightly asymmetrical and allowed more of the brilliant green underskirt to show, a dazzling effect, but one that somewhat compromised the original Madame X silhouette. The dress flashed green and black as Courtney strutted away, green and black and green again.

Lacey was sorry she hadn't discovered where Courtney had found the dress, before their little confrontation. She was sure there was a story stitched into every seam. *Not that Courtney would have told me. If she even knew.*

"We just got rid of your fake Madame X, and wouldn't you know it, here comes the X-Files," Lamont snorted.

Brooke Barton, Lacey's BFF and sometime attorney, squeezed through the crowd to reach them. Lacey considered her brilliant and crazy. Brooke was a conspiracy theorist to the bone, immersed in everything from alien abductions to Bigfoot to foreign spies among us in every branch and department of the government. The 'foreign spies' part was probably true, Lacey conceded.

Detective Lamont wouldn't admit it out loud, but he seemed to be having a wonderful time. Lacey knew he thought crazy people were good fun, as long as they weren't killing each other.

"Good evening to you too, Detective," Brooke said.

"Don't tease her," Lacey said. "Brooke hasn't had a promising intrigue in days. She's practically normal."

"In a world where women kill with stiletto heels, anything is possible," Brooke declared. "Scoff if you want."

"Scoff, hell, Barton," Lamont said. "I'm scared to death just checking out your killer heels."

"Don't worry, my wit is sharper than my stilettos," Brooke said. The heels were, in fact, a mere two inches—not high enough to fall off of—and they were hidden under her long, sleek, black dress. The only drawback to her garment was that it resembled a hundred other dresses in attendance. Brooke, with her long blond hair and regimented fitness routine, could be any beautiful, successful young attorney in the Nation's Capital. But she might have been the only one carrying a dossier of suspected alien life forms in her mental briefcase. And they weren't all congressmen.

In their pre-event confab, Lacey had argued for some color in Brooke's evening attire, but Brooke dismissed it on the grounds that all-black was appropriate for any lawyer, anywhere, any time. And her black gown would go with her boyfriend Damon's inevitable all-black, all-the-time, Geek Noir fashion vibe. Lacey sighed. *Two geeks in love.* At any rate, black was better than gray, another one of Brooke's favorites.

Although Damon Newhouse was what Lacey considered a fringe journalist, with his popular Conspiracy Clearinghouse blog on the Web at DeadFed dot com, he somehow managed to be a member of the White House Correspondents' Association. Lacey couldn't figure out how he could swing that, or the cost of the dinner ticket. But there he was. And Brooke was his date.

Damon materialized behind Brooke. He didn't bother with a tuxedo. He scoffed at black tie. Everything he owned was black anyway, so his black suit, black tie, and black shirt would do. He also sported a small black fedora. Damon was wiry, with delicate features, short, sleek black hair, sparse black facial hair, and serious black-framed glasses. He managed to look like a choirboy playing a hipster.

"Smithsonian. What's up?" he asked.

"Hemlines. Read it first in *The Eye.*"

"As hemlines go, so goes the economy."

"You have been reading my column."

"Did you ever doubt it? I'm always looking for hidden messages from the Mother Ship. I know you're plugged in." He whipped out his phone and grinned. "Hey, photo op." He directed Lamont, Lacey, and Brooke to crowd together for one of those golden-moments photos on Facebook.

"Lacey, what's Vic doing tonight?" Brooke asked.

"Keeping himself busy. He's meeting me here later, after this circus lets out."

"He was cool with the whole 'bring a source, not your squeeze' concept?"

"He said he wouldn't be caught dead at this soiree. Unless he was getting paid for it." It was a fib. Vic looked fabulous in a tuxedo and he would have attended in a heartbeat if she could have invited him.

"She's back," Lamont interrupted.

Lacey twirled in the direction of his gaze. "Who?"

"The magpie with the microphone. Your Madame Whatzit. Pretty poison."

Brooke and Damon turned in unison. Courtney Wallace had the same fevered stare in her narrowed eyes: intent on nailing sound-bites, counting face-time seconds in her head, silently rehearsing her on-camera patter. She was still hard at work recording live updates for Channel One News. She dismissed Lacey with a sharp twist of her head and a swish of black-and-green skirt.

"What was that about?" Brooke asked.

"Nothing, really," Lacey said, rolling her eyes. "Broadcast reporter. What can I say?"

"Wallace was trying to weasel out some style secrets about Smithsonian's getup," Lamont filled Brooke in. "They hissed at each other."

"Getup?" Lacey repeated.

"Dress. Outfit. Whatever. But Smithsonian, she asks, but she don't tell. Not when it comes to fashion and broadcast reporters." Lamont chuckled. "Me? I think some fashion voodoo is afoot."

"That's silly. Everybody knows about Lacey's gown, designed by the brilliant Gloria Adams, lost until Lacey brought her back to light. If Courtney doesn't know, she hasn't been paying attention. She is oh-so-faux a fashionista." Brooke reached for a flute of champagne from the tray of the hard-working waiter and lifted it high. "To Gloria! And to Lacey. No one would even know Gloria's name without Lacey."

"Wait a minute," Courtney yelled above the din, chasing a Hollywood actress trying to flee from her in the crush of the overcrowded room. She waved furiously at her photographer to follow her. "I only want ten seconds of your time! About your divorce!"

Lacey turned to watch Courtney's stalker act. The poor black-lace-clad actress was stuck by the door. There were too many people crowding in for her to get out. She was trapped, and Courtney was relentlessly elbowing her way toward her through the crowd.

Certainly there were times when a reporter needed to press a reluctant subject for a quote, Lacey thought, and the public's right to know justified being a little pushy. But she hoped she'd never been that desperate, and for nothing but a pointless celebrity sound-bite. *Is this what it takes to win an Emmy?* By now, Lacey's entire quartet was turning to watch the Courtney Wallace Show.

Something was happening around the charging TV reporter—a rumble, a movement, a reaction. Lacey stood high in her heels and craned her neck to see.

There was a loud crash of tumbling glasses and a bright spray of champagne, as sudden as an explosion. A shriek came from Courtney, drenched from head to foot. She and the champagne waiter had somehow collided, and she was now wearing the entire liquid contents of his tray. People were backing away from the mess, men brushing their wet tuxedo sleeves, women checking their shoes and dresses for damage from flying glass shards and the shower of alcohol. Lacey instinctively did the same. Brooke and Damon jumped backwards as Broadway Lamont danced out of the way of the champagne shower. He was light on his feet for a man his size.

"Much experience ducking whatever's thrown at you?" Lacey asked Lamont.

"Some. Police officer's life is a messy one. Blood, bone, slime, champagne. All play hell with the wardrobe. You might say I've developed a spill-avoidance ability."

"Remind me not to throw champagne at you. It would be wasted."

People around the drenched woman stopped talking. The unbroken glasses stopped clinking. Silence reigned for a moment, as if a ghost had blown through the patio doors with the rain. More waiters appeared out of nowhere and scurried to mop up the wet floor and broken glass.

"Did you see that?" Brooke finally said.

Hard to miss, Lacey thought. "I guess it's true that pride goeth before a fall."

Courtney's pride had surely taken a tumble. She stood stunned, surrounded by shattered champagne flutes, dripping in bubbly. Her lovely vintage dress was soaked from neckline to hemline and her hair hung in wet strings. Yet she still had a death grip on her microphone.

"Give her this, people," Lamont said. "She puts on a show."

Chapter 3

ALTHOUGH THE INCIDENT HAPPENED IN a flash, Lacey remembered it in slow motion.

The server, whom she recognized as a local stage actor in the role of a professional waiter, one hand under the tray, was smoothly weaving through the crowd on autopilot when suddenly things went off script. She could tell he hadn't planned to improvise. He seemed as surprised by this plot twist as everyone else.

Somehow he stumbled in the crush, falling toward Courtney face to face, tray first. He went down halfway and the tray went up and over. Two dozen full glasses of champagne went airborne, their contents cascading over the broadcaster and her glorious black dress with the brilliant green lining. Lacey gasped as the shower rained down, more concerned at the moment about Courtney's expensive vintage dress than she was about Courtney, who surely would dry without ill effects, albeit with a little shame. The waiter's expression was pure shock.

"Damn it! What the—?" Courtney's face registered confusion, then horror, then rage—not without many choice expletives that would be deleted from the tape if the moment ever made the news.

Her cameraman—Lacey had heard him called Eric Something— was still shouldering his camera rig, catching everything. Courtney's microphone finally tumbled to the floor as she tried to shake off the champagne like a wet dog. The crowd seemed to be waiting for the denouement, Courtney's twenty seconds of shame. Or was it just ten? Bystanders, mostly print reporters and their cherished sources, might have offered sympathy or help, even a dry handkerchief. But no, they stood and watched and said nothing, because it was Courtney Wallace, and she was not one of them. She was a broadcaster, and worse, a disgraced practitioner of "gotcha" journalism—now the victim of her own "gotcha."

The waiter recovered his composure before she did. He quickly and gracefully started picking up the mess. Slowly, a horrible realization struck Courtney: The camera was still on her. Her own camera, her own cameraman. There was the ghastly possibility this clip could end up as a blooper tape on her own TV station. Or worst of all, running endlessly on the Internet.

Camera phones came out and captured her reaction. Even Lacey took a photo. She really wanted a picture of the dress and that astonishing lining. She now regretted she hadn't taken a photo before it was spoiled.

It was clear what Courtney must do. She picked up the mike and cleared some sopping strands of hair out of her eyes. She nodded to her cameraman and smiled brightly into the lens.

"Well, folks, just a slip, a trip, and a fall. This story is all wet. But I'll be back with fresh updates throughout the evening as the President addresses the media. Reporting live from the White House Correspondents' Dinner, for Channel One News, I'm Courtney Wallace."

She signaled the cameraman to cut with that universal gesture, her fingers slicing across her throat. He put down his camera with a smirk.

"Way to go, Courtney," he said. "This one's a keeper. This will blow everyone else off the screen tonight."

"Shut up, Eric. Just shut up." Soaked and steaming, Courtney tried to make a quick exit from the cocktail party. It wasn't easy, but she elbowed her way to the door, dripping champagne at every step. Partygoers squeezed back to keep from getting dripped on, and, Lacey knew, to keep from being caught in the same camera frame as Courtney. She was followed closely out the door by another woman, presumably a friend or coworker.

Eric lowered the camera and turned his head. Lacey could see his shoulders shaking with suppressed laughter. *Ah, the rewards of broadcast journalism,* she thought. *From star to laughingstock in mere seconds.*

Lacey had never seen a news cameraman wearing a suit, and she didn't see one now. Eric was wearing a black sweater and black denim jeans, a concession to the formality of the event, and his long, glossy black hair brushed his shoulders. He looked Asian, perhaps Korean, and she could read his full name on one of the blizzard of press and identification cards around his neck: Eric Park. He smiled readily. His on-camera reporter having fled in shame, Eric went calmly about his business, capturing random video bites of the Correspondents' Dinner revelers.

"What's that smell?" Broadway asked her. "Don't smell like champagne to me."

Lacey sniffed the air. "Wet fabric? Old cloth? The scent of a century? Maybe the aroma of hopping mad broadcast reporter." She breathed in the pungent fragrance and that whiff of garlic caught in the air. It was the same scent she'd caught before, but stronger.

"The party's over. For Courtney Wallace," Damon said. "Glad I scored some priceless phone pics."

Brooke was more sympathetic. "She probably just wants to die."

One thing Washingtonians really hated was a scene. Any scene, especially an embarrassing scene in front of hundreds of strangers. Nevertheless, one woman's embarrassing scene is another's low comedy. There was a buzz of laughter rolling through the cocktail party crowd. Lacey felt a little sick to her stomach. Clearly many people thought it was hilarious, and that Courtney was only getting what she deserved. Still, public humiliation was hard to take. And the dress! That beautiful vintage dress didn't deserve that treatment.

The room started to empty out. The crowd looked for another party, another quick drink before the dinner. They would slowly make their way to the ballroom, armed with plenty of gossip. They had witnessed the blooper of the evening.

Damon took Brooke's arm. "I hear Matt Drudge is at the *National Journal* party. I'll introduce you."

"Catch you two at dinner," Brooke called to Lacey over her shoulder as they wandered out, chattering with excitement.

"I'll be right back," Lacey said to Lamont. "Ladies' room." Lacey figured Courtney would head for the nearest place where she could mop up the mess. Something else was bothering Lacey about the whole mishap, but she couldn't say just what it was.

"Following the rest of the story? Well, once a snoop, always a snoop. Don't get wet. I'll be here, testing the hors d'oeuvres."

Lamont leaned against the wall where he could take in the hubbub. He traded his empty champagne glass for one of white wine from the next waiter who came by with a tray of filled glasses. The champagne seemed to be gone, all wasted on the Wallace woman.

Lacey found the nearest women's restroom. It was suitably elegant, with marble floors and gilt-framed mirrors, but small, with just two stalls at an angle to the sinks. Two women were filling the space before the mirrors, and one of those women was Courtney. Lacey slipped into an open stall unobserved, just as another woman slipped out.

Courtney's companion was busier wringing her hands than wringing out her friend's soaked dress. Her own mustard-colored dress was eye-catching, but not as flattering as she might have hoped. It seemed to be a copy of a Nicole Kidman dress, with a mandarin collar and a keyhole cutout in the bodice. However, it might only work on the famous actress it was intended for. Lacey paused to make a mental note, an occupational hazard. She couldn't imagine that color looking good on anything but a hot dog. *In this case, a regulation little black dress would have been so much better.*

"Leave me alone, Zanna," Courtney snapped at her helper as Lacey peeked through the gap in the stall door. Zanna Nelson: Lacey recalled the name. She'd seen her once or twice as an on-air reporter on Channel One, but Ms. Mustard didn't seem to get a lot of face time.

Zanna apparently was Courtney's purse handler for the evening. She handed her a comb and a makeup compact from a sleek little silver bag and observed the other woman closely in the mirror. Zanna was pretty, in fact, much prettier than Courtney. She had long, straight, glossy brown hair that reached well below her shoulders. Her face was heart-shaped and her features even, with deep-set hazel eyes. Perhaps her only visual flaw was her small, cupid's-bow mouth. But she didn't have the exaggerated, outsized features that Courtney had, the kind of features that the camera loved. In person, Courtney looked more extreme. If they were fashion models, Zanna would be *catalogue*, while Courtney would be *editorial*.

Courtney was mopping her face with tissues, trying not to cry.

"Are you okay?" Zanna asked.

"Are you stupid? Do I look okay? I'm dripping wet. This is a freaking disaster! Oh my God." Her hair hung in strings and her makeup was streaked. She leaned in to the mirror and sponged her face with foundation. She was making it worse.

Zanna seemed accustomed to Courtney's dramatics. "I'm sorry."

"What are you sorry for? At least you're not soaking wet. Why is this happening to me?"

Courtney was fighting a meltdown, and possibly tears. Lacey didn't blame her. Any woman would be entitled, after that public disgrace. Still, Lacey hoped the vintage dress and the gorgeous green silk lining, champagne streaked and clinging soddenly to Courtney's legs, could be saved.

There was an atmosphere in the room that was giving Lacey a headache. That smell of garlic was back and even more pungent, as was the musty aroma of the sopping black gown. What was it about the aroma? She tried to remember.

"It's not that bad," Zanna said meekly.

"*It's not that bad,*" Courtney mimicked her. "No, it's not that bad, it's worse, it's a complete freaking catastrophe. I could kill that idiot waiter!"

"Let me help you." Zanna stood aside, still wringing her hands.

"Kill the waiter? Be my guest. Just leave me alone. I suppose you'd like to finish the rest of the story for me," Courtney sneered. "Well, you're not going on air for me tonight. This is my assignment. And if I go down with the ship, at least it's my ship."

"But Courtney, I'm just trying to help. If you're not feeling up to it, I could—"

"Don't you get it? I have to get back out there! I have to show my face in front of all those people! I have to prove I'm professional enough to finish this. Listen to me, I am fine. I will touch up my makeup and fix my hair and I will go out there and do my job."

Courtney rapidly smoothed her hair, twisted it into a ballerina's knot on the top of her head, pulled out a few damp strands by her face, and curled them with her fingers. It was an admirable save. The two women stood back, checking the results in the mirror. Zanna nodded in approval. Courtney shrugged.

Lacey decided this was her cue to join the party. She flushed the toilet behind her to serve as an announcement of her presence and stepped out of the stall.

"Is there anything I can do, Courtney?" Lacey asked.

"You! I don't believe it! You wouldn't even talk to me out there on camera, but now?" Courtney glared at Lacey in the gilt-framed mirror. "Now you want to *help*?"

"You know I couldn't talk. Not on camera. It wouldn't be professional," she tried to explain. "Are you all right? How is your dress?"

"I'm fine. The dress is fine. Everything is fine. Get out of here." Courtney didn't look fine. She looked furious. "You too, Nelson. Go away. Give me some space."

"This is a public restroom." Lacey wasn't about to be ordered away. Her head was aching, and she washed her hands for no particular reason while studying Courtney's dress and its saturated green lining. Courtney focused on redoing her eye makeup. Zanna stood watching, incapable of helping or leaving. The wet marble floor looked slightly greenish where the dress was still dripping.

Something about that color, that brilliant heart-stopping jewel shade, registered in Lacey's memory. And her headache. It made her think hard. The color, the aroma of garlic, Courtney's pallor, her throbbing head. Was it something about the wet vintage fabric? Was it mildewed, was it releasing some kind of mold? But no, the dress looked clean, if dripping wet. Could it be the green lining and not the dress itself? That lovely shade of green? Green, emerald green, bright spring green, like a green that Lacey had seen somewhere long ago, something with a lovely, evocative name. What was it? Something like—Paris Green. That was it. *Paris Green.*

Paris Green, Lacey remembered from school, was a dye discovered in the early nineteenth century. It was the first vibrant emerald pigment that was stable and widely usable. Even today, it was said that nothing could create exactly the same intoxicating green. Yet Paris Green had a sinister reputation: That beguiling shade of green was toxic when wet.

Lacey felt slightly woozy. She realized she needed fresh air. Was she just imagining this had something to do with the dress? Could it really be hazardous? *Impossible.* Paris Green hadn't been used in clothing in over a century. And this dress couldn't be that old. It was clearly a replica, probably from no earlier than the Forties. But she smelled garlic. *Hors d'oeuvres? Aromas from the hotel kitchen?* She shook her head to clear it.

"All right, Courtney," Zanna said with a sigh. "I'm leaving. I'll be right outside if you need me."

Zanna patted her sleek brown hair in the mirror and swept her mustard dress through the door, looking slightly ill herself. Of course, it might just have been the dress. *That mustard color would make anyone look ill.*

"Courtney, I don't know how to say this so it doesn't sound rude, but I think you need to get out of that dress," Lacey said. "I don't know what that lining was dyed with, but if it was something called Paris Green, and it's now soaking into your skin, it can't be good for you."

"Don't worry about me, Lacey. The dress will dry. Eventually. Besides, who cares? It's just an old dress. So what if it gets ruined?" She picked up the front of the black satin skirt and wrung it out in the sink. The lining clung to her legs.

Just an old dress. Lacey took a deep breath. "It's not that. It'll take forever to dry in this humidity. The dress might be making you ill."

"Really? That's really what you think?" She rolled her eyes and squeezed more liquid out of the skirt. "I think it's making you sick with jealousy that I look so good in it. You're not the only one who can rock vintage, you know."

But Courtney wasn't looking good. Despite her fresh makeup, her skin was shiny. She took out her powder and wiped a brush across her nose and cheeks. Her eyes had an unhealthy gleam.

"It's the lining. The emerald green lining," Lacey persevered. "Don't you smell that? That garlicky smell must be coming from it. When it's wet, Paris Green has that same aroma. I mean, according to what I've read."

"You're crazy. There's no smell. It's in your head." The pungent aroma of garlic filled the ladies' room.

Lacey sighed. She'd assumed that because the woman was, theoretically, a journalist, she would listen to facts.

"Listen, Courtney, depending on how old the dress is, or the lining, it might contain Paris Green, which was created in—"

"You wouldn't give me the time of day before and now you're giving me a lecture on fashion history? That's rich, Smithsonian."

Nobody likes a know-it-all. Cut to the chase, Lacey.

"Fine. If it is Paris Green, the dress could be dangerous. The dye is toxic when it gets wet. It may have even killed Napoleon Bonaparte."

"Really? Did Napoleon wear a green dress? If J. Edgar Hoover could twirl in a pink tutu, then anything is possible. But I'm hotter than either one of them." She looked feverish. Lacey knew she wasn't going to win this one, but she had to try.

"Some people believe the dye was used in Napoleon's wallpaper on Saint Helena, which was very humid. When it gets wet—or even just damp from humidity—the dye releases something called arsine gas. Arsine, as in arsenic. It can kill you, or at least make you sick."

"Likely story." Courtney was fussing with her damp hair. Lacey could see drops of pale green liquid on Courtney's exposed leg. "How could I trust anything you say about my dress? And how would you even know that?"

Now I remember why I try never to talk to this woman. "I know this because I do my fashion research." *Bitch*, she added silently. "And I don't know for sure. But I do know I'm getting a terrible headache in here. Aren't you? Wouldn't you rather take the dress off and be safe?"

"I'd rather take some aspirin. And a dry martini. Nice try though. Actually, it's something I might say on the air. 'Take the dress off and be safe!' I'll have to use that sometime. But I have no reason to trust you, Smithsonian. None at all."

"Trust your instincts then. How are you feeling right now? A little queasy? The hotel might have something you could wear. A uniform. Or maybe someone here tonight wore a trench coat that would fit you."

"That would make you happy, wouldn't it? Making me look ridiculous. Me, on camera in a maid's uniform and a trench coat at the fanciest event of the year. You'd love that!"

Maybe a little. "I'm trying to help. You could get sick. Very sick."

"I don't need your help. I'm not wearing some damn uniform or someone's old raincoat. I paid a fortune for this dress. I don't believe for a minute that it's toxic."

"No, I guess that's just you."

Courtney missed the jab. "Sometimes, Lacey, a dress is just a dress. Even a vintage dress." Courtney's green eyes seemed to glitter. Her cheeks were bright red beneath the powder.

"Fine, Courtney. Some people would rather be sorry than safe. And maybe the dress is just wet. Maybe that smell is your perfume. Maybe nothing will happen." *Other than starring on the YouTube TV Bloopers Channel, the Champagne Shower Edition, featuring Courtney Wallace.* "Good luck out there."

Lacey escaped the ladies' room. Lamont was waiting for her outside the door.

"You took your sweet time."

"What are you doing out here, Broadway? Picking up actresses?"

"Thought there might be bloodshed, the two of you in there together. Least some hair pulling."

"Sorry to disappoint. How about some fresh air?" Lacey noticed Eric Park was leaning against the wall with his camera rig at the ready, waiting for Courtney to emerge. Eric spotted her too.

"Hey, I'm Eric. Courtney's camera crew. Is she okay in there?"

"She says so. But I don't believe she's feeling too well. She's pretty pissed off, and she wouldn't let Zanna Nelson or me help. She's being really bitchy."

"Oh, she's fine, then. That's just her personality."

"You got my sympathy, man," Lamont said. "Have a good night."

Broadway Lamont pointed the way to the patio door, through another cocktail party. The crowds opened for them. They passed through the door to the patio beyond as their fellow partygoers parted like a sea around Lamont. He could have been mistaken for a bouncer, or a bulldozer.

A new waiter appeared at their side with a fresh tray of drinks. Cameras flashed and the cozy media hug that is the White House Correspondents' Dinner closed in behind them.

Chapter 4

"THIS MAY SOUND CRAZY," LACEY started to say. She swallowed deep breaths of fresh air. The rain had stopped, but a fine mist still hung in the air. Lacey didn't even care if her hair exploded from the humidity, she could always pull it back in a twist. She looked at Lamont and wondered if she should go on.

"I *hope* it sounds crazy," Lamont said. "I came for the floor show, and Ms. Courtney Wallace gave us a hell of an opening number. I want to hear all the crazy you got. Catfight in the ladies' room?"

"No, Broadway, not a catfight. But I have a funny feeling."

"Funny feeling, like clothing voodoo funny? Or whacked-out broadcast reporter funny?"

"Maybe I'm just hungry."

"I hear you. When do we eat?" Lamont's appetite was as large as he was. Whenever he dropped by the newspaper, ostensibly to speak with Lacey about a case, she suspected he was really there for the food editor's delectable daily dishes.

"There's something wrong with that dress. Courtney's dress."

"Are we back to that? That's your crazy feeling? I say there's something wrong with that woman. Period."

"The dress. I think it could make her very, very sick." It sounded ridiculous, even to Lacey.

"I'm listening."

"Have you ever heard of Paris Green?" She knew better than to give Lamont the whole fashion history lesson. "A very old dye, no longer used. It's made with arsenic. The thing is, it's fine when it's dry, but when it gets wet, it releases a toxic gas."

"Wet, like 'getting doused with champagne' kind of wet?" He inclined his head toward her.

"Yes. Like that. The lining of that dress, the part closest to her skin, is bright emerald green. It's the right range of color for Paris Green."

He swallowed the last of his wine. "Never heard of it. How toxic we talking here?"

"No idea. Not a chemistry major. But if the lining of that wet dress is poisonous and it's soaking her skin all night and she won't change into something else—"

"You know, Smithsonian. I got all the respect in the world for the way your brain works."

Really? she thought. *Since when?*

"But this time," he went on, "I think your imagination might be running overtime. You know how nuts that sounds, getting sick from some old-fashioned dye and a splash of champagne? Well, that's some crazy freak accident."

"If it was an accident," she said.

"Now you think it wasn't an accident? You think the waiter who plowed into her did it on purpose?"

What were the odds that someone who wore a vintage dress with a Paris Green silk lining to a cocktail party would wind up dripping wet?

"You're right, Broadway. It's completely implausible that something like that would still exist in this day and age. The dye was banned decades ago. Nobody uses it anymore, so far as I know." Her headache was almost gone and she was feeling better in the fresh air. "Maybe it's just Courtney's unique personality."

"You got that right. Smithsonian, I'm thrilled we're sharing a memorable fashion moment here, but when's dinner? I'm starved."

Lacey glanced at her Movado watch, a gift from her absent fiancé Vic, who was never far from her thoughts.

"Right now."

"Now you're talking."

Milling their way into the ballroom for dinner was an exercise in that favorite Washington pastime: celebrity spotting. Of course in the District of Columbia, innumerable politicians, pundits, and media figures counted as celebrities. Some people even counted in multiple categories, like Barbara Walters. Lacey scored early, spotting the most famous D.C. couple in a "mixed marriage," *Republican* Mary Matalin and *Democrat* James Carville, going down the escalator as she and Broadway Lamont were heading up. Lamont spotted pundit George Will chatting with them. A trifecta.

At the Correspondents' Dinner there were always those "news source" guests who could only be considered publicity stunts. Lacey spotted rock star Ozzy Osbourne and his wife Sharon, guests of one of the showier New York publications. Ozzy hid behind his dark sunglasses and long, stringy hair, while the formidable and slightly scary Sharon Osbourne glided grandly in a gown worthy of the Evil

Queen in Snow White, all sapphire blue satin and deep décolletage. Among the names Lacey heard in the excited buzz of the cocktail parties were Miley Cyrus, Jennifer Lawrence, Lindsay Lohan, Lady Gaga, and a gaggle of trashy Kardashians.

Keeping an eye open for any of the above, Lacey wondered how many celebrities cared even a fig about Washington or politics, or even knew where they were or why they were there. All they seemed to care about were their inch-long eyelashes. Among the television actresses, Lacey's favorite outfit so far was an above-the-knee white dress with a flouncy feathered skirt. It made her look like an ostrich. Her legs were appropriately long and skinny and she shed feathers in her path.

Most amusing to her was a photo op lineup of at least three sets of actors and actresses who were playing the President and First Lady on current television shows, although with more glamour and less gravitas than the real thing.

Male Hollywood heartthrobs were also on display. Brad Pitt and George Clooney were surrounded by female fans wherever they went, though Lacey thought Clooney looked smaller than he did on the big screen. On the other hand, and on the opposite end of the political spectrum, Tom Selleck appeared larger and grumpier. They both seemed slightly pained by all the attention. She thought she might have caught a glimpse of the entire heavily bearded cast of a cable hunting show, but she couldn't be sure.

Lamont nudged Lacey and they caught another peek of Wallace, back on her feet and berating her poor cameraman, Eric. Courtney was clearly on the hunt for more celebrities and still striking out. She caught Lacey and Lamont looking her way and turned her back. The woman really didn't look well. *Stress*, Lacey told herself. Courtney was just having a rough night.

Lacey and Detective Lamont had already gone through the Secret Service security checkpoints and metal detector stations to get into the pre-dinner parties, but now there was an additional check of their tickets against The List, just outside the banquet hall.

The Eye Street Observer had purchased two tables for the dinner. Unfortunately, second-tier newspapers like *The Eye* never received the prime tables. Those were reserved for the major newspapers, *The New York Times* and *The Washington Post* and their kind, and frothy lifestyle magazines like *Vanity Fair*, which also vied for the most outrageous guests. They specialized in bringing the latest D.C.

scandal victims, bad boy rock stars, and hot-right-now television personalities, many of whom had no conceivable serious link to news in the Nation's Capital. *The Eye* was exiled to the back of the room, as far away from the head table as possible. Lamont was heading confidently toward the tables in front of the dais when Lacey steered him back to humble Newspaper Siberia.

Peter Johnson, the Capitol Hill reporter, was already seated at their table. She suppressed a groan and wondered briefly who could have put them together. *Did they really want bloodshed?* Johnson was the last person she wanted to see, at this dinner or anywhere else. It was mutual. When he caught sight of Lacey he looked like he'd swallowed something sour.

Johnson was tall, and though he was on the thin side, he managed to look soft and pudgy. Lacey heard his only exercise was loitering in the halls of Congress and hefting mugs of coffee. He wore a respectable black tuxedo, but he'd already managed to spill something on the lapel. His shirt was a plain white button-down, rather than a tuxedo shirt, and his bowtie was crooked. His comb-over was sticking up, and he peered gloomily at her through his crooked glasses. *Johnson was geek before geek was chic.*

For tonight's event, Johnson had a minor congressman in tow, one Representative Purvis Daggett, from a Deep South state. Lacey wasn't quite sure which one. Daggett's accent was thick as barbecue, but his tuxedo ensemble was pristine. Lacey recalled him as a minor player on one of the budget subcommittees, but a major-league fundraiser for his pet causes. Johnson pointedly ignored Lacey, leaving her to introduce herself and Lamont to the congressman.

Daggett put out his hand. "Ms. Smithsonian, a great pleasure. I do believe you were the reporter who broke the story on Esme Fairchild?" he said. "Tragic story. Poor child."

"Yes, it was very sad." Lacey was flattered the congressman remembered it. Johnson seemed to choke on something. "Do you need some water, Peter? Perhaps some champagne?" She smiled brightly and Lamont laughed.

"We were all saddened by her untimely demise, especially seeing as how young Esme was an intern on the Hill," Daggett continued to Lacey, studiously ignoring Johnson. "She seemed so full of promise. Sometimes, I'm sorry to say, we let our interns flail around without the proper guidance in this town's political snake pits, such as she found herself in. Your story did her tragic demise justice,

I must say." He had obviously been in a few political snake pits himself. "Were you on that case by any chance, Detective?"

"Not my case," Lamont said. "The body was found south of Alexandria in a park, Huntley Meadows. The department does appreciate it on the rare occasion when Smithsonian finds murder victims outside of the District. Lacey here is like a dowser. Instead of water, she finds dead bodies. And fashion crimes. Sometimes even when they're invisible to the naked eye." He grinned.

"Thanks for the ringing endorsement, Broadway."

Daggett winked at her. He looked around the room and eyed the distant dais.

"You know, I have been to a great many of these events, but I don't believe I have ever been seated quite this far away from the President. Perfectly all right by me, you understand, he and I don't see eye to eye all that often anyway. I'd be just as happy if we were dining out in the hallway. Or across the street."

"Which we practically are, Congressman," Lacey said. The three of them shared a small laugh. Johnson looked mortified that Lacey and Lamont were charming his "date." He silently played with his silverware and gulped down ice water.

Cops reporter Tony Trujillo joined their table with his news source for the evening, an attractive police department spokesperson. Unsurprisingly, she was of the young single female persuasion. The only surprise was that she was a long-haired brunette and not a blonde, Tony's usual specialty. She wore a tight black dress and Tony was stylish in a crisp black tuxedo and black boots.

News editor Douglas MacArthur "Mac" Jones arrived next, with *The Eye*'s publisher Claudia Darnell at his side. The two of them had apparently excused themselves from bringing sources. Mac looked slightly grumpier than usual at being there. Although he was a mix of African-American and Caucasian, Mac hailed from California and Lacey knew he still found Washington puzzling, with its intricate strata of racial, political, and social classes. He would rather be at home with his wife and daughters, he told her, than at this "dog-and-pony show." It was a sure bet he'd leave right after dinner and pass on the post-event parties.

On the other hand, Claudia Darnell would undoubtedly be around for the entire evening. A woman of a certain age, which Lacey assumed was late fifties or early sixties, Claudia had the money and the moxie to keep the years away and the men close at hand. She looked ravishing, as usual. Her pale silver blond hair was arranged in a French twist, and her sleek fitted dress was bright red, a shade she favored. *Another rebel in color.* Diamond studs adorned her ears, and around her throat she wore a jeweled choker of rubies and diamonds, all real. She out-sparkled the jewels.

Claudia Darnell had survived her own Washington scandal, and like a phoenix, had risen from the ashes to spite the town that once turned on her. She wouldn't have missed making her annual appearance at the White House Correspondents' Dinner. However, Lacey thought she read in Claudia's expression dismay at the distant placement of *The Eye*'s tables. It must have felt like a slap in the face, being seated so far away from the dais and so close to the door. They did, however, have a great view of the color guard.

The paper's other designated table included a few veteran staffers, well-respected writers with terrible taste in clothes. *These guys are writers! Couldn't they look up "black tie"?* On the female side, a chubby legislative reporter wore a stretchy black dress with sparkly flowers over an apple-shaped figure that should not have been subjected to tight polyester. It clung to her lovingly. As a fun fashion bonus, her dress left a trail of glitter everywhere she went, much like the actress with her ostrich feathers. Another female reporter wore a fuchsia dress in a shiny faux satin with a full skirt and puff sleeves, from somewhere south of the Island of Lost Styles.

Luckily, LaToya Crawford, the Metro reporter and one of the few *Eye* scribes with a sense of style, showed up with her source guest, a handsome D.C. city official. LaToya was black and beautiful. Her trademark was her long jet-black pageboy with a patent leather sheen. Tonight she was wearing a canary yellow satin sheath that hugged her bodacious curves. Her eyes were made up like Cleopatra. LaToya always turned heads, but tonight her head turned at the sight of Detective Broadway Lamont.

He, in turn, resembled the proverbial deer in the headlights. A giant buck deer, about to become a trophy. Lacey knew the detective was afraid of nothing, except possibly LaToya. She took one look at her seat at *The Eye*'s tables in Far Siberia and turned to Peter Johnson. She put her hand on his shoulder, her purple nails digging in like daggers.

"Johnson, you don't want to sit here, do you? Why, you and Smithsonian might kill each other, which would be embarrassing, considering she's here with a homicide detective. Want to switch? You do, don't you?"

..⌐ nodded helplessly. "Do you mind, Congressman? The other table has the *real* writers."

"Musical chairs? Just like Congress." Daggett appeared to be used to being moved around. He grasped Lacey's hand gallantly in parting. "Ms. Smithsonian, I do hope we meet again soon. You can tell me all your secrets."

"You stole my line, Congressman," she answered and they both laughed.

"You guys are leaving? But this is the cool kids' table," Tony cracked.

Peter Johnson didn't look back. Lacey breathed a sigh of relief. She wouldn't have to deflect his sour vibes all evening. LaToya settled right in next to Lamont, and everyone else moved in turn.

"That guy give you any trouble?" Lamont asked Lacey.

She gave him an elaborate shrug. "He's out of shape."

"Don't let that fool you," LaToya said. "Johnson once ran the Marine Corps Marathon."

Lacey swiveled in her chair to take another look. "No way."

"Before your time," Tony said. "I've been seeing him at the health club around the corner, too. He once pitched for *The Eye*'s softball team. Before he switched to pitching doughnut holes."

Johnson, an athlete? That was hard to believe. She pushed the thought of him away and turned back to people watching. She spotted Damon and Brooke seated at a table across the room, one considerably closer to the dais. She wondered how Damon had snagged those seats. *Must be a conspiracy,* Lacey decided. He was buddying up to his table mate, Matt Drudge of the *Drudge Report*, who was also wearing a little black hipster fedora, a match for Damon's fedora. Apparently they were standard issue this year for the alternative press. *Must be the same conspiracy.*

She noticed Mac frowning at her. "I remember that blue dress," he said. "Last time you wore it you nearly got yourself killed."

And yet I survived. And so did my Gloria Adams gown.

"That was last time, Mac. Nothing's going to happen to this dress tonight."

"Wait. There was another famous dress adventure? One I didn't know about?" Lamont asked.

"Before we ever met, Detective," Lacey said.

"There's always another dress story with Lois Lane here," Tony added.

"You got another wacko dress thing going on? Here? Tonight?"

Mac inquired, his bushy eyebrows gathering like storm clouds.

"Oh, yeah," Lamont jumped in. "Not the one Smithsonian's wearing, though. The one Courtney Wallace is wearing. It's a good story, even if it ain't true."

"It's nothing, probably," she said. "But part of it is true."

Everyone stared at Lacey, then at Lamont. He picked up the narrative.

"First, the two of them got into a hissy fit."

"It was not a hissy fit. Exactly."

Under his shiny dome, Mac's bushy eyebrows started dancing. They had questions. "And?"

"Fine," Lacey said. "Wallace wanted to interview me on camera for *her* story on vintage couture. I refused. I'm not a celebrity. I'm not public property or fair game for her ambush sound bites. I'm a working journalist. Theoretically, I'm her competition, though I wouldn't dignify her with that title. And she's already had plenty of my input, through my columns in *The Eye*. She seems to have read my stuff closely. Very closely."

"This is that Wallace woman on Channel One, the one who's been copying your stuff?"

"You know about that, Mac?"

"Heard about it from my girls, Lily Rose and Jasmine. Never thought they'd care so much about clothing."

"Everybody cares about clothes," Lamont said. "Wallace is apparently wearing some fancy antique gown tonight. We were watching when some waiter took a dive and spilled a tray full of champagne all over her. Show them the picture."

Lacey pulled out her phone and displayed the picture she took of Courtney in the aftermath.

"Gives new meaning to the term drowned rat," Tony said.

"And that concerns Smithsonian greatly," Lamont intoned.

"The dress, right? Not Courtney Wallace?" Mac was catching on.

"Right. Here's the kicker," Lamont continued. "Smithsonian thinks the champagne could have activated some kind of antique poison dye in the dress. Hoodoo voodoo. Dangerous when wet. Sounds like a Fashion Clue to me."

"Not the entire dress." Lacey felt she was enduring this teasing with forbearance and good grace. "Just the green lining."

"Champagne does that?" Trujillo asked.

"Anything wet. Rain, water, coffee, whatever."

"What makes you think it's this dye?" Mac asked.

"The lining color. Brilliant green. There was once a toxic dye called Paris Green." She neglected to mention the smell or her headache. *Why confuse the issue?*

"Does that have something to do with Napoleon's death?" Tony asked.

"His wallpaper!" Claudia exclaimed. "Yes. One theory is that he was poisoned by the wet wallpaper. It was green. At some point after his death, they found arsenic in his hair clippings. But Napoleon was not the only one who had a run-in with toxic wallpaper."

"No?" Mac played straight man. "Do tell."

Claudia had a twinkle in her eye. "In the weeks before he died, Oscar Wilde reportedly said he and the wallpaper were fighting a duel to the death. 'Either it goes or I do,' he said."

"Sadly, we don't know what his wallpaper looked like," Lacey said. "Or whether it was Paris Green."

"We can imagine it was," Claudia said. "Makes a better story that way."

"You women are all in a conspiracy," Lamont said.

"I, for one, now can't wait to see what Ms. Wallace is wearing," Claudia said, ignoring him. "Is that her up there?"

Everyone at the table shifted to see Courtney stumble against one of the front tables. Eric Park quickly stepped in to steady her. He seemed to be trying to get her to leave. She staggered and shook her head vehemently.

"Has she been drinking?" Mac asked.

"I didn't see her drinking any champagne," Lacey said. "Just wearing it. I hope she's okay."

"Pretty embarrassing. Getting soaked by a waiter and losing your cool at this glamorous gala," LaToya said. "Motive for murder, I'd say. That waiter better watch his you-know-what. Good thing you're here, Broadway." She scooted her chair an inch closer to the big detective.

"Don't worry, it won't be murder," Tony said. "Courtney will probably just die of humiliation."

"She doesn't look healthy," Claudia said. "She shouldn't have to be working this thing tonight if she's sick."

"Nice dress, though," Tony commented. "A little limp-looking."

"Champagne will do that," Lacey said. "It's vintage. The dress, not the champagne. She's wearing it as part of her series."

"You don't think that dress really is harmful, do you, Lacey?" Claudia asked.

"I don't know, Claudia. I told her she should get out of it and wear something else. She wouldn't listen to me."

"Why would she?" LaToya said. "You're the competition."

"Well, then," Claudia said. "You warned her. She didn't listen."

"She looks inebriated to me. Hey, I see Hansen." Mac stood up and waved at the staff photographer. "Let's have him take that woman's photograph. For the record."

"Good idea, Mac. Just in case something awful happens," Tony said. "We are a newspaper, after all."

"Nothing's going to happen," Lacey protested. *I hope.*

"Long Lens" Hansen made his way over, draped with cameras and gear, as usual. He'd gone formal for a news photographer, which meant he was wearing his clean black jeans and black shirt and a black sport coat. He huddled briefly with Mac. A quick nod of the head and Hansen and his cameras were on the prowl for Courtney Wallace.

"If something does happen," Tony said to Lacey, "and you scoop Johnson on it, right here at the Correspondents' Dinner, he's going to have a stroke. And then we'll have to have pictures of that too."

"Nothing wrong with a little friendly competition," Mac said. "Johnson can take it."

"Ha. Wait till the book comes out," LaToya said, loud enough for the next table to hear.

"What book?" Lamont asked.

"*Terror at Timberline.*" Lacey shook her head as she said it. "Mac's title, not mine."

Mac yawned. He was bone tired after working many late hours on this pet project, an *Eye Street Observer* special publication recounting their recent adventures in and around Sagebrush, Colorado, involving the disappearances of several young women, later found murdered and dumped on lonely back-country roads.

Lacey had traveled to that remote Western town on a personal mission to exonerate an old boyfriend. She discovered the crime scene where the women met their fate, and Mac and Tony followed her to Colorado on the scent of that story. Although the book was Mac's brainchild, all three had been putting in a lot of after-work hours. Lacey supplied her first-hand account, her knowledge of the town, and its historical context, Tony profiled the women who had gone missing and the law enforcement efforts, and Mac was editing and braiding together their accounts into a single tale. It was a long-time ambition of his to produce a true-crime book from firsthand reportage by *The Eye*, and he was hell-bent for leather to complete it. The book would be available sometime during the summer, if they hit their editing deadline.

Lacey wasn't sure how she felt about the book. She admitted she was looking forward to seeing her name on the cover as a coauthor. However, what she had written was much more personal than she expected and she wasn't sure she wanted to let her readers peer that deeply into her psyche. Mac and Tony, on the other hand, were thrilled by the whole process.

"*Terror at Timberline*?" Lamont said. "Can't wait to read that one. My copy better be autographed by all three of you."

"We're still discussing the title," Lacey said. "It's a little tabloid for my taste. And it didn't happen at timberline, the line at high altitude where trees no longer grow."

"I didn't see any trees," Mac said. "We could have been on the moon."

"I can't wait to see this opus," Claudia said. "In fact, I'm throwing a book party for it at my house."

That was news to Lacey. "Really?"

"Absolutely. You'll be invited, Detective Lamont. If we can't celebrate our successes, what are we in this business for, anyway?" Claudia proposed a toast to the venture.

Mac seemed pleased. "If it weren't for Lacey's penchant for trouble, we wouldn't be celebrating a book at all." The entire table clinked their wine glasses in a toast.

As the talk turned to what a sensation the book was bound to be (which Lacey seriously doubted), she suddenly felt uneasy. She glanced over at the next table. Johnson shot her a look of pure venom. She felt almost a physical jolt. She was glad they'd all gone through Secret Service security checkpoints before dinner. *No weapons in this place tonight.*

Dinner arrived, diverting the table. The Washington Hilton's filet with a side of grilled shrimp seemed to satisfy even Broadway Lamont. The conversation ebbed and the wine flowed. Soon, everyone's focus was drawn to the head table as the lights dimmed and the show began. Lacey forgot about Courtney for the time being, though she did notice that LaToya Crawford was managing to scoot her chair around so she was sitting close to Lamont. Very close.

Spotlights lit the dais. The crowd hushed. Someone rose at the center of the front table, far away. Lacey shifted in her chair to get a better view. It was just another guy in a black tuxedo, though this one was obviously perfectly tailored.

It was the President of the United States.

Chapter 5

COURTNEY WALLACE WAS A TROUPER. Though suffering, she was still on her feet as Lacey exited the banquet hall after the dinner, with Broadway Lamont at her side. Courtney was still speaking into the camera in the hallway, giving her glassy-eyed wrap-up for the evening.

"For cripes sake, Courtney, give me a break," Eric said. "We're not even live now. Can we go home?"

"One more take," she insisted, wiping her brow with a cloth napkin taken from the dinner. "I stumbled over the beginning." Courtney leaned against the wall and took a breath, trying to find the strength to continue.

"You look awful," he protested. "They're not even going to use this footage. You wouldn't want them to. Go home. Get some sleep."

"She does look worse," Lacey whispered to Lamont.

"Flu. Going around," he answered. The flu was always going around.

"I hope so," Lacey said. "Not that she's sick, but that it's—something else." Working in the District of Columbia could wear down anyone's immune system. And inevitably, the Washington workaholics soldiered on, not caring who else they might infect.

The banquet hall emptied out quickly. Even the Secret Service was gone: The President had departed the premises. The barriers had been taken down and the metal detectors removed. Lamont paused to stare at the obviously sick television reporter.

He warned Lacey, "Don't give me no more of that 'ancient dress with a poisoned past' business. You sound like your buddy Newhouse. Next you'll be telling me it's haunted."

Lacey shuddered. "The flu," she agreed. "Probably just the flu."

Courtney grinned bravely into the camera. She tried to find her words, but they came out garbled. This take was worse than the last one. She slumped against the wall, closed her eyes, and slid down to the floor, unconscious. Eric lowered his camera.

Lamont was already on his cell phone to 911, barking instructions. A few dinner stragglers stopped and gawked.

"Give her some air, people," Lamont commanded and they obeyed. He knelt at her side to check her pulse. Lacey stayed with him, and LaToya materialized, eager to be part of the action. They waited for the ambulance to arrive. Lamont fixed Lacey with his detective stare.

"Paris Green, huh?"

"A remote possibility," Lacey said.

"Beautiful color," LaToya said. "This is the Paris Green you were talking about?"

Lacey nodded. "I just hope it's not the color of death."

Lamont glared at her. "Color of death, my ass. It's the damn flu. She worked herself into this state. Flu, stress, that wacky scene with the waiter and the champagne. And if it's that crazy dye of yours, then it's got to be some kind of bizarre, once-in-a-lifetime accident."

"Certainly once in her lifetime." LaToya smiled her most inviting smile at Lamont. He rocked back a step. "Hey, green isn't really my color. Don't move. I'll be right back." She went to reclaim her coat from the coat check as sirens headed their way.

When the paramedics stormed onto the scene, Lamont briefed them on the situation and the background. Lacey, at his elbow, took her opportunity to point out the extremely slim chance of a copper arsenate dye reaction or arsine gas as the cause of Courtney's illness.

"Garlic smell, possible arsenic toxicity. Duly noted, ma'am," was all the head paramedic said. He reached for a respirator just in case, and turned his attention back to the still-unconscious Courtney.

Vic Donovan found Lacey and Lamont standing at the side entrance of the hotel, watching as Courtney was being lifted into the ambulance. He put his arm around Lacey's shoulder and kissed her.

"What happened?" he said.

"I thought we were going to meet upstairs in the lobby bar," she asked.

"I heard sirens. I figured you'd be involved somehow," Vic said. "And here you are. Troublemaker. And I mean that in the nicest possible way."

The rain had stopped. The media protesters were long gone. She felt calmer just seeing him there and feeling his arm around her shoulder. She thought he was the most dashing-looking man she'd seen all evening, even though he wasn't in evening clothes. He was wearing the Bentley's leather jacket Lacey had given him for Christmas. With a deep breath, Lacey realized how tense she had been.

Lamont shook Vic's hand. "Donovan, you going to take Smithsonian off my hands now?"

"Hey, Broadway, you agreed to be my source date," Lacey protested. "You had a great time, admit it."

"I am honored to be your source date, Smithsonian. I wouldn't have missed it," Lamont said. "That is, the dinner, the President, the ladies in their fine, fancy dresses, the whole song and dance. Not to mention this sideshow with the Wallace woman. Experience tells me I should have expected something wacky to happen this evening."

"Wacky? What happened?" Vic said.

"Not completely sure yet." Lamont gave him a thumbnail description of Courtney Wallace's misadventure and Lacey's suggestion of the possibility of a poison dye. Not without a skeptical grimace or two.

"I just said it was a possibility," she said. "That's all I said."

"You believe that, Broadway?" Vic asked.

Lamont laughed, a big booming peal of a laugh. "Absolutely not. Except when Smithsonian is involved, I don't discount crazy."

"Crazy is always a good bet," Vic said.

"Hey, not my fault," Lacey reminded him. "I didn't spill anything on her."

"No one's saying it was your fault. And I look at it this way: There's always a silver lining. I can't wait to tell the guys at the office your latest theory." Lamont started to walk away. "You two have a fun evening. I'm leaving before any more mayhem happens."

"You're going to meet LaToya at one of the hot after-parties?" Lacey inquired.

Lamont squirmed inside his big tuxedo. "I don't know, Smithsonian. She's one very tasty-looking lady, but just between you and me and the fencepost, when I see her coming I don't know which way to run."

It was Lacey's turn to laugh. "Time to decide. I see a yellow dress coming this way."

Too late. LaToya found the big detective and locked her arm in his with a mile-wide smile. Lamont gave Lacey a shrug and a worried grin and went along peacefully.

"You don't have to go to a big after-party?" Vic asked her. "Not even *Vanity Fair*?"

"That low-rent ruckus?" She snuggled into his arms. "No way. You're stuck with me."

The legendary *Vanity Fair* and Bloomberg joint after-party was the most coveted invite of the evening, right after the Correspondents' Dinner itself, but no one from *The Eye Street Observer* was invited. Lacey assumed Claudia Darnell would certainly find her way into the bash. Claudia knew everyone who was anyone in Washington, and she'd have some handsome senator or ambassador lined up as her after-party date.

Lacey was glad the dinner was over, and she had no interest in another party that didn't include Vic Donovan. She was tired and a little deflated. Not just by her confrontation with Courtney and the worrisome aftermath, but by the emptiness of the celebrity worship she'd witnessed all night. Some of those celebrities were rock stars, TV actors, or movie stars, people who were legitimately famous, whether you loved their last epic or not, but others had done nothing to merit attention. They were simply famous for being famous. Or infamous.

Vic took Lacey to Firefly, a restaurant and bar on New Hampshire Avenue, just off Dupont Circle, for decompression and a nightcap. She leaned back in their booth, gazed at the birch tree décor and the huge tree trunk in the center, and ordered a coffee with cognac. Vic made it two. She felt the evening's anxiety slip off her shoulders. It was nice to have someone else's shoulders to lean on.

"Want to talk about it?" Vic caught her eye and smiled.

"Not me. Broadway covered the basics."

"I wish I'd seen that waiter-broadcaster collision and champagne spill. Not often you see a Charlie Chaplin moment like that. And then Lacey Smithsonian mentions a toxic antique dye no longer used. And there is the slightest, remotest, barest hint of a possibility the dye could still be present in this rare vintage dress?"

"The lining, not the dress. It's the right color for Paris Green. Just the lining."

"The lining. The color. The collapse. A fashion clue? Your specialty?"

Only Vic could tease her this way and still let her know he was completely on her side. Lacey was still trying to believe there could be some other cause for Courtney Wallace's sudden illness— exhaustion, anxiety, public pratfall, overwork, the flu. But Lacey's instinct, her nose for nuance, the thing her friends called her ExtraFashionary Perception, said the most improbable cause might be the right one. Her EFP was vibrating and she was suddenly interested in telling Vic all about it.

"Don't mock the fashion reporter, darling. You want fashion clues? I got your fashion clue right here."

Lacey Smithsonian's
FASHION *BITES*

Beating the Rain Game!
Or, *Don't Fear the Raingear*

April showers bring May flowers, but in Washington, D.C., May showers can bring a colorful bouquet of expletives, with little thought of the roses. Rain can dampen more than your outfit. It can totally hose your good mood.

There is no feeling in the Nation's Capital like standing in the four-foot spray of water from a passing Metro bus, one with a maniacally laughing driver who just scored ten points in his game of "Soak the Pedestrian." There is no frizz like the frizzy follicles blown up like a balloon by the constant mist of a Washington May. There are no cold feet like those soaked in a steady downpour of D.C. drizzle.

It's Eight A.M. Do You Know Where Your Umbrella Is?

If you have lived here for any time at all, you own a vast collection of umbrellas, bought in haste at street corners, purchased after dodging into drugstores between the raindrops, and as a last resort, grabbed for a few bucks at Metro stops as the clouds opened up and poured down upon you. Many of them you will lose, or have lost already. Others have turned inside-out in the gales, the spines have broken, the wind has blown them out of your hands, and you have tossed the battered remains in the next trashcan, where they will join others of their sorry kind.

You wonder why you can't find a simple plastic parasol among your possessions?

You have left them on the bus, dropped them on the Metro, forgotten them under your seat at the theatre, and abandoned them on the counter of the department store where you ran to address some more pressing fashion emergency. Thousands of umbrellas change hands and locations every rainy day in Washington, D.C., like a secret migration. They make their way into strangers' hands, into dark corners in closets and under desks and behind filing cabinets, and finally to dreary Lost and Found departments, from whence they are never retrieved. They fill the great Washington Graveyard of Lost Umbrellas, which is vaster than the Bermuda Triangle. It is to be hoped that these umbrellas are not all black, like your mood, umbrella-less in the rain.

So, shall we sing off-key of Spring's glories in our leaky waders? Shall we curse the skies that open up and rain down upon us? Or, shall we prepare for the inevitable with smart, stylish raingear? If you chose the last option, you are way ahead in the rain game.

Washington Rainwear Do's and Don'ts

Do invest in a smart pair of rubber rain boots. They come in a variety of colors and patterns, blue or red or yellow, but if that's too much visual adventure for your sense of propriety, you can always go with classic Wellies in English Garden Green. Simply swap them for another pair of shoes when you get to the office. You do have a few extra pair of heels and flats lurking under your desk, don't you? Next to that missing umbrella?

Do buy a good raincoat. You will need it here. Often. So buy one that is good quality and good looking. Unfortunately, when you find a great raincoat, one that is flattering and wicks away the moisture and remains unwrinkled, you will immediately see it everywhere in town, coming and going. A khaki trench coat? Another popular choice. You might think there's a Trench Coat Conspiracy to take over the Nation's Capital. On rainy days everyone on Pennsylvania Avenue looks like a trench-coated refugee from World War I. Take heart: Yours doesn't have to be khaki! Go crazy. Pick another color.

Do have several umbrellas on hand. Buy them in

bright colors or patterns, to lift your mood and help differentiate yours from the sea of gloomy black umbrellas filling every rainy Washington street. But don't get too attached to them. The life expectancy of the average umbrella in this town is short. See above.

Do have an emergency hair and makeup kit on hand. You will need these supplies to look polished for that important board meeting or Congressional hearing. Remember, never let them see you sweat, or with rain dripping from your scalp. So pack along your comb, elastic hair bands, hairspray, and pins to deal with a hairdo that has exploded and looks like a mushroom cloud erupting from your head. Wet wipes to clean up dark smears under your eyes are invaluable. Don't forget, a bit of foundation or powder and mascara can rescue melted makeup streaks creasing down your cheeks. Streaks happen.

Don't think that a mere newspaper or even that fat Senate subcommittee report is going to keep you dry in a Washington downpour. It won't.

Don't wrap yourself up in a big plastic garbage bag, not even a shiny black one. It looks sad and desperate. In this case, black does not equal *formal*.

And finally:

Don't reach for that cheap logo-printed plastic poncho you grabbed in desperation at the gift shop in one of the museums (probably the Smithsonian). Remember, a true Washingtonian never wants to be mistaken for a tourist! If you're caught in the rain here without a raincoat or an umbrella, just resign yourself to getting soaked to the skin and dripping wherever you go for the rest of the day, like a true Washingtonian.

Just like the rest of us in this town who've lost our umbrellas.

Chapter 6

O N SUNDAY MORNING LACEY HEARD the click of her clock radio just before the news came on. She yawned and lay back, enjoying the prospect of a lazy Sunday. With Vic. And no fashion clues.

"—Channel One spokesperson said Wallace appeared ill last evening at the White House Correspondents' Dinner. No foul play is indicated. Police are withholding further details pending autopsy results. Again, Emmy Award-winning local newscaster Courtney Wallace, dead at twenty-eight. Now, turning to the weather—"

"Dead?" Lacey opened her eyes wide and sat straight up. "Courtney is dead?"

"Was that you squealing?" Vic showed up at the bedroom door carrying two cups of coffee. He sat down on the bed and handed her one.

"I didn't hear what I just heard. I must have been dreaming."

"Scoot over. We'll dream together."

"It can't be true. Courtney's dead?"

"Sorry, sweetheart. Courtney Wallace shuffled off that mortal coil early this morning. I caught it on the kitchen radio while I was making coffee."

"Cause of death?" She held on to the warm cup and breathed the steam before sipping.

"Not announced. Details pending. Autopsy. You know the drill."

"Unbelievable. Courtney." Lacey tried to wrap her head around the news. She sipped Vic's delicious concoction and hoped it would clear her head. Vic had even steamed the milk with the adorable little frothing machine he'd bought her. The coffee was delicious, creamy, hot, and sweet. Normally, she would mentally compare the brew to Vic. He was very appealing this morning. This, she thought, could be the start of a great morning. But under the circumstances, she had other things on her mind.

"I tried to warn her," Lacey said.

"You can't be sure that Paris Green dye was the cause, you know."

"That's not what my gut is saying."

"It's Courtney's gut that'll have the last word. Autopsy,

toxicology, the poison will turn up or it won't." He pulled her into a hug. "Far be it from me to second-guess your gut, darling. But even if you're right, you warned her and she did not heed that warning. Who else could even have known there might be something hazardous to warn her about? You did your best."

The radio reported that it was going to be a beautiful day for everyone. *Everyone except Courtney Wallace.* Lacey switched the radio over to classical music on WETA.

"I need some Vivaldi. The news isn't going to get any better."

"Lacey, darling, I know you're going to keep going over everything in your head until you make yourself sick. Don't do it. Wallace's death had nothing to do with you. It's not your fault. You couldn't force her to change that dress, could you?"

"I wasn't very nice to her last night. I refused to let her interview me. I refused to go on camera."

"It didn't kill her. She was used to it. Besides, we've all refused to go on camera. We've all declined to be quoted."

Vic was speaking from experience. He had often declined to give Lacey information, back when he was the chief of police in Sagebrush, Colorado, and she was a green reporter. These days he was keeping a much lower public profile, and he shared a little more information with her. Vic had returned to Virginia to work with his dad as co-owner of a security company headquartered in Arlington. He and Lacey reconnected. Old feelings became new, and they were together at last. And Lacey had to admit the man made a mean cup of java.

Lacey pulled on a robe and took her coffee to the balcony of her apartment, where she never tired of her seventh-floor view of the Potomac. She had lucked out when she found this apartment building in Old Town, Alexandria. This time of year it was extra glorious. The tall willows on the banks might be weeping with joy that they were back in full glory. The oaks were leafing out. Ospreys, egrets, and blue herons were in flight over the river, and Lacey caught sight of a bald eagle soaring high above. Little sailboats from the unpretentious Belle Haven Marina were heading out for the day. Tour boats full of visitors headed across the river to National Harbor, while others were bound further south to Mount Vernon, the ever-popular home of George Washington. Yesterday's furious rainstorm had washed the humidity away and the day was bright and clear. Tourists would crowd the parks and the monuments and the streets of Old Town.

Lacey finished her coffee and went inside to shower and dress, leaving Vic to enjoy the balcony. For her, this was that time of year when the summer dresses were begging to come out. The light, airy summer frock she selected wasn't vintage, but it had a retro vibe in a bright coral with three-quarter sleeves and white trim. Vic was already showered and ready to go in jeans and a green shirt she had given to him. It matched his eyes.

There was just enough time for them to make the late Mass at St. Mary's. Vic wasn't very religious, but he was happy to go with her whenever she was in the mood. She took it as a pledge of his intent to walk her down the aisle. Lacey had prayers to say, but unfortunately the warbling soloist with the relentless piercing vibrato was making it difficult to focus. The soloist did, however, keep her wide awake, as last night's events played on a recurring loop in her head.

Afterward, she and Vic went to brunch at the Union Street Pub at the bottom of Old Town, a block south of bustling King Street. They were ushered to a small table overlooking the Union Street action.

"You're quiet," Vic said.

"I can't stop thinking about it."

"I'm not going to ask if you want to talk about it, because I know eventually you're going to talk about it until you've exhausted the subject."

"You know me so well."

"Just let me order first."

"More coffee then." Lacey yawned, covering her mouth.

"You had a big night. With the big guy himself, Broadway Lamont. And not with me."

"You know the rules. I couldn't invite you. I had to bring a source. I would love to have taken you."

"I could be your source. I'll make up all the news you can use."

She waggled her fingers at him. "Conflict of interest, my dear."

"That's what you used to say when I asked you out, back in Sagebrush."

"Huge conflict of interest. You had a wife. I'm not the one with a previous marriage."

Lacey had caught his eye when he was still married to, though separated from, his now ex-wife Montana. Lacey was a rookie reporter, fresh out of journalism school. He was an almost-as-green chief of police. Vic Donovan, dark-haired and green-eyed, towered over her, and she found him almost ridiculously handsome.

Montana tried her best to win Vic back, even though she had gone through a number of other men and other husbands, both her own and other women's. Lacey thought she was either completely ruthless, or an eternal optimist.

"I was getting a divorce. As I told you at the time. Besides, I'm not sure a Las Vegas marriage really ought to be considered legal. It's a gray area."

"Legal but tacky," she said. "Our wedding won't be tacky. I'll make sure of that."

"When?" he pressed.

"When? Not for a while." The waiter appeared at their table. "I'll have the crab cakes, please."

"Sounds good. Make it two." The server scooted off. Lacey rubbed her forehead.

"This thing with Courtney. It's bugging me, Vic."

"Especially with some screwy fashion aspect to the proceedings that only Lacey Smithsonian could possibly decode."

"It's a gift."

"Which keeps on giving."

"Why there?" Lacey took his hand. "Don't you think it's weird that Courtney's slide toward the Grim Reaper happened at the Correspondents' Dinner, of all places? Secret Service everywhere, all those metal detectors, cameras all over the place, wall-to-wall media? It's the most secure place in town. Maybe the world. Nobody gets in who's not on the List. Everyone has to submit personal information ahead of time, everyone gets checked, everyone gets screened at the security gates, all those guys with guns and earpieces. And yet—"

"It's not weird if it was an accident. You think it was deliberate?"

"Not exactly. Not yet. But if it was copper arsenate poisoning from Paris Green dye— And you can take that skeptical cop look off your face, mister. Just go with me here."

He smirked at her. "What cop look?"

"That one, and you know it." She imitated him, scrunching her eyebrows.

He smirked back at her. "Okay. You said it was an accident when the waiter with the drinks spilled his tray."

"That's the way it seemed. The waiter looked horrified. I didn't see anyone trip him or shove him, but the place was packed. I could have missed it. But why did he trip? Why was Courtney in his path at that exact moment? Why did she wear that dress when she could have worn any vintage dress?"

"Why do trees crash onto cars on the highway in a storm? That tree, that car, that exact moment?"

"Unanswerable questions, I guess."

Courtney's series of stories on vintage clothing on Channel One would be a place to start. Could the series have been some sort of punishment? An exile from hard news?

Fashion was not a beat that garnered respect. Lacey had discovered that firsthand. She started her career in news, not fashion. She was on her way to being a hard news reporter in Washington when she caught Mac's eye at the exact wrong moment. She was thrown into the fashion beat because the previous fashion editor, Mariah "the Pariah" Morgan, died at her desk, in her old-fashioned, oak desk chair. She'd been sitting there for hours and was in full rigor mortis by the time anyone noticed, and then only because she'd missed her deadline for a story. If not for that deadline, she might have sat there dead at her desk for days.

That was the kind of respect fashion got in D.C. And they never even got rid of the chair Mariah died in. The Death Chair sailed around the office from desk to desk like a ghost ship, an oaken Flying Dutchman on wheels. It always seemed to wind up back near Lacey's cubicle.

But what happened to Courtney?

"The biggest question right now is the dress," Lacey said. "How did a dress that I suspect was made in the early Forties, or maybe the late Thirties, happen to have a lining dyed a color supposedly not used since the late nineteenth century?"

"They stopped using Paris Green?"

"Long ago. After people found out how dangerous it was. I think maybe they still use it in fireworks, things like that, but not in clothes."

"You're the fashion seer. What do you think?"

"It looked like part of her series on vintage clothing. She'd been wearing a different vintage outfit for each story. I need to view all those video clips, I only saw a few on TV. They sounded suspiciously like they were cribbed almost word-for-word from my articles and columns in *The Eye*. However, Courtney reminded me last night that ideas are not copyrightable."

"In other words, it was okay to steal your stuff and change a few words."

"Basically, yes."

"She sounds like a lawyer, not a reporter."

"I've never seen anything quite like that Madame X dress of hers," she mused. "Where did it come from? And where is it now?"

"With her personal effects. It might go back to her family. Unless the M.E. hangs onto it."

"Champagne stains have to be taken care of right away. It'll be ruined. No one will want that dress now."

"You'd like to look at it, wouldn't you?"

Lacey peered out the window. "I don't know that it could tell me anything. But I'd like to see it."

"It will keep. If there's a way to see it, you'll find it. I have a better question on this beautiful day. When are we going to get your engagement ring?"

"My *what*?"

Weddings were in the air all around them. Lacey's friend Stella Lake had finally married Nigel, the man of her very specific and unusual dreams, despite all the odds against it. Brooke was paired up with Damon, again a dream that only Brooke could have dreamed. Felicity and Harlan, Marie and Gregor Kepelov. And Vic Donovan had proposed to Lacey, in the least likely circumstances she could ever have imagined. She stared at her left hand, which was still bare.

"You heard me." Vic was smiling. "We need a ring for that hand."

He wants to go ring shopping? "What's the hurry?" she asked.

"Darling, we're not getting any younger. I want to rock you down the aisle without a walker. When I see a ring on your finger, I might start to believe it's real. You have a history of fleeing men who ask you to marry them."

"One time! Gee whiz. That was all."

"One time, but you went two thousand miles!"

"Only eighteen hundred. Or so. And I was fleeing a terrible town!"

Lacey ran away from Sagebrush, Colorado, and the cowboy— correction, *rancher*—who proposed to her. It was a small town. People talked. Vic always made a bigger deal of it than it really was. *Maybe.*

"It's time to set up a home, Lacey," he said softly. "You and me. Together."

And shop for a ring? It was things like that—setting up house together—that terrified her. Vic reached for her hands. The feel of his hands warmed her skin, her heart, her soul. Lacey felt at home with Vic, without the need to set up house. Not just yet.

It was funny how love complicated things and simplified them at the same time. Perhaps it was because she feared losing her independence. Yet when she thought of Vic, she felt so at home with him. However, he had more money, a more stable career, a family business. She'd never be able to match him dollar for dollar with her reporter's salary.

What if the newspaper folded and she couldn't find another job? Papers were in a precarious position everywhere and *The Eye* wasn't making much profit, if any. Lacey didn't think she could switch to something like broadcast journalism, even though she had the cheekbones for it. Her heart would never be in it. Of course, there was her P.I. registration, for which she had worked harder than she expected. Could she switch careers? Would Vic give her a job as an investigator? Could they be a twenty-first-century Nick and Nora Charles? She liked that image. Minus Asta the dog, of course.

"We can get the ring," she said at last. "I'd like that." Lacey was grateful he hadn't simply surprised her with one. What if she hated it? She wanted to select the setting herself. After all, she planned to wear it for the rest of her life. She wanted to love it.

Vic's mother, Nadine Donovan, had already mentioned the "family jewels" from which any potential daughter-in-law would be welcome to choose. She knew there was at least one diamond that would be perfect. Well over a carat, a healthy size without being gaudy. *Okay, maybe just a little gaudy.*

"Is the diamond all right?" A frown creased Vic's forehead. The stone had already been taken out of the worn platinum solitaire setting. "It belonged to my grandmother. It worked for her. She was married for over fifty years."

Lacey laughed. He almost never betrayed fear, but he was worried she might object to his grandmother's gem?

"It's a wonderful stone."

"It's not like it's a chip or anything. It's a respectable diamond."

"Hush." She squeezed his hand.

"I've wanted you for such a long time."

"Me too."

For so many people in the world, it was hard to find love. Lacey thought of Courtney Wallace, so young and ambitious. Now she was dead. Lacey leaned across the table to kiss Vic.

"Let's go ring shopping," he murmured. "Can we do it this week?"

"I'll ask Mac for a day off." Vic looked like he was ready to go shopping right that minute.

"Good. We're going to Baltimore."

"Baltimore? Why Baltimore?" she asked.

"I know a guy there, a diamond specialist. Friend of the family. And we won't run the risk of running into anyone you know and freaking you out. I understand how emotional this ring thing is for you."

"I'm not that bad."

"Says the woman who wanted to have a secret engagement."

"It's been a busy time. And complicated." Lacey didn't want to admit he was right. Wearing a ring was a public declaration. She wasn't ready for it. Until now.

"I know you didn't want to step on Stella's wedding. But she and Nigel are off on their honeymoon. It's the perfect time for us to do this."

Her cell beeped. It was a text from Brooke, which she read aloud to Vic: "What happened re: Wallace? Theories? Need to investigate! CALL ME NOW."

Lacey put her phone away with a sigh. "Let's run away, Vic. Couldn't we just elope?"

Chapter 7

"I DON'T KNOW WHY SHE'S dead, if that's what you mean," Lacey told Brooke later that afternoon.

"Maybe she really was a wicked witch, and the champagne melted her," Brooke offered.

"Maybe you and Damon can rip the lid off wicked witches in the Washington media. Uncover a coven meeting at the Press Club. You'll have fun."

"With so many flying monkeys in this town, we'll never find them all."

They spoke on the phone as Lacey was walking home from lunch along the Potomac River. Vic had departed for his office to catch up on paperwork. She breathed in the May day. The warm air cuddled her. She adored Old Town, even though the Alexandria City Council was trying to destroy the picturesque waterfront and turn it into an exclusive millionaires' club.

"Well, witch or no witch, Courtney is dead and I'm sure *you'll* be investigating," Brooke said.

"Fashion reporter here. Remember? Not on the investigative beat. Or the conspiracy beat."

"I've heard that tune before."

"You have too much faith in me, Brooke. Besides, if I did come up with a theory, you'd tattle to Damon for his rag, although I don't know if you could actually call an online blog-slash-newsletter a real rag. It's a slur on rags."

"I'm hurt, Lacey. DeadFed is too a real rag. You know what I mean." Brooke never pouted for long. "What if I promise I won't tell Damon anything unless it's public knowledge or I have your permission?"

"He's there with you, isn't he?" A bright red cardinal swooped across the path in front of Lacey. She heard hushed voices on Brooke's end of the line.

"No, no, he's just leaving. I'm a free agent. Why don't I come over?"

"Come ahead, I'll be home in a few minutes. I'm going to chill." Lacey planned to catch up on the news stories about Courtney. It would be all over the media. She wanted to watch Courtney's entire vintage fashion series and see if she'd mentioned the Madame X dress or where she purchased it.

"I'll bring some wine. We need to debrief." Brooke sounded a little too excited.

"Debrief? You know I hate that word. Better to say 'brief' than 'debrief.' If *brief* means to supply information, *debrief* sounds like we'll be wiping our brains clean."

"Don't get your briefs in a bunch. See you soon." Brooke clicked off.

Back in her apartment, Lacey changed into a casual print skirt in blues and violets and a sleeveless purple top, comfortable for the weather, but not sloppy. Contrary to popular opinion among her friends and fans, she was not all vintage, all the time. She didn't want to wear out her favorite pieces, knowing how fragile some of them were, and there wasn't a lot of vintage casual wear left. The pieces that survived the decades were typically only the very best, things that women had saved for special occasions. Outfits from the Thirties and Forties, Lacey's favorite eras, were scarce and getting scarcer, and many were impossibly small, the size of modern children's clothes.

Often older fashions were recut and restyled to suit new designs, taken in or taken out, the shoulder pads thrown away. These transformations may not have been the best choice, but in tough times clothes were worn until they were threadbare and then cut up for rags or quilts, or the material was saved to be used another day. During World War II, posters and hand-stitched samplers advised Americans to *Use it up, Wear it out, Make it do, Or do without!*

The American people took wartime fabric rationing to heart, using and reusing their clothing. Lacey's grandmother and great-grandmother had made quilts of cut-up dresses and scraps of worn-out fabric. Only her Aunt Mimi treasured some special wardrobe pieces enough to keep them intact and pristine. Lacey eyed Mimi's trunk of vintage treasures (which doubled as her coffee table), where she often found inspiration. Instead, she booted up her laptop.

As she suspected, Courtney's recent news stories were easily found online, and Lacey was able to watch her every entry on vintage fashion. Courtney's theme was "Wearable Vintage in Vogue in Washington, D.C." The short segments were light and breezy and full of vintage eye candy, but Courtney's work still managed to irritate Lacey. Prior to Courtney's series, Lacey had written a feature series of her own in *The Eye*, highlighting local vintage stores—their strengths and specialties, the eras and types of clothes they carried, and how a vintage wardrobe could work in everyday life. Courtney cribbed a lot from Lacey's articles.

Five features on vintage were aired leading up to the Correspondents' Dinner, the last one just a few days before. The station treated these bits as the entertainment part of the news and replayed them on the Channel One morning feature-oriented show, "Wide Awake Washington."

Lacey wondered why this ambitious Emmy Award winner would pursue a series her station clearly considered to be nothing but fluff. More likely Courtney, for all her good looks and blond hair and Chiclet teeth, was being shifted off the news beat. A single Emmy wasn't that big a deal, anyway. Lacey knew broadcast journalists who'd won dozens of them. The one big political story Courtney screwed up must have had a far-reaching effect. It felt to Lacey like the ax was ready to fall, right before Courtney herself did. She skimmed through the features again on fast-forward, watching for clues in Courtney's clothes and presentation.

Courtney began her sartorial journey in the 1930s, wearing a beige-and-white-striped knit sweater and solid beige knit skirt, paired with brown pumps and a brown beret. She struck a pose, looking very much like that outlaw clotheshorse Bonnie Parker, of the bank robbing duo, Bonnie and Clyde. Bonnie didn't rate a mention, though, nor did the Great Depression or the end of the Flapper Era.

In the next piece, the sleek siren look was gone. The bias-cut Thirties fashions that hugged the figure changed dramatically, as the broad shoulders and nipped-in waistline of the Forties took over. Courtney wore a striking blue-gray pinstripe suit with red platform pumps, looking ready for the Senate press room—or *His Girl Friday*. But Courtney Wallace was no Rosalind Russell.

American clothing design in the Forties sent the message that women could shoulder the wartime responsibilities of the workplace and, indeed, the nation. While American men were at war, American women were taking over their jobs, and their need for a professional wardrobe fueled the historic rise of the American apparel industry. Courtney didn't mention any of this historical context. She just *oohed* and *aahed* over the shoulder pads.

For her segment highlighting the clothes of the Fifties, Courtney chose what Lacey referred to as the Lamentable Lampshade Dress. This one was a sleeveless cocktail creation in ivory taffeta which fanned out in an extreme lampshade silhouette. It looked painfully nipped in at the waist and flowed out into a full circle skirt. Lacey thought it looked just as preposterous on Courtney as it probably did in that postwar decade when men and society were shoving women out of their offices and back into the kitchen, to wear aprons and disappointment. Lacey was surprised Courtney hadn't donned pearls and a cocktail apron. Again, the television bites pulled the clothes out of context and ignored the larger world behind them.

"Don't eat if you're going to wear a dress like this," Courtney chirpily advised her viewers.

Moving into the Sixties, Courtney donned a simple yellow sheath dress à la First Lady Jacqueline Kennedy. The dress looked eminently wearable today, Lacey thought, though the matching yellow pillbox hat and low heels marked it as out of place and out of time. It was an iconic style, but Lacey didn't care for unconstructed garments that ignored a woman's basic shape. The Jackie Kennedy sheath dress would look good only on someone thin enough to pull it off. Courtney wore it well. But did she mention Jackie or JFK or the enduring style legacy of their brief, shining Camelot? Lacey watched and waited. Not a word.

The Seventies vintage piece closed Courtney's series with high-waisted bell-bottomed jeans and a white cotton bohemian top, its flowing sleeves embroidered in blue and lavender paisley. She completed the look with sandals and a lavender paisley scarf tied as a belt. It could have been worse. There were much more extreme fashions from that era, and this one managed to look fresh and pretty on her.

Lacey remembered her grandmother saying of the Seventies, "The whole world was having a costume party and I wasn't invited."

Courtney's series was one long costume party, without a hint of the worlds from which these clothes emerged. In each segment, Courtney merely demonstrated how vintage fashion was classic and wearable and could be found in stores here and there throughout Washington, Maryland, and Virginia. She never mentioned the Madame X dress, but she ended the last episode with a teaser: "Join me next time, as I once more travel back in time to explore more wearable vintage fashion at the White House Correspondents' Dinner."

Lacey grudgingly had to admit that she didn't own the vintage clothing territory. And television news stories were a flash in the pan that disappeared even more quickly than newsprint. In addition, the very nature of television news ensured that Courtney couldn't possibly explore any story in depth. Her stories were measured in seconds rather than column inches, and in those seconds she could only deliver the lede, a couple of the journalist's famous Five W's, quote someone on camera, smile, and sign off. The why and how of a story were usually the W's that got left out.

It was the why and how of Courtney's death that now nagged at Lacey. She didn't know why she felt so compelled to find answers. Perhaps it was guilt. She would have felt better if she'd left the situation with Courtney on good terms. Nevertheless, she didn't regret saying no to an on-camera interview. She had to protect herself, and sometimes feelings got hurt.

Could she have tried harder to convince Courtney to change out of that dress? Lacey didn't know for certain that the dress was the cause of the woman's death, but her gut said it was. Lacey kept coming back to the same questions: Where had the Madame X dress come from? Why was Courtney wearing it that night, at that exact moment in time, the same moment the waiter tripped?

And who exactly was the waiter? Lacey had seen him on stage in a play, a recent production of *A Midsummer Night's Dream* at the Folger Shakespeare Theatre. He didn't have a large part, but his sweet face and slight build made him a good fit for the role of Francis Flute, who played the lovelorn maiden Thisbe in the play within the play. Lacey called the Shakespeare expert with whom she'd seen the show, *The Eye*'s theatre critic, Tamsin Kerr.

Tamsin was always entertaining. She was tall and striking and had an austere, theatrical style of dress, usually in black. Her great mass of curly hair rested on her shoulders like a dark cloud, and her dark expression often matched it. She always managed to look regal, and in her career she had terrified hundreds of actors, directors, theatre producers, and not a few reporters. Lacey had heard the theatre community sometimes referred to her as "Killer" Kerr, but the life of a critic had its compensations: Free tickets.

Tamsin wasn't too excited by the show, Lacey remembered.

"Another season, another *Dream*," she'd commented at intermission. "At least it's not another modern-dress extravaganza with motorcycles and helicopters. Leave that to Arena Stage. And you should have seen the version with the swimming pools, half-clad actors shivering in and out of the water, slipping and falling onstage, splashing the audience. It was entertaining. Spectacle can be hilarious in all the wrong ways. It isn't always bad, it entertains the groundlings, but I hate it when the play gets lost."

Tamsin answered the phone with a single word.

"Speak."

"Tamsin? It's Lacey. Do you have a minute?"

"One or two. For you."

"I want to get hold of an actor who was in the *Dream* we saw together. *Midsummer Night's*, that is. He was one of Bottom's crew of rude mechanicals, the one who plays Thisbe. Do you remember his name?"

"Francis Flute, the bellows-mender. Oh, you mean the actor's name? Let me think." There was a pause. Tamsin had amazing, but rambling, recall and Lacey didn't interrupt. "Will. Will Something. He was rather droll as Thisbe. Will as in Shakespeare, but that wasn't the name, of course. It'll come to me. He played an androgynous Ariel in that ghastly Tempest-with-Bigfoot thing at Thesaurus Theatre last year."

"He's also a waiter," Lacey said.

"Of course he is, aren't they all? I used to see him waiting tables at Two Quail, but it has since closed. Unsurprising. Their service was glacial. Your waiter slips away for an audition and leaves your entrée congealing under the warming lights. He's waitering somewhere else now. Perhaps Trio's? But no, not Trio's. Next door or down the street. I believe I saw him before a show at Theatre J last week. A new restaurant. The Spotlight? That's it. It's theatre kitschy."

"The Spotlight. I haven't heard about it."

"All actors. Doomed to fail. But we'll see."

"How was the food?"

"Edible, but not memorable. I had the pasta, because you always assume they can't ruin the pasta. And yet, they *can* ruin the pasta."

"Thanks for the tip. Call me if you think of his name, would you?" She was ready to hang up.

"Wait, Smithsonian. Why do you want to know this Will Something? He's really just a spear carrier, you know, not a lead."

"He bumped into Courtney Wallace with a tray of champagne at the Correspondents' Dinner. Spilled it all over her dress."

"A clumsy waiter? Not a great calling card for an actor. Courtney Wallace. Now why do I know that name?"

"Television reporter." *And recently deceased.*

"Yes. Dreadful woman. Won an Emmy? Best performance impersonating a reporter, I believe. You know the type. Eternal ingénue, she'll never advance to meaty roles. She'll just flip that hair till we all have whiplash."

"Not anymore. She's dead."

"Dead? She's rather young to be dead. Though dying is easy, as they say. Tell me the plot, Smithsonian. What happened and how are you involved? You are involved, aren't you? Something to do with clothes, I hope. It drives the boy reporters mad when you do that. I love that. They have no respect for the rest of us poor scribes."

"I haven't done anything yet. It's just conjecture at this point."

"Conjecture away, I'm not an attorney."

"It happened last night."

"Ah, the Correspondents' Dinner, you said. I've never been. The Helen Hayes Awards are quite enough drama, or lack thereof, for me. But then, no one has died at the Helen Hayes. By the way, what did Will Something do, other than bumbling the bubbly?"

"Not sure. I just want to talk to him. Ask how he happened to trip."

"Was it on camera? That's always fun. You know what I mean. Not fun. Opportune." Tamsin's tone said she really meant it was fun. "Does it have anything to do with the Wallace woman's death? Wait. Did he bonk her on the head with the tray? A piece of glass struck a vital artery?"

"You've seen too many bad plays."

"Indeed, I have. At any rate that would be unmotivated, without a back story. Hence, dramatically unsatisfying. Therefore you must be seeking out the back story. The subtext."

"It must be interesting to see the world in dramatic context, Tamsin," Lacey said.

"Agreed. It would be if I did, but alas I don't. So pray, continue with your tale."

Lacey explained her theory of toxic fumes of Paris Green dye from the wet dress. "Just a half-baked theory at this point. The autopsy results aren't in yet."

"They wouldn't be. Clever way to kill someone though."

"You think she was killed?"

"I certainly would if I wrote plays. But in this case, a freak accident seems even more absurd. Is the poison asp in the bodice ever an accident? As a drama critic I vote for murder. And appropriate motivation. Good luck finding young Will."

"I appreciate it."

"I don't believe our Will Something is appearing in anything right now. I've seen every bad play currently running. He's Equity, I think, but you know theatre. You can make a killing but not a living, and all that. It's a hell of a life. Even if you're good."

"I imagine it is." *But theatre is also what people do for love,* Lacey thought. Kill themselves for a moment in the spotlight. Just like Courtney Wallace.

"Please call back with the climax and the denouement, when you know what it is. What we really need to know is whether this is the end of the play, or the beginning. Was Courtney's death the final curtain, or just Act One?"

Lacey promised an update and signed off. She searched online and found on *The Eye*'s web site Tamsin's review of the *Dream* they'd seen together. Francis Flute was played by one Will Zephron, Tamsin's "Will Something." Lacey called The Spotlight and asked for Will.

"Not here today." It was a bored woman with a flat Midwestern accent. "He's got a scene work class or something. He'll be working the lunch shift tomorrow. Like maybe about eleven? Not sure till when."

Good, another D.C. restaurant staffed with actors dashing off between customers to try and nail a part. Or nail a director.

"Do you have a phone number for him?"

"We don't give out personal information like that. If it's really important, I can get a message to him tomorrow. Or if this is like life or death, like about an acting gig—"

Lacey was glad it wasn't a matter of life and death. *Except for Courtney.* And it would be awkward to explain to the bored girl.

"No, thanks."

She decided to pencil in lunch tomorrow at The Spotlight.

Chapter 8

LACEY'S PHONE BUZZED, ANNOUNCING BROOKE'S arrival. She shut her laptop and opened the door to let in her friend.

"So what's the cause of death?" Lacey asked. "I assume that's your big secret."

Brooke's blond hair was pulled back into a braid, and her plaid shorts, athletic shoes, and yellow polo shirt told Lacey she'd either come straight from the tennis court or wanted everyone to think she had. Brooke's eyes sparkled with secrets to share. Lacey knew this could mean only one thing: She and Damon had their own mad theory about Courtney's demise.

"It was the *flu*," Brooke confided dramatically.

"The flu?" Lacey lifted an eyebrow. Just what Broadway Lamont suggested, too. "Just the flu? Really? That's an anticlimax. Is Damon's story online?"

"Not 'just' the flu. And of course it's online. Is D.C. the spy capital of the world?"

Lacey reopened her laptop and found the headline of Damon's Conspiracy Clearinghouse article on DeadFed dot com.

BROADCASTER DEAD AT 28! VICTIM OF 1918 KILLER FLU?

"Did he confirm that?"

"Of course he did. Confidential source."

Lacey suspected Damon's confidential source was *himself*. "Persuade me."

"It's not just any flu," Brooke said. "This is a pandemic flu, like the one that hit almost one hundred years ago. Damon thinks it's weaponized flu, genetically modified for rapid lethality, and it's being deliberately spread worldwide. But why and by whom, that's the real mystery."

"It doesn't have to be modified," Lacey said. "People in 1918 were healthy one day and dead the next."

"This one works even faster. Courtney was healthy when she arrived, and practically dead by the end of the evening."

"Maybe."

"There's no maybe about it! In 1918," Brooke explained breathlessly, "more young and healthy adults died of influenza than older ones, because they had a fatal overreaction of the immune system. They went into a state of emergency, called a cytokine cascade, meaning it wore them out, killing them at higher rates than older victims. Ironically, middle-aged people, though not the elderly, were more likely to survive. This year's highly weaponized flu resembles the 1918 strain in that young adults are dying in higher numbers. Those at the highest risk of death are between eighteen and forty-five years old. Like Courtney. And like us."

"Courtney fit the fatal profile," Lacey agreed, "but how could the flu, even *weaponized* flu, kill her so quickly?"

"Read the whole article," Brooke insisted. "You only read the headline!"

Of course, to Brooke and Damon the insidious conspiracy to spread a deadly new strain of Killer Flu was obvious. Or was Courtney already ill when she arrived at the dinner, and the gorgeous green lining of the black dress and the champagne spill, and Brooke and Damon's theories, all just irrelevant distractions? Had Lacey's ExtraFashionary Perception failed her, shorted out by a spray of champagne?

"It's too beautiful a day to stay inside and talk about the flu, don't you think?" Lacey said. "I need to get outside."

"As long as my cell phone works." Brooke couldn't stand to be completely unhooked from the Web.

"You know, Brooke," Lacey teased, "aliens are probably tracking you with your phone."

Brooke snorted. "Why use a phone when they can just read that microchip they implanted?"

They strolled down the river toward Dyke Marsh, a mile or so down the Potomac River bike path in the direction of Mount Vernon, only eight miles away. The earthy aroma of the river and the lush early summer vegetation accompanied them. Lacey was content to let Brooke talk and theorize at will.

"Maybe when Courtney was inoculated, she was dosed with the virus itself, instead of the immunization," Brooke suggested. "Maybe the virus was in the champagne. Or her microphone, always in her face. Or maybe it was in that crazy black dress."

"Maybe it was in the alien chip," Lacey said.

Brooke eyes lit up, almost seeming to buy it—until she saw

Lacey smirking at her. "You laugh. You've probably got one too."

The bike path was crowded with Sunday joggers and bikers until they reached Belle Haven Park at the marina, but it thinned out once they entered Dyke Marsh. A lone artist sat at an easel at a bend in the path, painting the boats and birds. Farther down in the marsh, just off the curve of the boardwalk, a violinist wearing green rubber boots stood in the tall grass, playing his fiddle in a concert for no one, or perhaps for everyone. He nodded to Lacey and Brooke as they continued to the end of the boardwalk. There was music in the air.

A breeze ruffled Lacey's hair. Now just south of the marina, they could see the full sweep of the Potomac, dotted with the marina's little sailboats, the larger yachts from up and down the river, the big sightseeing cruise ships heading for Mount Vernon, and of course the ever-present geese and gulls.

"You're convinced it was the flu?" Lacey said. "Alien or otherwise? Broadway Lamont thought so too. Not the alien part, though. Just the flu."

"Definitely the flu," Brooke agreed. "Genetically engineered Killer Flu. It's nationwide. Damon's really nailed it this time. But who are they? What do they want? And why choose Wallace? She wasn't even a real journalist! Why not *you*?"

Chapter 9

LACEY PLANNED TO EASE INTO work Monday morning. When it was quiet, Mondays at *The Eye* weren't that bad. She preferred the calm before the storm when the other reporters shuffled in grumpily, resenting the start of their workweek. On the plus side, after their brief storm of Monday crankiness, they would pick up their coffee and sit quietly in front of their computers reading Facebook and their email until at least eleven a.m.

It was just past nine, so she had time to prepare for the day. She took a deep breath before turning the corner into her cubicle. Harlan Wiedemeyer was already waiting for her. Short, chubby, and in love, he was often seen near the cubicle of his beloved Felicity Pickles, the food editor and his fiancée, who dwelled across the aisle from Lacey. Wiedemeyer paused in front of Lacey's desk with an announcement.

"Well, well, well, Smithsonian, seems that D.C. isn't the only place where crimes of fashion take place. Real crimes, I mean."

"Undoubtedly not. What are you talking about, Harlan?" She scooted around him. Did he know about Courtney? But no, he was on another story entirely. He waved the early edition of *The Eye* in her face.

"Some poor bastard died in a stiletto attack in New Jersey. I'm talking about a woman's shoe, a high heel. Not a pump, not a kitten heel, not a flat, not a Cuban heel. A stiletto heel as deadly as the blade of the same name, and wielded like a dagger by a vengeful female. Poor bastard never had a chance."

"I'm impressed. You've been reading my column. You know there are different kinds of heels. But it's a little early in the day for blood and guts, isn't it?" She hunted for her favorite coffee mug.

"Happened over the weekend, wire services were all over it. I wrote a brief for us. Bam to the back of the head with her stiletto heel," he continued. "Pithed the poor bastard like a frog in a tenth-grade science class."

Lacey lifted her head and stared at him. "Are you sure this really happened?" She wasn't sure 'death by stiletto heel' was even possible.

"Of course I'm sure. It's right here in black and white. Read my story. The accused murderer, some brazen jezebel with a foot fetish, is going to prison for the crime." He thrust the paper in front of her.

Brazen jezebel? What era is he from?

"They must have been really good heels." She studied the photos, the woman, her victim, and the blood-stained shoes.

"I'll say. Poor bastard." Wiedemeyer rubbed his head. "What's the world coming to? I could understand if she shot him with a gun. But a stiletto heel to the back of the head? Nobody expects that."

"No. Nobody does," Lacey agreed.

"And to add insult to injury, the poor bastard gave them to her. The shoes! They were a gift! This idiot couldn't win. He handed his killer the weapon of his own destruction. See, right there, it's in my lede."

"Nice lede, Harlan. But you don't have to worry. Felicity never wears high heels."

Lacey had only seen the woman in a pair of frumpy-dumpy pumps on the rare occasions she tried to "dress up." Felicity seemed to have an endless supply of clogs.

"You're right, Smithsonian. My pumpkin, my gherkin, my sweet Dilly Pickles would never harm me."

"Of course not." *Only your cholesterol.* Lacey watched him slip over to Felicity's desk and search for today's sugar-filled treats. He didn't find anything, but he had his own bakery bag with him.

"I understand you were at the Correspondents' Dinner this weekend when Courtney Wallace bought the farm." Wiedemeyer bit into what looked like a doughnut.

"She died later, at the hospital. Not at the Hilton."

Wiedemeyer was the reporter in charge of what the newsroom called the Death and Dismemberment beat. Lacey was sure it wasn't precisely that he was happy about Courtney's death; but as long as she had to die, he would be happier if it were peculiar or preposterous or truly disturbing.

"Tell me what you think, Smithsonian. Who offed the Wallace dame?" he asked.

"Harlan, how you talk. What makes you think it wasn't—" She hunted for a word.

"An accident? I already checked in with DeadFed."

She gripped the arms of her chair and sat gently down. "DeadFed. I've seen it. The general consensus is the flu. Killer flu."

"Maybe the virus was shot into her with the tip of an umbrella, like that spy."

"Not that again. Is that what Conspiracy Clearinghouse is saying?"

"I added the umbrella," Wiedemeyer said, proudly. "After all, it was a night for umbrellas, with all that rain. Newhouse says she was fine earlier, but on her deathbed by the end of the evening. He was an eyewitness."

"Thousands of people were eyewitnesses," Lacey said. "Damon is just imagining what happened. He doesn't *know*. He never knows anything. It's just another theory. He wasn't even there when they put her in the ambulance, he and Brooke were off schmoozing with Matt Drudge!" *There goes my Monday morning calm.*

"But you were there, weren't you, Smithsonian? Always hot on the trail of a crime. Drawn to it like a magnet."

Lacey took off her jacket, dark green with velvet cuffs. It was a favorite, a copy by her former seamstress Alma Lopez of one of Aunt Mimi's jackets from the 1940s. Underneath, she wore a vintage black crepe dress that never let her down. It was dressy yet businesslike, with white collar and cuffs.

"It's not a crime. We don't know that there was a crime of any kind. Besides, you don't look like you're hot on the trail of anything but breakfast."

He looked at the now-empty white bakery bag in his hand, crumpled it up, and tossed it in the trash. "I would have offered you a doughnut, but I guess I ate them all."

"You're worse than Winnie the Pooh."

He grinned, managing to look like a chubby monk. "I like honey too. By the way, you have a visitor."

Wiedemeyer's grin spread wide and became worthy of the Cheshire Cat. This couldn't be good. Lacey turned and saw Detective Lamont making his way up the aisle.

Lamont was eating a mini muffin and sipping coffee from Lacey's personal red-and-black FASHION *BITES* mug. She'd talked Mac into having a couple of them imprinted for her. The detective and the muffin indicated that Felicity Pickles, the food editor, was on-site with some new fattening delicacy. Broadway must have picked up Lacey's mug before she arrived. The detective could always just call her with a question, but he preferred to come to *The Eye* in person. He had a crush, if not on Lacey or on Felicity Pickles, then on Felicity's food.

"Broadway, what are you doing here?" Lacey asked. She indicated Mariah's Death Chair, waiting in the aisle. He rolled it over and settled in comfortably. The Death Chair didn't scare him.

"What? You're not happy to see me? And me—your star source and dinner date."

"Yes. Of course I'm happy," she said doubtfully. "I see you found my favorite coffee mug."

"I washed it for you too." He sipped coffee and munched happily on his muffin.

At least someone in Washington isn't grumpy this morning. She waited.

"Looks like you were right about the dye," he said between bites.

She felt her eyes open wide. "The Paris Green killed Courtney?"

Wiedemeyer jumped into the aisle between the cubicles. "Paris Green? Who's that? Like Paris Hilton?" He jumped backward when Broadway Lamont glared at him.

"I'm talking to Smithsonian here. Confidential, like. This is just a courtesy call, you understand?" he said to Lacey. "Not an official press release or anything."

"I understand." Lacey's news radar was tingling.

"Your poisoned-dress scenario, Smithsonian? Damnedest thing. You nailed it. Sounds like something only a fashion reporter would come up with. If it wasn't a strange mishap, maybe you'd be the perp." Lamont was playing with her. "Green is the color of jealousy, right?"

"Right. Me, jealous of a broadcast reporter? And you think I'd use a method that would clearly point to me?" Now she was playing with him.

"Nah, guess not. Too easy. Well, call it a tragic misadventure then. Wrong dress, wrong place, wrong tray of champagne. My department is calling it a freak accident. Pending the medical examiner's ruling, which is going to rule it a *bizarre* accident."

"Not a homicide?"

"No evidence of foul play. No suspects. Besides, you think I got time to get involved in some whacked-out medieval poisoning scheme? You find some murder plan like that, you take it to the suburbs. Tell them I sent you."

"Paris Green," Lacey pointed out, "was actually perfected as a dye in the early eighteen-hundreds, so that would make it more of a Regency poisoning plot, not medieval. Except they didn't know the dye was poison until much later." Lacey turned to where Wiedemeyer was still eavesdropping. "One thing, Harlan. This is my story, you got that?"

"You are vexing, Smithsonian," he replied. "Very vexing. This one sounds juicy. If you need a wing man on this, let me know." He sat in Felicity's chair and leaned back, his feet on her filing cabinet.

"Get ready, people," Lamont said, flipping open his notes. "The copper acetoarsenite in the dye, known as Paris Green, reacting to the champagne bath, produced a highly toxic arsine gas that sickened and then killed the victim. She might also have had the flu, weakening her system. Preliminary findings, pending further tests, of course. The Metropolitan Police are not releasing any information at this time."

"So it's a leak?" Lacey asked.

"Do not call it that." He shook his finger at her. "Out of the goodness of my heart, I thought I'd set your mind at rest, Smithsonian, seeing as how you took me to that swanky dinner. And you came up with the poisoned-green-dress theory."

Her mind wasn't at rest. All the questions still nagged at her. "You have the cause of death, but not the official determination of death by accident?"

"That will come. Eventually. The M.E.'s office takes their time. Because of Wallace's high profile, people are going to want an answer soon. Her news station is already pressing for it. On the other hand, the M.E.'s going to dot every 'i' and cross every 't.' Accident, not suicide, not homicide, I'm relieved to say. You don't have any hoodoo-voodoo fashion intuition about this one, do you, Smithsonian?" Lamont aimed his eagle-eye stare at her.

"Where is the dress now, Broadway? Did it go back to her family?"

"Funny you should ask." He drained the rest of her mug. "Once somebody, I don't know who, suggested that the dress itself could be a cause of death, well, that dress became very interesting to everybody. Now it has to be tested and verified and, who knows, maybe registered as a lethal weapon. That dress is in the custody of the office of the District of Columbia Medical Examiner."

"Can I see it?"

"Don't you think I gave you enough?" He leaned forward in his chair into her personal space.

"Yes, but—"

"No 'yes, buts,' Smithsonian. Sorry, no can do. It is sealed, not revealed. You think you going to get some kind of fashion vibration? That thing going to talk to you?"

"I just wanted to see the dress, the material. How it was

constructed and who made it. Do you think it will go back to her
family when the testing is over?"

"Not my call. They'll probably have first dibs."

"Thank you, Broadway. I appreciate the info." Lacey realized
she didn't have any coffee. Lamont had her mug. By now she was
practically craving an IV drip of caffeine. "The whole thing is so
weird."

"Weird like a freaky *accident*, right?" he said. "Say it for me.
Accident."

Lacey didn't have time to say anything before Felicity Pickles
bustled in with a self-satisfied smile. With her round blue eyes, ruddy
pink cheeks and glossy chestnut hair, she always reminded Lacey of a
china doll. *A chubby, badly dressed doll.* In addition to food and
Harlan Wiedemeyer, Felicity's other passion was themed sweaters.
Today she wore a typically shapeless cotton dress, in lavender. Her
matching lavender sweater was embroidered with purple violets and
yellow daisies. It lent her the air of a demented kindergarten teacher.

Felicity was starting early this week with the food festivities. It
wasn't even noon yet. Perhaps she planned to ask for a raise: Mac
Jones had a sweet tooth that wouldn't stop. Lacey could calibrate his
mood by the calories he consumed. More likely, Felicity's latest
calorie bomb was something she was considering feeding her guests
for her upcoming nuptials. Felicity carried a muffin tray, and Lacey
could smell bacon.

"Do try one of these, Detective." Felicity offered the tray and
Broadway Lamont scooped up a mini muffin. "Careful, they're hot.
Oh dear, I should have given you one of these breakfast muffins
before I gave you the dessert muffin."

"My stomach likes them no matter what order they come in. Like
they say, life is short, eat dessert first."

Wiedemeyer jumped up for his own muffin. She smiled and gave
him second pick.

"How do you like them, Detective Lamont?" Felicity asked.

"These, Ms. Felicity, are delicious." He licked his fingers and
she smiled. "Very tasty. Let's see, I taste eggs, bacon, and something
else."

"Walnuts for a bit of fiber, Asiago cheese, and a trio of secret
spices. These might just go on the brunch menu. The day after the
wedding."

Lamont heaved himself to his feet. "I'll take another muffin for the road, if you don't mind." He grabbed another and sat back down, in no hurry to exit.

Lacey was frozen in her tracks. "The day *after* the wedding?"

"Oh yes, it's going to be a multi-day event. Didn't I tell you?"

"No! What about the honeymoon?"

Weren't they supposed to scurry off and disappear for a month of so? Was Lacey supposed to give up the Sunday after Felicity's wedding too?

"After the festivities. Anyway, these breakfast muffins are so versatile, I can write about them now and pre-test for the wedding. Killing two birds with one stone."

Even though Lacey and Felicity had a tortuous history—they had disliked each other on sight—they were now "friends." *Sort of.* Lacey cleared Felicity as a suspect in the assault of a coworker, earning her trust. She had also *encouraged* Wiedemeyer to break the ice with Felicity. In the process, she helped mitigate, though not eradicate, his reputation as the office jinx, earning his undying gratitude. For Felicity and Harlan, Lacey's role in bringing them together created a debt of honor, and so she was now included in the wedding party as one of the bridesmaids and was unwillingly privy to nearly every detail of Felicity's wedding planning. Mostly about the food.

She couldn't think about that right now. Lacey hunted for another of her custom-imprinted FASHION *BITES* mugs: no luck. She picked up the one Broadway had used so she could fill it again.

"Why, thanks. Don't mind if I do. Black," Lamont said.

In the coffee room, she found a random clean mug for her own coffee and ran into LaToya Crawford, bouncing into the office earlier than usual.

"Lacey Smithsonian, girl, you gotta tell me what else you know about that Courtney Wallace! She's dead as a doornail."

"That's all I know. Well, basically."

"Must feel awkward, after your big fight."

"It wasn't that big a fight. But yeah, a little," Lacey admitted.

LaToya matched her high-heeled stride to Lacey's and turned the corner toward the fashion beat's cubicle, dressed in a hot pink sheath dress and pink and green striped high-heeled shoes. She didn't let the fashion world's tirades against "matchy-matchy" bother her, nor did she heed Lacey's usual caution against wearing too much pink in Washington, D.C. She went with her mood and today her pink dress was a banner headline that said spring was here.

Although the famous cherry blossoms around the Tidal Basin were gone and replaced by green leaves, the double cherries were still out and the azaleas and rhododendrons were running riot in shades of pink, purple, fuchsia, and white. LaToya seemed to be channeling Mother Nature in her ensemble.

LaToya stopped short when she spied Lamont at Lacey's cubicle. A slow smile lit up her face and she forgot all about interrogating Lacey about Courtney.

"Why, Detective Broadway, good morning to you. What brings you to our humble abode?"

Lacey lifted an eyebrow. She hadn't found out yet whether the detective and LaToya had hooked up after the dinner. If they had, maybe Lamont was also here to see LaToya. What if sparks had flown, the earth had moved, two hearts now beat as one?

Not another crazy wedding to get roped into.

Felicity made a welcoming noise. LaToya perched on the edge of Lacey's desk and leaned slowly and seductively over Lamont to pick out one of the savory muffins. It was getting very crowded in her cubicle, and a little steamy. Lacey gestured for LaToya to move, but she ignored her. Lacey grabbed her desk chair and held tight to her mug of coffee.

So much for my ease-quietly-into-the-workweek plan.

As if overhearing her thoughts, Mac joined the huddle in her cubicle with a full mug of coffee, the last cup in the pot. His mug also said FASHION *BITES.*

"Mac, you're early," Lacey said, grateful that Felicity had something for a hungry editor. "And with my missing mug. My life is now complete."

Mac fished around in the muffin tray, selecting one of each. He took one bite, before addressing the big homicide detective.

"Why are you here, Lamont? Besides Felicity's famous muffins. This can't be good news."

"Courtney Wallace."

"That screwy TV dame? Tragic. Weekend news department had a news brief." The small story appeared in the back of the Monday early edition news section. It was Mac's turn to give Lacey the side-eye. "Smithsonian got something to do with this?"

"It's not murder, if that's what you mean, but Smithsonian pointed the way. Credit where credit is due." Lamont indicated Lacey with his mug.

"How did she point the way?"

"Fashion clue. Paris Green. Killer dye. The dress did it."

Mac sighed meaningfully. "Follow up on this, Smithsonian. You've got the inside track. Check with Hansen. If he got some good frames of her, we'll run it front page. Color. Below the fold."

Lamont turned to Lacey. "You know how to play this, Smithsonian. Ongoing investigation. Preliminary lab results. Senior police official who asked not to be named. Blah blah blah. Run with it, but keep my name out of it."

"Thanks, Broadway." She was trying to gather her thoughts and write a few notes, but it was hard, in the crowded cacophony her corner had become.

It was Tony Trujillo's turn to follow his nose to the aroma of Felicity's cooking. Monday morning could sometimes be a traffic jam at the food editor's desk, but this was getting ridiculous.

"Now what?" Tony said when he spotted the detective munching a muffin with half *The Eye*'s senior staff crowded around Lacey's cubicle. The police reporter seemed to be out of the loop on this story. "What's Broadway giving you, Lois Lane, that he's not giving me? Wait a minute, this isn't about Courtney Wallace?"

"You can read all about it when I finish my story." Lacey turned to her keyboard, an expressive action that usually signaled to her fellow reporters to go away. It wasn't working.

"Funeral's on Tuesday," Lamont said.

"Tomorrow?" Lacey said. "Pretty quick work on that autopsy. Quick for the District, anyway. "

He shrugged. "So they tell me. People got to bury their dead and test results can take a while. Lab's got tissue samples, don't need the whole corpse."

"Does anyone else have the toxic dress information?" she asked.

"Not so far as I know. Not from me, anyway."

"Lunch is on me, Broadway. Say when."

"When can I join the two of you?" LaToya asked with a purr.

The detective grunted and reached for another breakfast muffin on his way out the newsroom door. The muffins were small. Broadway Lamont was large. LaToya looked after him longingly.

He'll be back, Lacey thought. *It's going to take a lot of those little muffins to fill him up.*

Chapter 10

LACEY WAS TOO BUSY TO thank Felicity (and perhaps LaToya too) for producing the delicacies that drew Lamont. She needed to get this story written, edited by Mac, and posted online before the other media knew what hit them. She had calls to make and details to confirm. Tony called the medical examiner's office for her. He told Lacey the spokesman wouldn't confirm the cause of death, nor deny it.

She checked first on Channel One News online to make sure their reporters didn't have this information too. They didn't. The station issued a brief news release on Courtney Wallace, Emmy winner, young, talented, and with a bright future in front of her, "mysteriously cut short by tragedy," "ongoing investigation, no official information at this time," et cetera. No mention was made of the suspected cause of death, or about why Courtney switched from hard investigative news to soft-serve.

Although the station must have had footage of Courtney's collision with the tray of champagne, it hadn't aired. Station managers were holding it back for some reason. Lacey didn't think it had anything to do with their taste or delicate sensibilities. It probably had more to do with Courtney's colorful language in the immediate aftermath.

On the station's Web site, a clip from earlier in the evening was playing without sound, but with a voice-over. Courtney was in the glorious Madame X dress, flashing her trademark smile into the camera, as the voice-over cut to her own signoff: "Reporting to you live from the White House Correspondents' Dinner, I'm Courtney Wallace, Channel One News."

That dinner was supposed to wrap up her series on vintage fashion, Lacey reflected. Ironically, it wrapped up everything for Courtney Wallace.

The station's news release to the print media did not include a photo of Courtney. Lacey remembered she'd taken her own cell phone shot of the immediate aftermath of the champagne incident. Her photo was clear and well framed. Courtney looked shocked, the waiter stunned, the spilled champagne dripping. She didn't know how her snapshot would compare to Hansen's professional DSLR pics, but it was raw and immediate. She emailed a copy of it to Mac to let him use his editorial judgment. After all, that's why he made the big bucks.

Lacey started typing. Her article on the demise of Courtney Wallace and her cause of death was edited and online in an hour, with her photo and one of Hansen's. It was sent as a Crime of Fashion special news report to *The Eye*'s subscribers.

LETHAL BLACK DRESS CITED IN TV PERSONALITY'S DEATH
By Lacey Smithsonian

Local television personality Courtney Wallace's sudden death following the White House Correspondents' Dinner Saturday night is being attributed by an unnamed source in the Metropolitan Police to a rare dye called Paris Green, used in the lining of her gown. The dye is made from copper acetoarsenite, and when wet, releases toxic arsine gas. This effectively turned her *little* black dress into a *lethal* black dress.

The weather may have contributed to the release of the dye's toxins, as it was raining and humid Saturday night. Additionally, in a mishap prior to the Correspondents' Dinner, Wallace's dress was soaked with champagne when a waiter spilled a tray of drinks on her. The unnamed source also noted that Wallace's health might have been in a weakened condition due to possible influenza.

The striking vintage gown Wallace wore was black satin with a visible emerald green lining. It closely resembled a gown worn in the famous painting by John Singer Sargent, called *Portrait of Madame X*. The portrait dates from 1884 and was both celebrated and controversial. The Madame X gown has been copied many times and has inspired countless imitations...

Life could be short and often brutal. The best intentions were seldom achieved. Love lost was a tragedy. Lacey stared at her ringless finger and Vic surfaced in her mind. She made her decision.

Her editor sidled into sight, heading for Felicity's desk. No doubt looking for leftover muffin crumbs.

"Mac, I'm taking tomorrow off," Lacey said. "I have plenty of hours of leave."

"Going to the funeral? Knock yourself out. If you're not back by Wednesday, I'm putting Kavanaugh at your desk."

"Yeah, you do that." She stifled a laugh. "That freckle-faced puppy doesn't know the first thing about fashion. Good choice, Mac."

Kelly Kavanaugh was young, full of energy, and she wanted to be a Serious Reporter in the worst way, which was, sadly, the way she wrote her stories. She bounced around the newsroom like a ping-pong ball, mostly filling in. She'd tried the police beat with Tony, but was shooed away. Kavanaugh was also interested in covering Lacey's fashion beat, but only when it involved real crimes. Her eyes crossed when it came to writing about trends and designers and social context. Accessories made Kelly cry. Shopping made her comatose. She had no knack for knits and she dressed like a sports reporter at a rag sale.

Lacey shook her head at the thought of Kavanaugh manning her desk, while she called Vic and made a date for ring shopping in Baltimore, after the funeral.

Within minutes, Lacey's phone started ringing. Her "Lethal Black Dress" story was being read online. The first call was from Channel One. Their news editor demanded to know where she got her information. Lacey's repeated "no comment" didn't give them what they wanted. Despite feeling bad about Courtney, she wasn't about to make it easy for the competition.

It was time to get some lunch and satisfy her curiosity about a certain actor. On her way out, Lacey caught sight of a pink-and-green blur. "LaToya, do you have a minute?"

"Sure thing. Help me fix my lipstick."

Lacey followed LaToya into the ladies' room, otherwise known around the newsroom as the Women's Conference Room, because of the amount of information that was traded there. LaToya grabbed her purse and took out a bright pink MAC lipstick and lip pencil that matched her ensemble.

"What's up, girlfriend?"

"Don't be coy with me, LaToya. What's up with you and Broadway Lamont? Did you connect with him after the Correspondents' Dinner? Inquiring minds want to know!"

LaToya paused to admire her reflection in the mirror. She carefully removed the remains of her old lipstick, then lined her lips.

"You would be talking about that delicious hunk of a man

you brought as your guest?"

"Yeah, yeah, get on with it."

LaToya laughed and slicked the lipstick on, right to left. She smacked her lips together.

"We went for an all-too-brief drink. After all the excitement with Courtney being shoveled into the ambulance." She blotted her lips, then reapplied. LaToya had a master's touch with makeup. "Alas, he left all too soon."

"Don't pout. You'll ruin your lip liner."

"Don't pout? Easy for you to say." She blew a kiss to her reflection. "I'm still pouting. I was perfection on Saturday. Ready and willing to extend our friendship into something a little friendlier. And the big man bolts. Just like that. I don't get it."

Lacey took out a comb and ran it through her hair. "Maybe you should tone down the, um, perfection a bit. Honestly, LaToya, I think he's afraid of you."

"A man that large, that fierce, that ferocious, afraid of me?" She tossed her cosmetics back into her purse and snapped it shut. "Story of my life."

"For the record, I know he finds you extremely attractive. Little bird told me. Well, a big bird."

"But not irresistible? Attractive but *resistible* is not what I am going for," LaToya said.

"I know. Maybe you just came on a little too strong."

"That man is a mighty bull elephant, and I should come on like a mouse? Well, I'm not giving up on Broadway Lamont. He is too big and tall and delectable to give up the elephant hunt."

"Don't let him know that."

"I hear you, girlfriend, but sadly, Lacey, subtlety is not my strong suit. Or maybe you hadn't noticed."

Lacey could hardly keep her face straight. "Give him time."

"I'll give Broadway all the time he needs. As long as it's still while I have my youth and beauty. I see he gave you a big beautiful story on Courtney Wallace."

"I gave him the fashion clue. And I'm grateful."

LaToya paused for a moment of reflection. "That's a terrible way to die. I mean, we've all worn fashion mistakes, and we've all died of embarrassment. But how many outfits turn on us and kill us? How many of us really die from wearing the wrong dress?"

"I think you just quoted one of my columns."

"I'm sure I did, I do it all the time. How do I look?"

"Perfectly awesome. Very pink."

"Good. I'm off to cover a city council meeting. And I might have my eye on a certain someone else if Big Bad Broadway doesn't work out."

LaToya sailed out the door. Lacey wondered if LaToya came from a long line of Amazonian women. She was fierce enough to be an Amazon queen.

Chapter 11

IT WAS A GOOD TWENTY degrees cooler inside The Spotlight restaurant than outside in the bright May sunshine. The decor was very theatrical, the perfect workplace for a waiter who wanted to be a Serious Actor.

The Spotlight was dark, painted in deep blues with stars, comets, and planets covering the walls. Booths lined the walls, with tables in the center. Every table had its own spotlight. It was impossible to ignore the giant lighting grids suspended from the ceiling, with theatrical lighting instruments and colored lights. It was too cute by half and Lacey was slightly afraid a grid would come crashing down, like the chandelier in *The Phantom of the Opera*.

She arrived at the restaurant just as it opened. The hostess ushered Lacey to a back booth in Will Zephron's section. The spotlight over her suddenly illuminated, a signal for her waiter, who might be preoccupied running lines from a play while pouring a patron's coffee.

Zephron was very young. Early twenties, Lacey guessed. Tall and thin with dark eyes and dark hair, there was a delicacy about him that would attract men as well as women, and, most likely, casting directors. Someday he would grow into a gorgeous man, she decided.

In Lacey's experience, there were a couple of types of actors who stood out from the rest. Some needed so much attention they sucked all the air out of the room. They always had to be on, to be the center of attention, and they were exhausting to be around. And then there were other actors who were so shy they could barely speak off stage. Some strange personal alchemy allowed them to shed their outer skin and take on another persona, but out of the spotlight, they could be exhausting to draw out.

Zephron turned out to be a little of both. He handed Lacey a menu mechanically, looking half asleep. Then she introduced herself and complimented his performance as Thisbe in *A Midsummer Night's Dream*. At last his smile came on full and he was in the spotlight.

"And I saw you the other night, too," Lacey said. "I was there at the Correspondents' Dinner. What happened with the champagne, Will?"

His smile faded instantly. "You saw that?"

"I did."

"Oh my God." He scanned the restaurant to see if anyone was within listening distance and sat down in the booth opposite her. "Nothing like that has ever happened to me before! I can handle a tray full of champagne glasses like that sleepwalking."

"You tripped?"

"No. I didn't." He scanned the room again, perhaps a little more dramatically than necessary. "I think I was pushed."

"In a crowd like that, wouldn't you be jostled all the time?"

"That's what you'd think, but not really. Carry a tray of drinks and people give you space. Nobody wants a tray of champagne or appetizers down their front. Besides, I've done this a lot, I'm always on my guard. This was definitely different. This was a shove and I was toppled, but I caught myself before hitting the ground."

Was there really a shove? Lacey wondered. It's always comforting to blame someone else, some anonymous person in the crowd.

"Did you see who did it?" she asked.

"I was too busy trying to stay on my feet and catch the tray, and this blond woman in a black dress was right in my way." He leaned against the back of the booth. "Honestly, I'm just glad I didn't hit more people."

"Do you think that shove was an accident?"

"No way. It was deliberate." Deep dramatic sigh. "It felt that way. God, I managed to spray champagne all over a television reporter! What a mess. Good thing it was the cheap stuff. They're not going to ask me to work a gig like that again. And I can use the money. Do you think the whole thing is on camera?"

Lacey wondered whether he was sorry to be involved at all, or regretting he wasn't the star of the show. In Zephron's mind, he surely was the star of this tragedy. After all, all the world's a stage.

"Probably, but no one's airing it. So you knew who she was? Courtney Wallace?"

"Is that her name? No. I don't watch TV. I'm in the theatre. I don't have time. I just assumed she was on TV because she was waving a microphone in people's faces and trailed by a guy with a camera. People didn't want to talk to her. Which is kind of odd, because people go to these things to get on TV, right? And she was really pretty."

The blonde thing. Always the blonde thing. "You probably are on film, or digital, whatever they were shooting that night."

"Don't remind me. I mean, actors always need exposure, but not that kind of exposure! If anyone catches that performance, I won't even be able to get a walk-on as a butler in a dinner theatre. God." He drummed his fingers on the table. "Why did you want to talk with me?"

"I'm a reporter, Will. A fashion reporter. For *The Eye Street Observer.*"

He looked puzzled. "Is this a fashion story? She isn't planning to sue me, is she? It was an accident. I didn't do it on purpose. And how bad could it be? Just a dry cleaning bill, right?"

A party of four sat down at a nearby table, and the spotlight above them illuminated. The hostess handed them menus. Will jumped up to get their drink order, then dashed off to greet another group coming through the door. He returned to Lacey, order pad in hand. She hadn't even looked at the menu.

"So that's all I know, Ms. Smithsonian. What can I get you for lunch?"

"Have the police talked to you?"

"For spilling a tray?! Why would the police want to talk to me? Oh my God, she is suing me. Or the hotel is. That hotel is never going to hire me again. Oh my God."

"No, Will. She's not suing. She's dead."

"No way!" He leaped away from her. Dramatically. "How could she be dead? She was fine. All I did was spill the drink tray! I was pushed!" He spun around as if looking for a camera, as if this were all an elaborate joke.

"People can hear you," Lacey said, signaling to the concerned hostess that everything was all right.

"Why is she dead? I had nothing to do with that. Or do you mean, they think I could be some kind of witness? I didn't see anything! All I did was—"

"Will. Calm down." Lacey lowered her voice as if she were talking to a child. "Courtney Wallace wore a vintage dress with a green silk lining. The silk was dyed with a substance called copper arsenate. A dye called Paris Green. When the champagne, or any liquid, soaked her dress, the wet dye released toxic fumes. Fumes full of arsenic. You can read about it in *The Eye.*"

"Are you telling me her *dress* was what killed her?"

"After the liquid hit it, yes." She remembered how queasy she felt in the tiny ladies' room with Courtney Wallace and Zanna Nelson. Lacey had no idea how Wallace could actually have kept that wet garment on for the rest of the evening. The woman must have started to feel ill very soon. But she was pumped full of adrenaline, anger, shock, humiliation—and her need for the story was stronger than her symptoms.

"So getting drenched in champagne killed her?" The color drained from Will Zephron's face. He put his face in his hands and rubbed his hair back. "You think they'll come after me now?"

"Who are they?"

"I don't know! The ones who were after her."

Has he been reading DeadFed? "I don't think so. It was probably an accident. Maybe someone just wanted to embarrass her and had no idea what might happen. Or maybe—"

"Maybe they used me as the weapon!"

"Who used you? Did you see something that night, Will?"

"O. M. G. I have to get out of here!"

He dropped his order pad on the table. Lacey handed him her card. He stared at it, pocketed it, and darted away. She saw him dash into the kitchen, dash out again with a backpack, and run through the restaurant's front door without another word. He didn't take her lunch order, either.

If Zephron was lying, he was a better actor than she thought. He seemed seriously shaken by the news that Courtney was dead. He left something to be desired as a waiter, however. Lacey figured she wasn't going to be served there anytime soon. She picked up her bag and left.

Outside the chilly Spotlight, the sun warmed her. She put her sunglasses on and breathed in the flower-scented air. Lacey had come to the restaurant in a taxi, but she decided to walk back to the paper's offices. She passed frothy rosebushes that hugged tiny gates and fences in the miniscule yards of Dupont Circle townhouses. The dogwoods were in full bloom, white and pink and proud. Spring seemed to be a reward for living through the rest of the year. She sneezed.

Washingtonians crowded Farragut Square on days like this. Many sat sunning themselves at the base of the statue of Admiral Farragut, surrounded by cannons. It was deceptively beautiful and calm in the Square, though it was the calm before the storm. The weathercasters predicted rain. Lacey loved marking the seasons and walking through the Square to get to *The Eye*'s offices, right across the street on the south side of Farragut Square; appropriately enough, on Eye Street.

"Hey, pal," a voice said, and Lacey turned toward the sound.

"Hey yourself, Quentin."

The formerly homeless man she'd befriended had finally secured a subsidized apartment, but he still panhandled to supplement his government assistance. He greeted her with a big smile on his beautiful dark face.

She discreetly slipped him a couple of dollars. "Lovely day."

"Thank you, pal. Yes it is." He leaned against a park bench, his face to the sun. "Terrible news about that television reporter, you know. Now, you know, I don't watch the television. I *read* my news. I'm a newspaper reader." He produced a copy of *The Eye Street Observer* to prove it to her. It was the Monday edition, with the news brief about Courtney Wallace. "And I get the paper for free. I'm an insider." He winked.

One of the staff always handed the good-natured Quentin a copy when the bundles arrived from the printer. He liked to keep current with the news, except on the occasions he forgot his meds and wound up in the hospital.

"Keep reading," she said. "Tomorrow's story gets more interesting."

"Thanks for the tip, Lacey. I'll put that on my reading agenda."

Lacey waved goodbye and he shifted his attention to another likely donor. She crossed the green space to Firehook Bakery and bought iced coffee, a muffin, and an apple. Her phone rang before she made it back to *The Eye*.

"Some friend you are," Brooke began without preamble. "You didn't tell me about the dress that killed Courtney. A poison dress! The Madame X dress? You didn't even give me a hint of what you were thinking! You knew all along that it was, how did you put it, a *lethal black dress*. Clever, Lacey, but very hurtful. Where's the trust?"

"Brooke, I didn't *know*. I merely suspected. When you started talking about a 'killer flu,' that actually seemed, um, more sensible. And if Courtney was coming down with the flu, it would explain why she looked so sweaty and glassy-eyed. Even Broadway Lamont thought it was the flu. At first. And if I *had* mentioned the dye theory, you would have told Damon and he would have run with it willy-nilly, before I could confirm it and write it for *The Eye*. And that's my job."

"Ha. You followed her into the ladies' room. You had a hunch."

"I was worried about that dress. I figured Courtney was wash-and-wear, but not that vintage gown."

"Then how did you come up with a poison dress? And don't tell me the police told you. They wouldn't immediately suspect a dye that 'hadn't been used in a hundred years or more.' And I'm quoting here."

"It had this strange aroma. Even before the champagne hit it. It could have been moist from the rain, or sweat, releasing the toxins. The smell was very faint at first. I had a funny feeling about the dress, about that green lining, that particular shade of green."

"The smell. Aha. It was garlic, wasn't it?"

"You just looked it up on the Internet, didn't you?"

"That's why it's there." Brooke's voice was frosty.

"Feelings aren't facts, Brooke. I didn't have the facts until today. You read the story."

"Broadway Lamont told you?"

"An unnamed source in the police department."

"Lamont. I thought so. I'm still mad, but tell me what really happened. Everything. I might just forgive you."

Everything? "I suggested to Courtney that she should change out of that soaking wet dress. That we could probably find something dry for her to wear, like a hotel staff uniform or some other guest's trench coat."

"I bet she loved that suggestion." Brooke chuckled. She wasn't irritated anymore.

"Who would? She accused me of being jealous. It was a beautiful dress. And she was angry because I wouldn't agree to an on-air interview."

"Do you think it was an accident?"

"What else could it be? By the way, is Damon going to write about this on DeadFed?" *Stealing it as we speak*, she thought.

Brooke practically smirked right through the phone. "As we speak."

Lacey raced back to the office. She had to see what nonsense Damon would spin out of her story this time.

Chapter 12

SOME MERRY PRANKSTER HAD PLACED a yellow road hazard sign on Lacey's desk:

~~SLIPPERY~~ DEADLY WHEN WET

The word SLIPPERY had been crossed out and DEADLY written above. Next to it was a printed copy of her story, with the headline scrawled across it:

LETHAL BLACK DRESS

"Hey! Who's the joker?" Silence. No one in the newsroom took credit for the impromptu display. Her next suspect was someone in the sports section, but Lacey wasn't sure they were literate enough to understand road signs.

A familiar whistle sounded nearby. Harlan Wiedemeyer was accompanied by the aroma of baked dough. She had her suspect.

"Did you do that?" she asked.

"Guilty. Pretty good though, huh? That Wallace dame needed a sign like that. Sadly, the majority of us poor bastards never take heed of signs and symbols."

"It's a little early in the day for hyperbole, Harlan. And besides I don't think a sign would have made a difference to Courtney."

"You never know. Maybe if it was in even bigger print?"

"Did you want something?"

"Just to congratulate you on a superb scoop on the Paris Green in the poisoned dress. Any suspects?"

"Did you not read the part about it being an accident?"

"Accident. Sure, go ahead, let's play that game." He peered into his bakery bag and inhaled the aroma. "You can trust me, Smithsonian. One-in-a-million accidents do happen. Almost never. Or some bastard did her in. Murder happens a lot. Course, she was a television reporter. They're like mold spores. You can't kill 'em all, they're everywhere." He took out a doughnut and bit into it.

"There is nothing new since this morning."

"Did you check DeadFed dot com? That Damon Newhouse has a way with words. Not our way, not our words, but his own way."

Wiedemeyer and his glazed puff of heaven shuffled off and she turned to her computer. Conspiracy Clearinghouse was bookmarked. The latest headline surfaced.

DRESS OF DOOM DOWNS DOGGED TV NEWSHOUND
By Damon Newhouse

Conspiracy Clearinghouse learned today that Channel One News broadcaster Courtney Wallace died Sunday morning after being soaked to the skivvies in the Dress of Doom she wore to cover the White House Correspondents' Dinner. With a lining as green as a poison apple, the so-called Madame X gown turned toxic in a strange chemical reaction when the liquid hit the fan, er, dress. Just a toxic misadventure? Or a kiss of death from a deadly Toxic Avenger?

The story was first reported by *Eye Street Observer* fashion guru Lacey Smithsonian. It has yet to be confirmed to CC by the Metropolitan Police...

And Damon does it again, Lacey thought. *The fastest fingers in the news biz.* At least Damon gave her credit and a link to her story. Lacey reached down to stash her purse in her bottom desk drawer and noticed a pair of black and white snakeskin cowboy boots heading her way.

"Hello, Tony." She straightened up.

"Hey, Lois Lane. How about escaping the Daily Planet for lunch?"

"I blew my lunch hour running down a source. But lunch with Jimmy Olsen? Tempting."

"I am not Jimmy Olsen. Nor am I Clark Kent. I'm even better looking than him, in my cape and tights." He smiled, using the grin to which she was immune, though many women in Washington were not.

"Not to mention modest," she said. "I do prefer Brenda Starr, you know. She has better clothes than Lois, and a sensational sense of style."

Tony Trujillo was a handsome and hopeless flirt. He and Lacey were pals with a friendship that would last for years, while his romances tended to expire early. Both were from the West, and Tony and Lacey shared a common sensibility. It wasn't often found in the Capital City, where everyone looked over your shoulder to see if someone more important had just walked through the door. But the two hadn't talked much lately. Lacey blamed *Terror at Timberline.*

"You could rock a Brenda Starr look. You just need the red hair. Have you thought about it?"

"I haven't, but my stylist has. Stella's pushed every color in the rainbow. I have resisted, but red is tempting. And I'd love to know how Brenda managed those great clothes on a reporter's salary. Guess you have to be drawn by a female cartoonist. So, what's up, Tony?"

"We haven't had a lunch out in a while, that's all."

That couldn't be all with Tony, but a real lunch would spare her from the muffin and the apple.

"Lunch. It's a deal. But it has to be at a place where they wait on you. No standing at the counter."

"You'll probably want a black orchid delivered to the table too."

"Wouldn't that be lovely? The world is in short supply of black orchids. Now, where?"

"Outside *The Eye*'s orbit. I don't want to be overheard by the random reporter."

"I thought you put Kavanaugh on night cops." She retrieved her bag and closed the DeadFed dot com site.

Tony looked around as if Kavanaugh might be listening. "*She's* Jimmy Olsen. Come on, Mustang Sally's outside and the meter runs out in ten minutes." He referred to his black Mustang ragtop, the true love of his life. "Let's hit the road before Mac decides there's more work to do."

"Didn't you hear, I already got a scoop today. 'Lethal Black Dress.' And it's only Monday."

"Braggart."

୦୫

It was the perfect day to sit outside at Café Le Ruche, the French café on a side street just south of the C&O Canal in Georgetown. Lacey generally disliked eating outside, blasted by the sun, the heat and humidity, and the exhaust of a thousand trucks. But Café Le Ruche was different.

The "pretty quotient" at the café was as high as the roses that climbed the walls. She and Tony sat under umbrellas at a two-top table. The waiter arrived with iced tea, along with a fragrant breeze. Lacey ordered the *potage Parisien* and *pâté maison*. Tony selected quiche, proving they were wrong about real men.

"What's on your mind, Tony?" Lacey asked. "It must be important or you would have spilled it at the office." Was he going to suggest they double-byline the Courtney Wallace story? He might kid her about her Crime of Fashion stories, but he usually wanted in if he smelled a scoop involving actual crimes. "Is it my latest story?"

"You're on your own with this one, Ms. Starr. I have a conflict of interest."

"A conflict?" Her eyes popped wide open. "You know something about the poison dress? Tell me."

"Not the dress. I went out with the poison apple herself, until I found the worm inside."

"You dated Courtney Wallace?" She was shocked. Perhaps she shouldn't be, knowing Tony's appetite for blondes. But Courtney? *The Wicked Witch of Channel One?*

"Inside voices," he said, even though they were outside. The waiter arrived with a basket of hot bread and butter and hurried away.

"Another one of your tall cool blondes? I never saw you with her. Couldn't have lasted long."

"No, not long. It was nearly a year ago. Thought we'd be good for maybe four or five dates." He had a system. Four dates, five dates, *finito,* forget about it. After that, he once told Lacey, you're practically picking out tea towels together.

"You are a cold rake, Trujillo."

Tony's particular "gift" was that his magnetism attracted women, then repelled them. He wouldn't be young and handsome forever, but he didn't seem to know that. He was lucky Washington had such a transient population, with a rapid turnover in available blondes.

"The way the world works."

"Not for everyone."

"Not for you and Donovan. I get that. I missed my chance."

"Oh please. Did you break up with her after five dates for a reason, or because her meter expired?"

"Hey, Lacey, I always hope it will be more, but that wasn't the reason. You think I was using her? She was using *me*. Courtney was scarfing my stories. I mentioned a couple things I was working on, and before I could file, they were on television with her shiny chompers smiling into the camera. Like a vampire."

"Did you want to kill her?" Lacey smiled her most fetching smile.

"Not in the permanent way. Maybe in print. She was a snake, but if people started killing all the snakes in D.C., this would be a ghost town. We had words. It wasn't pretty. I told her to go stick her fangs in somebody else and suck the blood out of another sucker."

"Was she upset?" Lacey understood about protecting your beat. She'd felt almost the same way about the late television reporter.

"Nah. Not terribly. I had the feeling she had another sucker, or suckee, waiting in the wings."

"Did this affair happen before her fall from grace?"

"You mean the Granville scandal? Right before it broke."

"You know the details?"

"Just what I read in the papers." He laughed. "She never talked about it. I followed the story because I knew her. She believed a rumor and reported it without verifying it. She made slips before. But this time, she tangled with the wrong dude, Thaddeus T. Granville."

"Long-time politico. Some sort of campaign wizard? Something like that?"

He gestured with another piece of bread. "That's his rep. Courtney torpedoed Granville and his candidate, a Senator Swansdown. Accused both of them of dirty tricks. Other stations picked it up. Story spread like wildfire. Turned out it wasn't true, probably a plant by his enemies. Courtney wasn't an investigative reporter, she didn't have the chops. She just repeated rumors, things she heard in bars, or maybe in bed."

"But the senator squeaked through, as I remember."

"Yeah, but there were ramifications."

"Refresh my memory," Lacey said. "What was the scandal about, the dirty tricks?"

"Washington's favorite subject. Sex. I'm guessing sex is so popular because all the workaholics never get any. Makes it that much more salacious."

"Details?" She sipped her drink.

"Right. Courtney, the Emmy winner, reported that Granville, the granddaddy of dirty tricks, was preparing to out the opposing candidate's wife as the former madam of an escort service, who'd cleaned up her act. Granville allegedly was going to publish a list of all the johns, including a number of congressmen. The story also alleged that the madam had been a high-level escort herself and was blackmailing her former johns to help pay for her husband's campaign."

"It's ringing a bell. Sounded plausible but none of it was true, right? And the candidate's wife attempted suicide?"

Tony nodded. "Took an overdose of something. Survived. But Courtney kept the heat on Granville and his history as a devious campaign mastermind. The focus was so hot on the campaign, Thaddeus T. fell on his sword for the good of all and resigned."

"This had to be after Senator Swansdown proclaimed he was one hundred percent behind Granville." Lacey knew the D.C. drill.

"Exactly. The kiss of death. Swansdown barely won. He would have lost if Granville had stayed on. But probably also because the other candidate's wife looked a little mentally fragile at that point, the candidate too. He lost and handed Swansdown the win. The day after the election Granville went public with some kind of 'proof' it was a setup, that Courtney had reported a fake story."

"Sounds like a Pyrrhic victory to me."

"And Granville was ready to torch the town, using Courtney as the torch. He stormed straight to the head of the station and screamed bloody murder. Demanded she be fired. There was an on-air apology, and Ms. I-won-an-Emmy was off the investigative team."

Lacey shook her head. "She hadn't even tried to confirm the story?"

"She was a woman in a hurry."

"Not anymore."

"About Courtney." He considered something and picked up a knife. "I wouldn't call what we had an affair. More of a hit and run. But yeah, it was right before her scandal. A few weeks. I wasn't sorry when it all went down. I thought it served her right. At any rate, I'm not going to write about her. Too close to home for me. I thought you should know." He stabbed at the butter.

"Thanks for telling me about this."

"Impressive scoop, by the way, Lacey. No one else would have tumbled to the fashion angle."

"It's not finished yet."

"Your interpretation or Mac's?"

She tore off a piece of bread and buttered it. "I would like to find out how Paris Green, a dye not used since the nineteenth century, got mixed up with champagne here in the twenty-first. And a vintage black dress that probably dates from the Forties. What's that all about?"

"You think this is another true fashion crime? Not just a random bizarre incident?" He leaned in with a smile. "Tell me, Brenda Starr, exactly how does a little black dress become a 'lethal black dress'?"

Chapter 13

TUESDAY WAS MUCH TOO PRETTY a day for a funeral. Courtney Wallace would probably have agreed.

Unlike so many transplants to the D.C. area, Courtney had grown up right in Washington's Maryland suburbs and went to college at the University of Maryland. She lived in nearby Arlington, Virginia, and her remains went home to be buried in Laurel, Maryland, less than twenty miles away. The graveside service would be private, but a memorial service was open to the public. Laurel was on the way to Baltimore, where Lacey planned to meet Vic later.

To reach both destinations, however, Lacey had to maneuver the infamous Highway I-295 through the District. It was a road where random bullets and detached car parts flew indiscriminately. Lacey once witnessed, and barely missed, an airborne hood from a speeding land yacht, an ancient American station wagon rusting apart at the seams. The car swerved around her, the hood barely latched and dancing up and down in the airflow. The careening wagon hit a pothole and the rusty hood disengaged, flew off, and glided, spinning like a scythe high above the line of cars, which dodged and dove all over the road to escape. She pulled off just in time to avoid a roof decapitation.

Today, however, was relatively calm on I-295, and the lovely vintage BMW that Vic had restored for her was purring flawlessly. It was dark green, but not Paris Green. But the thought of Paris Green made her fill the upgraded music system with Edith Piaf's music. With no one to hear her, she sang along.

Once she made it through the crush of District traffic and road construction, she was finally rewarded with the lovely Baltimore-Washington Parkway, miles of good road, stone bridges, and lovely spring-green trees, growing lusher every day in May. She could almost imagine she wasn't going to a funeral.

Lacey turned off on Fort Meade Road and swung into the town of Laurel. She parked at a medium-sized nondenominational church, unadorned except by large oak trees. She walked inside to what she assumed was the sanctuary, a large, plain, wood-paneled room with a tile floor. There were no pews, just plastic and metal chairs. There was no cross. Instead, there was a carpeted platform on which a podium rested, and red curtains pulled across the back wall. There were no candles or incense or stained glass. Lacey assumed that some people liked that degree of austerity in a church, but it felt chilly and soulless to her.

Several larger-than-life photos of Courtney were mounted on easels on the platform, and sprays of orchids were set up in front of the photos. With nothing else in the room to look at, the effect was rather like the First Church of Courtney Wallace.

Chairs were set up in rows, half of them already filled. Courtney's coffin was not there, open for the curious to stare into and snap a surreptitious photo of the body. Courtney's family seemed prepared, as they should be, for the shenanigans of which the press was capable. The family—her mother and brother—and assorted aunts, uncles, cousins, and friends were seated up front in the first two rows. Media cameras were placed off to the side.

Lacey hadn't expected Courtney's funeral to receive quite so much media attention, but all the major news outlets had sent a representative. One of their own had died and attention was due, if only briefly. Lacey even recognized a stringer for the *National Enquirer*, whom she'd seen before. He waved and smiled. Supermarket checkout stands would soon be filled with news of the freak accident of the Paris Green dye.

The other newspapers were playing catchup today on the story fashion reporter Lacey Smithsonian broke the day before. The local television stations, including Channel One, mentioned it that night, without crediting her original story. Conspiracy Clearinghouse pointed out that Smithsonian directed the police to the green lining, but concluded that the medical examiner's office might have figured it out eventually. Lacey wondered. The M.E.'s office in D.C. was notorious for *not* figuring things out. Oddly, Damon Newhouse was not there. He still had a part-time day job at a trade association that kept him in Washington. He'd tried to get on as a reporter at *The Eye*, but hadn't succeeded. Yet.

Lacey took a seat toward the back. A few heads turned her way. She recognized Eric Park, Courtney's photographer. He had thrown a sports jacket over his dark shirt and pants. She also recognized Zanna Nelson, whose press ID cards were hanging from a beaded lanyard around her neck. She was apparently covering the event for the station. Zanna's bow-shaped mouth was pressed into a frown, and she seemed subdued as she took a seat next to Eric.

Lacey took a moment to study her. Zanna was wearing a navy skirt suit with a crisp white oxford cloth shirt. She looked professional and appropriate, if a bit too typical. She wore black flats; the quicker to chase down a source, Lacey thought. Her long hair was pulled back into a ponytail.

You're not here to critique the mourners' clothes, Lacey reminded herself sternly. She promptly lapsed into a reverie about that very thing.

Very few people seemed to know how to dress for funerals. Members of the family might wear black, but the guests couldn't be counted on to follow suit. They might wear anything at all. Although if the family didn't wear black, it looked presumptuous for a virtual stranger to do so. It seemed to say, *I mourn your loved one's passing more than you do.*

Lacey didn't wear black. Instead, she selected a princess-style cocoa brown dress with sheer polka-dot sleeves. It was vintage, though not her usual period. This was an early Fifties dress, before the decade lapsed into its homemaker aprons and lampshade frocks. The sleeves and neckline were edged in pale pink piping, just enough color to give the outfit a bit of dash, but not enough to be inappropriate at a funeral. She wore brown heels, but left some pink-heeled sandals in the car for later.

A large shadow fell over her. She glanced up at the figure blocking the fluorescent glare: Detective Broadway Lamont had come calling. Nothing could hide his imposing figure, attired respectfully in a navy sport coat over a navy shirt, white tie, and gray slacks. She slid over one chair so the homicide detective could sit down next to her.

"That's the mother," he said in a low voice, indicating a woman in a dark gray suit with shoulder-length ash blond hair. She looked careworn, but the resemblance to her daughter was there. Lacey guessed her age at mid-fifties. Mrs. Wallace was standing next to a serious young man, who appeared to be college age. "That's the son."

The youth also looked like his sister, but his hair was darker. He was tall, a few inches over six feet, Lacey guessed. He and his mother flashed an occasional smile at a fellow mourner, but a heavy weight of sadness prevailed. A death in the family was never easy to bear, and far worse when the deceased was young.

Lacey lowered her voice. "Why are you here, Broadway? If you think it was an accident, and not murder, why come to the funeral?"

"Why not? Beautiful day for a drive. Shows respect. And when

Lacey Smithsonian is involved, it's always good for a story. I bet the boys at the office you'd be here looking for foul play. And foul clothes. Nice getup, by the way."

"Very funny." She'd like to meet those other Homicide jokesters sometime, though not during in an interrogation. "But you have to ask yourself, Broadway, how did this happen? Where did the dress come from?"

"What did you call it? Besides lethal. The Madame X dress?"

"It's a copy of the Madame X dress. It looks just like it, except for the green lining and cutouts, and raising the skirt on one side."

"Sometimes, Smithsonian, deaths don't get solved. Sometimes the weirdest deaths are just accidents. They make 'News of the Weird.' They win the Darwin Award."

"Perhaps the cleverest of those 'accidents' are actually murder," she countered.

"The perfect murder? No such thing, because people aren't perfect."

"Then why isn't every crime solved?"

"Because police aren't perfect either. Too busy. Too many bodies. Too little time."

The chairs were small and uncomfortable and Lamont shifted in his seat. The hall was filling up with media types.

"It wouldn't hurt to know the sequence of events," Lacey said. "After all, it still involves fashion, and fashion is my business. Not fashion with a capital F. Fashion for the rest of us. I want to know the stories behind the clothes."

He sat back, twisting again in the small plastic chair. "You get anything yet?"

"I talked to the waiter who spilled the drinks."

"You did? I didn't."

"He says he was pushed."

Lamont snorted in derision. "Course he's going to say that. Doesn't want to take responsibility for his own actions. Probably just tripped."

"Will Zephron is his name. He sounded sincere, but then he is an actor. Maybe he was just acting sincere. And when I told him Courtney was dead, it spooked him. He thinks he's next. Actor, you know."

"Dramatic type, huh? Actors are a pain to interview."

They fell into a silence of separate thoughts. Music began, a mournful bagpiper, and the crowd hushed. A middle-aged minister in a simple gray suit opened with a prayer. He made a few appropriate comments about Courtney Wallace and her love of the news business, including the highlight of her career—winning an Emmy Award for investigative reporting. He invited people to share their memories of the deceased.

It was curious how death laid not only regret and sadness at your feet, Lacey reflected. It also elevated the deceased in people's eyes. Death was often a "good career move" for artists and writers who never attained fame in this life, but made their name in the hereafter. Courtney would now always be young and beautiful, a woman who could have gone further, perhaps even achieved greatness, but for her life being cut short by tragedy. She would never grow old.

Courtney's brother, Richard Wallace, took the podium.

"When I think of Courtney, it is never on the news or as a television reporter. Not as a star or an Emmy Award winner. I remember my big sister at home, playing in our sandbox with dirt on her face and skinned knees—"

Lacey made a mental note to tell Vic. *If anything ever happens to me, do not allow my family to speak.*

A soloist sang "Amazing Grace," a song that always left Lacey cold. The bagpiper concluded with another Celtic tune, mournful but beautiful. Television lights and cameras caught it all, and then it was over. The mourners were invited to partake in refreshments in an equally uninspiring room next door.

"What's he doing here?" someone said, pointing to a newcomer at the door.

Lacey followed the pointing finger. Thaddeus T. Granville, the political operative who was the victim of Courtney's erroneous exposé, stood at the back of the room. Heads turned, as did cameras. The crowd hushed. Lacey was surprised by his presence at her funeral, particularly after what Tony had told her about the scandal. She edged close to hear what he was saying to a TV reporter. More reporters approached him with questions. His sudden appearance sent a ripple through the crowd. Nearly everyone in Washington had heard, or heard of, the damning news on Channel One, but few had seen the correction. Granville's reputation remained tarnished.

Granville was a former congressman from Louisiana with an unmistakable Southern-fried style and a drawl to match. Lacey thought he looked remarkably like Mark Twain, a resemblance that surely must have been cultivated. He was sixtyish, with a barely controlled head of curly graying hair, thick eyebrows that seemed to fly away from his eyes in wings, and a bushy mustache. His suit was a somber gray, but dandified by a pink shirt, pink bowtie, and pocket hanky. He cut quite the figure for the TV cameras. Lacey pulled out her notebook and pen.

"No hard feelings. Not now," he was telling a Capitol Hill reporter. "Courtney Wallace was impulsive and young. She apologized to me personally for her unfortunate inaccuracies in reportage, and that is all water under the bridge. Now she's dead. A terrible accident. It's very sad. Very sad."

Granville didn't look particularly sad, though. There was an air of triumph about him. It struck Lacey that he was quietly dancing on his enemy's grave, still managing to look gracious at the same time. Something Courtney might have done in his place.

Perhaps Granville was ready to raise his profile. With his timing and his presence, he was going to get air time on the news stations in Washington and Baltimore. He clearly had the media hanging on his words for a few precious moments. Lacey hadn't planned to write a story about the funeral, but she jotted down notes on what Granville said. When he left she slipped outside and, in the shade of an oak, called Mac. She gave him Granville's quotes. She returned to the church hall.

Most of the media quickly departed. They had gotten their story on Courtney, and a bonus with Thaddeus T. Granville. The crowd was halved. Lacey approached Courtney's mother and offered her condolences.

"She was so young and beautiful," Mrs. Wallace said, lost in a memory. "So bright, so full of promise."

Her brother Richard nodded in agreement. Something like exasperation crossed his face. "You're the one," he said. "You wrote the story about that horrible dress."

"I did, yes."

"How does a thing like that happen?"

"I don't know. I'd like to find out."

"You're the only one who wrote about it," he said accusingly. Lacey didn't know if that was supposed to be a good thing or a bad thing.

"You are her family, so the dress might come back to you. After the authorities release it." *If they ever do.*

"It won't do any good," Mrs. Wallace said, suddenly ferocious. "Courtney is dead. I never want to see that dress again. I hope they burn it."

So much for me asking to see it, Lacey thought.

"All we want is closure," he replied. "I don't know where she found that thing. She didn't usually dress like that. Courtney was way more casual."

With the dirt on her face in the sandbox, Lacey thought. He probably didn't know or understand anything about his grownup sister, the ambitious Washington reporter she'd become.

"There is no closure in death. There is only sorrow." Mrs. Wallace lifted her eyes to her daughter's picture, a glowing Courtney holding her Emmy. "She was a golden girl, but God chose her time on this Earth, and He chose when it ended. Courtney never liked to come home much. Not with her career and all. Now, she'll never leave us again. She'll be with her daddy in the family plot."

Her son put his hand on her arm and guided her away to a seat in the corner. Lacey declined to follow them. They seemed to have no information about the dress, or Courtney's death, or possibly even about Courtney's life. For them, Courtney had no enemies and no faults.

Mrs. Wallace was surrounded by other mourners, with other inane yet comforting things to say. Even if they disliked Courtney, they would praise her, perhaps feeling shame for their previous feelings. Death had that power over people.

Lacey headed to the refreshment table. Lamont was already there. She picked up a Styrofoam cup filled with tasteless black coffee. Although a few reporters approached Lamont with questions, he shook his head and put up his hand in warning. They stopped. He was not giving out quotes. To those who insisted, he repeated his mantra. "No comment. Tragedy. Just here to pay my respects."

Courtney's photographer edged over to the refreshment table. He drank down a cup of punch in one gulp.

"Hi. I saw you at the Correspondents' Dinner," Lacey said.

"I remember. You followed Courtney out of the room. After the—you know, the incident."

"I'm Lacey Smithsonian." She extended her hand.

"I know." He gulped down a second cup of punch and shook her hand. "Eric Park."

"You know who I am?" She was always surprised when people

recognized her. She liked to pretend she was anonymous, even after Mac put her picture at the head of her column.

"Courtney used to read your stuff."

"She did?" *As if I couldn't tell.* "Interesting."

"Yeah, she thought you'd found a good gig. A wide open beat. You investigate hard news as much as you do clothes and fashion trends. She said it was right up her alley."

"Really?" *Courtney was a copycat.*

"Oh yeah, she was a fan of yours. Imitation is the highest form of flattery."

"Sure." *No it isn't!* she thought. Fashion might be flimsy, but Lacey had found real things to say. About style and society and what people reveal about themselves in their wardrobes. She could read a person's history in what they wore. She found foul play in fabrics, secrets stitched between the layers of a corset, fashion clues that few could see. Most people didn't realize how much information they could glean with a single glance at someone's clothes.

To Lacey, Courtney's unflattering imitation was worse than the obvious theft of her ideas. Courtney didn't care that clothes told stories. *How could you call yourself a journalist and not care about stories?*

"Eric, did you accompany her on the entire vintage series?"

"Yup. I won the coin toss."

"I'm curious. Why did she move from investigative reporting to fashion? From hard news to soft? Besides the Granville mess."

He squirmed and reached for another cup of punch. "Here isn't the place to talk about it," Eric said, eyeing the big detective standing nearby, though he didn't seem averse to talking.

"Is there a better place?" She dug a card out of her bag and handed it to him. "Coffee?"

Eric measured her with his expression. "Do you have some feeling about her death not being an accident?"

"Why do you say that?"

"Because you're Lacey Smithsonian. Courtney used to say that the old clothes part of your beat wasn't that interesting, it was the murders you uncovered. She was pretty much in awe of that."

"The 'old clothes part' was always the key to the murders, Eric."

He tucked the card in his pocket. He smiled a slow, calculated smile. "Sure. I'm always up for gossip and a good latte. Ask Zanna

Nelson about Courtney, too. They were tight."

"How tight?"

"Best friends, I guess. Call me, we'll do coffee."

Eric swiped a petite tea sandwich from the table behind him on his way out. At the door he seemed to catch sight of someone he didn't like. He grimaced and slipped out. Lacey followed his look: A man impersonating a Ken Doll, tall and blond, was speaking to Mrs. Wallace.

"That's the boyfriend," Lamont said, suddenly standing behind her.

"Aha. He looks the part." Lacey took in the impeccably tailored gray suit, somber blue shirt, gray-and-blue striped tie, and pocket hanky. "I'm guessing he's a lobbyist or a lawyer for some interest group. Does he have a name?"

"Drake Rayburn. Lobbyist. Mouthpiece for some plastics association, or something like that."

"That fits. Ken to Courtney's Barbie."

The tall blond man directed a blazing smile to a comely brunette. Lacey recognized her as Eve Farrand, another broadcaster on Channel One. They shared a look over the head of Courtney Wallace's mother, a warm and intimate look. He leaned down and kissed Mrs. Wallace on the cheek, exchanged a few words of sympathy, and slipped out the side door with Eve, his hand in the small of her back.

"Whose boyfriend, again?" Lacey questioned Lamont.

"Man in motion. Not wasting any time, I guess."

They weren't the only ones who noticed Drake's escape with Eve. Zanna's gaze followed them, a look of longing on her face.

"Gotta go." Lamont tossed his cup and paper plate in the trash bin. "It's been real."

"Call me if you get any news, Broadway."

"Dream on, Smithsonian. One non-leak per non-homicide is all I got to give. On the other hand, you get some far-out hunch about Courtney Wallace, or old clothes, or anything at all, you call me."

"You said it was an accident."

"And I believe that. But just in case you got a theory, let me know before it hits the paper."

"Because you have to entertain the troops in the office?"

"That's right," he chuckled. "I'm the guy supposed to know things, even crazy-ass ideas like yours. And don't put too much store in what happens here today. People act funny at funerals. Don't mean they're killers."

Lacey watched Lamont exit without ceremony. Nearly everyone at the memorial service was rushing back to a job, work to do, deadlines to meet. Lacey seemed to be one of the very few who had the rest of the day off. But she noticed that at least one other mourner seemed to be in no hurry to leave.

Chapter 14

ZANNA NELSON WIPED HER EYES before picking up a cup of fruit punch.

"I'm sorry about your friend," Lacey said.

The woman jumped and the punch sloshed in her cup. "Oh. Thanks." She checked her outfit for spills and composed her face. "It's hard to believe Courtney is dead."

"Sorry I startled you."

"Deep in thought. You know. Courtney was so full of life. Fate was always so kind to her."

What did Fate like about her? That she was ruthless? Blond? Lacey put out her hand. "I'm Lacey Smithsonian."

"Zanna Nelson."

"I know you tried to help her that night. In the ladies' room."

"I did try." Zanna smiled sadly. "She never listened to me. But how could anyone help? No one knew what was wrong."

"I guess no one could."

Zanna stared at Lacey. "You wrote the story in *The Eye Street Observer*. You figured it out. The green dye thing, didn't you? How on earth did you know?"

"It was just a feeling at first." Lacey thought back to that evening. She gestured with the tasteless coffee. "And then I remembered something. It was a hunch."

"A feeling? A hunch? How did you come up with that? It was totally off the wall." Zanna looked perplexed.

"You know how it is, you're a reporter, right? Random bits of information float around in your head. Sometimes they coalesce, come together, create a storyline."

Where did her knowledge of Paris Green dye come from? The first time, she thought, was in a college class on costume history, where she remembered mishearing it as "poison apple green." It was a cautionary example of fatal fashions.

"Must come in handy when you write about the stuff you do."

"You've seen my column."

"Maybe once or twice." She tossed off a shrug and looked around the room, perhaps checking out who might be more important. She filled the cup again, turning her back on Lacey.

"Zanna, did you get a headache at the dinner, or feel strange? Or smell anything unusual? When you were in the ladies' room with Courtney?"

"Like bad perfume? Like those imitation designer scents? There was a lot of that going around that night." She turned back. "But I wasn't really paying attention. I mean, there was so much going on. Did you?"

Lacey distinctly remembered the oppressive feeling she'd had around the sodden dress, the smell of garlic and old wet fabric.

"Yes. That's one reason I thought she needed to find something else to wear. She didn't look well, she was stressed, her dress was soaked, and there was that odd smell about it. I thought at first it might be mildew, or the dress might be full of hidden mold."

"I don't know. I didn't smell anything extra strange." She looked sad and tired. "I was just concerned about Courtney."

"I know. We both were. Do you know where she found that dress?"

"She didn't share that information with me." Zanna swallowed the second glass of punch and made a face at the taste. "I was more interested in what I wore."

"Eric Park said you two were best friends."

"You talked to Eric? Well, we were, I guess. But I didn't know everything about her. Not every last little thing. Not like her clothes."

Judging from Zanna's aloof attitude, Lacey thought that could be true. "I heard Drake Rayburn was Courtney's boyfriend."

Zanna puckered her lips. The punch couldn't be that bad. "Occasionally. One of many."

"He was just comforting Eve Farrand earlier."

"Well. That's only natural." Zanna looked back to the side door as if expecting Rayburn to walk back in. "Excuse me, I have to go see about her mom. She's pretty broken up."

Lacey warmed up her coffee as she watched Zanna reach out and hug Mrs. Wallace. Courtney's mother started to cry.

"Lacey Smithsonian, you only go to the best places," a voice with a distinctly Russian accent said. She knew who it was before she saw him.

"Gregor Kepelov. Imagine seeing you here." The ex-spy seemed to dog her steps in the most unexpected places. "Did you know Courtney Wallace?"

"No."

"Why are you here, then? Just following me around again?"

"Always, Smithsonian." Kepelov grinned his odd crooked smile. "I am faithful follower of your reporting in *Eye Street Observer*. The manner of this death interests me too, as well as your proximity to the unfortunate woman when she suffered the fatal dose of champagne."

"My proximity? I had nothing to do with it."

He put up his hands in surrender. "Obviously! You are just lucky to be so often in the right place at right time."

"I'm not sure Courtney would agree."

Kepelov laughed. "The dress would also interest KGB, which exists no more. Except in spirit." Gregor Kepelov was a former KGB agent with a thick Russian accent who often talked of someday buying a ranch in Texas. It was his version of the American dream.

Kepelov had been shot and looked death in the face, and he seemed utterly fearless. He could easily blend into a crowd, unless someone looked at him closely. Stocky and well-muscled, he wore his pale blond hair cropped so short his round head looked almost bald. His facial features seemed a quarter-turn off normal, and his round blue eyes were icy, until he started talking about his fiancée Marie. Then they warmed. He was one of the oddest people Lacey knew, and it had taken a lot of work for him to earn her trust. But he had. *Mostly*.

"How did you know I would be here? Am I so predictable?"

"Is what I would do. We are alike in many ways. Also Marie said you would be here."

Obviously. Marie Largesse, his fiancée, was a psychic whose talents came and went, but she was positively savant about the rain and wind and snow. She was as accurate about the weather as a brass rooster weathervane. Apparently she had a reliable internal GPS where Lacey was concerned, too.

"She didn't faint, did she?" Lacey inquired.

"Not this time." Marie had a history of fainting whenever something bad was purportedly about to happen, like a death or an assault. She said whatever she saw in that medium's twilight was too awful to remember. Lacey was skeptical, but she paid attention to Marie's fainting spells.

"That's a relief."

"She has not collapsed in recent days. She has been working with Olga on whatever it is Olga teaches her. Personally, I think Marie is afraid to faint in front of Olga." He laughed. Olga Kepelov was Gregor's intimidating older sibling.

"I'd be afraid too. I thought your sister was going back to Florida."

"Unfortunately, she believes we need her. And though she finds us bothersome, and she does not like Marie's chicory coffee, she will not leave."

"You did get shot."

He shrugged. "I was wearing a vest. But I was, in her opinion, reckless. And now I will never hear the end of it from my meddlesome sister. Blood is thicker than bullets, it seems."

Olga had emigrated not only to the United States but also right into her brother's and future sister-in-law's lives. She was said to be some kind of weapons expert who consulted with law enforcement. Her brother's specialties in the KGB were surveillance and, Lacey had heard, assassination. They were a frightening family.

Lacey was unsure how Kepelov made a living these days, but he seemed to make himself useful in foreign policy circles around Washington and he dabbled in private security. He had even been a guest instructor in Lacey's private investigation course. Yet he also found time to be on the lookout for Romanov treasures to sell to Russian millionaires. His greatest desire was to locate a lost Fabergé egg. That, and a ranch in Texas. Lacey assumed one might lead to the other. *If the egg came first.*

"You wrote in your column that this woman's death was accidental."

"I was quoting an unnamed source in the police department. It's good to have friends in high places."

"Yes. Detective Broadway Lamont has been useful. However, you don't think the death of the television reporter was an accident?"

"I don't know what to make of it, Kepelov. How about you?"

"Gregor, if you please. We are old friends."

"Gregor." She frowned. "It's a little hard sometimes. With our past history."

"Lacey Smithsonian! I am wounded. Just because I happened to render you unconscious that one time."

"Kind of hard to forget, though."

"I tell you this. Holding a grudge is not healthy. Do I hold a grudge over the diamonds you found under my very nose? I do not. Most of the time. We are friends. It is our destiny to be great friends."

"So sayeth Marie?"

He helped himself to a plate of pastries. "The dress, how did you put it? 'Lethal Black Dress.' Very clever of you. This dress with the green dye is not an efficient way to kill. Yet it did. And so rare, so unlikely, who would not believe it was merely a cataclysmic mistake? Yet a poison dye would appeal to a certain kind of mind for a certain kind of death. The kind of death that is supposed to be considered a mishap."

"The KGB kind of mind?"

"Very possibly." He winked at her. "And others. The patina of misguided fate has great appeal as a cover for murder. What is your opinion?"

"It's more convenient for everyone if it was an accident."

"Just what a killer would want you to think." Kepelov smiled. His smile, though warmer and more frequent since he met Marie, still unsettled Lacey. It was the smile of a wolf evaluating a lamb. "But Lacey Smithsonian, what is your ExtraFashionary Perception telling you?"

"It took the day off. I only have questions. Where did the dress come from? Was it a random find in a vintage shop? Or was it a gift from the Evil Queen to Snow White?"

"Excellent. Origin of the dress is first step. And intriguing, yes? A fabric unused in over a hundred years. But you know yourself: Old fabric can be found."

"What if it really was a freak occurrence?"

Kepelov reached for a piece of crumb cake on the buffet table. "Even more unusual. The unusual is always of interest."

"Why do you care anyway?"

"Idle curiosity. Professional interest in obscure methods of death. Bonus: I like to watch you work. Harness your EFP for the service of justice."

"You're not as funny as you think."

He laughed and several people stared at them. He moved farther away from the table and she followed him. "They say Napoleon perhaps died from arsenic poisoning. Green wallpaper."

"I mentioned it in the article."

"You did." He nodded thoughtfully. "If there is more of this material in existence, a collector might be willing to pay for it. Particularly if provenance goes back a century or two. Perhaps a museum would purchase such an artifact. Or a dealer in curiosities." He finished the crumb cake and licked his fingers. "Many things are lethal. Guns, knives, bombs. Private collector in such weaponry would be interested and possibly willing to pay more. But to take possession of the very dress that killed TV personality Courtney Wallace…" He let the thought hang in the air.

"Cool your jets, Gregor. The dress is locked up in the medical examiner's office. And Wallace's own mother told me she wants it burned. The family doesn't want it, and they'll probably never get it back, anyway."

He raised his cool blue eyes to her. "Ah, most interesting information. I am grateful to you."

Now what is he up to? "Do you have a buyer in mind?" Lacey remembered a recent trip with Brooke to the Crime and Punishment Museum in the District, with its array of crime-related artifacts and weapons, and the Spy Museum, with its fascinating collection of spy tools and deadly devices. Kepelov sometimes hinted that some of his old handiwork was on display there, though he would never say exactly what.

"Who knows?" He reached across the table for a napkin.

"What does Marie say?"

His eyes darkened. "She says her dreams are washed in green. She woke up choking. She says, Beware the Green River, Smithsonian. But do not fear. I say: Gregor Kepelov, at your service."

Chapter 15

MARIE'S DREAM AND KEPELOV'S OFFER of help chilled Lacey. As usual, however, Marie's psychic hotline was short on useful details. Kepelov took his leave of her with an uncharacteristic hug.

Is Marie really turning him into a Russian teddy bear? Nah.

Lacey had to get out of that depressing church hall. She needed fresh air, air that had nothing to do with death. She took the wheel of her vintage green BMW and headed northeast, up the Baltimore-Washington Parkway to Charm City.

Unlike Washington, D.C., Baltimore always felt like a real city to Lacey. The Capital City sometimes seemed like nothing but stage scenery for the theatre that is American politics. The District, as beautiful as it was, produced mostly laws, red tape, paperwork, and hot air. Baltimore, on the other hand, worked for a living.

The downtown heart of Baltimore was solid and expansive, with huge old buildings marching down to the waterfront. She parked at a garage near the Aquarium at the Inner Harbor and met Vic, standing waterside, looking as dashing as a modern-day pirate in his jeans, black polo shirt, sunglasses, and leather jacket slung over his shoulder.

Vic caught sight of her and smiled. Her heart melted. Love sometimes grabbed hold of her and she found it hard to breathe.

"How about lunch?" he said, breaking away from her kiss.

"I'm starved." She kissed him again. "I assume you know a place?"

"I know a place." Vic didn't want to eat in the Inner Harbor area by the waterfront. Too full of tourists, he said. They hopped in his Jeep and he navigated the streets of Baltimore. Lunch was in the Mount Vernon neighborhood at a small French bistro. The food was delicious, the atmosphere romantic, and the service leisurely.

"How was the funeral?" Vic asked. "Any likely suspects?"

"Have you heard of Thaddeus Granville?"

"The political operative at the center of Wallace's dirty campaign tricks story. Yeah. Turned out the story was false. At least that particular story. There are others."

"Have you had dealings with him?"

"No, just heard tell he's a handful."

"Well, he popped up at the funeral today, spouting words of compassion. It caused quite a stir."

"Really?" Vic asked. "So he chose Wallace's service for his return to the fray?"

"In the flesh, and very nattily dressed."

"That man's got nerve. I give him that. What did he say?"

"He said all was forgiven."

"Now that she's dead."

"The media lapped it up."

"You included?" She shrugged and she caught him grinning. "So tonight he leads the news."

"And tomorrow, he is going to talk to me. At least, I plan to talk to him."

"Be careful, sweetheart. By all accounts, he's as dangerous as a snake."

"But smooth. Very smooth. For example: In the midst of the controversy, all the he-said, she-said, Courtney disappeared from the Channel One investigative team. Eventually turned up doing fashion features."

"And you think Granville had something to do with that?" Vic said.

"I know he held a grudge and he has influence. Other than that, the funeral was depressing, including the church," Lacey said. "Reminded me of a shoebox, only not as cheerful."

"No pomp, then?"

"No circumstance either. Guess who else popped up today? Gregor Kepelov."

"Kepelov? Did he expect to find you hiding some Romanov treasure?"

"Marie is having bad dreams. He is standing by to help me, if I need it."

"He thinks there's treasure somewhere," Vic said.

"I gather he wants to get his hands on Courtney's dress and sell it to the highest bidder."

"Like I said. Are *you* satisfied it was an accident?"

"I can't see Granville giving her a poison dress, even though he is a bit of a dandy. I think I'll follow up with Courtney's Channel One photographer, too. We're having coffee."

"You're not satisfied."

"Satisfied? 'There is no hope for the satisfied man.' That's a quote from Fred Bonfils, cofounder of *The Denver Post*, which was once a great paper. In this case, there is no hope for the satisfied woman."

"Not exactly what I've been dreaming of."

"I didn't say you couldn't satisfy me, honey." Lacey smiled. "Vic, I know this has taken us forever to go ring shopping, but do we have time for a quick stop first, after lunch?"

"You want to be—satisfied?" he inquired, with one lifted eyebrow.

She laughed. "Sweet talker. Not right now. Maybe later."

"How quick a stop and where?" Vic paid the bill. It was time for ring shopping.

"I happened to notice a little vintage store a couple of blocks from here."

"Why am I not surprised?"

"One of the shops Courtney mentioned on Channel One. The only one I haven't been to."

"Ten minutes?"

"That's all I need." *Unless they have some slamming Forties fashions.* She led the way down the street and he followed. She skipped up the steps to the shop, which was just opening for the day. The door said BVB, which stood for Best Vintage Baltimore. Vic stayed outside, grabbing some sunshine.

The store wasn't promising for Lacey's favorite era of vintage clothing, but it was illuminating just the same. The woman at the front counter told her the specialty of the store was the Eighties.

"The Eighties?" Lacey asked. "You're kidding."

"The kids, they love that stuff from before they were born."

"Me too," Lacey said, though she preferred the decades from long before she was born. Indeed, there were a couple of young women, in their late teens or early twenties, trying on vintage Eighties jumpsuits: pink and purple with huge shoulders and big white buttons, ready for their close-ups on MTV. The woman smiled and nodded, as if to say, "Told ya."

"I never expected to see so many jumpsuits. They're really big here?"

"You see, hon, here in Baltimore, what we want are outfits that are *all that*. It's a Baltimore thing." She gave her city's name the distinctive local pronunciation, which sounded something like

"Bawlmer." Lacey must have looked blank. "All that. You know, the total outfit, the one with all the style, the answer to all your prayers? Like, all that and a side of fries? My store, we got *all that*." She indicated the racks of clothing around the room.

"Courtney Wallace mentioned this store on the Channel One news."

"Oh, yeah, down in D.C. She was the TV woman? The blonde?"

"Yes."

"I remember her. Didn't see the story. Heard about it. I suppose I could Google it or something. Didn't something happen to her? She just died or something?"

"Yes. She died."

"One of my customers mentioned it. Sad to say, I would have paid more attention if she was from Baltimore. You know, local."

"Did she buy anything here?" Lacey gazed around the store. Courtney hadn't featured the Eighties. Perhaps if she'd had more time.

"No. She asked me a few questions, had her guy take some video, said she'd mention us on TV. I said fine, whatever. That was about it. How'd she die?"

"Wearing a dress with a green lining, which was toxic when it got wet."

The woman's eyes grew large. "No way! It wasn't polyester, was it? Because I never believed that polyester was that bad, even though some people say it was. I mean, I pretty much trade in polyester all day long, all this Eighties stuff. "

"It wasn't polyester. It was from a dye that was used in the nineteenth century."

"Oh. Seriously antique vintage. Well, what do you know?" She turned around and hung up a few garments. Apparently the woman, as well as her clothes, was living in the Eighties. What happened in the present didn't faze her.

One of the young shoppers brought two jumpsuits to the counter. A pink and a purple. "These are so cool! I can't decide. I guess I have to get both of them. They're all that, huh?"

The owner smiled brightly. "Cash or credit?"

As Lacey opened the door to leave, the woman called out to her. "Hey, if you really want to understand Baltimore and Baltimore fashion, the whole story, you gotta come to HonFest next month. I'll have a booth there."

"HonFest?" She'd heard about it, probably from Stella, her stylist. In "Bawlmerese," the Baltimore dialect, a woman dressed in a uniquely Old Baltimore style was called a *hon* (short for *honey*), and HonFest was a summertime street festival in their honor in Baltimore's Hampden neighborhood. Women competed for the title of "Bawlmer's Best Hon" in their curlers and bedroom slippers, tight lamé and leopard-print outfits, beehive hairdos, and cat-eye glasses. It sounded scary.

"You gotta go just for the beehives. It's a style statement nobody but Baltimore speaks," the woman testified. "It's all that. In fact, it's more than all that."

Lacey met Vic at the bottom of the steps outside.

"Did you find out anything?" Vic said.

"Not really. They may have 'all that,' but they didn't have what I was looking for."

⋙

"Victor, my lad. Welcome one and all."

A man small in stature, but large in personality, strode through the small jewelry store, arms outstretched. He threw his arms around Vic in a big hug, then leaned back to examine Lacey with some fascination. He was on the far side of sixty, with thinning gray hair worn in a short ponytail and a map of wrinkles around his grin. Slightly pudgy, he wore a gray vest over a white shirt and a jeweler's magnifying loupe slung around his neck on a lanyard. He was a jeweler with the air of an aging hippie.

"Good to see you, Reese." Vic put a protective hand on Lacey's shoulder. "May I present Lacey Smithsonian. Lacey, this is Reese Evans."

"You may. I am so pleased to meet you, Ms. Smithsonian." Evans took Lacey's hand in his. "Victor, this is the first time you have graced my shop with a sweetheart. Where is my calendar, I must mark the date. I wondered if I'd ever see the day. And you, Vic, what's your secret with the ladies?" He winked at Lacey.

"My secret," Vic said, "is that there's only one lady."

"And the lady is a rose. And a rose by any other name would smell as sweet."

Vic turned to Lacey. "He always talks like that. With flourishes."

"Come in, come in. Ms. Smithsonian, welcome to my shop. It's not very grand. A family tradition, just modest Welsh watchmakers. It was a way to escape the coal mining. We've been here in Baltimore for the last hundred years or so, but we can't seem to escape this city."

"It's a great city. And it's Lacey, please." She gazed at the cases full of glittery delights, full of anticipation.

The shop was in a long narrow building in Fells Point, so carefully tucked away it might not be noticed at first. Sprays of spring flowers decorated the one large window, full of the shiniest current offerings, earrings, necklaces, and bracelets, as well as rings and watches. Lacey wondered how these two men met.

"I have known Sean Victor and his family for many years now," Evans was saying, as if reading her mind. "My father sold his father a very fine watch, oh, more years ago than I want to say."

"Seventeen jewels," Vic said. "Or was it twenty-one? My dad still wears that watch. A Longines. He bought it after his first really big case."

"Twenty-one jewels sounds very impressive," Lacey said, wondering precisely what that meant. "And you have other jewels, too?"

"Yes, you could say that. We have made wedding rings, just for example, for more than a century. We made Vic's mother's ring and his grandmother's too. You get to know good people like the Donovans. So when I had a problem, I took it to Victor."

"It was nothing, really," Vic said.

"This guy, he would say it's nothing. But that's not true. We had a thief inside the company, a dirty little embezzler. And he made off with a few emeralds and rubies too." Reese Evans shook his head. "Obviously, that's not the kind of thing you want announced to the world. Victor has always been the soul of discretion." He slapped Vic on the shoulder.

"Some things are better handled in-house," Vic said modestly. "We simply kept it inside the family, so to speak. But we came on another matter today, Reese. We're thinking about resetting a stone."

"For a ring," Lacey said.

"An engagement ring," Vic clarified.

Lacey held her breath. *This is really happening.*

"Well, that is something to celebrate." Evans's mouth spread in a wide grin. "Great news! Congratulations, Victor," he said. "And best wishes to you, my dear. Do you have the stone with you?"

Vic nodded and pulled a small blue velvet bag from his inner jacket pocket. The jeweler opened the bag and set the diamond on a black velvet board. He picked it up with tweezers and examined it with his loupe.

"I remember this stone. First I will have to clean it. You can't really see the beauty of a diamond when it is dirty." He motioned them to two chairs in front of a glass counter. Evans cleaned the stone and returned it to the velvet board. "See how it sparkles now. It's a very fine stone. No chips. No visible flaws. Good color. Now, make yourselves comfortable."

"Lacey would like a new setting," Vic said.

"Of course. I remember the old one. You would need a new one in any event." The jeweler winked at Lacey again. "And you are particular about what you wear on your finger?"

"Yes, I am. A bit."

"A bit?" Vic poked her.

"I chose *you*," she said.

"It's a good thing you did," Vic said, "because I'd already chosen you."

"Why shouldn't you be particular?" Evans said. "It will grace your hand for years to come. You will see it and cherish it every day of your life. As Juliet said to Romeo, 'My love is as boundless as the sea...' "

"Reese. We only have today to do this," Vic said.

Evans just laughed at him. "Your grandmother would not hear of a new setting. We replaced the prongs and the head several times, but she insisted on keeping the original band. She was sentimental. It was set in platinum, but something tells me you don't particularly like platinum, do you?" he asked Lacey.

"Did you tell him?" Lacey poked Vic this time. But it was probably the gold hoop earrings that gave her away.

"No. I swear. He only knew we were coming today."

"Victor didn't need to tell me anything. I can tell," Evans said.

"Do you read auras too?" she asked.

"I do. Yours is gold," he answered.

"The diamond will stand out better in a gold setting," Lacey said. "I prefer gold to silver. Or platinum." *I'll leave the platinum to my friends and everyone else in D.C.*

She was about to say something more, when he put up his hand to stop her. He took her left hand and studied it a moment. "You don't want a typical setting."

"You're right. I don't really care for a solitaire."

"Ah yes, so lonely. I have some unusual settings, if you would like to see them. Victor, do you have a preference of your own?"

"Whatever Lacey likes. No matter how gaudy," he teased her.

"You might regret those words, mister," she replied.

The jeweler reached below the counter and withdrew a tray of rings, some with stones and some without.

"Just to give you an idea," Evans said.

"Bling," Vic said. "Let me put on my shades."

The jeweler placed the tray on the table and picked up a setting to show her. "We can take the stone and set it gently in the setting, like this, to see how it would appear. Be careful though, the diamond is not secure."

"Perhaps a thicker band?" she said.

"Of course. You want the world to see this ring."

"Everyone but my mother," she said.

She glanced at Vic. He looked like he was in pain. *Hey, this was your idea, buddy!* She held back a giggle. She eased the first ring onto her finger for size. It was dazzling. She tried on a half dozen for comparison, each with a comparable stone, but none were quite right. Lacey was beginning to feel like Goldilocks, when she peeked into the jewelry case and saw something in the estate jewelry section. Her gaze was drawn to an antique gold ring with a coral rose in the middle. The coral was cracked and chipped, but the ring wrapped round it like leaves around a flower. There was something about it.

"What about that one?"

The jeweler withdrew the ring from the case. "You are thinking without the coral, and with your diamond?"

"Yes. Maybe."

He nodded encouragingly. "Let's see. This is easily remedied." With a small tool he popped the coral out of the ring. "Don't worry, I can put it back, but the coral is damaged. It should be replaced anyway." With tweezers, he carefully set Vic's family diamond loosely in the center. "Ah. Very nice. You have a good eye."

Lacey took the ring and slipped it on her finger. "It's gorgeous." It felt right on her finger. She was glad her manicure was fresh. Like so many of her vintage clothes, this ring seemed to already belong on her hand. It fit perfectly and wouldn't even need resizing. She gazed at Vic with a smile.

"Are you sure?" he asked. Lacey nodded. She didn't speak for fear of choking up.

Vic picked up her hand. "Reese, this is the one. Our engagement ring. But what about a wedding band?"

"It doesn't come with one, does it?" Lacey managed to say.

"I could make one for you," Evans said. "A thinner band that would dip below the ornamentation and fit snugly with the golden leaves. It could be plain, or it could carry some smaller diamonds, if you like."

Lacey's head was spinning as the jeweler explained that he could fashion a complementary filigree band that would make it a set. Vic agreed that two rows of smaller diamonds set in the wedding band would pull the pair together, and were, indeed, absolutely necessary.

She could only nod in agreement. *This is the ring. This wedding thing is really going to happen.*

"The size is perfect, but you can't have the engagement ring today, I am sorry to say. I must make sure this lovely diamond is rock solid in the setting, as it were. I'm going to build up these prongs and strengthen the band to make sure it is just right before I hand it back to you." He assured them it would take no more than a week, the wedding band a little longer.

"Do you know anything about the ring's history?" Lacey asked.

"Only that it came from a very happy home. And that it is going to another one."

Vic escorted her outside to the waiting sunshine before returning to the jeweler's tiny office to conduct business. She turned to him and said, "He would have to say that it came from a happy home. I nearly choked up."

"It probably did come from a good home, he's dealt with the same families for generations. I'm just relieved he didn't say it was haunted."

"Tell me again, why I'm marrying a smartass?"

"Because you love me." He kissed her.

"I seem to remember now. See you later." She kissed him back and reluctantly let him go.

Besides the selection of their rings, Vic had other business to conduct with Reese Evans, something about a background check on a potential employee. Before heading home, Lacey would have some time to check out the quaint Baltimore shopping area of Fells Point, and a vintage clothing store, a shop that Courtney had visited for her feature series. Perhaps the Madame X dress had come from Baltimore. It was a long shot. But it was *all that* and then some.

"It doesn't feel right to let you go after this," Vic said. "We should be going home together. With that ring."

"Next trip to Baltimore, we'll come together."

"Meet me in an hour at the Daily Grind, before you drive back to Old Town," he said. "You're sure you'll be okay for an hour on your own?"

"Vic, honey, do you know me at all? I have a store to explore. A vintage store."

"Just don't trip over any bodies or try on any poison dresses."

"But the poison ones are the most compelling. I love that shade of green."

Chapter 16

LACEY WAS ON THE HUNT. She was slightly chagrined to be following in the footsteps of a broadcast reporter, especially one who had so often copied her own lead. However, she consoled herself with the fact there was more to this story than could fit in a twenty-second news bite.

Killer Stash was a popular Fells Point vintage store, the shop where Courtney Wallace found the Sixties dress she wore on Channel One, the shift style popularized by Jackie Kennedy. The Sixties weren't Lacey's favorite period, because she thought the styles weren't particularly flattering on her. But the store was bound to have other clothes, and possibly information.

Lacey had been to Killer Stash before, but most of the clothing it carried was a little more recent than she preferred. Like Best Vintage Baltimore, "vintage" to them meant anything pre-1990. The small store was packed with clothes, and the vibe was friendly. Lacey spotted the sales clerk, a young woman who obviously loved the 1950s, as evidenced by her vintage leopard-print wiggle dress. She had artistically penciled black eyebrows and thick cat-eye liner that made her eyes look enormous. Her black tresses were tamed into a modified beehive wrapped with a red ribbon.

Her name, she said, was "Veronica. Like in the Archie comic books, the early ones."

Lacey introduced herself and complimented Veronica on her commitment to style.

"Fifties," Veronica said, knowingly. "The Eighties are very popular here right now, but I prefer the Fifties. Because I have a *waist*." She pointed to her tiny middle, encircled by a narrow red patent leather belt. "You really need an excellent waist to rock the Fifties."

"Agreed. You're certainly rocking it. Did you happen to talk with Courtney Wallace for her Channel One series on vintage?"

"You mean that blond woman who died in that dress?"

"The TV reporter, yes."

The clerk's eyes grew even larger as she opened them very wide. "Is that weird or what? I mean it looked like a really pretty dress on TV, and that lining is wild. But to die for a dress, it's just so wrong.

People always say things like, 'That dress is to *die* for,' but no! It's just a dress! You know what I'm saying?"

"I do." Lacey was happy to have found someone who liked to talk. "Did you sell anything to her? To Courtney Wallace."

"Not me. I wasn't in the store that day. But between you and me and the rest of the world, that woman was a bitch. That's what Betty said. Isn't that funny, Betty and Veronica working together? Like the comics. And Betty is a blonde with a flip. But we get along. There's no Archie coming between us. Oh my God, did you hear about what happened to Archie?"

"Um, yeah. Tragic. So it was Betty who waited on Courtney?"

"Yeah. She told me this Courtney person was acting all high and mighty and everything. She even talked Betty out of that cute yellow Sixties number that Betty was saving up for. And the perfect pillbox hat that went with it. Even the *shoes*."

Lacey leaned in a little. "How did she manage to do that?"

"Betty said she threatened not to mention us on TV. Went all bitchy on her. As it was, she gave us like two seconds or something. The yellow dress was on that mannequin in the window. So of course it caught her eye. It was like she wanted it all for free just for a tiny mention on TV, but that wasn't going to happen. This is Baltimore, hon. She had to pay. Everyone's got to pay. And now she's dead." Big sigh. "I mean it was weird, on TV she was all hard-charging with her funky anchor-woman-crossed-with-a-prom-queen hairdo. Must have used a ton of hairspray and not in an ironic-I-have-to-keep-my-beehive-in-place kind of way. It was stiff, like the rod up her you-know-what." Veronica patted her own beehive. "I don't wish ill on nobody, but you know, maybe it was her karma. Karma ran over her in a Paris Green dress."

"Oh, so you read my article in *The Eye Street Observer*?"

"Was that you? You're the one? You're Lacey? Oh my God! Are you kidding me? I totally read Crimes of Fashion, like every word! I think it's on a bulletin board in the back room. Would you sign it for me?"

"Be happy to. Do you think it was an accident? Her death?"

"Why? You think someone slipped her a poison dress on purpose?" She put her hands on her hips, considering it. "Like instant karma or something? Who knows? I don't know if karma cares. Karma just wants the job done, you know?"

Lacey thanked Veronica and signed her clipping like a regular celebrity. She strolled a couple of blocks to the Daily Grind coffee shop facing the harbor, admiring colorful petunias in hanging pots. The warm breeze felt like kisses on her skin. She was tired. She felt emotional. The day had been a roller coaster. The memorial service, running into Kepelov of all people, then lunch and ring shopping with Vic, strange new vintage stores to explore, and all topped off by the philosophical wisdom of Veronica at Killer Stash. She wished she had her engagement ring right now.

After avoiding it for so long, now suddenly I miss it. Instant karma?

She was craving something sweet and hot and chocolate to take the edge off her mood. She was sipping the velvety smooth brew when Vic walked through the door. He threw her a huge grin, bought himself a coffee, and sat down beside her.

"Sorry I couldn't wait," Lacey said, kissing him. "It was either this tiny hot chocolate or a giant chocolate chip cookie. This might be more forgiving."

He leaned down and kissed her, then pulled up a chair. "You talked with the clerk at—what's the name of it?"

"Killer Stash. I spoke with the Philosopher in Chief. Veronica, like in the Archie comics."

"What did she think of the Lethal Black Dress?"

"That it was weird, that Courtney was snotty, and that the killer was probably instant karma."

"She could be onto something. In death, darling, karma is often part of the equation."

"Karma's a bitch."

Chapter 17

WHEN SHE OPENED HER BEDROOM curtains Wednesday morning, Lacey couldn't see Maryland across the Potomac River. It had been towed away in the night, or else it had disappeared in the gray morning's fog and heavy rain.

She selected the easiest thing she could think of to wear, a lightweight two-piece suit from the Forties in dark violet crepe. The skirt was plain and flared. The elbow-length jacket, which buttoned so it didn't need a blouse, was a work of art. There was a bit of smocking at the yoke, under which were small shoulder pads. Small bands of embroidered flowers, red, blue, yellow, and green, created four horizontal stripes on the jacket, which precisely matched the sleeve bands. The waistline eased out into a short peplum. She selected her lightweight white trench coat and umbrella, pulled on her bright red rubber rain boots and grabbed a pair of wedge shoes for the office and in case the rain lightened up.

Many people found the rain in D.C. depressing. Not Lacey. After growing up in a place with relentless sun, blindingly bright days, and air so dry it hurt your lungs, she enjoyed the peace and solitude of a gray, rainy day. There was the usual griping at the newsroom that the weather was miserable, humid, and stuffy. Lacey loved it. But coffee was essential.

She called Thaddeus Granville's office as soon as she filled her FASHION *BITES* mug with the sludge from *The Eye*'s coffee maker. To her surprise, a receptionist put her call straight through and Granville agreed to meet with her at four that afternoon. There were certain conditions: an informal chat, off the record, no recording devices. Lacey agreed. At this point, their chat would be merely informational anyway. His public comments at the funeral were already tucked into a brief story in today's paper.

Lacey was itching to walk outside and plan her interview strategy, and to escape the newsroom, which was full of grumpy weather complainers. She combed her hair and tucked it back into a chignon at the back of her neck, picked up her cardinal-printed umbrella, and fled outside to the rain.

She wound up a few blocks from *The Eye* at St. Matthew's Cathedral, breathing in the scent of incense and candles. The hustle and bustle of the District stayed outside the doors. Lacey was often surprised at the people she saw at St. Matthew's, which today included several reporters and section editors from *The Eye*. Newspapers were supposed to be bastions of atheists and nonbelievers. Yet here was a cadre of cynical journalists seeking the quiet serenity of the Cathedral during the workday.

Perhaps it was the peace that drew them there, among the marble pillars and stained glass and statuary. Lacey didn't stay for the midday Mass, but she left feeling confident she could nail the Granville interview and not let him intimidate her.

Outside, the rain let up, leaving a fine mist in the air. The gray sky and slick pavement intensified the color of the flowers around the trees and in planters around the city. Farragut Square was empty of the noontime lunch parties of the day before. Office workers scurried to and from their jobs. Lacey detoured to Firehook Bakery for a cup of decent coffee to bring back to the office.

Her calm lasted precisely until she returned to the newsroom. Mac poked his round head around her corner of the news world just as she was hanging up her raincoat and booting up her computer.

"What are you looking for, Mac?" she asked, as if she didn't know. "If you're looking for the calorie queen, I haven't seen her lately."

Mac stared at the latest of Felicity's offerings, but he seemed reluctant. It had not been nibbled. "Is it fair game?" he asked, wistfully. "Has she photographed it for her column yet?"

"I don't even know what it is. Or want to know." She did suspect, but she thought Mac should find out for himself.

Lacey half believed Felicity lived in a gingerbread house in the woods, where she lured unsuspecting reporters to fatten them up on her muffins and tarts. But Felicity had no need of a gingerbread house. She simply dropped a trail of tasty crumbs leading to her desk, where *The Eye*'s reporters were drawn as inexorably as Pavlov's dogs were drawn to that bell.

Felicity had free rein to use the fully equipped kitchen on the executives' sixth floor for her food column experiments. These executives were seldom seen in the flesh, at least not in the newsroom. Perhaps, Lacey thought, they were locked up in calorie-laden captivity in Felicity's fattening pens at the gingerbread house. *One could only hope.* Today, however, Felicity hadn't personally baked this dish upstairs. Rather, she had *built* it, so to speak, with the aid of the Krispy Kreme Doughnut Company. The final creation was an impressive mound of glazed doughnuts, stuck together with icing and sprinkles. On the very top was a small statue of a tuxedoed groom, standing atop a miniature Krispy Kreme doughnut truck.

"What is it supposed to be, exactly?" Mac asked.

"The groom's cake, of course," Harlan Wiedemeyer announced from behind him.

It was common knowledge around the office that Wiedemeyer was a devotee of the famous Krispy Kreme "Hot Doughnuts Now," as well as a fan of their no-longer-hot doughnuts, anytime at all. His tie was often iced or sprinkled with the remains of the latest Krispy Kreme seasonal offering. He'd been transported to Doughnut Heaven when the company opened a shop at the Dupont Circle Metro stop, within walking distance of *The Eye*'s offices. Felicity appeared right behind him.

"Groom's cake?" Mac said, lost in wonder. "Wow. It's—it's—"

It's a carbohydrate and sugar volcano, Lacey thought. And if the miniature statue on top truly represented Harlan Wiedemeyer, it should have had a round tummy. She felt dismayed. *I can't believe you have to have a groom's cake at a wedding these days. Surely, Vic won't expect one of those. Will he?*

"I think that is the most beautiful groom's cake I've ever seen," Wiedemeyer was saying. "Felicity, my sweet bread-and-butter Pickles, you have outdone yourself." He delicately removed the groom-and-truck cake topper with one hand and snatched a doughnut with the other. This seemed to be the all-clear signal. Mac grabbed a second doughnut, while Tony popped his head around the cubicle wall.

"Felicidad," Tony sighed. "Doughnuts. What would I do without you?" He lifted a fluffy puff of dough and calories. He bit into it with great contentment.

Lacey briefly wondered if Tony dropped all his blondes because they couldn't cook. If that was the case, he needed to find himself a tall, skinny, blond Felicity. *If there was such a thing.*

She turned her back on the groom's doughnut cake extravaganza, sipping her coffee, telling herself that being strong was better than giving in to temptation.

"Um, Lacey," Felicity began tentatively.

"No, thanks," Lacey said, without turning around. "Looks fabulous, really. But I have coffee."

"It's not that. I have a small request. A teeny, tiny little request."

No. Lacey turned, reluctantly. The last time Felicity had a request, she was accused of assault and Lacey had come to her aid. There were witnesses, all staring at Lacey and Felicity, contentedly munching their doughnuts like a herd of cows. Watching their beloved bringer of fatty foods and the fashion reporter who always seemed to be getting into trouble.

"Request? What kind of request?"

"Well—" Felicity said, with a fluttery hand gesture. "You wrote that column. About how a vintage wedding dress can be made over into a one-of-a-kind gown?"

"Yes. I did write that." *In a moment of weakness.* "Do you have a vintage wedding gown? Maybe your mother's? Grandmother's?"

Lacey wrote that particular Crimes of Fashion column after a small snafu left her friend Stella's wedding gown in tatters, almost on the eve of her wedding. The point of the article was that there were alternatives to the giant Wedding Industrial Complex and their overpriced, cookie-cutter white gowns. If someone had a little creativity. And a good seamstress.

However, Lacey was fresh out of great seamstresses willing to remake a wedding dress. Her favorite, Alma Lopez, had sworn never to sew a stitch for Lacey again after one particular incident. It made her sad to lose Alma, but Lacey understood completely. A maniac had gone berserk in Alma's shop with sharp implements and made a slash of things. It was scary. It was sort of Lacey's fault. Alma was not in a forgiving mood.

Something even worse could happen to Felicity and her wedding dress, Lacey thought. *After all, she's marrying the original office jinx of* The Eye Street Observer.

"No. I don't have a vintage dress. Right now." Felicity's voice jolted Lacey out of her musing. "But I've been thinking about finding one. You said altering a vintage dress could be way cheaper than going to one of those big wedding dress shops." She made it sound like an accusation.

Felicity? Dress shopping? Live and in person? Felicity was a dedicated online and catalogue shopper. Her wayward outfits and her seasonally themed sweater collection testified to the dark power of the Web. She'd once mentioned that the thought of going to a bridal shop with the snooty salesclerks and their unspoken judgments terrified her.

"Um, I did write that, but—"

"I want to go shopping for a vintage wedding dress. With you, Lacey."

Me? Dress shopping with Felicity Pickles? Lacey could hardly wrap her mind around it. *What have I done to deserve this? And how can I tell her that a plus-sized vintage wedding gown is among the rarest of all creatures? It would be like hunting a unicorn. A plus-sized unicorn.*

"Shopping?" Lacey was appalled. "Together? You and me?"

"Anytime is good. As long as it's right now. I like white, but I'd be willing to consider something pastel." Felicity's voice sounded a note of desperation.

"Right now?" *Think fast, Lacey.* "What about your maid of honor? It's really more of a maid-of-honor kind of thing. I bet she'd love to go with you."

"She's in Pittsburgh. Besides, I can't wait to order a bridal gown. We've kind of moved the wedding up."

"Moved it up!" It was suddenly hard for Lacey to breathe. "And it's going to be three whole days? You said it was going to be in September. In Pittsburgh." If it were in the fall, Lacey could put off thinking about it. Now it was practically breathing down her neck. All three days of it.

"We think a summer wedding here would just be so much nicer," Wiedemeyer put in. "Outdoors. In July. In D.C."

"A July wedding! Here? Seriously? Pretty steamy." More than steamy. *Insanity.* It would be like having a wedding inside an oven. *In a gingerbread house. In the woods.*

"Steamy like our love," Felicity said, beaming at her intended.

You didn't really just say that, did you? A wedding in a torrid D.C. July would make dresses stick to the skin. Hair would droop or frizz. Makeup would melt. Tempers would flare. "What about the bridesmaid dresses?" Lacey managed to say.

"Hillary, you know, my maid of honor, she's working on that. She'll be in touch with you soon."

Lacey had no idea who Hillary was. She could hardly wait to meet her. "I don't know, Felicity, there just isn't a lot of time to find something you like and get it reworked and—"

"Lacey, you saved my life once. You can do it again. Besides, it's just *clothes*. It'll be a snap for you."

"Just clothes?" *Just stab me.*

"Exactly. We could go shopping today. Over lunch."

"Lunch!" Lacey's head was spinning.

"I'm sure Mac won't mind if we take a long lunch. In a good cause."

Mac stood waiting, munching another doughnut. If Felicity was unhappy, she would stop baking. It had happened before. The inmates of *The Eye*'s asylum had been miserable. There would be no decadent delicacies, no fattening desserts, no savory casseroles, no little sugar-filled pick-me-ups. And if there was no food, Mac would be unhappy. Nobody wanted an unhappy editor. Unhappy editors barked orders and made unreasonable demands. Felicity gazed meaningfully at the towering doughnut concoction on her desk.

Lacey reached for her bottle of Advil. She swallowed two pills with the last sip of the brew in her cup.

"Well, Mac?" *Please say no. Please, please, please…*

"Yeah, sure. Go for it." Mac's eyebrows settled complacently under his bald dome. "Felicity's food section is finished. Take a couple hours."

Lacey grabbed her raincoat in a daze. "I have an interview at four on K Street. With Thaddeus T. Granville. I can't be late."

Mac looked suspicious. "The political fixer? About what? Clothes?"

"Possibly. That'll do."

"This will be such fun, Lacey! We'll take my new minivan." Felicity had insisted on replacing her old, exploded minivan with another one just like it. In gray. "You'll love it. You want to drive?"

The humiliations just keep coming.

Chapter 18

"I AM NOT DRIVING YOUR great gray whale of a minivan, Felicity. Just drive."

Felicity took the wheel and headed the minivan straight toward Polly Sue's vintage store in Takoma Park, Maryland, a suburb sometimes referred to by Washingtonians as "the People's Republic of Takoma Park." It was known, among other things, for its political correctness and a popular farmer's market.

"Why here?" Lacey asked, as Felicity maneuvered her gray van into a too-small space in the rain. Lacey closed her eyes and hoped she wouldn't hear the sound of metal on metal. She didn't. Felicity was a pro minivan commander, speeding north through D.C.'s maze of streets and traffic and road construction and Presidential motorcades in record time. Lacey was fine, except for the motion sickness. They jumped out and darted through the rain into Polly Sue's.

"Because you mentioned this one in a column, silly, and then Courtney Wallace did one of her Channel One spots from this store. She made it look like fun."

So Courtney was responsible for Felicity's sudden interest in vintage attire. It figured that Felicity would take Wallace's word over Lacey's.

"It's much nicer than that Killer Thingy store up in Baltimore," Felicity went on, "according to Courtney."

"You mean Killer Stash?"

"Whatever. And there's an organic market near here that I want to check out."

Of course. There would be food involved. Lacey closed her eyes and rubbed her forehead. "What are you looking for in a dress?"

"Something cheap. You'll find the perfect thing for me, I just know it."

That was the funny thing about Felicity. She'd been planning the menu for her wedding reception practically since the moment she met Harlan Wiedemeyer. Granted, she hadn't made any firm decisions, but she was doing something about the food every single day. Felicity refused to believe that the guests didn't really care about the menu at the wedding. Certainly not as much as this bride. But this was one bride who didn't care nearly as much about the dress.

"Any particular color? Ivory, cream, snow white? Length? Style? Look? Period?"

"A white dress. Pretty. Something that fits. What about you, Lacey? What kind of dress would you have, if that handsome Victor Donovan of yours ever gets around to asking you to marry him?"

Good old Felicity, always managing a little dig. Well, I have my own secrets. So there.

But Lacey froze at the thought of choosing a wedding gown. Wasn't it enough to decide on a ring? She wasn't hung up on what everybody else was wearing. She could always wear her lovely Gloria Adams dress, though it was blue. She liked the idea of a light-colored wedding gown, although the Morning Glory Blue was a bit intense.

"I'll know it when I see it," she said.

"That's how I feel too."

Sure you do.

Polly Sue's was one of Lacey's favorite vintage stores. They displayed a healthy selection of mid-century clothing, with some nice older offerings from the turn of the twentieth century, the early 1920s and 1930s. There were even a few wedding gowns, including a tiny Victorian number, meant to be worn with a waist-cinching corset. It looked like it might fit a child, but not a full-grown, twenty-first-century woman. They looked through all the racks, but Polly Sue's had nothing in Felicity's size, not even a housedress. In fact, it would be difficult even for Lacey to fit into many of these tiny dresses.

Lacey introduced herself to the new saleswoman, dressed in nerdy but severe all-black and big square black-framed glasses, and asked if there was anything in back, or set aside, in a larger size. It didn't even have to be a wedding dress. The answer was no.

"Courtney Wallace came here," Felicity said. "She mentioned your shop on TV."

"Yes, but she didn't wear anything she bought here," the saleswoman said.

"What did she purchase?" Lacey said.

"Evening gown. Thirties. Not the one she died in, thank God. We like to be known for our killer style, but not, you know, literally."

"Do you happen to know where she found the dress she wore to the White House Correspondents' Dinner?"

"The Madame X dress? That's what you called it, right?"

"That's right." *Another reader.*

"Great dress. Good name for it, too. No, I have no idea. I pretty much know all the shops in the area. There's one possibility though. There's a new vintage shop in Del Ray in Alexandria. The kind of shop that's open when the mood strikes."

"Really?" *How do I not know about this?* Lacey thought she knew all the vintage shops around town.

"Ingrid Something. Allendale. Ingrid Allendale. Brand-new shop. Used to do most of her business in Charlottesville, but I heard she recently moved back home to take care of her parents. Her stuff is amazing. I don't know where she finds it. She's more of a curator than a seller. Her stuff is that good. But good luck finding her in. Better call first."

Lacey took down the address and phone number and gave the woman her own card. "I have a question. What's up with all the Geek Chic these days?"

She eyed the collection of distinctly nerdy clothes and black-framed glasses. The saleswoman sported an austere version of the same look, like a Beat Movement librarian.

"Geek is what Washington does best. Wild, isn't it? Go figure. People are embracing it. Making it cool. Making it chic. Wearing it with a hip, self-aware irony."

"Not everyone."

The woman laughed. "True. And self-awareness is asking a lot. But hey, if it sells, we're there."

Felicity sighed deeply, signaling to Lacey that she was ready to leave. Her round doll face fell into a frown. She was pouting. Outside, Lacey tried to smooth Felicity's ruffled feathers.

"It's just one store." *One down and heaven only knows how many more to go.* "Don't be so glum."

"I thought it would be easy."

"Easy? Felicity, shopping is never easy. Style is not easy. Sloppy is easy. Comfortable is easy. This is your wedding. You are looking for a wedding gown. It's once in a lifetime, if you're lucky. Weddings are not easy. They are hard. They take a lot of work."

"You sound just like your column." Felicity put her minivan in drive. "Let's get to that market. I've heard they've got great organic veggies."

While Felicity was inside scooping up organic goat cheese and other sundry healthy foods, Lacey stayed in the car and prayed for inspiration. She jotted down a few notes for a column on Washington

Geek Chic, which made her snicker. Suddenly, she thought of something that just might help in Felicity's hopeless quest for the unicorn, that perfect cheap vintage wedding dress. It was a risk, however. She didn't want to insult Felicity.

Oh, go ahead, insult her, she thought. *She insults me all the time.*

The food editor hopped into the driver's seat after setting two bags of healthy, politically correct, organic groceries in the back.

"I can't believe you didn't want to come inside. They have incredible stuff. Samples too."

"My head is throbbing. Listen, Felicity, I have one thought left. This is a long shot, and the dresses might not be vintage, but a few bridal shops sometimes donate their older sample sizes to certain Goodwill stores. There's a sale on them this week, a June-bride promotion. I wrote a news brief about it in the paper." *And promptly forgot about it.*

Felicity's eyes lit up. "Real bridal gowns? At Goodwill? Why didn't you tell me?"

"You wanted a vintage gown. Remember? Something pretty?"

"I don't care about that! I just don't want to spend a lot. Really? Goodwill? We have to hurry," she wailed, "those dresses could all be gone by now!" Felicity checked the map on her phone. There was a participating Goodwill store within striking distance.

"You have to know they won't have every size in stock," Lacey warned her. "They may not have your size. These are manufacturers' samples. Some might be soiled, damaged, or store returns. But it's my last idea. Take it or leave it. "

"I'll take it." Felicity gunned the minivan in the direction of the Northeast D.C. Goodwill store, near New York Avenue. "This better work."

There was a threatening note in her voice. She was a bride in desperation.

Inside the entrance of the store, under the harsh fluorescent lights, they were greeted by a large rack full of fluffy bridal gowns. Oddly, the rack, crammed with snowy white frocks, seemed to have been ignored by Goodwill shoppers, as if bridal gowns at a thrift store were too kooky to contemplate. On the other hand, maybe this was just a midday lull in store traffic. In which case, they needed to act fast. Lacey started at one end, Felicity stood paralyzed at the other.

The first few dresses Lacey looked at had obviously been worn before. One was torn and stained. *Wine or tears? Oh no, I hope this isn't the Bridal Rack of Broken Dreams.* Lacey prayed these dresses were not all donated by heartbroken widows, jilted brides, or bitter divorcees. She certainly wasn't going to voice her bad-luck fears to Felicity. She pressed grimly on. Time was of the essence. Lacey dared not be late for the Granville interview.

A quick inspection revealed that most of the other garments still had the original tags. Lacey breathed a sigh of relief: Samples! These unsold dresses weren't exactly going for a song, but they were marked down by hundreds of dollars, some by thousands. Most were only a year old, last year's styles, and Lacey was surprised by their quality.

"It's sort of overwhelming," Felicity said.

"Focus, Felicity. I need some direction from you. What do you want? Beading? Ruching? Plain? Fancy? Neckline? Sleeves? No sleeves? Off the shoulder? Long? Short? Ball gown? Mermaid?"

"Yeah. Sure. Whatever. Something that fits." Felicity nodded helplessly, her blue eyes wide.

"Great." Lacey tried not to roll her eyes. There was freedom, and a gin and tonic, in her future. She simply had to live that long.

Because they were samples, most of the dresses were sizes eight and ten. But hidden in the middle of the white tulle forest Lacey found some sample gowns made especially for the "full-figured" woman. The brand seemed to be called "Curvaceous Bride." Lacey zeroed in on them. There were three possible sample gowns that just might fit Felicity, with minimal alteration: a beaded ball gown, a mermaid style, and one in a sleeker A-line silhouette with ruching on the sides. All three were clean, new, unworn, and had sweetheart necklines. *Take it or leave it, sweetheart.*

Felicity grabbed the fluffiest one, the ball gown, and charged toward the dressing room with Lacey right behind her, struggling to carry the other two dresses. Those two had straighter lines and might be more figure-flattering, but Felicity was dazzled by the ball-gowned princess who suddenly appeared in her mind. Lacey tapped her foot while she waited, worried that Felicity was either frozen again in panic or mesmerized by her mirror image. She worried about her four o'clock interview. Her previous serenity had flown.

Finally, Felicity emerged, in a flurry of ruffles and lace and beading. She lifted the heavy skirt and made her way to the mirror, heavy brown clogs smacking the linoleum. She seemed not to notice that she was dragging the skirt on the floor. It needed to be hemmed an inch or so for safety's sake, depending on what shoes Felicity chose. Lacey hoped they wouldn't be clogs, of any color whatsoever.

"I can't reach all the buttons. Could you?" Felicity turned and Lacey fastened the rest, adding lady's maid services to her personal shopper duties.

The elusive fluffy white unicorn of a gown fit Felicity amazingly well. The beaded sweetheart bodice was more flattering than Lacey expected, and the bell sleeves with delicate lace kindly covered Felicity's upper arms and flared just below the elbows. There was a glittering, bejeweled, sky-blue ribbon belt that fastened around the waist. The dress commanded attention, and space, and could not be ignored. Scarlett O'Hara with her many hoops would have nothing on this skirt. Felicity looked like a doll stuck in a cake, a cake with layers and layers of fluffy white icing.

"Perfect," Felicity declared, in love with her image, even in the unflattering fluorescent lighting and wavy mirror. "And look at this blue belt. I just decided this is my color for the wedding. It matches my eyes. Harlan loves this color."

"This is the one?" Lacey couldn't believe her ears. "You've decided? Really? Just like that?" Felicity had changed the wedding cake plans at least twenty times. But Lacey shouldn't have been surprised: Felicity simply picked the dress most resembling a giant *dessert*. "Do you want to at least try on the other two?"

What am I saying, Lacey thought. *Take the dress and run!*

"Nope. This is it, Lacey. I'm sure. I'll tell Hillary to find bridesmaid dresses in this blue color."

"You could let your bridesmaids choose their own dresses. In the same color."

"What? Choose their own dresses? Don't be ridiculous."

"That's what a lot of brides are doing these days." She knew it was a vain hope. She would soon be wearing one of those bridesmaid dresses.

"Lacey, Lacey, Lacey. Don't you know anything about weddings? The dresses have to go together, they have to *match*. I don't know how you can write a fashion column without knowing that."

"How indeed." How could Lacey be here at Goodwill, shopping for wedding dresses with Felicity Pickles? The world was topsy-turvy. "You should at least try on one other dress. To make sure this is your favorite." *Somebody shut my mouth, please.*

"But this *is* my favorite! I don't want to let it go. What if someone snatches it away?"

The store was empty, the bridal rack deserted, and Felicity had the only dressing room in use. It wasn't exactly bridal mania, with desperate women going *mano a mano* over the last white dress.

"Okay. This is the dress. But you're going to need special underwear for that dress, too."

"Special underwear? What kind of underwear?" Felicity looked baffled. "Why?"

"Look at yourself. Your bra straps are visible. You'll need a strapless bra, one with support. Major support. Like a corset, or a merry widow. New, not used, in your size. With a professional fitting. It is absolutely essential. Do you understand? And let me make this perfectly clear, Felicity: You're on your own for that shopping trip."

Felicity ignored her, staring at the person she loved most in the world: herself. She spun around to see the back view.

"Oh my God," she exclaimed. "It's beautiful. I love it. Harlan will love it. Harlan will faint."

I may faint. Any minute.

"Now all I need is a tiara and a lace veil," Felicity added, gazing hopefully at Lacey.

"Up to you. And proper undergarments and the right shoes and a dozen other things. None of which you will find here." Lacey realized she hadn't had lunch. She needed protein. Her head hurt again.

"Are you sure?" Felicity peeked around her toward the dress rack, as if bridal undergarments might magically appear there.

"I'm sure." Lacey sneezed. Spring was in the air and so was the pollen, not to mention a rack full of dusty wedding dresses. "Let's buy this dress and get out of here."

"You're not getting sick, are you? I can't get sick. I've got things to do."

"Sick?" It was a chance to escape. "Yes! Very sick." She faked another sneeze. "I should get back to the office. Cold coming on. Or the flu. That Killer Flu that's going around. Shall I undo your buttons?"

"No! Don't touch! And don't sneeze on me! I can manage."

Felicity bustled off to the dressing room and emerged in record time, her arms full of the dress, its voluminous skirt spilling onto the floor. She didn't seem concerned about sweeping a muddy thrift store floor with her wedding gown.

"You'll probably want to take it to the cleaners," Lacey pointed out.

"Why? It's brand-new."

"Right. But the skirt is wrinkled, it has smudges from your hands, and you're dragging the hem on the floor."

"I can iron it. I'll sponge out the spots. I don't want to take it to a dry cleaner. It might shrink."

"Fine, Felicity. Fine."

Lacey's head throbbed as they loaded Felicity's big purchase into the minivan. She texted Vic as they pulled away.

"Dinner?" All she had to do was get through her interview with Granville first.

Vic texted back. "Where and when?"

"Steak at six," she texted. "Rare. Anywhere."

Felicity was racing her minivan back to the office like a woman possessed.

"If you're getting sick, Lacey, could you breathe out the window?"

If you open this window, I'm jumping out. "So, Felicity," she said, "you really don't mind buying your wedding dress at Goodwill?"

"Mind?! I'm thrilled!" Felicity shouted over the roar of the speeding minivan. "The tag doesn't say Goodwill, it says 'Curvaceous Bride.' I'm keeping the tag for my scrapbook. I have my dress and it was a steal. And so easy! Now all I have to do is find a veil and a tiara and some shoes and stuff. How hard can that be? I mean, come on, Lacey, this was a *snap*." She laughed. "And you made this wedding dress thing sound so hard!"

Lacey Smithsonian's
FASHION *BITES*

Eastern Standard Geek: *A Primer*

Washington, D.C., is legendary for having more spies per square mile than any other city on Earth. But I'm willing to bet it also has more geeks per square foot than any other place on Earth. Many wear a style I've affectionately dubbed Eastern Standard Geek.

You may have pondered this popular fashion statement on the Metro, or on the streets of Dupont Circle, Capitol Hill, or Adams Morgan. Or in the fast-food restaurants on M Street while you grab your lunch. You may feel moved to imitate this look, to fit in with the local geeksters. Pay no attention if you hear the occasional snicker.

Timeless (and clueless) geekiness has always been in style in the Nation's Capital. But "Geek Chic" is now the hot look in hip boutiques and vintage shops inside and outside the Beltway. Is it really chic? Is it merely "preppy" on steroids, or "nerdy" with a degree in an obscure field? Is Geek Chic the silent uniform that rules the street scene of D.C.? Could your personal look be the True Geek Chic, or a distinctive subspecies? You be the judge. I offer a formula for the elements that go into the unique D.C. Geek Chic look, so that you, the dedicated follower of fashion, may recognize it. Or imitate it.

The Math of Eastern Standard Geek

Is there a mathematical equation that describes this look? Why yes, there is! Let's go to the chalkboard.

Capitol Hill drone *times* preppy squared *plus* tech nerd *plus* advanced degree *minus* social and sartorial skills *equals* Washington D.C. Eastern Standard Geek.

The absentminded Georgetown professor, the Foggy Bottom think tank geek, the Capitol Hill drone, the Congressional aide, intern, and assistant, these are all classic examples of the Eastern Standard Geek. Male or female, young or old, or any variation, all are from educated backgrounds and work, study, and play in a uniquely Washingtonian social setting. They are far too busy and important to care about what they look like or what they wear—or they choose to *appear* to be.

That self-aware choice is what turns un-ironic Eastern Standard Geek into Geek Chic. The true ESG is generally happy merely to have gotten dressed. So what if your socks don't match? If the tie clashes, or the tights are torn? These anti-style visual keynotes are the security blanket of Eastern Standard Geek, also known as the look of the Prematurely Serious.

Today's Eastern Standard Geeks are teched out with tablets and iPhones and smart watches. They no longer carry leaky fountain pens in a pocket protector in their polyester shirts. They don't merely wear glasses, they wear Google Glasses. They are secure that their facts and figures are straight, even if their seams are not. They are more casual and less self-aware of their chosen look than are the Geek Chic.

Three Shades of Geek: Geek Chic, Geek Noir, and Hipster Geek

The poster girl for *Geek Chic* is the "sexy librarian," the coolly sophisticated woman who turns into a Geek Goddess when the spectacles are tossed and the pinned-up hair tumbles down.

The poster boy for Geek Chic, bespectacled Clark Kent, is the prototype Chic Geek, although more muscled. The man from Planet Krypton was aware of the costume aspects of playing Clark Kent and the importance of urban camouflage. Beneath those square suits and glasses, and that "Yes, Chief," and "Gosh, Miss Lane, would you like some coffee" attitude, he was Superman! With his glasses off, his hair was a shiny blue-black with an adorable curl on his forehead, his eyes were bluer than blue, and his physique is what Geek Chic aspires to when the lights are low.

Geek Noir is a subset of Geek Chic. It sports the same basic style notes, only darker. It wears black and wants to look *dangerous*. It pretends to be edgy. But this is D.C., so edgy belongs in the theatre or the 9:30 Club, not in the halls of Congress, or in the K Street lobbying corridor, or at high-priced law firms.

Hipster Geek is basically Geek Chic with an attitude and a little hipster fedora. Hipsters are too cool for school. Geeks love school. You know who you are.

Geek Chic Do's

Argyle sweaters and socks, sweater vests, cardigans, Oxford cloth shirts, and bow ties.

Plaid is acceptable, but in only one item at a time: the shirt but not the pants, or the pants but not the jacket. Especially avoid three or more different plaids worn together.

Khaki is not merely acceptable for Geek Chic, it's practically required. Wear it in shirts and slacks and additionally, for the women, skirts.

Navy jackets or blazers in good condition are always acceptable, and in fact, often required. Tailoring is a friend to this look.

Penny loafers polished to a high gloss. Pennies are optional, though a true Geek wouldn't see the point.

Geek Chic Don'ts

Geek Chic does not involve clothes held together with tape, safety pins, staples or bread wrapper ties. Those are in the purview of the Nerd. No short-sleeve polyester shirts, no hanging hems, and no knuckle-dragging sleeves, please. No high-water trousers. Capris are different. *Really.*

No pleated-from-the-waistband slacks or skirts. Geek Chic does not mean adding ten pounds to your waistline, even if you are a 90-pound weakling.

No mashups of a multitude of patterns, stripes, and plaids. The person wearing a trio of conflicting plaids may be a genius, but their style statement says, "I am insane." Compare and contrast: Clark Kent and the Nutty Professor.

Messy electro-fried hair with a mind of its own is reserved for Albert Einstein.

Dear Fashionable Reader, if you choose to go Geek in any variation, be aware of what your look is saying. Wear what you mean and mean what you wear. The essential difference lies between your personal style statement and clueless imitation.

Geek guys and gals of the Nation's Capital, you with your horn rims, your bow ties and suspenders, your high-flying hipster ponytails, geek on! Let your Geek flag fly, whether Geek Chic, Geek Noir, or Hipster Geek. We can't stop you, and we may learn to appreciate you yet, you nerdy style rebels.

Besides, we need you to fix the printer.

Chapter 19

THE OFFICES OF THADDEUS T. GRANVILLE perched high above a corner of K Street, Washington's bustling hotbed of lawyers and lobbyists. The suite was large and appropriately intimidating, though more modern than Lacey expected. There were no antique, rococo, or Southern antebellum touches, as there were on the man himself.

The floor-to-ceiling windows looked down from the fifth floor on the street below. There was no sound from the K Street traffic. The furniture was sleek and chrome with a mid-century feel, upholstered in smoky blue and set against pale gray walls. The latest news magazines were placed with precision on the glass coffee table.

The receptionist was young and blond and well-dressed, in blue and gray, as if coordinated with the decor. She placed a call and delivered Lacey to Granville's corner office, which was furnished in the same manner. He came around the huge lacquered desk and offered his hand. They shook.

"You have lovely offices," she said, because it was the thing to say.

"Thank you. I selected the space myself. You work hard in this country, you can wind up here. In the corner office." There was a hint of self-satisfaction in the air as he swept his arm around.

She wasn't sure she wanted an office like this. Granville's suite was too antiseptic and stark for her. Nothing warm or personal, no bookcases, no books. The difference between a newspaper's office and a lobbyist's was vast. Lacey rather enjoyed the controlled chaos of the newsroom and a never-ending availability of stimulation. And reading material.

Granville, on the other hand, was more interesting than his space. He was the peacock in his pen. He wore a blue seersucker suit, a pale lavender shirt, and a blue-and-pink bow tie. A lavender hanky peeked out of his pocket. On his feet were baby blue bucks, without smudge or crease. His graying hair was in its trademark Mark Twain tangle, which probably took his stylist hours to achieve. His mustache was trimmed. Lacey detected a hint of woodsy cologne. He looked like he should be sipping a mint julep on a Southern porch with white pillars, instead of holding court in a K Street lobbying firm.

"How do you do, Ms. Lacey Smithsonian," he drawled, his Deep South accent smooth as honey. "You must be the star style writer at Claudia Darnell's paper. Do give my regards to Claudia, by the way. She's quite a lady."

"Thank you for seeing me, Congressman." Thaddeus Granville was many years out of public office, but in the etiquette of Washington honorifics, once a congressman, always a congressman. Until and unless you rose higher on the ladder of public office.

"My pleasure."

"I see you've broken out the summer wardrobe early. Very dapper, I must say." Lacey couldn't help herself. She was fascinated by anyone as dedicated to expressive personal fashion as he obviously was.

"My seasonal plumage. Why wait until Memorial Day? All of this color makes me a *character*, of course," he acknowledged with a smile. "I like it when people notice my efforts. I expect them to. In my business, it is important that people remember me. Not to mention that people have come to expect a certain standard of dress from me. I try not to disappoint." Lacey knew that pressure well herself. "Besides, seersucker makes good sense here in the semi-tropical District of Columbia. Would you care for tea? I generally find a cup restorative at this time of day."

"No, thank you."

"Let me know if you reconsider."

He checked his pocket watch, and in one second, at precisely four p.m., the receptionist came in with a tray. On it were a china teapot and matching cups. She placed it on the chrome coffee table between them. He waited to seat himself and ready his tea until Lacey took a seat opposite him.

"Ms. Smithsonian, what brings you all the way to K Street?"

"It's only one block from Eye Street, Congressman. And you went all the way to Laurel for Courtney Wallace's funeral."

"No beating around the bush. Good, I don't like to waste time either. I did go to her funeral. As did you. I read your story about her 'lethal black dress,' as you called it, in *The Eye Street Observer*. Oh yes, I do read your newspaper. And I saw your small story this morning. I was gratified that you quoted me correctly. I keep up personally on all the major newspapers and broadcast and online media, particularly since the—*incident* with Ms. Wallace. Your original article was very informative, too." Granville seemed amused.

"Toxic fabric, a dye which may have contributed to Napoleon's demise? A very baroque method of death."

"The police think it was an accident."

He dropped a sugar cube into his Earl Grey tea and stared at her. "You don't think so?"

"Frankly, I don't know what I think yet, Congressman. You didn't like Courtney Wallace." She leaned forward.

"That's putting it lightly. I had no reason to like her, or respect her. That young idiot tried to destroy me. Without a clue, which makes it worse." He burst out laughing. "In short, I despised her. But I didn't put her in that dress. I may have some small reputation as a mastermind of the subtle art of politics, but I didn't choose her wardrobe for her. Nor could I fathom such a bizarre method of revenge. If I were so inclined."

"Revenge?"

"Revenge. You do not suffer the slings and arrows of a media harlot like Courtney Wallace without hoping for some opportunity to even the score. But I would have wanted to do it in some way so that she would have to live with it. Not die with it."

"You didn't want her to die?"

He smiled. "Not at all. Living, and suffering, is more instructive. I know from experience. Her contract at Channel One was coming up for renewal. I was in a position to know it wouldn't be renewed. No matter what kind of spectacle she pulled out of a hat. She tried to dip below the radar, with soft news features. Change her profile. It did no good. She would soon be through in television. Heaven knows she didn't have the chops to be a real reporter. Washington was not being robbed of a future Woodward or Bernstein."

"We agree on that," Lacey said. "But she didn't get that chance."

"Fate, it appears, took her destiny out of my hands. And hers." He shrugged and stirred his tea.

"Why did you go to the funeral?"

"Simple. To get the last word. Important in this game we play."

Does he really think this is a game? Lacey wondered. *He might.* "You're not sorry she's dead, though."

"No. I'm not. My comments are not for the record, of course. As we agreed."

"If I want to use something, I will run it past you." At least he hadn't demanded "deep background." Politicians and reporters often had very different opinions as to the definitions of "off the record," "background," and "deep background."

"Fair enough. Her funeral was an opportunity for me to be the bigger man. I took it. I could look gracious, and indeed, I was feeling gracious. No matter our sins, any death is still a loss and her family is grieving. Yet as you know, after her character assassination on me, I had to do what I could to save my career."

After his run-in with Courtney Wallace, Granville reinvigorated his career with renewed energy, lobbying and giving seminars about the havoc that irresponsible, free-wheeling journalists could wreak on unsuspecting victims in the public eye, and how to recover from slander and scandal. They turned out to be very popular among politicians and CEOs.

"Do you think somebody planted that story? Someone used her?"

"Very likely. She believed one of my enemies. Someone lied to her and she didn't dig for the truth. Now, however, everyone knows she betrayed all tenets of responsible journalism by slandering me with a blatantly false story."

"You quit the Swansdown campaign."

"The campaign I was running, yes. That was a disaster, after Wallace spread her pack of lies. My candidate was not happy either, though he supported me. He knew there was only one way to regain his traction. For me to leave."

"That must have been very hard."

He stirred his tea vigorously for a moment. "As if I would ever attack the family of an opponent. For all I know his wife might well have been a madam, or an escort. Makes no difference. It's out of bounds. Every political neophyte knows that. Whatever the candidate does or had done is fair game. But their family and relatives? Hands off."

"His wife took an overdose."

"Regrettable. Wallace's damage spread far and wide. I lost my best clients."

"You've made a remarkable comeback."

"Yes. I have." Whatever Granville might have been guilty of, it did not seem to be false modesty. "I had to find a new passion, a new direction in my life. However, I'm not about to thank Wallace for that. I was very comfortable in my old life."

"You have lectures and workshops, a successful speaking career."

"Presentations on the pitfalls of an unrestrained press. I counsel people and corporations on how to deal with the media, before, during, and after they've been scorched by them. A reputation, once wounded publicly, is difficult, if not impossible, to recapture. In my case, the damage was exacerbated when the other media picked up her allegations. Television, newspapers, magazines, the Web. All of them had an opportunity, indeed an obligation, to check their facts and report the truth. And they did not."

"You have recovered, though."

"In part. Only because I knew how it could be done. It has cost me."

"And now she's dead."

"Yes, she is. And I am alive to fight another day." He waved his tea cup for emphasis. "Are you sure you won't join me? Earl Grey. It's quite nice."

"Thank you, but I've had too much caffeine already."

"I take it you're following up on your article on the so-called 'Lethal Black Dress.' I must confess, I think that was a clever turn of phrase." He smiled again. "What else did you call it? The Madame X dress?"

"It did seem to be a copy of that famous dress. But I haven't determined yet if there is more to the story."

"It would be a good story though, wouldn't it? If you found out that someone really had managed to kill her, in such a strange way, in such a safe place. Some fiend, foisting hazardous haberdashery on unsuspecting fashion victims?"

"I don't think my editor would let me run with that headline." *Although with Mac "Terror at Timberline" Jones,* she thought, *you never know.* "At any rate, curiosity is one of my failings."

"Then you must *not* be the cat that's killed. Tell me, Ms. Smithsonian. Am I to expect a visit from the police?"

"Not that I'm aware of. The police believe this is a one-in-a-billion freak accident."

"That's where the smart money is. For the record, I had nothing to do with the death of Courtney Wallace. In any case, my approach to problems has often been called 'ham-fisted' and 'hammer-wielding.' I have no grasp of anything so devious and clever as lining a dress with poisoned fabric, though I can appreciate the concept in an academic sense."

"Do you think there's a possibility it was murder?"

"Theoretically, I suppose. In fact, I believe Courtney Wallace was done in by a most peculiar twist of fate. If it was by a deliberate act, the perpetrator strikes me as probably female. Poison is most commonly a female weapon, I believe. Poison and clothes? Stitchery and witchery, if you like."

"Do you know anyone capable of killing her? Female or otherwise?"

"Seems to me finding someone like that would be more up your alley than mine. You have a decided talent for discovering the macabre in a yard of material." He finished his tea and set the cup down carefully. "I've heard it said that Courtney stole many of *your* ideas. I wouldn't think you would particularly care about why she died, or what really happened. After all, a sneak thief and character assassin is dead. Peace reigneth once more in the land."

"I want to know what really happened. And I might be more curious about that dress than about Courtney. That's probably a personal failing too."

"Ah, yes. The curious cat. An honest answer. Thank you for that. And for coming to me to ask your questions, not just pulling the answers out of the air. You can be sure I will be following your every story."

Was that a threat? If it was, Granville could certainly deliver a threat with a charming smile.

"If I want to quote you, Congressman, you can be sure I will call to confirm."

"And I will welcome your call, Miss Smithsonian. Any time. We'll meet again for tea."

Chapter 20

"IT'S WILL ZEPHRON. YOU KNOW, the actor, from the thing? Can we meet?"

"Why not?" This day was feeling like it would never end. "Can you come over to *The Eye*?"

Lacey was on Seventeenth Street heading back there when her cell phone jingled. She skipped the short cab ride in favor of walking. By the time she left Granville's office, the sun was out and steam was rising from the streets.

"I can't. I'm auditioning at the JCC this afternoon and I'm up next. Meet me here? I've remembered something about that night."

Apparently it was too top-secret to relate over the phone. Lacey didn't really mind, she generally got better information face to face.

Lacey turned around and headed up Sixteenth Street. The Jewish Community Center and its well-regarded professional theatre were less than a mile away, and hailing a cab at rush hour was a lost cause. The walk also allowed her to think about what Granville had told her. On the surface it didn't seem like much.

The young thespian was waiting on the steps of the JCC, the stately building on Sixteenth Street, not far from The Spotlight Restaurant. Auditions apparently were still in progress and Zephron had just finished his. He wore black jeans, black shirt, and black running shoes, indicating he took his work as an actor seriously, or perhaps he had an additional part-time job as a mime. Slung over his shoulder was a battered leather messenger bag, presumably full of play scripts and head shots.

"You ran out on me," she said. "The other day at the restaurant."

"Sorry about that. I was totally blown. My mind, I mean." He rubbed his hands through his hair, then grinned sheepishly. "Forgive me."

The actor was more in control now, but there was no telling when he might fly away again. She suspected he'd been rehearsing what he was going to say to her. Dramatically, with sincere emphasis here and an earnest nod there. Cue the winning smile. Perhaps he had decided he was at the center of a great big story and he didn't want to miss his moment. Perhaps he really was scared.

"I've been trying to reconstruct exactly what happened. At the

Correspondents' Dinner," he said. "To see if I could remember any more about the, um, incident." He paused and took a breath. He sipped from a bottle of water before resuming. "I don't want to be responsible for someone's death. I'm haunted by her. By Courtney Wallace. She wants justice. She screams at me in my dreams. But at the time I was just pissed off because I spilled the drinks. I keep replaying it in my mind."

"You told me that."

"I know, but now I'm really *feeling* it. It's scary. Someone pushed me. I'm sure of it."

"Did you remember anything more? Like who pushed you? Can we narrow it down to a man or a woman?"

Sitting on the steps of the JCC on a pretty afternoon after the rain with a breeze spraying pollen on her was certainly better than returning to the office, she told herself. Even if she had to sit through Zephron's one-man show on a slightly damp step.

"I was in waiter mode." Zephron stood and mimicked holding a tray. He reached out and offered imaginary drinks to imaginary partygoers. Lacey took one. "Just cruising along. Seeing what I could use. You know what I mean. For my craft. My acting. It's character work. A dinner like that, I get to observe all the Washington types and the Hollywood types together. For instance: George Clooney was there with his girlfriend or fiancée or wife, or whatever of the moment. He looked great, but you know what's strange? I'm taller than Clooney, and well, obviously younger, but he looked so small."

"I saw the knot of women surrounding him," she said. "I couldn't tell his fiancée from the rest."

"Me neither. There were other big-name actors too, a lot of them. Most have probably lifted a tray at one time or another. I couldn't see it with Clooney though."

"See what? Him waiting tables?"

"No, the charisma. The fabled thing he has. Maybe it just shows up on screen, not in person. Sometimes it's like that. And vice versa. Some of the greatest stage actors don't have the right stuff on camera. Like people who are beautiful but don't photograph well? Clooney had this distant look. Bored out of his gourd while trying to seem interested and amused. He's into politics, I guess, so he goes to this important dinner, but he still has to play the movie star. It's old hat for him, so he's always looking past you. Like this."

Zephron posed in his impersonation of the Clooney bored-but-half-amused look. He wrinkled his forehead in concentration, but let his eyes wander in every direction, seeking someone more important to schmooze with.

"That's good." Lacey laughed. He might not really remind her of Clooney, but he had captured a look, a distinctly Hollywood-meets-D.C. moment.

"Thank you."

"You're digressing."

"I know. I'm using my sense memory to reconstruct the scene." He inclined his head slightly. "Clooney was surrounded by women. Not all movie stars. Frumpy reporter types too."

"Thanks a lot."

"Not you. You're different. I remember you. You were in a fabulous blue gown. Period piece, right? I don't see you playing the groupie. I'm talking about the rest of them, media worker drones in their stretchy black dresses from discount stores. I've seen actresses look better borrowing random costumes from the backstage shop in the dark. Courtney Wallace was hot too. Her dress was different, sexy. You called it something?"

"The Madame X dress."

"That's it. I was watching her. She glided into the room just before Clooney worked his way out. He wouldn't talk to her. He put his hand out like 'stop.' The cameraman caught it all. I felt a little sorry for her, being dissed by that guy on camera. I don't usually talk to people at these things, but I've seen some clips of her now, since it happened, and she seemed friendly on television. Big smile." Zephron lifted his imaginary tray. "Ms. Wallace, would you care for champagne? But she didn't even look at me. Most people at least nod. A lot of people say 'Thank you.' Even George Clooney smiled and said 'No, thank you.' I felt disrespected in a big way by her. That's the key."

"What's the key? Being disrespected?"

"How I *felt*. That's how I can reconstruct the event. Through my emotions. She made me feel low, depressed. A nobody waiter in a crowd of important people. It stung. I am somebody. People are going to remember me someday."

Celebrities could do that, Lacey reflected, especially at an event where people fawned over boldface actors and politicians. They sucked energy out of the room, as if it were their due, and they left people like Zephron downgrading themselves, feeling even less important than when they walked through the door. It could be a dangerous feeling.

"What was she doing? Who was nearby when it happened?"

Lacey figured if someone had managed to convince Courtney to wear the dress with the Paris Green lining, he or she could find a way to slam into a waiter with a tray of drinks at precisely the right time. And they wouldn't leave the scene. They would stay to witness the champagne spill. To see Courtney's humiliation. They might even be on camera. The tool didn't have to be Will Zephron, it could have been any waiter in the room, anyone in the right place at the wrong time.

Or was the waiter included in their plans? Did they recruit him to spill the drinks on her? No, Lacey thought, it was too risky to involve a third party. Especially an actor who couldn't keep his mouth shut. It would be better to manage it alone, without anyone else knowing or suspecting.

"She was trying to snag interviews for TV, so she was scoping out the important people. Like everybody else. Because she had a microphone in her hand and a camera guy behind her, she assumed people would talk to her." Zephron mimicked her. "Oh, hi! I'm Courtney Wallace for Channel One and I'd just *love* to ask you about your *dress*. It's *fabulous*! Is it Givenchy? Armani? Versace? Gucci? Pucci? Hoochie-coochie? As if anyone in that crowd would be wearing a real designer."

Except me. And maybe some of the Hollywood imports. "You said someone pushed you."

He closed his eyes and reached behind him, discarding the imaginary tray.

"Yes. Two hands, one in the middle of my back, one on my elbow. Fast and hard. And then—" The imaginary tray came back. He demonstrated how the tray went up and over as he spilled the champagne glasses.

"They pushed your elbow up?"

"Like it was hinged. Well, it is hinged. But I wasn't expecting it."

"The crowd was practically elbow to elbow. Someone could have stumbled against you," she suggested.

"No. If someone stumbled, they would be off balance and they probably would have fallen. Or grabbed at me to hold on. They didn't. No one actually fell down, not all the way. Not even me. So whoever pushed me was *not* off balance. It was deliberate."

"Does your sense memory tell you anything else?"

He closed his eyes again in thought. "Small hands."

"Are you sure?"

"They felt small. Or maybe they were fists. Pushing just hard enough to set things flying."

"In which case it could have been a man or a woman."

"The other television reporter was there." He rubbed his temple, as if that helped.

"Zanna Nelson?"

"Who's that? No, I'm talking about Eve Farrand. The dark-haired one with the sexy growl. I saw her on the news last night and remembered she was there. She wore something light that night. Maybe white? That's why I noticed her. She was with a guy. Tall. A pretty boy." *Said one pretty boy about another.*

"I don't remember seeing Eve there," Lacey said. *Or Drake Rayburn, her pretty boy.* After first telling Lacey he never watched TV, now Zephron seemed to know quite a lot about the players.

"Why would you? You were looking at Courtney Wallace, like everyone else. God, how embarrassing. Even more embarrassing than it was for me. Eve Farrand dodged out of the way when the champagne flew. I remember seeing her feet running to the back of the room, near the doors to the patio."

"Her feet?"

"Hey, I was bending over, picking up broken champagne glasses. I saw the light-colored skirt and light high-heeled sandals. That funky beige nail polish too, I remember that. But she didn't leave. Her dress wasn't ruined, so I guess she stayed to watch Courtney's moment of mortification."

"Reporter's instinct. Could she be the one who pushed you?"

"No idea. I didn't see her till I saw her running. But right then everyone was running, scrambling out of the way."

"Anything else you remember? Your emotional memory?"

"Courtney. Screaming at me. The bitch. It wasn't my fault. I felt sick to my stomach. And there was this funny smell. A little like onions or garlic? It wasn't the hors d'oeuvres."

Lacey marveled at how Courtney Wallace had changed over the course of Zephron's re-enactment, from glorious to horrible, from a beautiful, friendly TV personality with a microphone and the ability to bring someone out of obscurity, to a high-handed bitch. All in the time it took to break a glass.

The Will Zephron show was winding down. The wind picked up. Lacey stood and stretched.

"How long did you work that evening?"

"Not much longer. The cocktail parties were breaking up, everyone was leaving to go in to the dinner. I was exhausted, humiliated, bummed out. They didn't need me after that anyway. After the big dinner event, everyone who's anyone heads to the *Vanity Fair* after-party. Did you go?"

"I gave it a pass," she said. *Ah yes, the party to which neither I nor anyone from* The Eye Street Observer *was invited.*

"It wasn't a bad gig until I was pushed," Zephron reflected. "Everything went south from there. Are you going to put all of this in the paper?"

"If I do, I promise to get it right, and I'll spell your name correctly."

"Could you mention that I'm an actor? Equity, by the way." He reached into his messenger bag. "And if you need a photo, here, take one of my new headshots."

Chapter 21

"HARD DAY AT THE OFFICE, dear?" Vic smirked at her from across the table. "You went shopping with Ms. Pickles! Good God. Are there photos documenting this unlikely occurrence? I say, pics or it didn't happen."

"Boy, I hope there aren't any pics." Lacey slumped in her seat.

"Sometimes your better nature gets you into trouble."

"It had nothing to do with my better nature. It had everything to do with keeping my job bearable. And getting cornered, like a rat in a trap. Not very noble, I'm afraid."

"You still get points, just for going. And you found her a dress. Bonus points."

Lacey was so tired she could hardly concentrate on the menu. She set it down and leaned against the back of the booth. The waitress quietly materialized.

"Filet mignon, medium rare, please. And a gin and tonic."

Vic took her to a new steak restaurant in Arlington, not far from his Rosslyn office building. The décor was warm and comforting, all dark wood with a pressed-tin ceiling and windows overlooking the lights of Georgetown. The wood-burning grill smelled wonderful. Lacey turned off her cell phone. The world would be fine without her for one evening.

"Same. Thanks. Oh, and a baked potato, loaded." Vic handed his menu to the waitress, who departed. "Consider it your good deed for the day," he said to Lacey.

"It better count for more than that. Felicity wouldn't even try on the other dresses. They might have looked better, you know. At least the one she picked fit. A miracle. For which I'll take those bonus points."

"At least she'll be dressed."

"I have to admit, on her wedding day every woman should be able to look as ridiculous as she wants to. Whether she's jumping out of a plane in a Supergirl cape, or riding a unicorn, dressed as a fairy tale princess. Or in a dress that looks like it could swallow a room-sized wedding cake whole."

"Think of how entertaining this wedding will be." He took hold of her hand. "And how much nicer ours will be."

"If we run away. I'm still trying to find a way not to be a bridesmaid."

"Is that nice?"

"Oh, Vic, I'd be doing her a favor too. She'd be just as relieved as I would if I could wiggle out of it. She knows it, I know it, and everyone at *The Eye Street Observer* knows it."

"And break Wiedemeyer's heart? He thinks you and Felicity are the best of friends. And I personally can't wait to see what she'll make you wear. I bet it's something—*poufy*. Maybe even *froufrou*."

"You think it's funny now, Victor Donovan. I will look fabulous in froufrou, if I consent to wear froufrou. I will be *too too* froufrou."

Vic was still laughing when the gin and tonics arrived. "Darling, you'll be beautiful no matter how outlandish the outfit."

"Outlandish? If the bride's dress is merely insane, the bridesmaids will have to look bonkers. It's a law of the universe." She detected the aroma of steaks, heading their way. "At any rate, I might have found a lead on where Wallace found that fatal gown."

"Still chasing the story? Sorry. Of course you are. Lacey, sweetheart, I realize you're going to chase this into the ground, at least until you run out of leads, or steam, or villains. I just want to tell you to be careful. I want to tell you stop, but I won't. So I'll just say—beware of old clothes. "

"Vintage. Not old. Vintage clothing. I'm glad you understand that a woman's got to do what a woman's got to do." She sipped her drink. "It bugs me, you know, the freak accident part of it."

"As odd as it seems, it could have happened that way."

"As you said before, if a tree is struck by lightning and falls on your car, that's a freak accident. Bad luck."

"Or the Wiedemeyer jinx."

"Granted. Or an act of God. The emerald green lining of that dress was not an act of God, Vic. Somebody deliberately put that dress together, a hundred years or more after the dye was known to be toxic. Who and why, and how did it get onto Courtney Wallace's back?"

Vic raised one dark brow. "You're hypothesizing."

"And how I could not know about a vintage clothing store in Del Ray? It's practically in my backyard."

"I sense a field trip coming on."

"Definitely."

"Sweetheart, you are the only one who cares about that dress."

"I am not. Kepelov, for instance."

"What's Kepelov got to do with it?"

"He wants to get his hands on it and sell it to a museum, I gather. He's always a little hard to follow. But he wants to sell something to somebody."

"He'd sell his grandmother's babushka if there was a buck in it," Vic said. "Or a ruble."

"Good luck on that, Vic. Wallace's mother says she wants it destroyed."

"As would any mother. But in Kepelov's world, it may be a commodity. I suspect he was always a secret capitalist, even in the KGB. What's the EFP saying?"

"EFP? Are you making fun of me?"

"No way. Your friends have mentioned it so often, it's sunk in. I believe. However, if you have any of those feelings, the ones that go hand in hand with danger, tell me. Call me. Let me in on it." He was beginning to sound like Broadway Lamont.

"I'm not Spider-Man, I don't have spidey senses."

"No, you're a lot spookier than Spider-Man. Cuter, too."

"Thanks. In this case, something in my gut is telling me there's more going on here than meets the eye."

"I was afraid of that." Their steaks arrived, sizzling. "Whatever you have in your gut, darling, let's replace it with a steak."

Chapter 22

HARLAN WIEDEMEYER WAS DANCING ON air the next morning at the office. He was also dancing down the hallway. Lacey knew one of the little known secrets about him: He was once the leader of a retro-swing band, Harlan and His High-Stepping Hipsters. When he was happy, he ate doughnuts, he sang, he danced. When he was unhappy, he just ate doughnuts.

Mac was smiling. Tony had a spring in his step. Harlan Wiedemeyer was twirling. It could mean only one thing: Order had been restored to the universe, and Felicity Pickles was baking.

"You've done it again, Smithsonian," Wiedemeyer sang out. "My Felicity Pickles, Dilly Pickles, my sweet little gherkin, has a bridal gown. I don't mind telling you we were all taking bets on how long it was going to be before there was a food fight."

"Bets? Thanks a lot." *Where is my coffee cup?*

Lacey was glad she'd dressed easy today, in another Forties favorite, a V-neck navy dress with embroidered flowers asymmetrically placed on one hip and one shoulder. The skirt was flared for easy movement. The three-quarter sleeves were cool enough for outdoors, yet they covered her arms under the air conditioning vents.

"It could have taken days, Lois Lane," Tony opined, lured by the scent of almonds and cinnamon. "There could have been bloodshed."

Lacey ignored Tony and addressed Wiedemeyer. "Did she show it to you?"

"Are you crazy? That's bad luck. No use inviting trouble." The irony escaped the resident jinx.

"I'm sure it will be a big happy surprise for you, Harlan," Lacey said.

"People make their own luck. Mmm, smells like some kind of cake," Tony said, retrieving a precut square of this morning's treat.

One crisis solved, and another was brewing. An ill wind (or Felicity's baking aromas) blew Peter Johnson their way. He strode into the newsroom as if he were a media star of the marble corridors of Congress, glorying in the minutiae of federal regulations and the quirks of obscure politicians.

"You!" He shouted at Lacey.

What now? The paper's reader algorithm must have shown a readership spike over her story on Courtney, while his ponderous "all the news to snooze" must have put them to sleep.

"What is it about you?" he went on. "Where you go, disaster strikes. Not once, like lightning, but repeatedly. When are you going to leave this alone?" He threw a copy of her updated story at her. It fell to the floor at his feet.

"This is about Wallace, I presume?"

"Smithsonian doesn't cause trouble." Little Wiedemeyer braved Johnson's wrath. "She discovers it, celebrates it, revels in it. She has a nose for news. She finds stories you never could."

"Said the jinx." Johnson backed up a few steps from the shorter, chubbier man.

"Then beware my superpowers, you sorry bastard."

Johnson turned to Lacey, his voice quivering. "The White House Correspondents' Dinner is the most high-profile event of the year. And you go and ruin it."

"Who? Me, or Courtney Wallace with her unfortunate death, or the poor waiter who bathed her in champagne?"

"The spotlight belongs on the President. The dinner, the dignity of the press corps."

"The spotlight lands where it lands, Johnson. And let me try to wrap my head around the dignity of the press corps pandering to sleazy, second-rate celebrities to make the evening newsworthy. By the way, your zipper's undone."

Johnson turned a dangerous shade of purple as he half turned and fumbled with the front of his pants. "My sources are asking me about this story as if it were important. Not just one story, but a follow-up? It's a desecration of the front page."

Mac stormed up the aisle. "Johnson, go back to your sour grapes and rewrite that turkey of a story you gave me. This time, try it in English."

"What about her?" Johnson whined. "What are you going to do about her?"

"Smithsonian? I'm going to let her get back to work. People read her stories."

"My stories are vital!"

"To what? National security?" Lacey cracked. She always seemed to get on his last nerve without even trying. It was time to fight back. "Or do you have a dissertation on Herodotus's potty training you'd like to share with us?"

Johnson started to sputter. He loved to bring up Herodotus, the ancient Greek historian, for no apparent reason. Johnson crumpled up the paper in his hand and threw it at her, glaring with all the intensity he could muster behind his glasses. This time his missile went almost to its mark.

"Johnson, I said *move*," Mac ordered. "Go back. Rewrite. Fix your mess." Johnson retreated, glaring daggers at them all.

"Thanks, Mac." Lacey had a champion in Mac. *At least this morning.* She momentarily forgot her irritation with Felicity as her editor reached for a piece of almond cinnamon Bundt cake with thick cream cheese frosting. While Felicity's cake might mollify Mac, it wouldn't stop Johnson, who lacked the capacity to enjoy anything so trivial as food. *Watch your back, Lacey,* she thought.

Was Johnson fearful for his job? That might explain his behavior. These days, every reporter had reason to worry. Newspapers folded faster than lawn chairs after a picnic. For that matter, if the print news biz faded away, what would Lacey have to show for it?

She couldn't waste any more time on Johnson or her dubious future. She had leads to follow. A vintage shop in Del Ray. A woman named Ingrid Allendale. A dress with a Paris Green lining. And a cameraman who might have seen something.

Lacey pulled her notebook out of her bag and flipped through it to her contact information for Courtney's Asian cameraman, Eric Park.

Chapter 23

IF ERIC PARK WAS ANYTHING like "Long Lens" Hansen, the top photographer at *The Eye*, he would notice everything. At least Lacey hoped so.

Hansen was a quiet observer, a man of few words. He saw the world through his camera lenses and spoke through his photographs. Judging from the photos he took of Lacey, he had a particularly wicked sense of humor. He hadn't caught her slipping on a banana peel yet, but he'd come close.

Eric, on the other hand, turned out to be a chatterbox and a gossip—Lacey's favorite type of source. They met for coffee near Judiciary Square. He had to shoot a story with Eve Farrand at a Senate hearing, but he said he had time first for a quick meet.

When he arrived, Lacey was in line at the counter, behind someone who ordered *two* double caramel latte macchiatos with soy milk and whipped cream, some very complicated additional instructions, and apparently, no irony.

"You said you were buying, so—" He favored her with a grin.

"Not a problem. Order anything you like. But not two of them." She tilted her head at the two-latte lady.

"Only kidding. I can handle a latte, even on my salary." He checked his watch. "Eve ducked out for what she calls a 'quick' manicure before the hearing. I figure I got an hour."

"You're not attending the whole hearing?"

"Why bother, Eve never does. She picks up the preprinted testimony and then tries to get a quick quote on camera from some senator when it's over. And those beige nails of hers are very important."

"Beige nails." Will Zephron had mentioned that detail, too. She didn't know what shocked her more—wearing beige nails or skipping out on covering a hearing. True, most hearings on the Hill were ninety-nine percent snooze, but that one percent could be full of newsworthy surprises and pithy quotes.

"She's into them. Like corpse hands," he said. "It's Eve's latest thing. She's trying to wear beige, or cream, or camel, on camera, so she looks different from everybody else. Complements her dark hair, so she says. It looks 'rich and competent.' Yadda yadda. The nails are part of her new look. I hear her on her cell all the time, talking with her girlfriends and ignoring me. She thinks I don't listen to her babble on. But I do." He grinned. "Or maybe she thinks I'm deaf."

"Stocking up on cocktail chatter?"

"Exactly, or just blackmail."

"Dodging a hearing, though? Wow. She could get blindsided if some witness goes off script. Or a senator keels over dead."

"It's her story. I just follow her lead."

Broadcast is very different from print, Lacey thought, not for the first time.

Lacey was one of those tiresome old-school reporters who covered meetings from beginning to end. When she covered the occasional Hill hearing, on such subjects as safety concerns of textile workers or the budget for the fashion museum in D.C., she arrived early, grabbed all the printed testimony and press releases, read them, and then watched the entire hearing, waiting patiently for those rare moments when a witness or a congressman or senator said something unscripted and genuine, or memorably stupid or offensive, or admitted something they hadn't planned on admitting.

But then, Lacey didn't get to Capitol Hill that often. She was aware there were the occasional print reporters who ducked out of an endlessly dull meeting for a haircut or a shopping trip and still hammered out a barely passable story. Peter Johnson sprang to mind. She tried to scrub her thoughts of him, but he had sullied her day.

She paid for their coffees. Eric picked up the cups and followed her to a table.

"Eric, I was wondering—how did you team up with Courtney? Were you always on stories together at Channel One?"

"No. Just turned out that way for her vintage clothing thing. The photographers drive the cars and the cameras, the reporter drives the story. Usually, it's kind of luck of the draw. Keeps it interesting. If your reporter du jour is a dud, better luck next time."

"What was Wallace like?"

"Drama queen. All wrapped up with being Courtney, that's for sure. But it wasn't hard work for me. I was just the camera guy on board that day for the first piece. She liked the way it turned out, so we wound up teamed together for all of them, so they would have a cohesive look. The lighting, the editing, that kind of thing."

"Did she have more fashion pieces planned?"

"Just the dress at the dinner. That was it. All she wrote." He nodded and sipped his coffee. "The Correspondents' Dinner was supposed to be the final piece, the wrap. Turned out it was. She might have been planning something else, but she didn't tell me."

"You weren't there when she bought the Madame X dress?"

"Nope. Don't know where she found it. She kept that one under wraps. Pulled it out of the hat, you know? She just showed up in it at the dinner."

"The moment she got drenched with all the champagne. Did you see anything? Or get any video of it?"

"If you mean, did I see anyone slam into that poor chump of a waiter, I didn't. I've been wondering about that too. Mostly I have Courtney's back, chasing some actress. Courtney dodging through the crowd at top speed, me zig-zagging after her, my camera rig bouncing around. I caught up with her just as she got nailed with the drinks. A few great seconds of her dripping wet, yelling and screaming. A bit of the waiter. Nice clear footage, tight on her, well lit, Courtney dropping F-bombs on the world. The station will never use it. Some cop looked at it, though. Nothing there but Courtney."

"Which cop, do you remember?"

"Detective. Didn't catch his name. Some big black guy."

Some big guy named Detective Broadway Lamont, I'll bet. Holding out on me!

"No smoking gun in your footage? That's too bad."

"I know! Would that be great? But you said 'footage'? Too many feet in that footage, not enough room. I was stepping on feet all night. You really need steel-toed boots at those things. My guess is the waiter just got his feet tangled up in somebody else's and over he went."

"Sounds like the likeliest story," Lacey said, not mentioning Will Zephron's take on the incident and the small hands or fists he felt pushing him. "By the way, who exactly decided on the vintage series? The station?"

"Courtney. She had to sell the idea to them. Slow news day stuff. She was looking for a regular kind of feature gig, a signature sort of story, after she screwed up big-time."

"The Thaddeus Granville story?" Lacey wanted confirmation by name.

"That's the one. Boy, am I glad I was nowhere near that one. Look, I don't really know how far the fallout went. The suits upstairs were in an uproar. There were contract issues and legal issues.

Granville was breathing down their necks with a possible lawsuit. It looked like she wasn't going on air again. At all. Ever. And then she did. She thought she could escape the chopping block by going in a whole new direction. It worked too, for a little while."

"Was she grasping at straws, choosing fashion?"

"Maybe." He licked the froth off the side of his cup. "The rise and fall of Courtney Wallace. Her contract was coming up for renewal soon and she was tap dancing as fast as she could to stay on."

"What were her chances?" Granville told Lacey there was no chance. She wanted Eric's take on it.

"A long shot. A very *long,* long shot."

"Did Courtney have enemies? Other than Granville?"

"You mean, did anyone want to kill her at the Correspondents' Dinner?" He laughed. "Yes, I've been reading your stuff. Really, who knows? Lots of jealousy going around in this biz. Hey, did you know Courtney was reading your column as background for her series? She said fashion was easy. After all, look at Lacey Smithsonian." Lacey felt her temperature and her eyebrows rise. Eric put his hand up. "Just quoting."

"Right. If Lacey Smithsonian can do it, anyone can do it." It wasn't the first time she'd heard that.

"Hey, that might be what Courtney thought, but it's not what I think," Eric said. "You've done some really cool stuff. Not just the fashion stuff. The sword-cane dude might be my favorite. Death threats! Explosions! How interesting is that? Solved murder cases too. There's more than meets the eye to the fashion beat, right? Too bad you don't get to do it all live on camera."

"Oh, there's been an embarrassing picture or two. I can't tell you how happy I am that my whole career isn't on YouTube."

He laughed again and pointed an imaginary video camera at her. "And the diamonds in New Orleans? Wow, that was a killer story! What's up with those? Did they ever decide who gets to keep them? I'm pretty sure Courtney was hoping for a big story like that. Something like that might have saved her ass."

Those diamonds had been hidden for nearly a century. Many people had looked for them. Courtney could never have stumbled onto that story. *Not in a million years.*

"Last I heard, the State Department and the Kremlin were still dancing a tango over ownership and who gets to show them off first. And *The Eye* wants to be prominently mentioned as their discoverer.

If the diamond dust ever settles, I'll write a follow-up."

"Then you pop up with that Madame-X-poison-lining-lethal-black-dress thing. I didn't see that coming. Wild."

"You read my story?" Eric was a guy, and they generally didn't read about fashion.

"Are you kidding? Everybody at Channel One reads your stories now. They're about Courtney and she's dead. Hits way too close to home. You know that dress really did look like the one in the Sargent painting. Courtney never made the connection. I didn't either, until you made it. If Courtney really had what it takes for fashion, she should have figured it out. Or at least suspected something. You did."

"It's kind of a special talent," Lacey said.

"I feel bad for her. Looking back, I can see she was getting sicker and sicker all night and maybe I should have dragged her out of there. But she insisted on sticking with it. My job is to follow wherever the on-air talent wants to go."

"What did you think of her vintage clothing series?"

"Different than the stuff I usually shoot. I liked the juxtaposition of now and then. I wanted to shoot some of it in black and white, with shadows."

"Film noir?"

He gestured with his macchiato. "Right. Shadows of venetian blind slats across Courtney wearing some classy old gown, that kind of thing. I kind of got into it."

"Sounds cool. I didn't see that on the news clips."

"Wasn't there. Some things you try just don't make it."

"Too bad. Was she happy with the series?"

"Guess so. She was all about finding stuff that would look good on her."

"She succeeded," Lacey said. "Especially the black dress."

"The Madame X dress. You have an interesting mind, Lacey."

She smiled at him. "It's the clothes. They carry messages, if you pay attention. I'm not talking about the message I see a lot around this town, of total anonymity and the desire to wear what everybody else wears. If you put a little of yourself into your clothes, you can use them to reveal things that are personal and meaningful about you."

"And that dress of hers said, 'Drop dead!' So you think someone put Courtney in that dress on purpose?"

"I'd like to find out. And that is totally off the record, Eric."

"I get it. You can't let it go until you've figured it out. You're that kind of reporter." He seemed to think this was a lark. "Want to make a wager?"

"Never take a sucker bet. I just want to put it in context. Clothing messages are all about context. Freaky accidents are freaky by their nature. Freaky means out of context."

"Do you think someone killed Courtney on purpose?"

"It's about a zillion to one. I just have a bad case of curiosity."

"You can't let it alone, can you?"

Lacey laughed. "Are you interviewing me?"

"Nah, I'm just the camera guy right now. But hey, I'm curious too. Someday I could be on the other side of the lens. Promise to tell me if you find out?"

"You and the rest of the world." It would never cross Lacey's mind to call the broadcast media to scoop her own story. Never, ever. "Anything I find out goes to *The Eye* first."

"Too bad people only believe what they see on TV," he teased.

"Ouch." She pretended to spill her coffee on him.

"Come on, Lacey. Just give me a heads-up, in case persons unknown are gunning for another Channel One reporter. Or God forbid, a photographer." He grinned. He had a great smile, bright and guileless.

"Will do. On another subject, Eric. How is it, working with Eve Farrand?"

He whistled. "She's a piranha, man. If there's blood in the water, it'll draw her like a shark."

"Did she like Courtney?"

"Like a shark likes a baby seal. She didn't take Courtney's beat and her boyfriend out of love and friendship. Two cats hissing. They mostly kept their distance. But they had a big screaming fight right before the dinner. I have no idea what it was about, but people said they could hear their voices shouting in the ladies' room."

Women's Conference Room. "Really? So Eve was at the Correspondents' Dinner too?"

"She was there. She wasn't working it, though. Took the new boyfriend under cover. Apparently they wrangled seats at one of the big magazines' tables. With Bloomberg, I think."

Eve had a definite vision for her image, the brunette who wore cream and beige in a city of black and gray. Courtney's boyfriend and the beat—were they just stepping stones? Would she just as easily step over Courtney? Would she push a waiter with a tray of drinks?

Timing was everything in television. Timing was everything in Courtney Wallace's death. And Eve's rise.

"So Courtney's gone and Eve is on the ascendant. Where does that put Zanna Nelson?"

"Zanna? Nowhere in particular. She's a pinch hitter, been there a couple of years trying to get a toehold."

"I haven't noticed her on TV much."

"She gets on-camera occasionally. You know, filling in for reporters on vacation."

"She was friends with Courtney?"

"Yup. Courtney's little puppy dog. Zanna wants a TV career bad."

"What are her chances at that career?"

"Please. Many are called, but few are chosen. Everybody in broadcast wants a shot at being on air. And on-air talent would kill for a shot at being an anchor. Lifetime gig, if you do it right. Once they get their feet behind that desk, that's where they die, man. If they can age gracefully enough. Zanna? She's lucky to get the occasional on-air story. She dreams of being an investigative reporter."

"Why not? She's very pretty."

"Pretty, but she shrinks in the lens. I don't know how to explain it. She becomes forgettable. Cold. She has a small mouth and a small head, that's part of it." He shook his head and took a moment to swallow some coffee. "She can work her butt off behind the scenes, but she doesn't have what it takes to be on air. I don't know if you can quantify the magic it takes, the presence, the whatever, but you can see it in someone or you can't. Courtney had it. Zanna doesn't. She bores the camera."

Lacey digested this. It echoed something Zephron said. "How's she been since the funeral?"

"Quiet. Everyone's been quiet. The ghost of Courtney haunts us all." Eric slurped his macchiato. "Listen, I bet you don't know this. Courtney and Zanna and I all lived in the same big group house right after college, six years ago. Went our separate ways after that, and then we all wound up back together at Channel One."

"That's curious."

"Well, maybe not so odd. We all went to U of Maryland to study broadcast. Knew each other in school. Reconnected in D.C. after the cap and gowns bit. We were all going make it big in the Nation's Capital, man." He laughed again. "We fell into these rigid little roles in that house. Like a sitcom or something. Strange times."

"Courtney was the queen?" Lacey was sure of that. She looked like a prom queen.

"Yeah," he agreed. "Queen bee of the hive. She was always leaving messes and I was always cleaning them up. Literally, I mean. That woman wouldn't be able to tell you what a vacuum does. Except make her run away like a cat."

"So she's the queen, you're the sidekick and all-around fixer. And Zanna, what was her role? The jester? The puppy dog?"

Eric mused for a moment before answering. "She wanted to be queen too. Same ambition, but not the same talent. She was prettier than Courtney, or she certainly thought so. But not as smart, not as magnetic. Zanna had this strange conception of herself."

"An example?"

Eric stared into the distance. "I keep thinking of this one thing. All that time ago, Courtney was sort of invited to an exclusive cocktail party once with some major D.C. celebrity journalists. You know the type, old dudes like Bob Woodward. Watergate. All that. Courtney knew one of the organizers, so she had an in. No big deal for me, not being invited. I didn't need to hear that old gasbag pontificate."

"Who does? The man interviews dead sources! I mean, allegedly."

"Graveyard Bob, they call him. Zanna wasn't invited either. The minute Courtney walked out the door, dressed to kill, Zanna had a fit, a total crying jag, about how it should have been her. How she was the one who cared about Washington politics, not Courtney. How she, Zanna, was just as qualified. More qualified. She was prettier, she was smarter, she was going to be a Major Investigative Reporter, with capital letters, and Courtney was nothing but a face. On and on. I never saw anything like it. Crying and screaming, totally out of control. Zanna and I, we were friends at school, we were housemates, but I didn't know what to do. I tried to talk her down. All that drama for not being invited? She was acting like Woodward and Bernstein broke her heart or something. She didn't even *know* the old dude. Apparently he was her hero and maybe this was her one and only chance to, like, kiss his phony investigative feet. Go figure."

"Sounds really embarrassing. For both of you." Especially for a guy like Eric, who seemed so easy-going and good-natured.

"I was mortified. For her, for me, for everyone."

"She probably was too. Afterwards."

"No idea. I finally left. Slammed the door. Went to some movie. When I got back, she was still at it, her 'I'm the best, why can't I get noticed' tirade. By then she was drunk. Made a pass at me before she passed out." He blinked. "I moved out pretty quick after that. I didn't want to get caught between the two of them in whatever psychodrama was going on."

"Cinderella goes to the ball and Cinderella's forgotten step-sister has a meltdown," Lacey offered.

"Never thought about it like that, but you're right." He checked the café as if making sure Zanna wasn't around. "I used to think maybe Zanna had a thing for Courtney, romantically, you know. But I'm not sure that was it. I think it was just—"

"She wanted what Courtney had," Lacey said. "What Courtney was. Her career, her clothes, her men, her looks?"

"Right. Because she deserved them." Eric's phone rang. He answered it. "Showtime! The new Queen commands. Long live the new Queen. Gotta go."

"I appreciate you talking to me."

"No problem. This was fun. We should do it again. Next time I'll buy. Don't wear any poison dresses."

Eric shouldered his gear, saluted her, and left.

Chapter 24

BACK AT THE OFFICE, JOHNSON ratcheted up the hostilities. It was war.

Lacey didn't know it until Mac marched to her desk and told her to pull up the editing queue on her computer screen. Mac pointed to her latest story. After calling Granville briefly to clear the few comments that he made on the record, she had written a brief update to his reaction to Courtney's death, and the aftermath of her story on him.

"This doesn't make any sense. None," Mac said. "Did you write this glop?"

Impossible. What glop?

She read the story that carried her byline. The Granville story was full of mistakes. It was garbled. Lines were missing, others were turned inside out. Names were swapped and misspelled. Crucial words like *not* had been deleted. It was full of idiotic sentences she never would have written. She felt ill. She glanced up to see Johnson peeking around the corner, looking smug. As the substitute political editor, Johnson had access to the editing queue. Lacey suspected Johnson didn't know that she knew that.

"This is not what I wrote, Mac."

"It's not?"

"Barely a word of this is mine. Maybe the words *and* and *the*." She marched over to where Johnson lurked. "You changed my story! You colossal jerk!"

He shrugged. He didn't deny it, nor did he admit it. He merely looked victorious. "Why would I bother? You write crap. Just look at it. And you're milking this story to death."

"Mac. Take a look at this." She pulled up her original draft on her screen to show her editor. Some reporters routinely deleted their old drafts after filing. Lacey never did. "He messed up my lede. He put in false information. And he misspelled Thaddeus and Granville. He deleted lines, he added things that make no sense at all. Look for yourself. This is what I wrote. I'll send you a fresh copy." She faced Johnson. "You're sabotaging me and you know it."

"I'm trying to improve you. Maybe someday you'll learn to write a good story."

If I had fangs, I would rip your throat out.

"You are pathetic. You are slime. And you couldn't write your way out of the *Federal Register*."

He flinched. Other reporters stopped typing, deciding the floor show was more interesting than their stories. Mac stared at Lacey's screen. He grunted. His eyebrows knit together in storm-cloud formation. Thunder and lightning were in the forecast.

"Smithsonian, resend your original story. Johnson, you and I are going to have a chat. Right now. My office. Move."

Johnson blanched and followed Mac meekly, while Lacey refiled her story.

She was so angry she was sure she was glowing red-hot. *How could he think he would get away with that stunt?* Peter Johnson was becoming more than a pain, he was an enemy. He wanted her to look like a fool, and he was reckless enough to try something that stupid. He was trying to undermine her work, her confidence, her reputation. She had apparently committed the sin of turning the media social event of the year into her personal scoop. The sin of being a better reporter than Peter Johnson.

As if that would be hard to do. Johnson was a hack, hanging on by sheer seniority in a possibly terminal industry. Sooner or later, he was going to find himself out in the cold.

"Mac ought to just fire his bony ass." LaToya had walked into the middle of the action and watched it all like a hawk.

"Dream on." Lacey was so angry her hands were shaking.

"Listen, girlfriend, it's not you, it's him. He's about to snap. If it wasn't you showing him up, he'd be after someone else. I just hope we don't find him up on the roof one day with an AK-47."

"You're serious? I've worried about the very same thing. You're saying it's not just me?"

"Goes way deeper than you. You're just the red flag. You're the match to his deadwood. And that book thing you and Mac and Tony got going on, that's got to sting Johnson's sorry butt."

"*Terror at Timberline*, or whatever it's going to be called?" Lacey had been worried about that, since the night of the Correspondents' Dinner. Any mention of the book-to-be made Johnson turn purple with suppressed rage.

"Exactly. Johnson's been blowing smoke for years that he's working on a book."

"Him? What kind of book?"

"Who knows? Something boring. Something political. Or—" She lowered her voice. "Maybe even *poetry*. He's mouthed off about that. Can you imagine the dreck he'd write?"

"Poetry?" Lacey made a face. "That figures."

LaToya shook with laughter. "Yeah, poetry about Herodotus."

"Rhymes with hippopotamus." Lacey shook her head, trying to force the thought out of her brain. "Herodotus the hippopotamus?" Nope, it was stuck there now. It was viral. "Herodotus, hot to trotamus. Oh, the very thoughtamus!"

"I mean, have you ever read his stories? Herodotus the Hippopotamus would be so much better. But then Mac comes up with this book idea and it's really happening, at lightning speed, and guess who's right at the center of it? Why, Lacey Smithsonian. Again. One thing about Johnson, he talks all political correctness, he's Mister Liberal Social Consciousness. All peace, love, and brotherhood. But he is not about sisterhood. He can't stand it when one of the *women*, especially one Lacey Smithsonian, bests him at his own gig."

"You're beginning to sound like Broadway Lamont."

"Probably because we're soul mates. Detective Lamont just doesn't know it yet. Here's the deal, Lacey. You keep me in the loop about Broadway, I'll watch your back with that lunatic, Peter Johnson. And my fingernails are longer and sharper than yours, girlfriend."

"Deal," Lacey said. "There's a lot to be said for being fierce."

"Pinky swear," LaToya demanded, raising one perfectly manicured pinky. Lacey raised hers and they linked them in that ancient playground oath.

Lacey's cell phone rang. She didn't recognize the number. LaToya strutted off and Lacey answered.

"Hello, Lacey. This is Veronica. From Killer Stash. You left me your card?"

"Hi, Veronica, what's up? Did you think of something else?"

"Not exactly. I was reading *The Eye* today and I realized you're not the only one looking into the dress. I thought you should know you got some copycats on your trail."

"Really? Who?"

"Don't know, but after you left the other day, like maybe half an hour, a couple people came in asking about the Madame X dress. Course I didn't tell them anything."

"Can you describe them?"

"Not really. They were, I don't know, boring looking. Like, in suits."

"Like cops?"

"Nah. Not that boring. Like, I don't know, good looking but nondescript, kind of? Not from Baltimore, that's for sure. But they wanted to know what you knew about Courtney Wallace."

"Men or women?"

"One of each."

"Like reporters?"

"Yeah, maybe. But they didn't seem that smart. And you were here first and I respect that."

"Do you think it was someone from the *National Enquirer*?" Lacey had seen their stringer at Courtney's service. The guy could have a female partner.

"That would be so cool! Don't know. But I'll be watching the stand at the grocery for sure, now. Just thought you should know." Lacey thanked her and Veronica hung up.

Lacey knew it was possible someone was simply on the same investigative track she was, trying to fill in the blanks in the story about Courtney after her funeral. Or could it be a coincidence? She didn't know what to make of this news flash, but she didn't like the other possibility: Someone had followed her to Baltimore.

ɔ3

"Have a seat."

Before she could leave for her next destination, Mac called Lacey into his office. Both of his extra chairs were filled with papers, reports, and stacks of old *Eye Street Observers*. She moved the smaller stack from one chair to the other, dusted the chair with her hand, and sat down.

"What's up, Mac?"

He coughed and cleared his throat. "This thing with Johnson—"

"I don't know what it is with him," Lacey interrupted. "He sees me and he goes berserk." She noticed her front-page story on the cause of Courtney's death was on Mac's desk. It looked as if it had been crumpled and then straightened out. She suspected it was the paper Johnson had crushed into a ball, and Mac had restored it.

"I know, I know." Mac nodded. "His last stunt is a firing offense. But I can't summarily fire him. Much as I'd like to. Nobody plants a false story or sabotages a colleague at this paper. That includes Johnson. However—"

Here it comes. "The Newspaper Guild contract?"

"The Newspaper Guild contract. I have to go through the proper channels."

Her heart sank. That could take forever. "But what about Johnson?"

"He's taking a ten-day leave. At my *suggestion.*" That meant it was an order. "Starting immediately. He needs a rest."

"A rest? He needs a padded cell."

"We'll be discussing matters with the Guild. Claudia agrees with me. I just thought you should know."

"Who's going to cover his beat?"

"There's Kelly Kavanaugh."

"Heaven help us." Lacey could just picture Kelly storming the Hill in her shabby khakis, with her overabundance of enthusiasm and deficit of reporting ability. "On the other hand, she can't be worse than Johnson."

"You might want to tell her how reporters are expected to dress on the Hill."

Lacey knew talking to Kavanaugh about clothes was like talking to a puppy, but the Capitol Hill press galleries had certain dress requirements. No shorts, no flip-flops, and definitely no jeans. Jackets, dresses, or suits were expected, and no bare sundresses without a jacket or sweater.

"Yeah, that ought to be fun. Maybe I should take her shopping too. At Goodwill."

Mac smiled for the first time since the Johnson incident.

Chapter 25

INGRID ALLENDALE'S SHOP, DECADES, WAS Lacey's only slender lead on the origin of Courtney's Madame X dress, and it was her last scheduled stop before going home. She'd called and got an answering machine, but the recording said the shop would be open until five. She barely made it.

She parked on Mount Vernon Avenue, the main drag of Del Ray, and checked the address on her phone. Del Ray wasn't her own neighborhood, but it wasn't far from her beloved Old Town, and it was charming, in its own way. Less snooty, less expensive, less ostentatiously historic. More neighborly and more down to earth, and with a wealth of shops and restaurants on the avenue.

Distracted by the line for ice cream snaking out of the Dairy Godmother, Lacey almost missed the small, discreet sign: *Decades*, in an antique gold script on a brown background. She hadn't noticed it before. She climbed the narrow steps to the shop, nestled unobtrusively above a music store. The occasional sour note of violin lessons penetrated up through the floorboards.

The store was full of artificial trees and paper-leaved vines, hung with twinkling lights that made Lacey think of fireflies. The shop was small, but the clothing was thoughtfully displayed, and not crammed so tightly together that a customer couldn't get a good look, which was one of Lacey's pet peeves about most vintage stores. The place had an elegant, upscale feel that might have been snooty enough for Old Town, had Ingrid not been so welcoming.

"I'm glad you found me," Ingrid said. "I plan to get a bigger sign. That one is too hard to see."

"Good for your exclusivity, though."

"Exclusivity can put you in the poorhouse," she said with a smile.

"True. Anyway, I got a tip you were here. From Killer Stash, in Baltimore."

"How sweet of them. I've only been here a couple of months," Ingrid said. "I came up from Charlottesville. I'm still unpacking and deciding where to put things."

Like most lovers of vintage, Ingrid clearly dressed from her own stock. Her heart-shaped face, red lips, dark eyes, and short, dark, curled hair, rather like a sculptured cap, evoked another era, as did the dress she wore, a late Thirties bias-cut frock in a black and pink print. Almost like a demure Betty Boop. She appeared to be mid thirty-something.

"You must be Ingrid. I'm Lacey Smithsonian," she began.

"So nice to meet you. I recognized you from the photo on your column. I like the pieces you write about vintage clothing the best. And you wrote that article about the death of that TV reporter? Frightening. And fascinating."

"You won't mind if I ask you some questions?"

"About the clothes? Of course not."

"I'm particularly interested in the Madame X dress, the one Courtney Wallace wore the night she died."

Lacey pulled out an enlarged photo of Courtney from Hansen's archive. It was Courtney in full broadcast diva mode at the Correspondents' Dinner: one hand on her hip, big smile blazing, thrusting her microphone at some unseen celebrity. Unfortunately, the dress looked limp after the dousing. Ingrid took the photo from her.

"The Madame X. Oh, dear. This must be after the champagne hit it." She sighed deeply, sadly. "I noticed it looked like that dress in the painting too, with a few slight differences. Yes. It came from my shop. Right here."

Lacey felt a thrill. She had finally found a thread, and now she would pull it to see where it led her.

"Courtney didn't mention your shop on Channel One, though."

"I'm rather glad now that she didn't. She was here all alone. I guess she was saving the dress for that dinner, as part of her big finish. Perhaps she meant to say more about it and didn't get the chance."

"What can you tell me about it?"

"I sold it, and not for a song, but reluctantly. I didn't want to sell it to that Courtney Wallace person, but she was so insistent, so relentless, I feared I would never get her out of my shop unless I gave in."

"Why didn't you want to sell it?"

"Oh, I didn't mind selling it. It was selling it to *her* that gave me pause. This may sound funny, but I have deep feelings about my clothes."

"It doesn't sound funny at all. Not to me."

Ingrid smiled and moved behind the counter to lay the photo down flat. "Yes. You understand. I like your dress, by the way. High

Forties. Side zipper under the arm. The shoulder and hip embellishment firmly places it there. This dress always puts you in a good mood, doesn't it?"

"Always. I wear it when I don't want to worry about what I'm wearing."

"I can tell. Let me see here." Ingrid turned to her private stock she kept on an upper rack behind the counter and pulled out a pale gold gabardine jacket, with beading on the collar and breast pocket. "This would be fabulous on you. Early Forties, possibly late Thirties. One of a kind. Came from the same batch as the Madame X. Perfect for a cool spring day. And we're having a lot of those just now."

"It's lovely. Does it have a skirt?" Another connection. Lacey was drawing a picture of the woman who owned the Madame X dress and this jacket. They were exquisite.

"Alas, I was hoping it might turn up in that batch, but it never did. It was probably worn without the jacket and simply wore out."

"What about chocolate colored slacks with this?" Lacey suggested. She reached for it delicately, running her fingers over the beautiful weave of the gabardine. "I don't know, it looks pretty snug."

"Try it on, I think you'll be surprised."

Lacey gingerly put one arm through one sleeve, listening for ripping seams. No rips. That was promising. Then the other. To her surprise it fit like the proverbial glove, only better. The heavy satin lining gave it weight and a proper drape. She looked around for a mirror.

"Right over there," Ingrid said.

Lacey moved to the mirror and assessed her reflection. The buttery gold color picked up the highlights in her hair. It was perfect.

"I'm in trouble now."

"Does that mean you like it?" Ingrid was smiling gently.

"Not just *like* it. I love it. I might have to have it."

"I'm so pleased. It's really not that expensive. And certainly not the kind of thing you could pick up at the mall."

"You've convinced me." Lacey slipped it off and handed it over to be rung up. "You were saying that you didn't want to sell the Madame X dress to Courtney Wallace."

"Right. I thought something bad would happen—to the dress, not the woman. Almost a premonition. She insisted. I ignored it. I wish I hadn't."

"Something bad did happen."

"I am seldom wrong." Ingrid wasn't boasting, simply reporting.

"You haven't talked to the police about it, though," Lacey asked.

"Not even after you heard she died?"

"No one has asked me anything. Except you. Anyway, things like premonitions would just confuse the police. Why borrow trouble?"

Indeed, why borrow trouble? Lacey had borrowed quite enough already. "Do you think it was a freak million-to-one accident, as the police do?"

"I do not. For one thing, the lining of that dress, when I sold it, was not green. It was never green. Certainly not Paris Green. I would never knowingly resell a piece dyed in Paris Green. No, the lining was white. Pure white silk, to flash through the cutouts in the skirt."

"White?" Lacey felt an electric current run through her. "So Courtney, or someone, changed it. When did she buy it?"

"Three weeks ago."

"Did she say anything about replacing the lining?"

"No. Not that I recall. But the white lining was in bad shape. It was a silk that had shattered. The fibers had deteriorated. Happens unpredictably with silk, sometimes just from hanging in the closet all those years. A shame."

"Do you know where the Madame X dress came from?"

"I do. My stock comes from various places. Dead stock, when I can find it." Ingrid referred to vintage clothes that had never been worn and still had the original sales tags attached. Dead stock was highly coveted by some vintage collectors. Others believed if a piece hadn't sold the first time around, there was something wrong with it, style-wise.

"That's rare stuff."

"True. People occasionally come through the door with a big bundle of clothes. From an armful, I might find one piece I can use. There have been times when other dealers have gone out of business and I've bought entire store inventories, but that's rare too. That particular dress and your new jacket came from an estate sale in Richmond last fall. An old woman died, I suppose, and her family sold everything through an estate sales house. I'm sure they thought she was crazy for keeping all those antiquated clothes, the families usually do, but my God, some of them were couture! New York, Paris, Milan. Beautiful pieces. That dress was made for her. Your new old jacket, too."

"Even though it seemed to be copied from the painting, which was 1884, I'd say the dress was made in the early Forties," Lacey said. "The turn of the decade, before the wartime government regulations restricted fabric, especially silk."

"Precisely. Before all the silk went into parachutes. Just what I was thinking. That metal zipper on the side, too, very common in the early Forties. Possibly late Thirties. Very classy at the time, definitely influenced by Hollywood. I wonder how she looked in it, that woman. Very glamorous, I would guess."

"Do you know her name?"

"No. I received no information about her or her family. The estate sales people might know. I have their number somewhere. I'll find it for you."

Every decade of fashion borrowed or incorporated details from earlier ages, but the Madame X copy could not have been made before the twentieth century, Lacey knew, because it wasn't until 1913 that the modern zipper appeared on the scene. By the late 1930s, metal zippers were commonly used in men's pants and were beginning to be used in women's dresses. Only later did plastic zippers supplement metal.

Courtney had changed the lining. So the Paris Green silk might have been much older than the dress. Possibly from the mid nineteenth century, as bizarre as that seemed. Unless someone managed to dye a batch of vintage silk at a much later date. Lacey tried to visualize the Madame X dress with a white silk lining. It might make better sense, stylistically. So where did the Paris Green silk come from?

"You wouldn't happen to have a photograph of the dress?" Lacey inquired.

"Funny you should ask. Yes. I keep a photo inventory of all my stock. Oh, not so much the common threads, cotton skirts and pants and so on. But all the dresses, suits, jackets, hats, all the substantial pieces. I have an online store too. They're all on there."

Antique clothing meets the twenty-first century, over the Internet.

Ingrid moved behind the counter again and opened up her laptop. She turned it around for Lacey to see. The Madame X dress was modeled on a mannequin, with the skirt pinned to the upraised hand to show off the cut-out pattern, the playing card suits. The lining was snow white.

"You see, it's unique, beautifully designed, expertly stitched, most likely by a professional seamstress, possibly in New York or Paris. It's not mass market. There were no tags. I've never sold anything else quite like it." She sighed.

"I can't decide which lining I like best," Lacey said. "The white or the green."

"The white. It never killed anyone."

Ingrid printed a copy of her photo for Lacey. Side by side with Hansen's photo of Courtney, the change in the lining color made a striking difference.

"Do you mind if I use all of this in a follow-up story?"

"You're welcome to. Would you mind mentioning the location of my shop?"

"I'd be happy to."

"Nothing wrong with a little notoriety, and publicity." Ingrid smiled slowly. "I think I'll wear more of a noir look for the rest of the week. Please enjoy the jacket."

With her beautiful new-yet-vintage gold gabardine jacket in the car and the new knowledge that the original dress lining had been replaced, Lacey's EFP was humming.

She had tracked down the store where the dress was purchased. She had found the thread she'd been looking for. But how could she keep pulling it? Now she knew there was a brief window of a few weeks in which the lining switch must have occurred. But that just opened up more questions. Did Courtney know what she was doing? If not, who did? And where did the old green fabric—or the brand-new dye—come from?

Courtney Wallace's dress told a story, but Courtney had listened to only a fraction of what it had to say. Lacey wanted to hear the rest of the story. Curiosity, as she often said, was her failing.

And it killed the cat.

Chapter 26

SOMEONE ELSE KNEW THE LINING material had been switched. Maybe that person knew even more.

The Madame X dress design details were complicated, and if Lacey and Ingrid Allendale were right, it was more than seventy years old. No amateur would attempt such a delicate job as relining the entire dress. It had to be a professional seamstress or tailor. Whoever it was, they weren't talking, at least not to the media. No one had come forward to say they'd neatly stitched in the cause of death. Perhaps, like Ingrid Allendale, they didn't want to borrow trouble, or feared they might be implicated in Courtney's death, even without intending it. Or there was a chance whoever it was knew exactly what they were doing and would never come forward.

Nothing is ever easy, Lacey thought.

At least she was finally at home in her apartment, lying on her deep blue velvet sofa, and not at her desk in the newsroom. Phone calls could be made anywhere. Even in a prone position. Even though she found it hard to concentrate.

She tried not to be distracted by a bag of delicious treats she picked up at the Cheesetique. The so-called cheese boutique in Del Ray was far too tempting and far too close to Ingrid's vintage shop, and Lacey found it impossible to pass by without stopping in. Once inside, the aromas of delicious cheeses from many lands and a gnawing hunger from missing lunch drove her to purchase far too many assorted cheeses, meats, olives, and crackers. And a bottle of Virginia Riesling that the girl at the counter recommended to complement them all.

Lacey would rather plan an intimate dinner for two than think about death, but the Paris Green mystery wouldn't solve itself. Her cell phone was in her hand. She thought about calling Courtney's coworkers, like Eric Park or Zanna Nelson, to ask where she usually took her clothes for alterations, but Lacey didn't think about it very long. If they were any kind of newshounds, even broadcast newshounds, they would wonder why she was asking, connect her question to the infamous dress, and launch their own hunt. Lacey decided against it.

Courtney's family was next. It was a long shot. Lacey called

Mrs. Wallace to see if she knew anything about the lining, or if she knew where Courtney might have had the dress altered.

The woman was polite but brief on the phone. She had no idea where her daughter would have gone for tailoring. Indeed, Courtney never told her what dress she would wear to the dinner. Perhaps it was meant to be a surprise, she said, her voice breaking. They didn't talk about clothes much.

"I hate that dress," Mrs. Wallace added. "If it weren't for that dress, and that idiot waiter, and that ridiculous dinner party, my baby would be alive."

Unless it wasn't an accident—and if the dress had failed, someone would probably try again.

Lacey wanted to make sure she covered the waterfront. She asked one more time. "What's going to happen to the dress?" *Did she really plan to burn it?*

There was a pause. "My hands will never touch that dress. I will never see that dress. I have no idea."

"I'm sorry for your loss, Mrs. Wallace." Lacey ended the call. She decided against calling Courtney's brother. If her mother didn't know anything about her daughter's wardrobe, the brother certainly wouldn't.

Courtney seemed to have had a remote relationship with her family. Lacey formed a picture of a woman who couldn't wait to leave her little Maryland hometown for the bright lights of nearby Washington. Someone who might say, "I'm too busy to come home, Mom, but you can always see me on TV!"

Who tailored Courtney's dress? Did they know it was a toxic time bomb? Ingrid didn't know, nor would the estate brokers who sold it to her; the dress still had its original lining when they last saw it. Short of calling every seamstress in the D.C. area, there was only one more person Lacey could think of to ask about the green lining. And that person did not want to talk to her.

"Hello, Alma? It's Lacey—"

"Lacey Smithsonian, the answer is still no. No, no, no. I am sewing for you no more. Never. *Comprende?*"

"This is not about me, Alma. I promise."

"And none of your crazy friends either. It was even worse with that crazy Stella and her crazy dress."

"I'm so sorry," Lacey started. She was saying that a lot lately.

"Sorry? I'm lucky to be alive!" Alma was just getting started too.

"And I'm grateful. I just have a question. Please don't hang up. Do you remember Courtney Wallace?"

"That TV reporter who died." There was a snort on the other end. "Another crazy friend of yours? Did you get her killed too?"

"I didn't get anyone killed! Listen, this is about the dress she was wearing."

"The one that killed her? I'm not surprised to hear you're involved."

Lacey paused to take a deep breath. Alma was entitled to a little rant. Anyone would be entitled. Maybe it would make her feel better.

"I had nothing to do with it," Lacey said. "She bought the dress from a vintage store I didn't even know about until today. I just found the store. What I need to know—"

"You going to tell me there's another haunted dress? Everything is haunted when it comes to you."

"That was a Russian shawl. And it wasn't really haunted. I don't think. And the original silk lining of this dress was shattered, so Courtney had a new lining put in. It would have been a tricky job. She must have taken it to a local seamstress. That's who I'm trying to find."

"Where? Virginia or D.C., or heaven forbid, Maryland?"

"Courtney lived in Virginia. I'm guessing it was someone here."

"It wasn't me, if that's what you want to know. Someone else sewed in the poison green lining. And don't you be asking me to do such a thing, Lacey Smithsonian!"

"You have been reading my column."

"Maybe I was bored."

"Do you have any ideas?"

"My only idea is I don't sew for you or anyone you know, ever again. Now I ask people, 'Do you know Lacey Smithsonian?' before I agree to do any work for them. If the answer is yes, I say no."

She's really milking this. "I never meant to put you in danger, Alma, you know that. I simply thought you might have heard something through the grapevine."

"You think we got a union? Maybe a newsletter? You think we keep poisoned material on hand so we can sew it into our clients' clothes? Now that I think about it, maybe I should get some, for the next crazy dress for Lacey Smithsonian. Except there's not going to be a next one!"

Patience, Lacey.

"Alma. You are the best seamstress I know. There is poetry in your hands, Alma. And I am sorry from the bottom of my soul that you were involved with such a bad scene with Stella's dress. I hope you are feeling better now." Lacey also hoped that Alma had the same curiosity most people had. She prayed Alma would want to know the end of the story. "How is your shop? Back in one piece?"

"Humph. My place will never be the same. And after all those news stories about me and your crazy business with that *loquisima* woman, I'm busier than ever. I suppose I could ask around among my ladies, see if anyone heard anything or handled that green silk. Probably scared they're gonna die after touching it. Maybe I could make a couple of calls. For their own safety, not for any other reason."

"That would be great, Alma. I owe you."

"Yes, you do."

"If you turn something turn up, I will give you credit. In the paper."

"That would be a start." Alma hung up the phone. In the best of times, she was not one for sentimental goodbyes.

Lacey checked the time. Vic would be there shortly. He had taken her to dinner the night before. It was her turn tonight. It was a perfect evening for a dinner *à deux* on her balcony. The harsh sun that blasted the balcony during the day had receded behind the building's other wing. It was now lovely, and the Potomac River far below was as blue as the evening sky.

Lacey spread one of Aunt Mimi's linen tablecloths on her petite bistro table and set up a small banquet, arranging the cheese and the other expensive items from Cheesetique. She could have called it tapas, but that seemed pretentious. *It's really just a picnic on the balcony.*

Work often made her too tired to cook anything more complicated than popcorn or scrambled eggs. Occasionally, she produced a splashy dessert to impress Vic's mother, but most of the time, she was a simple eater. This comparative feast on the balcony was in recognition that it had been a tough week and she deserved a break. She spent far too much money at the cheese shop, but at least all she had to do was open the packages and chill the wine. And there would be leftovers. She changed into a simple sleeveless yellow and white dress and touched up her makeup.

Vic arrived as the clouds and sun turned the sky into a

spectacular pink, orange, and purple display over the river. He kissed her at the door.

"You're a wonderful appetizer, honey," Lacey said. "We're eating outside." She led the way, after retrieving the wine from the refrigerator, and a corkscrew. He followed. He gave her a hug and lifted the wine bottle. His gaze took in the table, the food, the candles, the river view.

"A picnic high above the river. What's the occasion?"

"You're here." She held on to him for a few minutes.

"And so are you. And you're in one piece. I'll celebrate that." He opened the bottle and poured it into a couple of rose crystal goblets, another gift bequeathed to Lacey from Aunt Mimi.

"It's been a weird week." She stretched her back and took a deep breath.

"Does this weirdness involve your hunt for the origin of the killer dress? The dress to *dye* for? The poison-apple-green Gown of Doom?"

"You think you're smart, don't you? Well, you are. And it is. And I found it. Right here in Alexandria. A little vintage shop, hidden away, practically invisible to the naked eye."

"I had every faith in you. Good work." Vic glanced at the assembled banquet and checked a label on an exotic cheese. "By any chance, was this miraculous find anywhere near the Cheesetique? My guess is the vintage shop's in Del Ray, close to Mount Vernon Avenue?"

"You must be psychic."

"Simple deduction is an art form." He grinned and handed her a goblet of wine. They admired the Technicolor clouds over the Potomac. A few white sailboats were heading back to the Belle Haven Marina for the night. They sipped the Riesling. It complemented the cheese, just as the Cheesetique promised. A warm breeze ruffled her hair. She leaned against him. This was the first time Lacey felt herself really relax since she'd heard Courtney Wallace was dead.

"Do you want to hear about the great gown hunt?"

"So our evening is dinner al fresco and a game of Clue?" He seemed amused.

"You guessed it. The killer is Colonel Mustard with the wine bottle on the balcony. I give you Exhibit X." Lacey produced from her shoulder bag the photograph of the Madame X dress in its original form, with the white lining. "What do you think?"

"Isn't this part supposed to be green?"

"Very good. Courtney herself changed the lining. Or had it changed. Part of my big discovery. I spoke with the woman who sold the gown to her. When Courtney bought the dress, it looked like this. White silk underskirt. Not green. I give you Exhibit Y." She placed Hansen's photo of Courtney on the table next to Exhibit X. "Voilà. Green lining. I don't know where this Paris Green material came from, or who replaced the white lining. Yet. The original lining was in tatters. It's called shattered silk. The big question is: Did the person who changed it know what they were doing?"

"That's a lot of questions. I'm sure you're working overtime to come up with a theory. You realize, sweetheart, it could still be a peculiar once-in-a-lifetime accident. Cops say so."

Lacey nodded. "And if it was, then it would be even sadder if Courtney had a hand in accidentally causing her own death."

Above the river, an osprey soared and dived down for a fish in the river. Lacey filled a small plate with cheese and meats and popped a salty garlic-stuffed olive in her mouth. *This is perfect,* she thought. *Now that Vic's here.*

"The poison's in the dye and the dye is in the dress lining," Vic said, looking through the things on the table. "And Colonel Mustard is nowhere to be seen."

"No. But here's some Dijon, if that's what you're looking for."

He put some salami on a cracker, topped it with a little Colonel Mustard, and popped it in his mouth.

"Life is sad, darling. We make split-second decisions every day. Many of them go wrong. Some of them dead wrong. The only saving grace is that we don't know everything that's going to happen. What fun would that be? Life unfolds."

"Like a dress. Like a mystery." She leaned over and kissed him, thinking what a wonderful mystery it was that Vic Donovan had walked back into her life years after they first met.

The evening deepened to a clear blue, and a big round moon rose gold over the Potomac. It was time to forget about work and Courtney and killer dresses. And Colonel Mustard.

Chapter 27

FRIDAY MORNING, WHICH GENERALLY LED to *date night*, always made Lacey feel like dressing up, even for her newsroom coworkers. Unfortunately, there would be no date tonight. Vic had some kind of urgent computer maintenance to oversee at his security firm's offices, because the IT people needed to do it after office hours, and he wouldn't be finished until late.

Unfortunately, Friday inspired many of Lacey's coworkers to wear their idea of "Casual Friday," which she considered the bane of the working world. And in Washington, D.C., achieving the ideal mix of casual yet businesslike often produced truly awkward outfits. The last day of the work week looked like a grab bag at *The Eye Street Observer*. Casual Friday also led to a general downward slide in standards of dress, until it contaminated the whole week. Lacey ignored the thought and concentrated on the big issue of the morning: *What should I wear today?*

She wasn't the kind of woman to let a new purchase hang forlornly in the closet. Not when she had a lovely new vintage jacket she was dying to wear. She paired her "new" gold gabardine jacket from Ingrid's shop with a brown tank top and a brown and gold patterned skirt that flared out and floated around her knees. She wore a pair of kitten-heeled sandals in brown and tan and white, and she pulled her hair off her face with a pair of gold beaded combs and let the back fall down her shoulders, over her gold necklace. Red lipstick added the final touch of "war paint." She was ready to face the world head-on once again. Aunt Mimi would have approved.

She rode into the District on a Metro car full of mismatched Casual Friday office workers and tourists. She couldn't be quite sure who was who. At the newsroom, armed for the day with a stiff latte from the coffee shop, Lacey's first call was to Detective Broadway Lamont.

"Smithsonian, you made my morning. Does Ms. Pickles have a delicious new dish I should be taste testing?"

"Haven't seen her yet. This is just to let you know what I found out about Courtney's dress. Like you asked, remember? Three weeks ago, the lining was white. It was not Paris Green."

"What're you talking about? Courtney Wallace's Madame X

dress? That old thing? Ancient history. Unless it gets up on its hind legs and tells me it was foul play, I am officially bored with that dress."

"The white lining was innocuous and safe. Maybe a bit musty. The silk was in bad shape. Shattered, but not lethal. When it was changed to green, it became potentially deadly. Update for you. That's all."

He grunted. "Doesn't prove anything."

"Not yet. I'm writing an update for *The Eye* and I just wanted you to confirm that the death is still officially accidental."

"Unofficially freaking *freak* accidental. M.E.'s office hasn't officially ruled. Could take a week or two." He paused. "By the way, how do you know the lining thing was swapped out? Can you prove this?"

"I have a photograph from the woman who sold Courtney the dress."

"You've been busy, Smithsonian."

"So have you, Broadway. You watched the Channel One tapes."

"And they didn't tell me anything except it was an accident. The new lining thing is interesting. Makes for good newspaper copy. But that alone don't change a thing from the department's point of view."

"Maybe not, but it does advance the story. Do you have a comment?"

"Not for the record. Call me when Felicity is baking some new goodies."

Why doesn't she start her own fan club? "This isn't about food, Broadway."

"Too bad. I haven't had any breakfast yet. You call me when you got means, opportunity, a suspect, a motive, and preferably, a muffin. I know you're heartbroken, Smithsonian, but I still don't see any crime here."

"I'll give your regards to LaToya." Lacey hung up. *That ought to scare him.* If something suspicious developed, Lamont couldn't say she hadn't told him. She turned to her computer and started her update on the Madame X dress alterations. One paragraph in, she received a text from Alma Lopez.

"Meet me at G Street Fabrics at Seven Corners if you want to know more. Eleven a.m."

Why not just call me? Oh, that's right, she's not speaking to me.
Lacey checked her watch and marched to Mac's office.

"I have to leave to check on a lead."

"A lot of that going on lately. What's up?" He leaned back in his chair and put his feet up on a tall pile of papers that Lacey suspected were a draft of *Terror at Timberline.* "Something important? Like a story?"

Mac was always casually, and badly, dressed, so it was hard to tell if Casual Friday meant anything to him. He wore rumpled khakis and a Madras plaid short-sleeve shirt, topped with a zip-up sweater vest in mud tones. Formal black socks duked it out with his garish running shoes with neon green and orange stripes. A red-and-white Washington Nationals ball cap perched proudly on his desk. He actually wore it, and not just on game days—when he wasn't wearing his new Stetson. Lacey averted her eyes.

"Possibly. I might find out something else about the Madame X dress. Something I apparently can't get over the phone."

"You're still on that dress thing?"

"Call me obsessed. Obsessed with the dress."

"Who are you talking to?"

"Alma Lopez."

"Where's my Maalox! Isn't she the one who got her seamstress shop trashed? From your last little misadventure? She was not happy with you. Or this newspaper."

Lacey avoided his gaze and stared out the window overlooking Farragut Square. "Yes, my former seamstress. She's, um, warming up to me."

"Probably warming up to burn you at the stake. I'm sending Trujillo with you."

"It's not necessary." Lacey folded her arms in self-defense. "I don't need Tony on this, Mac, it's my story."

"Ha. You got another true crime of fashion? Possible murder?"

"I didn't say *murder.*"

"You don't have to say it, you think this death is suspicious. It's written all over your face. Yeah, that expression, right there. You can't let this thing go and now you're off all alone to— Where are you off to?"

"Alma wants me to meet her in Falls Church. A fabric store."

"Thought she was never going to talk to you again."

"I got lucky. She might have an idea who altered Courtney Wallace's dress."

"Lucky." His bushy eyebrows lifted, but he was interested in spite of himself. "Smithsonian, you got a bad track record for getting into trouble. Don't bother arguing. It's a known fact. You be careful this Alma Lopez doesn't stick a pair of knitting needles in you. I want you and Tony to buddy up on this."

Lacey tried to protest, but he stopped her with a glare. He stood and marched toward the inner window of his office that overlooked the newsroom, his eyes finally settling on his quarry. Mac stepped outside his door and hollered for Trujillo. Then he reached for the Maalox bottle on his desk and took a swig.

"I thought you were trying to cut down on that stuff," Lacey said.

"How can I, with you around?"

☃

Tony insisted on driving Mustang Sally. Lacey agreed grudgingly, because it simplified the trip to Falls Church, Virginia. It would take too long to Metro back home to Alexandria and retrieve her car, or to take the Metro out to the East Falls Church stop and grab a cab to Seven Corners. And his black Mustang convertible was a much cooler ride.

"Nice threads, by the way." Tony was possibly the only man at *The Eye* who would notice. "Hot date tonight?"

"Nope. Just trying to eradicate Casual Friday," she said. "One Friday at a time."

"Good luck with that. You tilt at windmills too? Astride your mighty winged pig?"

"Constantly. And she's a very well-dressed pig."

Tony was wearing black denim pants, black shirt, and a light leather jacket. Black lizard-skin cowboy boots featuring stitched longhorns were his footwear du jour. He liked to look as sharp as Mustang Sally.

G Street Fabrics was a mecca for seamstresses, a local chain, the best fabric stores in the area. Once located on G Street in Northwest D.C., they had moved to the suburbs years before and kept the name. Alma specified the store at Seven Corners, a shopping center at a major seven-way intersection that tangled Northern Virginia traffic converging from every direction. Tony didn't let Seven Corners scare him. He gunned Mustang Sally up Arlington Boulevard. Lacey closed her eyes and hung on for dear life.

"Hey, we made it in record time," he said, pulling into the parking lot.

"No kidding." Lacey unhooked her safety belt. "I'm more impressed with the fact we aren't dead. You could wait for me in the coffee shop." Lacey pointed to the Barnes & Noble bookstore next door.

"No way. Mac said to stick close. You are not getting out of my sight line."

"It's not dangerous, Tony," she argued. "It's a fabric store. I'm just meeting a source. And you have a conflict of interest on this story, remember?"

"I have no interest at all, much less a conflict. Fabric is not generally a lethal weapon. Except when it is, Ms. Lethal Black Dress." Tony matched his steps to hers. "That's always the way with you comic book heroines. Take kryptonite, for example. It's not dangerous until it is dangerous. Until you have a homicidal maniac gunning for you. That's when it's dangerous and newsworthy. And I guess you've forgotten the famous Beltway Snipers? Seven Corners was one of their shooting galleries. So I go where you go, Wonder Woman."

"You're just jealous. You've already bowed out of this story. No double byline, remember?"

"But if you become the target of a mad sniper, then *you've* got the conflict of interest, and *I've* got a big story."

"That's convenient. And untrue. I can always write a feature on being shot at while *very* well-dressed," Lacey said, while Tony held the door for her.

G Street Fabrics was in the basement level of the shopping center, accessed via an escalator. There were no windows down below, which gave it the feeling of a bunker, a very large, fabric-filled bunker. Tony was mesmerized by the rows and rows of bolts of fabric. He stationed himself on a chair nearby, where he could keep an eye on her and the front door, without cramping her style with her source.

Lacey wanted to wander through the aisles of materials, the bolts of brightly colored cloth and patterns, the raw material of fashion. She told herself to stay on point, but she was soon lost in contemplation of how various fabrics would look in several of Aunt Mimi's unfinished patterns. *If I only had a seamstress.*

Alma found Lacey deep in thought in the silk aisle. As always,

Alma was striking, in dark jeans with high heels, topped by a crisp white tailored shirt and a wide belt cinched at the waist. Her sleek dark hair was pulled back into a ponytail, tied with a scarlet scarf. Her makeup was minimal, but her lips were bright red and large silver hoop earrings completed the look. She was carrying a small white paper sack.

"Alma, hello," Lacey said. "Nice to see you. Why are we meeting here?"

"I have things to buy here and I don't want you in my house. Not after the last time. You are *mala suerte*."

"Okay, okay, I get it. I'm here. What do you have for me?"

"I made a few calls."

"Anything turn up?"

"It seems that a friend of a friend of a friend of mine did some work for this Courtney Wallace woman."

"Your friend is the one who switched out the lining?"

"She did. It was a big job, a couture gown like that, complicated pattern, and not much time. The old white lining was shredded. Came apart in her hands."

"And the replacement lining fabric, the Paris Green silk? Where did she get it?"

"Supplied by the customer."

"Courtney Wallace brought the material with her? Are you sure?"

"That's what she said. The friend of a friend."

"What's her name? This friend of a friend?"

"She doesn't want you to have her name. Here." Alma thrust the package into Lacey's hands. "Call her Anonymous."

"I don't understand." Lacey peeked inside and pulled out several pieces of brilliant emerald silk. She gasped at the richness of the color. Tony jumped up from his chair at Lacey's gasp. Lacey warned him back with a look.

"This is the material that was left over," Alma said. "It may be pretty, but it's poison. It already caused that woman's death. My friend of a friend doesn't want it. I don't want it. You're so interested in this, you take it."

"It's only dangerous when it's wet," Lacey said. Alma glared at her. "Of course I'll take it. I appreciate this, Alma. Did this other seamstress have any idea where Courtney found it?"

"I don't know. I didn't ask her. She just told me this Courtney woman was in a hurry to have the dress finished. That's no surprise. Everybody is always in a hurry to have their sewing finished. No one comes in and says, 'Take your time.' People like Lacey Smithsonian come in and say, 'Can you make my crazy friend's crazy wedding dress even crazier? And can I have it yesterday? And by the way my friend's *loquisima* stalker will come and try to kill you?' Oh, wait, you didn't tell me that part."

"I'm so sorry, Alma. Your creations have always been quite lovely. "

"The price of beauty can be too high." Alma wore her superior expression.

"Yes. Much too high," Lacey agreed. "Particularly in this case. Thank you so much, Alma."

Alma lifted her shoulders, then dropped them. "I had to get rid of this evil fabric. My duty."

"It was very good of you to call me."

"So tell me. What have you found out, Ms. *Eye Street* Reporter?"

I knew she'd be curious. "You know as much as I know, Alma. Could I talk to the woman?"

"She doesn't want to talk to you." Alma quickly glanced past Lacey's head and then looked away.

"Wait." Lacey turned around. "Is she here?"

Alma pressed her lips together in a tight line. "She wants to remain anonymous."

A petite woman peeked out from behind the button aisle and walked shyly to Alma's side. She was pretty and about Lacey's age, with black hair and dark eyes and a short edgy haircut set off by large gold hoop earrings. She wore a tight black T-shirt and black cropped pants and sandals. They stared at each other for a moment.

"Alma told you everything," the woman said. "I don't know anything else."

"I'm Lacey. What's your name?"

"You're not going to use it, are you?"

"My editor prefers it, but I don't have to, in special cases. I'll call you a confidential source. Promise."

"Well, don't use my name. Please. My name is Lola Gallegos."

"Courtney went to you?"

"I did a few small jobs for her. Before," Lola said. "Tailoring, some hems, ripped seams. The woman couldn't sew on a button. She got my name from someone. She told me at the time. I forget who. I get most of my work from referrals."

"She asked you to put in a new lining?"

"Yeah. She brought the material and the Madame X dress with her the same day."

"The Madame X dress," Lacey repeated. It seemed that a lot of people had read her article.

"I was surprised. This woman, I don't think she ever saw a fabric store. She said a friend gave it to her. It wasn't brand-new material. Just all folded up, in a paper sack. That sack, with the leftovers."

"How could you tell it was older?" Lacey opened the paper sack full of remnants and peeked inside. Lola pulled out a sliver of the Paris Green silk with two delicate fingers.

"Feel it. It has a different feel from silk you buy these days. Heavier. A little stiffer, maybe? Nice stuff. Pretty color. Except for the being deadly part. I never heard about that kind of dye before all this."

"I don't suppose she mentioned who the friend was? Or how the friend happened to have it?"

"Nope. They never tell me that stuff. Only that it was vintage, so it would go better with a vintage dress."

"Was it difficult to reline the dress?"

"Very. But rewarding. Complicated, but interesting too. Clothes aren't made with that kind of detail today," Lola said. "Working on a dress that old, that precisely put together, it was a challenge, a lesson. I like a challenge sometimes. It was really a piece of art. No tags. So it wasn't factory, it was handmade. If I knew it was dangerous, I never would have taken it on, you know. Or I would have at least charged double."

"Why did you come here with Alma today?"

Lola ran a hand through her hair. "Alma called me, asking all these questions. She was curious about it." Alma snorted, but Lola continued. "I told her, yeah, I worked on the dress, but I wasn't going to say anything to anybody after someone died in it. Anyway, Alma told me about you and what you write. How you listen to the fabric. You hear what the clothes say. I thought that was pretty cool. That's it, pretty much. I guess I was a little curious too."

"Okay." Alma turned to Lacey. "We're done. You satisfied?"

"I'm indebted," Lacey said. "To both of you."

"Good. We don't care what you do with it. Just don't use Lola's name, or my name without permission. And don't use that material in any clothes. Course, there's not really enough left. Just scraps."

"That dress, the bodice, the full skirt," Lola said, "it took a lot of fabric."

"It's a gorgeous color." Lacey stared at the scrap she pulled out. It was soft and cool to the touch. "Thank you."

Alma and Lola moved off into the recesses of G Street Fabrics to purchase supplies and, no doubt, discuss the "crazy fashion reporter." Tony appeared at Lacey's side.

"What have you got there, Brenda Starr? Kryptonite? Plutonium?"

"Practically. Kryptonite is green too." She handed him the paper sack and he peered into it cautiously. "It's not a gun, Tony. It won't go bang. It's just Paris Green silk."

"Unless it gets wet, right?"

"That's right," she said, and he tossed it back like a hot charcoal. Lacey returned the scrap she had handled and tucked the package into her purse.

"I guess the water balloon fight is off," he said with a smile.

"You got that right, buckaroo."

He bought her a latte at the bookstore next door and they discussed Courtney and her fatal fashion disaster. Tony applauded her investigative instincts. Lacey was dissatisfied. What did she really have? *Not much.*

The dress itself came from an innocent source. The deadly lining material came from the victim herself and had been changed by an innocent seamstress. There was no way to tell it was dangerous when wet just by looking at it. Lola Gallegos didn't know, nor did Alma Lopez. The occasional needle prick or scissor mishap was as dangerous as the sewing business usually got, leaving aside what happened to Alma and her shop. Lacey now even had the leftover silk, in telltale Paris Green. But no suspects. Not even proof of deadly intent.

Courtney hadn't even believed it when Lacey warned her about the dye. In fact, she was highly annoyed. Even if she'd listened, would she have believed the danger was real? After all, the fabric was old. She might presume the poison had lost its punch. And who could predict getting drenched in a sudden champagne storm?

That was the question. *Someone* could indeed have predicted that storm. Because—if Lacey was right—someone arranged for the Paris Green silk, and that same someone arranged for the champagne shower. *Who was this someone?*

Remembering the phone call from Veronica at Killer Stash, Lacey turned in her chair and stared into the bookstore. She felt as if someone was watching them.

"What's up?" Tony asked. "You act spooked."

"Making sure no one followed us here." She explained about Veronica, the odd couple who asked about her at Killer Stash, and the possibility of other reporters trailing her for a piece of the story.

"Don't think so. First of all, this story's interesting, but it's not 'all that.' No blood? No suspects? Takes someone with a really quirky brain, like yours, to even follow the clues. And I can guarantee you no one could keep up with Mustang Sally through that Seven Corners traffic out there. I'll prove it on the way back. Let's hit the road."

Chapter 28

BACK AT HER COMPUTER AT *The Eye*, Lacey returned to the Crime of Fashion story she started writing that morning.

LETHAL BLACK DRESS ALTERED BEFORE BROADCASTER'S DEATH
By Lacey Smithsonian

The Eye Street Observer has learned that the lining of the dress worn by the late television broadcaster Courtney Wallace at the White House Correspondents' Dinner was replaced in the weeks leading up to her death. The new lining was colored with the toxic Paris Green dye blamed for Wallace's death, the dye that turned Wallace's black gown into her now-notorious *lethal black dress.*

The original lining of the Madame X gown was white silk and was still intact when Wallace purchased it, according to the owner of an Alexandria specialty vintage shop where the dress was last sold. Decades shop owner Ingrid Allendale told *The Eye...*

Lacey asked Hansen to photograph the material she brought back with her, and after he'd finished she put one small scrap of the pretty green silk in a plastic baggie and tucked it in her purse. She didn't know whether she would have a use for it. The rest she stuck in her locking file drawer. She sent Hansen's best photo of the fabric scraps and Ingrid's inventory picture of the original dress to Mac, who was soon peering over her shoulder, reading her draft copy.

"You're saying that, in a way, Wallace was apparently responsible for her own death," Mac said. "You're looking into where it came from? Seems to leave some loose threads, doesn't it? Pun intended."

He glanced at Felicity's desk, but the offerings were sparse. He settled for half a blue-sprinkled doughnut from today's test version of Wiedemeyer's groom cake.

"There's got to be more to the story," Lacey agreed. "I don't know if I can find it. After all, Courtney's not talking."

He nodded. "Stay on it, as long as there's a fashion angle."

"You're all heart, Mac." *At least Johnson isn't here to screw up my story.*

"That's what they tell me. Curious though. This Wallace woman. She wins an Emmy and lives. She gets caught peddling a phony scandal story, and that doesn't kill her. She tries to walk a mile in your high heels on the fashion beat, and before you know it, she's dead."

"How many times have I told you this beat is deadly?"

He ignored her. "Are there any cookies around?"

The sound of flip-flops smacking the newsroom floor interrupted them. Mac and Lacey stared at Harlan Wiedemeyer, who was wearing the flappy footwear. His Casual Friday bulky jeans and fire-engine red, extra-large, Washington Nationals T-shirt didn't do him any favors.

"When did you start wearing flip-flops to the office?" she asked him.

He looked puzzled. "It's Friday. It's almost summer. Duh. What's the problem?"

Lacey would have said *your big hairy toes*, but she refrained. Felicity, who generally wore frumpy-dumpy black pumps, was also slapping the floor with flip-flops. Her white legs hadn't seen the sun in months. She was wearing bright blue culottes, a white T-shirt and a bright blue sweater with kittens embroidered on it. The kittens wiggled when Felicity inhaled. No one had worn culottes in years. Or those particular kittens on sweaters. Lacey was transfixed.

Felicity was carrying a platter of some kind of almond-cream-filled pastry. Mac's focus zoomed from her feet to the tray in her hand. He took one and sauntered off.

Lacey, however, could not take her eyes off the sky-blue toenails and fingernails of the food editor. Apparently Felicity had spent her lunch hour getting a manicure and pedicure. *At least they're not beige.*

"What do you think, Lacey?" she asked. "I'm trying blue nails to match the blue band in my wedding dress."

"When you look back at your wedding photos in years to come, Felicity, I hope you will be kind to yourself."

"I think they're adorable." She admired her hands and licked pastry icing off her fingers.

"It's your wedding. You have the right to wear whatever you desire."

Felicity grinned. "Blue it is."

I blame Casual Friday. Casual Friday is the Devil.

Lacey flashed forward to the wedding of Felicity and Harlan Wiedemeyer. She could imagine the headlines:

QUEEN OF COOKIELAND WEDS KING OF KRISPY KREME
HAPPY COUPLE HONEYMOONS ON SUGAR MOUNTAIN

Before technology transformed the journalism game, a newspaper reporter competing for a scoop would have to race back to the newsroom with the story, type it up on a clattering manual typewriter, confirm it by phone with her sources, get it past her cranky editor, and take it to press, after which a giant machine would mate her story with ink and newsprint, and a newsboy would hawk it on a street corner the next morning. But these days, Lacey's scoop would be online in a matter of minutes, as well as in the next day's printed paper. Other media could then choose to pick it up, copy it, run with their own story, or ignore it, but in any event, it was still her scoop.

Within minutes of the updated story hitting the wire, her phone started ringing. Brooke was the very first.

"Do you just sit staring at the screen until my byline pops up?" Lacey asked.

"No way. I have you in my alerts. I get pinged every time you update a story."

"Impressive," Lacey acknowledged, even as she found this news intimidating.

"I know. I love technology."

"You too? That makes one of us."

"You didn't tell me about the latest development," Brooke said. "And what fun, a new vintage store for you to explore. Did you buy anything?"

"Maybe." Lacey brushed imaginary lint from her lovely new vintage jacket.

"So why didn't you call me? Sharing is caring!"

"I just found out about the fabric today, Brooke, and I was on deadline. Just finished writing it up. Obviously." The previous night, after she discovered Ingrid's shop, Lacey was busy with Vic, playing Clue, and other games for two. That was no time to update friends.

"Okay, theoretically let's say I forgive you," Brooke breezed on. "Incidentally, I also have something else on my mind. There's a new art exhibit opening at that gallery, you know the one, in Old Town tonight. You'll love it. With Stella away, we mice can play. And I can pump you mercilessly about everything you know."

"The Somerset Gallery? Tonight?"

"I know it's Friday, and it's last minute. But Damon is busy tonight catching up on DeadFed business. And I can't look at another brief today. Vic can come along, if he wants to."

"Vic's got a work thing too. I'm not going to see him until tomorrow."

"Then it's just us. Girls gone wild. Well, semi-wild."

A chance to turn off her brain, grab a glass of bad art gallery wine, ogle bad art, and put this whole Lethal Black Dress story on the back burner? Quality downtime with her wackiest best friend? *Well, one of the wackiest.*

"Love to. What time?"

She arranged her rendezvous with Brooke for six-thirty and clicked off the phone. It rang again. Lacey didn't recognize the number.

"Hello?"

"My dear Lacey Smithsonian, I knew you could do it," a distinctively deep Russian voice said. "You have advanced the story. Bravo."

"Kepelov, you've been reading my stories again."

"Gregor, please. I always read the Crimes of Fashion news. Not before I met you, of course. Now, I do not miss it. If a body falls in the forest and no one is there to see it, does it wear a designer dress? Lacey Smithsonian will know. Today, look at me: Fashion plate. Okay, you cannot see me right now, but trust me. I am one very stylish guy."

Lacey closed her eyes. *Kepelov: Threat, menace, or nutcase?*

"Why are you calling me, Mr. Stylish Guy?"

"The material, of course. The poisoned fabric you have received from your clueless seamstress. I wish to purchase it from you after the story is finished."

Lacey opened her eyes and wondered where she'd put her Advil. "No, Kepelov. Gregor. You are ghoulish. That fabric is a killer. Besides, it's just scraps, and it's filed. Filed and forgotten."

"Too hot to handle? And yet I, Gregor Kepelov, have a use for it."

"Involving profit, no doubt."

"Capitalism. Is American way of life."

And death? "It's not really mine to give or sell. Definitely not. It's part of an ongoing investigation."

"If you change your mind, call me. Please. And Marie has a message for you."

"What's the message?" Maybe Marie would be free tonight and she could join Lacey and Brooke at the art gallery. *Girls Night Out.*

"She says: Stay safe. Green River is flowing. That is all."

"That's it?"

"That's it."

"And what does that mean, exactly?"

"No idea."

"Thanks, Gregor. I'm sure that will come in handy."

Lacey hung up and the phone rang again. Another number she didn't recognize. She picked it up reluctantly.

"This is Lacey Smithsonian."

"Is it true?" Eve Farrand demanded. "This is Eve Farrand."

"That's a nice preamble," Lacey said. "Hello, Eve."

"I'm talking about Courtney's dress. The lining was altered just before she died, according to your story. Is that true?"

"No, obviously not, I write all sorts of errant nonsense just to confuse people. Of course it's true, Eve. I assume you read my story online. Didn't you see the photo?"

"Yes, I saw it." Her voice deepened into phony intimacy. "Lacey, you and I just want the truth, don't we? It's very convenient, don't you think, you finding this obscure vintage store and your unnamed seamstress?"

Aren't we chummy all of a sudden, journalist to journalist!

"Convenient? It wasn't convenient at all, it took some digging. Investigative work. And my unnamed source is going to remain unnamed. But Ingrid's shop is located in Del Ray in Alexandria. Open to the public, as it says in my story."

"Sorry for how that sounded." She didn't sound sorry. "I just mean, Courtney was one of our own. We take her loss personally at Channel One News. You and I should be working this story together, don't you think? If there is a story beyond this."

Invite a broadcast reporter in on my scoop? Sure, I'll simply hand it to you on a silver platter. What nerve! Of course Eric Park had asked the same thing, but they had bonded over coffee and gossip. And she'd only promised (jokingly) to tip him off if she thought he was in danger.

Lacey didn't want to play this game with Eve. Still, she needed to be cautious about what she said, and what she might learn. Did Eve have a larger hand in events than she was revealing? Maybe she was probing to see if Lacey was holding back information. And there was the remote chance that Eve knew something more and didn't realize it. If so, maybe Lacey should play the game. A game of her own.

"The truth. You're right, Eve. That's the main objective for all of us." She checked her watch. It was almost four. "It's a little early, but why don't we meet for a drink or coffee, and discuss this?"

"I hope there's a way we can work together on this."

"Who knows?"

"I'm seeing a friend in Georgetown at five. We could meet there a little beforehand. Martin's Tavern on Wisconsin?"

"I know Martin's. If you're seeing Drake Rayburn, I'd like to meet him too."

"Oh." There was a pause. "You know about Drake?"

"I saw you together at Courtney's funeral service. I'm a reporter. I *notice* things."

"Well, don't spread it around, okay? We've been keeping a low profile."

"I see," Lacey said.

By showing up together at her funeral? And the Correspondents' Dinner? Maybe they left in separate motorcades.

"He'll be there at five."

"I'll see you at four-thirty, then."

Lacey hoped she could kill two birds with one stone.

Not literally, of course.

Lacey Smithsonian's
FASHION *BITES*

Casual Friday:
Let the Counterrevolution Begin!

Believe it or not, "Casual Friday" is not a national holiday mandated by Congress. On the contrary, it is an insidious conspiracy, perhaps instigated by Levi Strauss & Co., to convince you to wear your worst worn-out blue jeans, baggy shorts, and shabby logo T-shirts to your workplace, and to disregard common sense.

D.C. is where the seat of government *sits*. Do you really want the seat of your government flying by the seat of its baggiest old khakis? The ones that need a few more patches? And wouldn't it really make more sense to have Casual Monday instead of Casual Friday? After all, breezing into the work week is much harder than sailing out of it. I hereby propose scrapping Casual Friday in favor of Dress-Up Friday and Easy Breezy Monday!

Washington: Not Wired for Casual

The biggest problem with Casual Friday in a place like Washington, D.C., is that our Washingtonian workaholics are not wired for it. They don't have a business casual wardrobe, much less a casual wardrobe, or even a casual attitude. They don't have a sense of the middle ground between Brooks Brothers and Goodwill. They are used to going straight from work to dinner to the theatre to drinks to home without stopping to change their suits until they toddle into bed, presumably in their neatly ironed pajamas and name tags. Nothing else can explain the Washington phenomenon of seeing so many men (and women) all buttoned up with their ties still tightly knotted at 11 p.m. after the show.

When faced with the mandate of Casual Friday, *some* of these same buttoned-down professionals will, in the blink of an eye, go straight from crisply suited and vested on Thursday to a Friday morning office look that says, "Dude, I'm waxing my surfboard, why do you ask?" If your wardrobe contains *zero* choices in that vast area between *buttoned-down* and *let-it-all-hang-out*, please don't let it all hang out where the rest of us are trying to work.

Business Attire: Survival of the Best Dressed

Darwin was right. Professional dress has evolved over the millennia for a reason. Professional dress assures us that we're professionals dealing with professionals. It reassures us that our professional business is well in hand, in a professional manner. For instance, when you go to the bank on a Friday, you want to be assured that your money is as secure there as it was on Monday or Wednesday. If your teller is dressed as if he's waxing his surfboard between customers, you might worry that a decimal point will land in the wrong column while he's mentally boogying on the beach. Maybe your savings account is out casually shooting the curl (or whatever it is surfers do) with your casually surfer-themed banker. Maybe they'll run off to Tahiti together some Casual Friday and never be seen again.

Casual Friday is an insidious dressing-down that has spread this lack of regard for appropriate attire to the rest of the week. Casual Friday has turned into Casual Everyday. The trend must be stopped, or at least slowed. Many D.C. workplaces have resisted or reversed Casual Friday, and you can too. Be on the lookout for these Casual Friday eyesores, and just say, "No!"

Too Much Information: Tops that reveal the most intimate tattoos, deep cleavage, ripped abs, or hairy chests, and shorts that show off hairy legs and purple veins. What's perfectly natural on the beach is distracting in the office. If I'm too distracted by your lack of attire to pay attention to your presentation, neither one of us is getting any work done.

Sandals and Hairy Frodo Feet: All feet are not created equal. That's why shoes were created, to protect, conceal, and beautify them. If your feet resemble Frodo's or you have odd-looking toes, or *extra* toes, be merciful. No one wants to look at curled yellow toenails or peeling heel callouses, not even your own. And on others, once you've seen ugly feet, they can't be unseen. *My eyes, my eyes!*

Baggy Shorts and Saggy T-Shirts: If "man capris," baggy cargo pants cut off below the knee, and blown-out T-shirts are really appropriate in your workplace, then you're probably waxing surfboards at the beach. Lucky you! The female counterparts to this look are the too-short shorts and too-tight tops that make us all wish we were at the beach too. Wearing our shades. With our eyes closed.

Pajamas and pajama-like outfits: This look proclaims that not only did you roll out of bed late, you dashed straight to work without noticing you were still dressed for Dreamland, not Friday in Foggy Bottom. And that you don't care. Even on college campuses, going to class in your flannel jammies bottoms and surgical scrub tops looks silly. If the message you want to send with your outfit every Friday is really "I'd Rather Be Home in Bed," why not stay in bed?

So join the Casual Friday Counterrevolution this Friday, and dress up instead of dressing down. You'll be doing your part to turn this menace around. Together we can stop the conspiracy known as Casual Friday, one Friday at a time.

Chapter 29

SOMETHING WAS BOTHERING LACEY ABOUT Courtney. The woman's troubles started long before last Saturday night, before the White House Correspondents' Dinner. Was there a connection?

What if the whole news scandal wasn't just about Granville and the senator? Not completely, anyway. Had someone planted the story to bring down Courtney Wallace? Did that person understand what the fallout would be? Maybe Courtney was the objective and Thaddeus Granville and Senator Swansdown merely collateral damage. Or a bonus.

Lacey called Granville. The best information gained from an interview was usually at the very end, when she put her pen or recorder away, and the subject would say something like, "By the way, did I mention…?" Or she would ask, "What didn't I ask that you'd like me to know?" She wasn't sure whether she'd asked the man in the middle of the Swansdown scandal everything she should have. She decided to take another shot.

"This is an unexpected pleasure, Ms. Smithsonian," Granville said. "Something on your mind?"

"There is, Congressman. A loose end or two. Do you know who gave Courtney Wallace the spiked information on Senator Swansdown's campaign? I know she never revealed her original source, at least not on TV."

"My dear, I have kept myself up at night, long into the night, pondering that same question. With my brandy and my cigars. I don't know. I have more than enough enemies to go around. So does the senator. However, I thought it quite interesting that Drake Rayburn, Wallace's sometime companion, worked against us heavily and often bent the facts to his purposes, though he never quite lied. It's a useful skill. I did wonder if he fed the story to her somehow, on the theory that the phony scandal would backfire and create sympathy for his own candidate. It's a crazy idea, but Courtney Wallace wouldn't have known the difference. Or cared."

"I didn't realize she dated him that far back."

"Nobody 'dates' anymore, do they? I hear people merely hook up."

"So they tell me," she agreed. "If Courtney dated Drake at the time of the scandal, and if she got the info from him, whether he twisted it or not, it would be a major conflict of interest."

"Why, Ms. Smithsonian, are you the last living member of the press to care about conflict of interest? I thought that scruple was out of fashion in your field."

"You're making fun of me."

"Oddly, I'm not. I'm paying you a compliment."

"Thank you, Congressman. There's one more thing, and this is a big 'what if.' What if Courtney was the real target? What if her unnamed source for the phony scandal story really wanted to sink *her* career?"

"And not the senator or his wife, or myself?" He sounded shocked. *Every victim thinks it's all about them.*

"I'd say you were definitely part of the equation. But what if she was the primary target, not you?"

"My word. That's devious. Rather like handing a letter bomb to a mail carrier with the intent to blow up the carrier, not the target it's addressed to. And if the so-called target catches the blast as well, who cares?" He paused. "That would be a hell of a thing. Not unheard of, I suppose, in the dirtiest kind of politics, but Courtney Wallace was just an inconsequential little whelp. Ignorant and thoughtless. Hardly someone worth targeting for destruction."

"Perhaps not everyone would agree."

"And if that were the case, you think the Correspondents' Dinner was the last act of this little drama?" He started to chuckle. "Clever. I don't know that you are right, but you are one different kind of thinker, Ms. Smithsonian."

"So I've been told. I appreciate you letting me know about Rayburn's connection to the election, Congressman Granville."

"My pleasure. Thank you for your very interesting call. You've given me things to ponder over brandy and cigars. You may call me Thaddeus, you know, all my friends do. If you are ever in need of a job, look me up."

೧೮

Martin's Tavern was serving libations the day after Prohibition ended, and every day since. It was a legendary Georgetown hangout on the corner of Wisconsin Avenue Northwest and N Street, with a list of famous patrons that included presidents, senators, speakers of the house, and spies, among other notables. Decades of secrets, political and otherwise, had been whispered over beer and cocktails poured by four generations of the Martin family.

The Tavern's décor included Tiffany-style lamps, dark wood, and hunt country prints. It felt cozy and inviting, a place where anyone might say—or overhear—almost anything. No wonder Drake Rayburn and Eve Farrand liked it. Lacey cautioned herself not to spill too many of her own secrets here.

It was quiet when she arrived. She knew the bar would fill up later, after the workday was over and date night began, which in workaholic D.C., even on a Casual Friday, started later than in the rest of the world. And ended sooner. Eve was already there, at one of the wooden booths near a window looking out on N Street. She sipped a glass of white wine, the ubiquitous drink of Washington career women.

Lacey ordered a soda and lime at the bar, so she could chat without alcohol impairing her clarity. She slid into the booth opposite Eve, who lifted her glass in greeting.

"Hello, Eve. Good choice, I've always appreciated this place. First, how about some ground rules? Everything we say is off the record. For now, anyway."

"Works for me."

Other than the corpselike beige fingernails Eric Park had mentioned, which were unsettling, Eve Farrand was perfectly groomed and conservatively dressed. Lacey was glad that Eve chose a flattering pink lipstick, instead of beige to match her nails and complete that *undead* look. The television reporter wore a cream-colored knit skirt and matching sweater edged in black, and her top featured a knitted rose at the side of the neckline, strikingly outlined in black. The outfit complemented Eve's smooth complexion and glossy dark hair. Her deep brown almond-shaped eyes were lovely. Physically, Lacey thought she was more striking than Courtney Wallace.

"Nice story you wrote, Lacey. We're running with our version."

"I suppose you took a camera crew to Ingrid's shop after I broke the news?"

"We did. She was informative. I have to admit she didn't tell me anything she didn't tell you. But it made a nice news bite. It'll be leading the news tonight."

"That will make Ingrid happy. The publicity, I mean. She told me she was afraid she was too hard to find." *And yet I found her, and you didn't.*

"And you have the rest of the lining material? I saw the photos in *The Eye.*"

"The leftovers. Just scraps, really, but obviously a match to Courtney's dress. By now, they could be in the possession of the paper's attorney." They weren't, one scrap was in her purse and the rest were locked up in her desk, but they could be. *Maybe they should be.* Lacey thought about turning the material over to their attorney, or Mac, so she wouldn't have people hounding her for it.

Eve nodded. "It's very peculiar, isn't it? The whole thing."

"Yes. Did you know where Courtney took her alterations?"

"No. She certainly didn't tell me anything. I'd have guessed some dry cleaner with alterations on site. But you found the woman. I didn't even know the dress had been changed. Hats off to you." She sounded annoyed.

"Just working my leads. I understand you and Courtney had a screaming fight right before the Correspondents' Dinner."

"We did?" Eve scrunched her brow in concentration.

"You were overheard. You were in the ladies' room. Not criticizing, just reporting. I had words with her too, though no one screamed."

Eve shrugged. "Screaming fight is an exaggeration. Words were exchanged. It happens. Tensions run high before a broadcast, a big event like that."

"But you weren't working it, and she was. What was the argument about?"

"Who knows? I don't remember."

"Why don't I believe that? I remember most of my recent fights."

Eve set her wine glass on the table. "It was about Drake, of course. Courtney hadn't come to terms with the fact that she and Drake were over. That he's with me now. That we're, you know. Dating."

Or just hooking up? "And Courtney dated lots of men?" Lacey thought about Trujillo, who always preferred blondes, and who hooked up with Courtney.

"She was an equal opportunity dater. But apparently she was more into Drake than anyone suspected. Even Drake."

"Did you hate Courtney?"

"Hate is a strong word, Lacey. I never liked her. It was an instinctual thing. A gut feeling not to trust her. But hate? Honestly, who has the time? You couldn't have liked her much either."

"I didn't care for her series on vintage clothing," Lacey said. "It was far too close to what I'd written for *The Eye*."

"Those are the breaks. You use what you find."

"Or steal. Where television is involved."

"Where *journalism* is involved. Let's talk about your story. How did you track the dress?"

"It's a beautiful dress. It was the capper for her vintage clothing series, and the dress had to come from somewhere. I started pulling on threads. And I had a little luck."

"Better luck than Courtney. I find it odd and tragic that Courtney had a hand in her own death. It's unbelievable. She was only twenty-eight. Only a year older than me."

"Too young to die," Lacey agreed. "I wonder who gave her the Paris Green silk."

"You said it was a friend."

"That's what the seamstress told me Courtney said. But that's all she knew. The fabric was exquisite. Why wouldn't someone want to use it for themselves?" *Unless they knew*, she added silently.

"Maybe it wasn't their color." Eve lifted her wine glass, then stopped it in midair. "Maybe they knew it was dangerous?"

Lacey shrugged and let Eve think about it. "Did Courtney buy the silk from the so-called friend? It wasn't the type of fabric you could buy in a store. That dye's been off the market for at least a century. If someone gave it to her, didn't Courtney question it?"

"A friend doing her a favor with an old dress that needed help in a hurry? No way. People don't question their good luck," Eve said. "Maybe they should, but they don't. Courtney never did. She took everything as her due."

"Was the material a Trojan Horse, a present with a nasty surprise?"

"On purpose?" Eve frowned.

"I've been thinking. Courtney's bad luck began a year ago."

"You're talking about the Swansdown-Granville scandal?" Eve shuddered visibly. Clearly it was a bad memory. It reflected negatively on Channel One News.

"That story started Courtney's long, slow slide, didn't it? Losing the plum investigative slot at the station, getting pushed aside, trying to find a new beat. She had bad luck ever since."

Eve cocked her head to the side, thinking. "I could never figure out why Courtney wanted to do that vintage fashion series. It seemed a pretty desperate bid to save her job. No one else cared about it, and we always need features that aren't time-sensitive, so it was wide open for her. But after I read your stories, I figured it out. You solved some actual crimes. Big stories. Murders. And Romanov diamonds? Quite a find. Courtney would have killed to do stories like that."

"Once in a lifetime," Lacey answered. It made her feel suspicious that Eve had suddenly looked up her online dossier.

Drake Rayburn of the pretty boy looks materialized at their table with a beer in hand. Eve scooted over so he could sit next to her, giving Lacey the opportunity to study them side by side. Unlike so many couples in D.C., who seemed unevenly matched, Drake and Eve were perfect together. At least visually.

His expertly cut blond hair, worn just a tad long and combed back, gleamed with gold highlights. His features were even, his eyes blue, his smile a toothpaste commercial. Lacey decided that close up he was almost too perfect-looking. He put out his hand toward Lacey. His manicured nails were impeccable.

"I'm Drake Rayburn. Call me Drake." He gave her a dazzling grin. "Rayburn is a congressional building."

She took his hand. "Lacey Smithsonian. It's a museum."

He laughed. Drake's manner was as smooth as his wrinkle-less forehead. *Botox?* The most popular cosmetic procedure in D.C., according to a dermatologist she interviewed for an article on skin care. More and more men indulged in the chic paralyzing agent, as well as women. In Congress, as well as on K Street.

Lacey, however, included in her story a troubling study that found people who'd had Botox displayed less empathy. It was as if the Botox paralyzed not just their wrinkles, but their ability to feel for others. *Just what Washington needs, congressmen with less empathy.*

Drake smiled. His teeth were extraordinarily white, almost blue. He left Lacey unmoved. For lack of a better word, he seemed antiseptic. A picture of Vic settled in her brain. His unruly curly hair, the crinkles at the corners of this eyes when he smiled. The very thought of him, his rugged handsomeness, stirred her. He wasn't afraid to work with his hands and get them dirty, if necessary. He would never be a Botox poster boy.

Drake jumped right to the chase. "You're talking about

Courtney? I have to admit, it makes me uncomfortable, now that she's not here anymore."

"Have you seen my story?"

"Good piece. Eve told me about it."

Because heaven knows you wouldn't have read it on your own, Lacey thought.

"That bizarre dress," Drake went on. "You found out a lot. But I thought that story was over. An accident is an accident, right? As wild as it was."

"Lacey thinks it's possible her death was not an accident," Eve said.

Drake looked alarmed. "Not an accident? You're not saying someone was after her?"

"I'm just looking at what happened," Lacey said. "Courtney had a bumpy year. Someone planted poisoned information that damaged her career. Journalistic hazard. People try and use us all the time. But what if someone also engineered the poisoned fabric? Maybe the same someone."

"Don't look at me. I don't know anything about fabrics and dresses." Rayburn laughed nervously and sloshed his beer.

"Someone was playing dirty tricks last year," Lacey said. "And it wasn't Granville."

"Just because it couldn't be proven, doesn't mean Granville wasn't up to his usual nasty tricks. He's always guilty of something. Only not this time. Apparently not, I mean," Drake finished awkwardly.

For coming on so smooth, Lacey thought, *this guy sure rattles easily.*

"Drake has a point," Eve said. "And the senator did win."

"Just barely. Not to mention the collateral damage."

Drake took a deep breath and patted Eve's hand. "If you ask me, Granville came out of it pretty sweet. He's making a lot of money with all his media-bashing lectures. He goes on TV to play the celebrity victim on talk shows. Besides, Courtney and I weren't really going out then. I mean, we'd gone out a few times. We didn't make it exclusive until later and that didn't last long."

"You were dating when the scandal broke."

"Off and on." He swallowed some beer. "Not exactly dating. You know."

"Hooking up?" she asked. Drake nodded, looking away.

Granville was right, Lacey thought. "Were you her source for that story? Knowing it would fall apart and discredit her?"

"No! Besides, what a risky maneuver that would have been! You'd have to be out of your mind to try that. Anyway, I mean, Courtney was always asking questions. She was a newshound. But she didn't know what 'off the record' meant, and she was careless. I assume she overheard some crazy rumor and just ran with it." He looked as panicky as anyone could with a forehead full of paralyzing Botox.

Drake echoed what Tony told her: Courtney reported whatever she heard, without confirmation. Motive for murder?

"Maybe someone didn't appreciate her lack of discretion."

"What are you getting at, Lacey?" Eve demanded. "Someone planned all of it, all the way back? And if Courtney was a target for being on the investigative team, then I could be a target now too?" She looked conflicted, horrified at the thought of being in someone's crosshairs, but intrigued by the attention.

"Who knows? I'd watch my back if I were you, Eve. You have to look at all the possibilities to get to the heart of the story." Lacey thought she'd given them something to think about, but nothing they shouldn't have thought about already. "I have to run. Thanks for the chat."

What did I get here? Except gossip about Drake Rayburn's unnaturally smooth forehead, and the impression that he might not be the brightest graduate of lobbying school. He certainly acted like a man with things to hide, but then he was a Washington political operative, so that came with the territory. If he was the one who planted the fateful scandal story, knowing it would be discredited, his target was probably Swansdown or Granville, not Courtney. After all, he was working for Swansdown's opponent. Or was damaging Courtney along the way just a twofer?

Eve, on the other hand, was very bright, and very careful. And a little afraid. Of what? That Lacey would scoop her on the story? Or find out something more damaging? Or was she dogging Lacey's steps and worried Lacey would find out?

"Hey, one last question," Lacey asked as she stood to go. "Did you two take a trip up to Baltimore after Courtney's funeral service? To a little vintage store?"

"No! No, we didn't. Not us." Drake and Eve shared a guilty look.

Lacey walked to the door of the tavern without a backward glance.

Jealousy was always epidemic in Washington, D.C. Lacey thought of Peter Johnson, trying to sabotage her story out of pure jealousy, and her stomach turned. It might not be exactly the same situation, but Lacey and Courtney might have had something in common.

Among its aliases, jealousy is called the Green-Eyed Monster. Was the Green-Eyed Monster that hunted Courtney that particular shade known as Paris Green?

Chapter 30

THE SOMERSET ART GALLERY WAS on lower King Street in Old Town Alexandria, just blocks from the river. Although it looked small from the street, the space was deceptively large. Located in a historic building with wide plank floors and handsome molding, the rooms rambled back to the alley and into the storefront space next door. For this warm spring evening, the colonial-era fireplace focal point was filled with an extravagant bouquet of flowers.

Visiting an art gallery always made Lacey feel arty, and her chandelier earrings fit her mood. She changed into comfortable black slacks, a black silk top, and sandals, and because it was a little chilly, she added the beautiful vintage gold jacket. She walked the mile to the gallery in the heart of Old Town. Brooke would be happy to give her a ride home after dark. The young barrister was no doubt breaking speed limits on the George Washington Parkway, but Lacey still beat her to the gallery.

The exhibit featured the work of three artists, one established, one new to the scene, and one who had almost disappeared from memory, all local to Northern Virginia. Lacey wasn't familiar with any of them. One painted childlike landscapes that played with perspective, featuring tall skinny trees and whimsical creatures. Another's work was aggressively abstract, and the third had made her reputation as a 'modern Impressionist,' at least according to the notes next to the paintings.

A table near the entrance held refreshments, the ubiquitous art gallery wine, cheese, and crackers. Lacey picked up a plastic glass of white wine that was not terrible, but not good either. She briefly wondered why so many receptions offered mediocre chardonnay. *Perhaps because it's cheap enough to give away.* On the other hand, the cheese was excellent. *Aha*, she noted from a small sponsorship sign, *the Cheesetique scores again.*

Bright lights drew her attention to the rear of the gallery, and Lacey followed the lights. The gallery director was being interviewed on camera by two more of her favorite persons of interest. Zanna Nelson might not have what it took to be a star broadcaster, but she was wielding the microphone and Eric Park was her cameraman.

I can't seem to get away from these people. Lacey watched until they wrapped it up. Who was following whom? Were they the mystery "copycats" who followed her to Baltimore? But Eric Park would have mentioned that to her, wouldn't he? Or was it Nelson with some other partner? Or Eve and Drake? They'd all look a little "boring" to Vintage Veronica at Killer Stash.

Lacey waved to Eric when their few seconds of on-camera time were over and the bright video lights were turned off. His hands were full of equipment, but he acknowledged her with a smile and a nod. Zanna Nelson handed Eric her mike and stopped short when she saw Lacey.

"Hey there, Smithsonian. We seem to be crossing paths these days. That's quite a jacket. Looks old."

"Vintage is the term. What's the story here tonight?"

"Just another gallery opening. Feature for tomorrow morning's Wake Up Washington," Eric said. "You've been busy with that dress story. White lining? Green lining? I thought you were going to tip me off."

"I said I'd tip you off if you were in danger," Lacey countered with a smile. "Wear any green dresses lately?"

"What have you two been up to?" Zanna asked, looking from one to the other.

"We had coffee yesterday," Eric said, laughing. "Waiting for Eve to get manicured. Beige, you know."

"Interestingly enough," Lacey said, "this jacket came from the collection of the same woman who first owned the Madame X dress."

"No way!" Eric's eyes opened wide.

"So is that what you call a fashion clue on your beat?" Zanna reached toward the jacket, but pulled her hand back. "Better be careful this one hasn't been dyed with poison too." She checked her watch. "Gotta run. We have to get back to the station. Come on, Eric."

"Lacey, we'll talk," Eric yelled over his shoulder on their way out the door. He sped up to match Nelson's trot.

"Lacey!" Brooke rushed in through the front doors moments after they rushed out, looking flushed and lawyerly in her navy pinstriped suit, relieved by a yellow blouse and matching pocket hanky. "Sorry I'm late. The Parkway was a parking lot."

"You're not, really. I just got here. I walked along the river. First relaxing moment all day."

"Hey, great jacket. I sense the sexy vibes of your latest vintage purchase."

"Let me tell you about it." Lacey showed it off for Brooke and held forth on the stitching, the beading, and the versatility of her new-yet-old gabardine jacket.

Brooke and Lacey had been fast friends ever since Lacey had arrived in D.C. four years before. At the time, Brooke seemed quirky but almost normal, for a conspiracy-obsessed Washington lawyer. What's a little conspiracy between friends? However, since falling for Damon Newhouse, Brooke, who once held whatever Lacey told her in confidence, was turning into Damon's eyes and ears.

"Any *new* news?" Brooke asked.

"Depends on what you mean by news. Everything I know is in today's paper."

Lacey wasn't about to share with Brooke her new idea that Courtney may have been targeted by persons unknown long before the White House Correspondents' Dinner. She'd hit Eve and Drake with it, to gauge their reactions. But she didn't want to see Damon use it on DeadFed before she had a chance to explore her theory.

"Uh huh. Not even a scrap of gossip?"

"After this week, my brain is empty. What's up with you? Are you all right?"

"I don't know. I'm feeling bored, Lacey."

"With Damon, or the lack of a good new conspiracy to pursue? Tired of time travel? Bored with Bigfoot? "

"You can joke. I'm never bored with Damon. We're on the same frequency, somehow. I guess I just need a change of pace. A vacation."

"Is that why you suggested the art show?" Lacey asked. "A mini vacation for the evening?"

"More or less. A client sent me a postcard for the exhibit. She's a collector, so it won't hurt for me to look prepped, knowledgeable. When I realized the Somerset Gallery was right here in Old Town, I thought of you. And you and I haven't gotten together recently. I miss you."

"Me too. I'm glad you suggested it. This is such a pretty place," Lacey said. "Do you know any of the artists?"

"Nope. I don't get modern art anyway. Or post-modern art. No use pretending. I know what I like when I see it. I like paintings to look like something." They stopped to contemplate an abstract canvas, a spray of crimson on a pavement-gray background. "I'd rather not look at something that resembles blood spatter, unless it *is* blood spatter. And then only if it proves my client didn't do it. If I had such a client."

"I'm with you. Who needs pointless blood spatter? You might as well watch TV and destroy your attention span. But I do like those." Lacey strolled over to a dreamy landscape, one of the Impressionist paintings. "Look at the colors. No blood spatter in this."

"I can get behind this one," Brooke agreed. "It reminds me of someplace. But I have to stand back a bit. And squint my eyes. Oh, very nice."

Lacey was drawn to the landscape. There was a river in the painting, a ribbon of bright emerald green. Marie Largesse's cryptic warnings about a green river, delivered via Kepelov, echoed in her head. But how could a random painting fit the jigsaw puzzle of a deadly dress? *It's just the color*, she told herself.

There were those who claimed that no one, with all of the twenty-first century's technology at their fingertips, had managed to find an exact match for the legendary emerald hue of Paris Green. Yet the brilliant greens of this landscape came close. They evoked the shimmering green of the lining of the Madame X dress.

"What does the program say about the artist?" Lacey asked.

Brooke read from her brochure. "Here it is. 'The artist, Jillian Hopewell, followed in the footsteps of the great Impressionists. Inspired particularly by Cezanne, she worked diligently in her relatively short life to approximate the master's color palette and his love of the color green.' It *is* very green."

"Is that it? That's all?"

"Just that the artist died almost three decades ago, in her forties, and lived and worked in Great Falls, Virginia. There are five pieces of hers here. You like it?"

"I do. Very much."

"This one costs two thousand dollars," Brooke said. "Shall I have them wrap it to go?"

"I believe I can admire it from afar."

Lacey picked up a brochure and a postcard for herself. Brooke returned to the refreshment table for some cheese. She took a sip from her plastic glass of chardonnay and blinked. "Oh my."

"That's what I thought," Lacey said.

"I don't know where they get that stuff. But they serve it everywhere." She put the glass on the cleanup tray and glanced back at the painting that Lacey admired. "You know, that color reminds me of Courtney's dress."

"Yes, it does. A bit."

They examined Jillian Hopewell's other paintings. All landscapes, some larger and some smaller. All featured heavy doses of green.

"I'm curious, Lacey. Where did you hear about Paris Green in the first place? I never heard of it before your story in *The Eye*, and I read all sorts of bizarre stuff."

Lacey shrugged. "College. I took a class on costume history from the theatre department. I took it as a lark, as an antidote to all those dreary math and science requirements freshman year. And I loved it. It was a great class."

Lacey explained to Brooke that she'd found the course fascinating, every minute of it, from sumptuary laws which forbade certain clothing to various classes and sexes, to the strange career of Paris Green, also known as copper acetoarsenite. Bits and pieces of clothing and costume lore stayed with her, and after Broadway Lamont confirmed for her that Courtney's dress lining was dyed with the toxic pigment, Lacey had done a little more research.

Paris Green was so called, supposedly, because it had been used to kill rats in Paris sewers, but it was also lethal to everything from mosquitos to human beings. Throughout the nineteenth century it was found in fabric dyes, artist's pigments, wallpaper, fireworks, and even candy wrappers, and in pesticides well into the twentieth century. But Paris Green was too dangerous. It had been off the market in any form for decades.

However, if a landscape painter like this Jillian Hopewell got her hands on the basic ingredients, perhaps she could have mixed it herself. *After all, where there's a will, there's a way.* Lacey had watched a video on YouTube demonstrating how to make Paris Green and other highly toxic pigments. *Maybe not the most dangerous thing on YouTube,* she decided, *but it'll do.*

Lacey looked again at the Impressionist painting of a river in the woods in springtime. It wasn't set in Cezanne's world, but closer to home. When she stepped further away, spots of blue became flowers, almost a carpet of them. It reminded Lacey of Riverbend Park, on the Potomac River upstream from D.C., which erupted in the spring in masses of blue flowers: Virginia bluebells. The bluebells would be thick in the park right about now. Maybe she could convince Vic to see them with her.

"I suppose you'll be looking at everything through green lenses now until you figure it out," Brooke said. Her inner prosecutor was popping out. "Isn't that right?"

Lacey smiled. "I think I know where this landscape was painted. That's all."

Riverbend Park lay above Great Falls on the Virginia side of the Potomac. And while sunny weather on a spring weekend would bring the crowds out to Great Falls, Riverbend was much less well-known, a little more remote, a little more secluded.

The last of the sunlight was sifting through the front windows of the gallery. Lacey could probably make the trip to Riverbend Park tomorrow, she realized. Her weekend was free of *The Eye* and Vic promised he was all hers Saturday and Sunday. A picnic among the bluebells might not solve the mystery of where the artist's pigment came from, but perhaps she could see that familiar landscape from the artist's perspective. And forget about The Dress for a while. After all, even if the dress was somehow deliberately engineered to kill Courtney, the motive seemed obviously personal. There was no reason to suspect someone was systematically targeting Channel One broadcasters, or anyone else, no matter what Eve and Eric might worry.

"Yoo-hoo. Calling Planet Lacey. So where is it?" Brooke interrupted her reverie.

"Riverbend Park, up above Great Falls."

"You can tell me all about it over dinner. How about that Thai restaurant by the waterfront with the great mojitos?"

"The one overlooking the river? I love that place."

"Let's go. I have to get the taste of this cheap wine out of my mouth."

಄

Later that evening, back in her apartment, Lacey searched the Internet for Jillian Hopewell. Information on her was scant. There was a very brief biography on Wikipedia, consisting mostly of the information that was printed on the postcard. The artist was born in Virginia, traveled the world, and returned to her roots before she started painting. There was nothing about her background. Her Impressionist paintings featured locations in Virginia, where she made her home, and the best known were her "Riverbend Series of landscapes." She was never famous, but she was remembered among Virginia artists and collectors and had carved out a small, satisfying career. Or at least that's the way it sounded.

One thing that stood out was Jillian Hopewell's admiration for Cezanne, who often used Paris Green in his art. Lacey pulled that thread on the Internet and found that Cezanne's chronic ill health was attributed by some to the toxic pigment. Several days before he died, he had been working outside for hours in a downpour. He collapsed and never recovered. His death was attributed to pneumonia. But Lacey wondered if there was another contributing factor.

Simple pneumonia—or Paris Green?

Chapter 31

IT WAS LATE SATURDAY MORNING when Lacey stopped at her favorite deli in Old Town and packed a picnic lunch into the car: a variety of sandwiches, ham and brie, roast beef, mozzarella and tomato, chicken salad, potato salad, pickles. She added chips and apples and sodas, and a couple of brownies for dessert. She loaded it all into her little BMW and drove to Vic's townhouse. She surprised him.

"You want me to see the bluebells? I think I already saw one once." Vic greeted her at the door, yawning, barefoot, and shirtless, in nothing but a pair of old jeans that fit in all the right places. He was sleepy from babysitting his company's computers half the night. His dark hair still damp from the shower, it curled around his neck and one dark curl fell over his forehead.

She almost lost her desire for a romp in the woods. There might be other romps to be had. She kissed him, backing him up to the door.

"Late night?" she asked.

"Yeah. System crash."

"What about *my* system? I had no one to crash with. Besides, you're not the tech guy."

He rubbed his eyes. "No, but we geniuses in the security business have to guard against even the hint of someone planting a bug in the computer. Or spyware, or whatever. So even though I trust these guys, I had to hang out with them till the cows came home. And you? Have a good time with Brooke last night? Plotting something? Zombie takeover of the world?"

"Been there, done that. But I kept thinking about you. So I packed this great picnic. You and me?"

"And the mosquitos?"

"Lounging on a plaid flannel blanket under the trees. And bug repellent."

"Dining in the wilderness. I get it. The bluebells are calling you."

"Come with me, Vic, honey. Just the two of us."

"Promise?"

She kissed him. "Cross my heart."

"When you put it that way... I guess I'm coming along. How's the car?"

"Full of goodies. And I'm driving."

It was a pretty drive up the river and through the woods, and past the ever-proliferating suburban mansions. The week's hard rains had cleared away the thick humidity of early summer, and the scent of the fresh-washed woods was delicious. She and Vic emptied the trunk at the tiny parking lot of Riverbend Park, with the Potomac River gleaming in the sun just a few yards away. He lugged the cooler.

"What did you pack in here? Gold bullion?"

"Just the food. And drinks. It's full of ice."

"For the record, ice is heavy."

Lacey picked up the blanket and tote bag with plastic glasses, plates, and silverware. They marched to the picnic grounds. She was just happy he was here with her, and it was a beautiful day.

The Potomac at Riverbend was deceptively flat and serene, just a mile above where it tumbled over the wicked rocks at Great Falls. Down by the river, the delicate blossoms of the Virginia bluebells were small, but the plants grew thick and they wound through the woods, creating rivers of larkspur blue among spring-green leaves. There would be time for a picnic and a walk around the park, up the river and over the hills, past the little pond in the woods.

They opted against setting up on the lawn, which was still soggy from the week's rains. Lacey spread her flannel blanket from the trunk of her little BMW over a picnic table. She sat on the bench and watched her fiancé. Her heart caught when he grinned at her. She set the table and laid out the feast.

"Good stuff. Why, Lacey, are you trying to seduce me?"

"I don't have to try, big fella."

"You remembered the potato salad?"

"And potato chips, just in case."

"A woman after my heart."

"Sorry, no fries. Just so you know, Vic darling, it is not a federal law that you must have some sort of fried potato with every sandwich."

"Says you. I've got Irish in my blood, I need my spuds. This looks wonderful. What's the saying about the way to a man's heart? Through his stomach?"

"Let's just keep the organs in their proper places." Lacey was glad the park seemed so quiet and uncrowded. She wanted Vic to herself.

"You brought enough for an army."

"I wasn't sure what you wanted. I can always take the leftovers to work. Feed them to Felicity, for a change."

She opened an herbal tea and poured it into a plastic goblet. Vic gazed into the green distance behind her.

"By the way, why are we here?" he said. "Still on the Madame X beat?"

"Off the beat today. I just want to let my mind wander. And my feet."

"Good. Not that I don't love hearing about patterns and fabrics and killer dye." He picked up half a roast beef sandwich. "Tasty. You make good deli, darling."

"I'm the best." She selected a ham and brie sandwich. "Actually, I need inspiration. I need the bluebells. I need to think. If you close your eyes just a bit, you can imagine this whole scene as a painting."

"That painting is getting crowded. We've got company." He stared at something beyond her shoulder.

He's kidding. She frowned, but didn't look. "Don't tease me."

"I wish." Now Vic was frowning.

"Inspiration! Always a good idea." The speaker was Russian. He was directly behind her.

"Kepelov?" Lacey spun around to see Gregor Kepelov in a polo shirt, plaid shorts, and a pair of running shoes. Perched incongruously on his large round head and short cropped hair was a cowboy hat.

"At your service, Smithsonian. Donovan, good to see you."

Just behind him was Marie Largesse. In this setting, the woods, the flowers and the river, Marie looked like a fugitive from a Russian fairy tale. Or at least what Lacey assumed to be a Russian fairy tale. Sweet-faced Marie was lush and zaftig, and her long black hair, curlier than ever, fanned out as if electrified by the river's current. Her eyes were large and dark and her lips red. She wore a dress of blues and purples and, in case it was chilly, she carried over her shoulder her prized possession, a hand-embroidered Russian shawl given to her by her fiancé. It had been handed down through the Kepelov family and was said to be haunted. Marie was not Russian, she was part Cajun and hailed from New Orleans, but she said she could feel the lives of the Kepelov women stitched into it.

What are they doing here?

"Now, cher, don't get mad at me," Marie said. "I told Gregor you'd be here. Crashing your party was my idea."

"And you knew—how?" Vic asked.

Marie tapped the side of her head and smiled.

"Right. Psychic," Lacey said. "Then you probably knew this was supposed to be a romantic afternoon for us. Not that you're not welcome. You want a sandwich?"

"Some things are more important than romance," Kepelov said. "Though I love romance, life is more important. We are here to protect you. Not that Victor Donovan is not a great protector. Marie convinced me to come."

"Thanks a lot, Marie," Lacey said. Marie laughed and sat next to her on the bench. The newcomers eyed the spread.

"Potato salad?" Kepelov asked. "What kind?"

"Help yourselves," Vic said, amused. "Lacey brought enough for everybody. She must be psychic too."

"Y'all didn't know why you brought all this, did you?" Marie said. "Now you know."

No brown-bagging it this week, Lacey thought.

Kepelov selected a chicken salad sandwich and made himself at home. "It is good to be with friends. You don't say it on the outside, Lacey Smithsonian, but you know we are good friends. Our lives are entwined. You, me, Marie, Vic, all of us. Stella too."

"Kepelov, you're beginning to sound just like Marie," she responded. "And you're right, I don't really say it on the outside. Or the inside."

"Okay. We're all friends. We knew that already," Vic added. "But can we get to the point? What's this about protecting Lacey?"

"Marie had another vision," Kepelov said matter-of-factly, munching one of their sandwiches.

"I'm so sorry, Marie. Did you faint?" Lacey asked. She felt Vic beside her tense ever so slightly.

"No, no, not this time," Marie said. "I am learning from Olga and Gregor how to stay with the vision but keep my distance, and not be so afraid that I lose consciousness."

"Olga scares her more than the spirit world," Kepelov said.

"Gregor, cher, Olga scares everyone, even you. And, Lacey, I became very dizzy and frightened for you. You were caught in a green river."

"I'm sorry, Marie. I know you mean well, it's just—" Lacey gazed at the bluebells. "How could anything seem threatening on a day like this?"

"Yes, I know, a perfect afternoon for a stroll with the one you love. I felt compelled to warn you."

A phone call wouldn't do? Lacey wondered.

"I thought in person was best," Marie said, as if answering the unasked question.

"Okay. What was the vision?"

"Paris Green. You were being washed away down the river. In a river of that color green."

They all looked at the broad, quiet river. There was a thick layer of floating pollen on the calm places. It created a bright green haze on the water, like one of the shades in Jillian Hopewell's Riverbend paintings. Lacey's spine contracted with chills. She willed them to go away. The chills laughed at her and stayed. The river up here looked placid enough, but it was deceptive. The current swept relentlessly downstream toward the dangerous rocks of Great Falls.

"Tell me more about the vision, Marie," Lacey said. "Please."

"Well, let me recollect." Marie closed her eyes and took a deep breath. "You were walking in this park. Among the trees. Among the bluebells. And a lovely but poisonous cloud of emerald green liquid—you know, if clouds could be liquid—came upon you violently, and pushed you. You fell and skidded down the hillside into the water. Now, when I say a cloud, I think that image represents something else. Could be a person, could be—I don't know. Something else."

That's the problem with Marie's psychic visions, Lacey thought, *they're always a visual puzzle.* They could mean anything. Or nothing at all.

Vic drew Lacey close. "Where was I?"

"You were following her, to your own doom, sucked down into that place from which no one returns. I started to choke, you see. I couldn't breathe because you couldn't breathe. I pulled out of it. So that was all I saw. But I didn't faint."

Lacey reached out and squeezed Marie's hand. "Thank you."

On the one hand, Marie's prophesies always seemed crazy, except when they were weather predictions. On the other hand—her crazy visions did sometimes come true.

Kepelov cleared his throat. "You told Victor you were thinking." His cool blue stare was unsettling. "Thinking about what? The dress?"

"I came to be with Vic. I'm a little tired of that dress. And who knows, the medical examiner's office will probably have it destroyed, eventually."

"But you have some of the lining material. And not to worry about the dress. I am in negotiations."

"What negotiations?"

"With family of dead woman. Museum I know is very interested in the dress. Middleman position is tricky, but often pays handsomely."

"You approached Courtney's family to buy the dress she died in?" Lacey was appalled. "I can't believe the M.E.'s office would actually let it go. It's dangerous! And you want to buy it from them? How could you?"

"This is a problem? The family do not want the dress. Understandable. But they have a right to demand it. If they have a good lawyer, and a good reason, and now they do. Yes, Mrs. Wallace said many things about the dress. She hated it, it is evil, it should be destroyed. And I, Kepelov, pointed out that Courtney Wallace would not want her legacy to disappear after death. The dress is part of her legacy. A lesson, a warning. Her mother started to listen. She changed her mind. She is working with me."

"You have some Russian nerve there, Kepelov," Vic said with a smile.

"True. I am not shy. Also I can be charming," Kepelov gave an elaborate shrug. "Courtney Wallace—her death was tragic. But! She died young and beautiful and well-dressed and doing what she loved. Approximately. Her Madame X dress, if displayed appropriately in proper setting, can tell that story. What better legacy for Ms. Courtney Wallace? Better she should be forgotten?"

"Lacey," Marie broke in, "her spirit wants to live on in memory, and she wants the truth to be found. She has no problem with thousands of people at a museum seeing that dress and learning about her death. She was in the public eye in life, after all. She doesn't want to leave it."

Very convenient excuse.

"Also consider. At time like this," Kepelov continued, "her family needs money. Her insurance policy from her work? Won't last forever."

"You know this how?" Lacey asked.

"General knowledge."

"You're a ghoul, Kepelov."

"Gregor, remember?" He took no offense. "Not a ghoul. A middleman who can make some good come out of a bad end for all concerned. Her story is a cautionary tale for the world: Don't wear poison dress. Don't get it wet. And perhaps: Watch the waiter when you have enemies."

Lacey snorted. "Who's the buyer?"

"You will be happy to hear. Famous American museum." He beamed at them. "I resisted urge to sell to Russian museum, run by ex-KGB acquaintance. Old friend, but the trust is gone."

"Aha! The Crime and Punishment Museum?" Lacey prodded.

"Cannot confirm or deny until it is done deal, as they say. Are you going to finish that potato salad?" Vic handed it over. "Tell us why we are here, Lacey Smithsonian."

"Can't I be here just because it's beautiful and the weather is perfect for a quiet, romantic evening?"

"Of course, if you were anyone but Lacey Smithsonian. When your EFP kicks in, it is all about the hunt. You will not rest until you solve the mystery of the death of Courtney Wallace."

"Leave my EFP out of it."

"Everyone knows about your EFP," Marie said. "You have uncommon intuition when it comes to clothes. It's a gift, cher, and believe me, I know about gifts, even when they are unwelcome."

"Theories are theories, but everything about the woman's death points to an accident," Vic said. "An unusual accident, I give you that."

"Pity. Dress of deceased will be more valuable if murder is involved."

"Now, Gregor, cher," Marie began. "Sometimes we try not to say everything we think."

"Is true!" he protested.

Lacey lost her appetite. She wrapped the rest of her sandwich and put it away in the cooler.

"You all enjoy. I'm going for a walk in the woods."

Chapter 32

"HOLD ON!" VIC THREW HIS unfinished lunch in the cooler. "I'm coming with you."

"We're coming too," Marie said. "That's why we're here."

"So glad you could join us." There was just a hint of sarcasm in Lacey's tone.

"We are probably saving your ass. Be grateful," Kepelov said.

"Prove it, and I will be."

"Now, children, don't squabble," Marie scolded. "It's still a lovely day."

After handing out the remaining brownies for the walk, Vic packed up the rest of the food in Lacey's tote and locked it the trunk of her BMW. She put an extra bottle of water in her backpack. They found the sandy hiking path at the edge of the woods and headed up the river. Vic and Lacey led the way, with Marie and Gregor a few paces behind them. The Virginia bluebells became lusher and thicker the farther they went. The sun dipped behind a high hill to the west, creating deep green shadows among the leaves. A rustle in the forest startled Lacey and she stopped.

"Turkey buzzard," Vic said, scanning the woods.

Lacey pulled the postcard of the Jillian Hopewell painting from her pocket and showed it to him. "I really came to see this, Vic. Nothing spooky at all. The exact spot where this was painted must be at a bend where the river cuts in. Not far from the trail to Carper's Pond, I think."

"Is that the little pond up the hill?" Vic pulled out his trail map from the visitors' center. "Yes, but the river cuts new bends and landmarks every year. This exact spot might be hard to find."

Marie took the postcard and studied it. "The artist who painted this—her light is almost gone. Look, she painted with the same green color you wrote about. You're right, Lacey. There is a connection to the dress."

"I knew it!" Kepelov said.

"How could there be?" Lacey said. "Tell me, Marie, what is the connection?"

"Oh my. I don't know. That is your journey to find."

Typical. Lacey thought Marie was slightly overplaying the

drama of the moment.

"All that from a postcard?" Vic asked. "And what do you mean, her light is going?"

"Almost ready to cross over," Marie said. "She's cutting the tether to this earth."

"You mean when she painted this?" Lacey asked. "She died years ago."

"Marie is beautiful to watch, is she not?" Kepelov said with admiration. "Together we learn more. There is a connection from the dead woman's dress to dead artist's painting? Let us find out."

Lacey didn't even know what she expected to see. Her new companions muddled her thoughts. She turned toward the Potomac, just a few feet to their right. The path's edge hugged a rise of rocks over the water. Beyond the rise, the cut bank fell steeply several yards to the water's edge. The bluebells, the trees, the river, it was all breathtaking.

She had no sense of danger until a large rock hit her in the right shoulder and threw her off balance. She fell forward and skidded down the embankment through the mud. Marie screamed. Vic shouted her name and slid down after her. He grabbed hold of her by one outstretched leg and slowed her skid. She caught herself on a big rock, just before she would have tumbled into the river. She clung there, trembling, inches from the water.

"Up there, Kepelov," Vic shouted up from the water's edge. "Find whoever threw that rock!" Kepelov looked at Marie.

"You go, Gregor," Marie said. "I'll stay right here with Lacey."

"Lacey, are you okay?" Vic held her close, both of them covered with mud and leaves. "Where are you hurt?"

"Just find the creep. Go. Seriously, I'm fine!" Lacey was shaken and scraped, but nothing felt broken. There was a crashing sound above them as Kepelov took off running through the trees. Vic nodded and scrambled up the bank to follow the big Russian. Marie gave her a hand back up to the path.

Her legs were scratched and cut from her slide over rocks, mud, and downed tree limbs. Lacey felt a stinging in her shoulder and warm liquid dripping down her back. She reached around to touch the place where the rock had caught her. When she pulled them back she saw blood on her fingers. Her sweater was torn and her skin was broken. Her very first thought was not of the pain or the blood or the injury.

You bastard! You ruined my sweater! She was very glad Marie was there. She was also glad she was wearing a generic black sweater top, and relieved she hadn't chosen a vintage sweater or blouse. She had more black sweaters. It was one of her style rules: *You can't have too many black sweaters.*

"You all right, Lacey?" Marie brought her back to the present.

"I'm bleeding a little," she commented unnecessarily. She turned around and let Marie pull off her backpack and inspect the wound.

"Not too bad. It's a shallow cut. Just good pure blood, cleaning out the wound. See how close you were to the edge?" Marie's expression was ever-so-slightly smug. "You could have toppled into the water. Vic surely would have gone in after you. And you might both have been swept away. Drowning in the green river."

"I get the picture. Thanks, I feel so much better now. I'm fine, Marie."

Lacey reached into her pack for the water bottle. She poured it over her shoulder to cleanse the wound and thought how smart it would be to have a first-aid kit. *And maybe a bulletproof sweater.* She folded her scarf into a triangle and knotted it around her shoulder to cover the tear in the sweater and the seeping blood.

They perched on a large rock by the sandy path, exhausted. They sat in silence. They could hear nothing from the woods but the sound of birds and rushing water. No one came up or down the path, and there was no trace of Kepelov or Vic, or even of the direction they'd gone. Marie might have been communing with the spirit world. Lacey just tried to order her thoughts.

"Thank you, Marie, for coming to my rescue. I appreciate it, even when I don't say so."

"I know, cher. I know. You'd do the same for me."

They sat silently again. Lacey contemplated how a perfect day could spin so out of control, yet remain so beautiful. There was a fresh rustling in the trees above them on the wooded hillside. Lacey turned her head at the sound. It was Vic, followed by Kepelov.

"They got away clean, whoever it was." Vic was disgusted. "We talked to a family in the parking lot. No one saw anything useful."

"Is always the case," Kepelov said. "Even when they do see something, nobody sees nothing."

"I have their names and a phone number, I'll follow up with them. They did get a glimpse of a car tearing out of the lot. Gray, no one saw the plates."

"Typical anonymous gray car, like bat out of Hell," Kepelov grumbled. Then he smiled slowly, which always had a disquieting effect on Lacey. "Good work, Smithsonian."

"What on earth could you possibly mean by that?" Lacey felt stupid for being hit by a rock.

"Congratulations. You, and our mysterious rock thrower, have just proved that death of Courtney Wallace was no accident. Why else try and put you into the river? You are getting too close. Killer is becoming nervous. Making mistakes. Classic. Your theory is proven. Well done!"

"You don't have to sound so happy about Courtney's death," Lacey said.

"Don't misunderstand. I am never happy about death," Kepelov said. "Never. But that Lethal Black Dress you wrote about? Price just went way up."

Chapter 33

"**O**UCH! THAT HURTS!"

"You could use some stitches." Vic was cleansing her wound as gently as he could, but it still stung. He closed the tear with wound closure strips.

"So could my poor sweater. I'll be fine." She was too tired to even think of going to an emergency room. The wound stopped bleeding, eventually, and it only started hurting again when Vic cleaned it. The cuts and scrapes on her legs and hands were all superficial, though they stung like fire when Vic cleaned the mud from them.

They were at Vic's place. Lacey studied the room. It was comfortable, but very masculine and decorated with way too much brown. The sofa was brown leather, the walls were taupe. She wondered how wedded he was to that particular shade of mud. *Mud! Mud is the last thing I want to think about today.*

"You're nearly done." He kissed her neck and applied an antibiotic cream and a cotton pad, and taped over it. "There."

"Why did you take the rock?" she asked him. "You can't get prints off it. Probably not even DNA, right?"

"Call it a sentimental gesture. It has your blood on it. Also it's a weapon, and I witnessed the assault. Chain of custody. Just in case."

Vic bagged the rock when they left the park, and they reported the incident to the park police at the visitors' center, who were sympathetic but unimpressed. The rangers said it was probably just some kids, they probably didn't mean to hit her, and they took off, running scared. She found their explanation hard to swallow.

"I just wanted the two of us to have some time alone today. A romantic little picnic." She leaned back on the sofa.

"There will be other picnics, other rendezvous. And who says this isn't romantic? Me, dressing your shoulder wound. Sharing bodily fluids. That's pretty intimate."

"Good to know, and thank you." She switched positions, careful to avoid the sore shoulder. "I love you, Vic. And it's eye-opening to know that someone hates me."

"Hates you, or else is afraid of you. Kepelov is right."

"Really? Kepelov?"

"Kepelov didn't survive in the KGB by being stupid. He just looks that way. We can conclude that there is more to Courtney's death than mere accident."

"Someone thinks I know more than I do? Darn, I wish I knew what that was."

"We have to find out what it is, and why they are so afraid of what you're going to find out. Then we'll find out who it is. And stop them in their tracks."

"We do? We will?" This was a switch. Vic usually wanted her to back off from any investigation that put her in danger.

"Don't think this will stop at rock throwing. And you won't stop doing what you do, either. So I hold my lecture and we go forward, together, not back."

"You're going to stick with me, then?"

"Like glue." He nestled in closer.

"I'm safe here tonight?"

"Very safe. Except from me."

She laughed and kissed his neck. She snuggled into his chest. An image of Peter Johnson surfaced in her thoughts. Had he really pitched on the softball team? But Johnson pitching rocks, at the river? At Riverbend Park, well outside the District? Outdoors? He seemed allergic to the outdoors. At the moment, however, he was the only person she could think of who actively hated her.

"It could just be this idiot at work, you know, and have nothing to do with Courtney."

"Shall I beat him up for you?"

"I already beat up his ego. So, sure, knock yourself out. Knock him out too, while you're at it."

"Who is this creep?"

"Peter Johnson. Capitol Hill reporter. You've seen him." Lacey explained how Johnson sabotaged her story, his escalating jealousy over her beat, her book, her very existence, and how she was afraid he might start doing more to stop her from scooping him, to harm her job.

"That guy?" He grimaced. "Sweetheart, he's too out of shape to run that fast through the woods. And if he's trying to screw with your work behind your back, he's the passive-aggressive type, not someone to throw a rock."

"That's what I thought. But I heard he ran the Marine Corps Marathon a few years ago with some tubby congressman. They trained for it together for a year and Johnson wrote a series about it in *The Eye*. It was a big deal right before I moved here. He also pitched on the office softball team once. So we know he can throw a little. Maybe not major league."

"In that case, I'm definitely checking this jerk out. Find out where he's been hanging." Vic looked grim.

"And if it's not Johnson, then there's someone else who hates me. But how would anyone know I would be at Riverbend? Other than clueing into the psychic hotline, like Marie?"

"Maybe you were followed. Maybe all the way from your place, to the deli, and here, and then they followed us to the river."

"All day? And we never noticed anything? That doesn't make me feel any better."

"Leave that aside for a minute. Let me see that postcard."

She gingerly reached into her pocket and retrieved it. It was slightly the worse for wear.

Vic studied it, turning it over front to back. He assessed the photo and read the biography on the back. "That name sounds familiar." He concentrated, his eyebrows knit together. "She's dead?"

"According to the gallery last night, and all the sources I found on the Web, and her small entry in Wikipedia."

"Says she lived in Great Falls." He tapped his head with the card. "Nadine might know her."

"You're kidding. Your mother?" Lacey rubbed her forehead. "Why am I not surprised? Does she know everyone in Washington, D.C., and all the suburbs too?"

"Never underestimate Nadine. She has a wide variety of acquaintances. I might even have met the artist myself when I was a kid, maybe that's where I heard the name. Nadine was always having some sort of soiree or other, artists, writers, symphony conductors. She loves creative types. Probably why she likes you. And I like you too." His grin was back.

"If we ask your mother any questions it will just make her curious. You know that. Why do we want to know? Are we interested in buying a painting? Or in taking up painting? Or is there something else, something darker and deeper? Mystery and murder, perhaps?"

"That's very good. She'll like that. She's curious, like you. She'll always find out. Do you want me to call? Satisfying my mother's curiosity is the price we have to pay for her information on this artist, if she has any."

Lacey lay back on the sofa. "Yes, please."

Vic picked up his cell. She looked at her hand. The ring was not yet on her finger. Vic had said nothing about it. Reese Evans, the Welsh watchmaker, was taking his time with the setting.

She was very comfortable where she was now, on Vic's sofa. But she could feel herself frown in concentration. Lacey and Vic had never even discussed where they were going to live after they were married. Whenever that was going to be. She mentally compared his place to hers. Hers possessed much more personality. *Not all of it good.*

Lacey's apartment building was pretty ratty, that was impossible to deny. The wood parquet floors needed refinishing. The kitchens were tiny. The window air conditioners worked about half the time. The plumbing was fragile. There were cracks in her walls from an earthquake which also damaged the National Cathedral and the Washington Monument. In its favor, the building had not actually fallen down.

Her complex of apartment buildings on the south edge of Old Town Alexandria were built in the late 1940s, during the Cold War years, and were reputed to be "bomb-proof." Luckily, despite the cracks in the walls, they had proven to be earthquake-proof. On the outside, the red brick buildings were ugly and industrial-looking. On the inside, the apartments were light, airy, and fairly spacious. Vic's townhouse, by contrast, was comfortable and new and had a big, modern kitchen. But it was in the burbs, deep in the suburbs, and it made her feel isolated. At home, she had the river, right beneath every window.

Vic hung up, saying, "See you tomorrow." He tapped Lacey on the hand. "We're set. Brunch after church. Hey, what are you thinking? You have a funny look on your face."

She met his eyes. "You haven't said where you want to live. After we're married."

He smiled. "I suppose you have sentimental feelings about that shack in the sky where you live."

"It has a river view, Vic. I can see the trees greening in the spring."

"We have trees out here too. I'll show you one tomorrow."

"It's in Old Town, where I can walk to everything."

"You don't like my place? You can walk to downtown McLean from here."

"It's okay. But about the décor, darling," she said. "It's, um, brown. You seem awfully fond of neutrals, Vic. I'm not very neutral. You sure you like me too?"

"You're not neutral at all, Lacey. You're vivid. And I love you." He chuckled. "You can paint this place pink and purple for all I care."

"You wouldn't mind? I probably wouldn't paint it *all* pink."

"I think my manhood can take it." He leaned closer to her. "It's just a house, Lacey. I'm not wedded to it. I will be wedded to you. But your apartment won't work. It's too small for the two of us."

It certainly seemed like a lot of room when Lacey moved in. "I don't think I can live in the suburbs."

"We can move closer to Alexandria. Rosemont. Del Ray. Maybe even Old Town, if we rob a bank to pay for it."

Rosemont, full of azaleas in the spring and so close to Old Town, had possibilities. She pulled him down and kissed him.

"About your manhood—"

Chapter 34

THE NEXT MORNING HER SHOULDER ached from the rock's blow. The blood stopped seeping sometime during the night, though the bandage was soaked through. The rest of her body joined her shoulder in a conspiracy against her. She was sore all over and jarred by the experience at Riverbend Park. And the restless night left her feeling hollow-headed.

Sunday morning should have been more relaxing. But wondering who might be stalking her, ready to throw stones, made her tense. *It can't be the same person who was after Courtney,* she told herself. *Or Peter Johnson?* Subtly engineering a poisoned dress, vandalizing her story in the paper's editing queue, and throwing a big rock out of the woods were such radically different kinds of attacks. *Wonderful. Just how many enemies do I have out there?*

Vic instructed one of his operatives to keep close tabs on Johnson, who turned out to live in Silver Spring, Maryland, near the Metro stop. Lacey worried about what this surveillance would cost, but wisely kept quiet. She knew Vic wouldn't care about the cost. So far, the initial report was that Johnson slept late and had a lot of beer cans in his trash.

Lacey's chosen form of bravado was to greet the day wearing a light blue sundress with a natural waist and a vintage vibe. She wore a short navy jacket over it to cover up her bruised and bandaged shoulder, and sandals, dressy but comfortable. Vic put on black jeans and a pale blue polo shirt and spent half an hour checking over their cars to make sure no one had tampered with them. After Mass at a big suburban church in McLean near his townhouse, they headed to his parents' house for a late brunch.

Lacey liked Vic's mother. Nadine could be overwhelming, but sweet, and Lacey was interested in keeping her future mother-in-law happy. She was much closer geographically to Vic's parents than her own. And closer emotionally, as well. *There, finally a happy thought!*

Nadine greeted them with hugs. She was slightly taller than Lacey and very trim. In her early sixties, she looked at least a decade younger. Looking at Nadine in her best suburban hostess mode, no one would suspect she adored rodeos, commotion, and classic cars, especially her giant 1957 Cadillac Eldorado Biarritz. Nadine Donovan grew up a cowgirl in Nevada, though she'd left that life a long time ago. She traded the West for the glossy patina of the Washington, D.C., matron and a happy life with Vic's dad, Sean Daniel "Danny" Donovan.

Impeccably groomed, Nadine wore pale linen slacks and a silk shirt and pearls. Her dark hair was styled in a smooth bob, just a little longer than the standard Helmet Head hairdo so popular in the District of Columbia, and her manicured nails showed off a large diamond ring and wedding band. Nadine's wardrobe favored Brooks Brothers and St. John's knits, but her pampered exterior belied her steely core.

She took Lacey's hand and stared pointedly at the empty ring finger, but said nothing. She knew something was up with them romantically, and Lacey knew she knew. Nadine smiled.

"No news there, I see," she said.

"You'll be the first to know, Nadine." Vic stepped in and kissed his mother's forehead. "When there is something to see."

"It's so delightful you could make it today. I know you two are happy to see me," Nadine teased. "But what's the ulterior motive? Anything new on the lethal lining of the Madame X dress?"

"I'm flattered. You're keeping up."

"What else would I be doing?"

"Well, Vic said you might have known a local artist, Jillian Hopewell," Lacey began.

"Jillian. Yes. I haven't heard that name in a while." Nadine looked into the distance for a moment. "I knew Jillian. We even have one of her paintings, a small one. But what does this have to do with your dangerous fashion beat?"

"You do know her?" Vic said.

"I *knew* her. Men never pay attention, do they?" She laughed.

"And you have a painting of hers?" Lacey asked.

"In the guest bedroom. It's an early one. I bought it at one of her gallery shows. Years ago, now. Your father, Vic, was cruel enough to say he hoped it would increase in value after she died. He didn't care for it. Thought it was too garish. Hence, the guest bedroom."

"What does it look like?" Lacey asked.

"I'll show it to you after brunch. A landscape, painted somewhere around here, along the river. I liked it because of the vibrant blues and greens. It's not garish at all. It's no great work of art, I suppose, but it's sweet and soothing, goes well with the room."

"What do you remember about the artist?" Vic asked.

"I used to talk to her at events, gallery openings, things like that. She came to some of my soirees. We were friends, I suppose. Jillian wasn't a very warm person and she always looked ill. There was a gray cast to her skin. As I said, it wasn't too long after we met that she died. She had a terrible cough, though she didn't smoke. There was a strange intensity about her that drove some people away, I think. Of course she'd had three or four husbands, so there was something that drove them to her as well. More than anything, I think, she wanted to be remembered, to be a great artist. At any rate, the art world doesn't take too kindly to woman artists, as you know."

"There's a blanket statement," Vic said.

"True, nonetheless. Wait, come to think about it, I met her for the first time many years before that. When her name was Jillian Holstein."

"Holstein?" Lacey said. "I didn't find that on the Web."

"A different husband. That one didn't last long. There were several other married names, I'm thinking, before Hopewell. That was her last name. Sounds more hopeful than Holstein, don't you think?"

"Maybe she didn't care for the dairy cow connection," Lacey suggested.

"Who would?" Nadine said.

Lacey planned to keep her own name after the wedding. While she thought Donovan was a lovely name, and in Washington she was forever having to explain that she bore no relationship to the famous museum, Smithsonian was her name, and her byline, and she planned to stick by it.

A Cockney ancestor of hers named Smith changed the family name upon immigrating to America, because he thought Smithsonian sounded richer, classier, tonier. America was the land of opportunity, and so the English Smiths took the opportunity to become the American Smithsonians. All except for Lacey's Great-aunt Mimi. Mimi fell in love with that hit movie of her era, *Mr. Smith Goes to Washington*. In fact, she went to Washington herself, and changed her name back to Smith.

Lacey pushed the name-changing issues from her mind. *Getting married is so complicated.*

"Jillian died in the late Eighties, I believe, though it might have been later," Nadine was going on. "By then she was gaunt. Like a walking skeleton. Every time I saw her she looked worse. Terrible to watch."

"Do you remember anything else about her?"

"She really could paint, until she grew too weak. She always took great pride in her color sense. Her hero was Cezanne, as I remember. She loved the Impressionists." The same information as the postcard. "What's this all about?"

"Nothing, really."

"Don't nothing me, Lacey Smithsonian. Something's up. You pull a name out of a hat from years ago and say it's nothing?"

"I saw her work at an art gallery show in Old Town. Last Friday, with Brooke."

"Jillian, in a gallery showing? After all this time?"

Vic handed her the postcard. "We think it looks like Riverbend Park," he said.

"Her Riverbend collection," Nadine said, studying the postcard. "She was painting those landscapes for years, all up and down the river."

"We were there yesterday, at the park," Lacey added.

Nadine gave them a coy smile. "Lovely place for a cozy picnic. Are the bluebells in blossom?"

"Could have been cozier. We had company. And someone threw a large rock at Lacey's head," Vic said.

"For the record, it didn't hit my head." She winced at the memory. Her shoulder ached. "I'm all right."

"Well, hell! Who would do such a thing?" Nadine asked. "Is this about that awful dress?"

"We've been asking ourselves the same question," Lacey said. "Vic took out after whoever it was, but whoever it was got away."

"Was it a big rock?" Nadine said.

"Big enough to throw and big enough to hurt," Lacey said. "Winged me on the shoulder."

"My God, what if it had hit you in the head and given you a concussion?" Nadine said. "Thank goodness Vic was with you."

"Or she could have gone into the river and over the falls," Vic added.

"You two optimists keep chatting," Lacey said. "I have a headache coming on."

"Oh dear," Nadine said, concerned. "Do you need to lie down, dear? Can I get you something?"

"I don't have a concussion. I'm fine. I'll just have an impressive scar to show off. Besides, Vic cleaned it and kissed it and it's all better." She kissed him on the cheek and headed for the sofa.

"Another exciting near-death escapade. I should go picnicking with you two." Nadine made herself comfortable on the sofa next to Lacey and sorted through the newspapers on the coffee table. "Your father and I have had our share of scrapes and we came out all right in the end." She opened the LifeStyle section in *The Eye Street Observer*.

"What are you looking for?" Vic said.

"What Lacey wrote today. If she's in trouble, it's probably because of something she wrote, don't you think? Goodness, I never would have guessed that writing about clothes could be so dangerous. It makes them ever so much more interesting."

"Fashion is murder in this town," Lacey commented dryly. Her shoulder started to itch. Nadine scanned Lacey's story on the substitute lining in the Madame X dress.

"Very interesting, and very clever of you to put this all together, Lacey, but what on earth does your Riverbend Park experience have to do with that dress?" she asked.

"No idea. But there might be a connection, somehow. My friend Marie Largesse would say that the universe sometimes demands synchronicity."

"Your Marie would also say it demands sustenance. Shall we have brunch?"

Nadine led them into her formal pink dining room. The sweetness of the soft color was cut by the dark mahogany dining furniture. Brunch was set up on the buffet with pink patterned china plates, napkins and silverware, goblets for orange juice, and cups for coffee from the silver coffeepot. The selections included an egg casserole, sausage and bacon, biscuits with butter and honey, and a selection of jams.

"Wow," Lacey said. "Quite a spread."

"Don't let it fool you, it's all a big show. She's just putting on airs," Vic joked.

"Don't be impertinent, Sean Victor."

Vic's dad entered, looking spiffy in his khakis, a pale blue shirt, and Top-Siders. Danny Donovan had a full head of white hair, he was as tall as his son, and he had the same green eyes.

"So nice of you two to join us," he said.

He winked at Lacey and gave her a big hug in greeting.

"This is lovely," Lacey said. "You've gone to so much trouble."

"Not at all. Help yourselves. Now tell me all the latest intrigue," Nadine said. "And what is the connection between this universal synchronicity and people throwing rocks at other people?"

ᘗ

After brunch, Nadine led the way upstairs, over a lovely oriental carpet runner that led to the guest bedroom. Decorated as if it came from the pages of *Architectural Digest*, the room featured ivory grass cloth on the walls, deep green drapes, and a queen-sized bed with a padded green velvet headboard, flanked by matching ivory porcelain lamps on matching bedside tables. A comfy leather armchair deep enough to get lost in cozied up to a bookcase full of books. *Okay, Nadine, you just won me over. I'm moving in.*

"I change the covers and pillows, depending on whether the company is male or female," Nadine said.

"And if she has two people staying," Vic said, "the female covers always win."

"I don't mess with it," Danny said. "Decorating the house is Nadine's territory." Vic confirmed this to Lacey with a look.

"It's very pretty," Lacey said. "I'd love a room just like it."

Nadine indicated a small painting over the dresser. "There it is. Our painting by Jillian whatever-her-last-name-was at the time."

Lacey leaned in to get a closer look. In the lower right-hand corner was the tiny signature. "Jillian Hopewell."

There was something about the painting that was familiar. The scene, but there was also something different. It was delicate and reminded Lacey of Japanese prints. She took a closer look. It wasn't painted on canvas.

"It's silk," she said at last. "She painted this one on emerald green silk."

"Oh yes. Didn't I tell you?" Nadine played dumb. "She'd been experimenting on different mediums. Canvas, wood, tile, fabrics. Not velvet, I am happy to say. An Impressionist Elvis on black velvet is just too awful to think about. But this was so delicate and bright. No idea what I paid for it. Probably not very much, I'm sorry to say."

"It's a little too bright, I always thought," Danny said. "Looks good in here, though. Where I don't see it."

Vic stared at it. "I remember this now. It looks like this spot could be up around Riverbend too."

Lacey retrieved from her purse the small scrap of silk that she'd been given by Lola Gallegos. She compared it to the background of the painting.

"It's a color match."

"My goodness, do you suppose it's from the same material as the dress?" Nadine's eyes were bright. *She's been waiting all through brunch to spring this on me,* Lacey thought.

"What does it mean, Lacey?" Vic asked.

"It means I need to find out more about the artist and her stash of green silk," Lacey said. "That's a little difficult, I'm afraid, as she's no longer with us."

"Perhaps Marie could hold a séance," Vic said. "Go right to the source."

"Do you need to borrow the painting?" Nadine offered. "I have a tote bag it should fit inside."

"There are textile experts who could compare the silk," Danny said. "Now what's this all about, just by the way?"

"Could it be dangerous?" Nadine looked hopeful.

"Nadine, don't get your hopes up," Vic said. "We just won't get this thing wet."

"The gallery postcard says she lived in Great Falls."

"Actually out in the woods, but it's not very far from Great Falls. I could show you," Nadine said. "I've been there. Of course that little house of hers could be gone by now, what with all the mansion construction going on up there. You'd hardly know the place. Who's up for a drive up the river?"

Nadine looked like a cat sipping cream.

Chapter 35

"NADINE, ARE YOU SUGGESTING—?" DANNY said, with a knowing grin.

"It's a perfect day to go for a drive," she said. "In my big old Caddy, the Pink Flamingo. Who's with me?"

"I knew it would come to this." Vic squeezed Lacey's elbow. "I suppose you're up for it?"

"A drive in that giant pink Cadillac? Are you kidding? I'd love to," Lacey said.

"No use trying to stop a pink tornado," Danny said. "I'm getting my hat."

Nadine put Lacey up front in the passenger seat, Vic and his dad in the back. She pulled out of the garage and put the top down.

"You boys don't have to come, you know. You could stay home and watch the game. I'm sure there's some kind of game on television. I'd be perfectly disappointed if there wasn't."

"Drive on, darling." Danny pulled his snappy fedora down over his forehead.

Vic grinned behind his shades. "Let you two run off alone with fashion crimes, poison dyes, and a big pink Cadillac? I don't think so, ladies."

Nadine tucked her hair under a scarf, à la Grace Kelly, donned her pink sunglasses, and tuned the radio to oldies. She was definitely Old Hollywood star material. Lacey tied her hair back in a ponytail to brave the top-down open air.

People don't go for a drive on a sunny Sunday afternoon in a pink 1957 Cadillac Eldorado Biarritz if they want to remain anonymous. Vic and his dad, both private investigators and security professionals, slouched down in the back seat, trying to look inconspicuous. *Or maybe just cool.* Cars on Chain Bridge Road honked and drivers waved, when they weren't staring and pointing and taking photos. Nadine waved back gaily. She had a no-holds-barred driving style, and like the captain of an ocean liner, she was in her element. A few turns took them onto Old Dominion Drive, then Swinks Mill Road, and Georgetown Pike sped them out of McLean, Virginia. They cruised the Pike past the turnoff to Great Falls Park, and Nadine turned right onto Riverbend Road.

Although a few modest original homes and old farmhouses remained along the road, the woods and rolling hills were being rapidly transformed by immense mansions, all competing to show off the new money it took to build them. Nadine turned off Riverbend onto a side road and pulled into the drive of a small white one-story frame house. It needed a little paint and TLC, but it looked inhabited.

"What do you know?" she said, getting out of the Caddy. "It's still here."

"Amazing. It was a long time ago," Danny said. "This property's got to be worth a lot now."

They had just reached the tiny porch when the front door of the house opened and a scruffy man who would look at home on a motorcycle stepped outside. He was big and burly, but not fat, with a full black beard and jet black hair that grazed his shoulders, wearing a T-shirt with the sleeves cut off, faded jeans, and heavy black boots. Black tattoos snaked down both well-muscled arms, and a gleaming black Harley Davidson sat by the side of the small house. He strode toward the car.

He grinned at Nadine. "Hey lady, that is my kind of car. Fifty-six?" He had a friendly smile to go with his bouncer-at-a-biker-bar looks.

"Fifty-seven. Sorry to interrupt you," Nadine said.

"A beauty like that can interrupt me anytime," he said, clearly meaning the car and not its occupants. He stuck out a hand, still eyeing the Caddy. "I'm Michael. Big Mike, if you're looking for a mechanic. What can I do you for?"

"I'm Lacey. We were hoping for some information," Lacey said. She shook his offered hand, clean except for a little grease under his fingernails.

He reluctantly shifted his gaze from the Cadillac to her and Nadine. Vic and his dad brought up the rear in their shades. Lacey knew they were both carrying concealed weapons. For that matter, she thought, Big Mike probably was too.

"You lost? Looking for the park, right? It's just down around the bend. Go back to Jeffery Road and turn left, watch for the sign."

"No, we know our way around, thanks," Nadine said. "My name is Nadine, this is my family. I used to know a woman who lived here, in your house. Jillian Hopewell?"

"The artist lady?"

"That's her. Did you know her?"

Michael shook his head. "Heard my folks talk about her. They knew her, somehow. Bought the house from her. I was in high school at the time. Actually, they bought it from her ex-husband. She was dead by then. I guess he still owned it, or she left it to him, something like that."

"I suppose there's nothing left from when she lived here?" Nadine said.

"Not much, though it was a real mess when we got it. The place was full of her stuff. Canvases, paintings, whatever. My mother was in a state. Supposed to be all cleaned up before we moved in, but the guy didn't do it. I guess the folks didn't holler too much though, they got a sweet deal on the house. Just me here now."

"Did that stuff include paints and other materials?" Lacey asked.

"I guess. She was a painter." Big Mike shrugged. "There was a couple of boxes and like a big trunk or something. Pictures, easels, lots of junk laying around. My folks put it all in a storage shed out back, and then her family hauled it away a few months later. Except for one painting. My mother liked it, so she kept it. Rent on the shed, I guess."

"Where is her ex now?" Vic asked.

"Oh, man. That was a while ago. Last I heard he moved to Florida with his new honey. Wacky old guy. Gerhardt Hopewell, his name was. Course, he'd be pretty old by now. Hey, that painting's still here though. You want to see it? It's inside."

"That would be lovely," Nadine said. "Thank you, Michael. I visited here years ago. Before she died, of course. The house looks the same."

"We never did much to it. Worked for us the way it was." Michael opened the door for them. "Don't mind the mess." It wasn't terribly messy, though it did smell a bit like beer and motor oil. The house consisted of the living room, dining room, kitchen, bath and two small bedrooms. The décor consisted mostly of TVs and guitars. "Great little house. Sweet and petite. Works for me."

"Very pretty out here in this neck of the woods," Nadine said.

"Except for all the damn McMansions popping up and crowding everyone out. Blocking the sun."

"I was surprised to find this house still here. It was so long ago that I last saw Jillian."

"Believe me, they keep trying to get us out. Me and the few old homesteads still standing. Flashing their money at us. Those people think this house is a pimple on their perfection. That's from a song. But I don't want to move, even though the property taxes are killing me. Thank God, I got solid employment. I fix Harleys, work on some cars, play a little music. Here's that painting I told you about."

There was a smoke-blackened fireplace on the back wall of the front room, above which hung a large-screen television. To the side of the TV there was a large painted landscape, obviously by Jillian Hopewell.

"That looks familiar," Danny said. "Larger than the one we have."

"Cheerful, ain't it?" Michael said. "And green. That's what my mom liked about it. Said it reminded her of why they moved out here. Beautiful green country. Before all the Richie Riches moved in. Another kind of green here now. Greenbacks."

"Part of her Riverbend series." Lacey leaned in to examine it. The picture had a bit of soot from the fireplace, but the vibrant greens and blues still shimmered. "This one is painted on silk too."

"Yeah, that's what my mom said. Real pretty green silk. You wouldn't be interested in buying it, wouldja?"

"Not today," Lacey said.

"I could let it go for the right price." What was a family heirloom between friends?

"Let me think about it. Where did Jillian paint?"

"Over to the dining room." He led them into a bright room with a long farm table in the center. The table was covered in neatly organized motorcycle parts. "The light's real good in here. Careful you don't step in any oil."

The airy room faced south, with big windows on three sides and light streaming through them. It felt like a sunroom. It would be a lovely place to work, though awfully warm in the summer.

"Is that the same shed out there?" Vic asked.

"Yep. I guess that's where she mixed up paints and stuff. Want to see it?"

Lacey wondered why Big Mike was being so friendly, offering all these strangers the nickel tour. Perhaps he didn't have much company out here. More likely, it was the magic of Nadine's pink Cadillac.

"Absolutely!" Nadine was halfway out the door, as if she expected to find a nice shiny skeleton.

The group trooped outside. The old corrugated metal shed had double doors that stood slightly ajar. Inside were a couple of Harleys in various stages of disassembly, more parts, workbenches, and a heavy scent of motor oil. Big Mike had made himself at home here too.

"You have a nice setup out here," Vic said. He and his dad stepped into the shed. "You do your own machining?"

"Oh yeah, man, you can't trust those bandits at the big machine shops! I do everything right here so I keep the cost down and…"

Lacey and Nadine wandered around the shop while the men talked about cylinder heads and camshafts. There was not much of Jillian Hopewell to be seen here, just a few ancient paint splatters on the walls. An old galvanized wash tub hung on one wall, stained green and specked with paint. Had she also dyed her own silk for her work? Lacey could imagine it. The men rejoined them and they stepped out into the sunshine.

"I'm indebted to you for the tour, Michael," Nadine said. "The place is just as pretty as I remembered it."

Lacey was sure Jillian Hopewell hadn't done motorcycle repair on her dining room table, but it was the right thing to say.

"Why y'all so interested in the artist?" Michael asked. "I mean, she's long gone, right? No disrespect or anything, just wondering."

"She was a friend, and she lives on in her art," Nadine said.

"I saw her work in an art show in Alexandria the other night," Lacey said. "And Nadine said she'd known her and knew where she lived and painted. So here we are."

"We have one of her paintings too," Danny said. "Not nearly as large as yours."

"No kidding? Mine's a big one? Are they worth anything?"

"One of hers at the gallery show had a price tag of two thousand dollars," Lacey said.

Michael whistled. "For something like that?"

"Doesn't mean it will sell," Danny said, ever upbeat about art.

"So that picture of mine might come in handy for a rainy day." He stroked his beard. "An original Jillian Hopewell!" Michael escorted the group back to the Cadillac and looked lovingly at Nadine's big pink car.

"Thanks for your time, Michael." Vic opened the passenger door and offered Michael his hand.

"No problem, happy to do it. Nice to meet y'all. Man, I love these old cars. Nothing cooler than a big old finned Caddy. She's a beauty."

He put his hand on the fender and gently stroked it. Nadine and Lacey shared a look.

"I call her the Pink Flamingo. Would you like to check her out?" Nadine inquired.

He grinned. One side tooth was missing. Nadine popped the hood latch. Big Mike lifted the hood and made grunts of approval.

"Whoa! Oh man, that's the original mill, isn't it? With the dual quads!" He whistled again. "She's real clean. You take good care of her."

"You want me to start her up?"

He put both thumbs up. "You bet." Nadine turned the key and pressed the accelerator. "If you ever need any work done on her, you let me know. I work on cars too, not just Harleys. Man, she really purrs. You think maybe—?"

"Hop in. We'll take a little spin, but she only purrs for me, Michael. I am her only driver."

"Understood, ma'am. You're the boss."

Danny just smiled at Vic and Vic smiled back. They didn't say a word. Nadine and her big pink Caddy had made another conquest. Big Mike hopped in the front passenger seat, sunglasses and big grin in place. Lacey sat in the back between Vic and his dad. Nadine pulled the Caddy out of the driveway and pointed her hood ornament at the open road.

ଔ

"You didn't have to drive him all over the countryside," Danny remarked after they dropped Michael back at his house and headed back to the Donovan's place in McLean. "You could see West Virginia from where we turned around."

"Just thanking him for the little home tour." Nadine smiled at her husband, a cat-licking-cream smile he knew very well. Danny was now in the front seat, Vic and Lacey snuggled in the back.

Vic snickered. "Thank you, Nadine. It was a fascinating afternoon. And now I know where I can get all my motorcycles repaired dirt cheap. If I ever get one again."

"Don't taunt your mother," Nadine said sweetly.

"You had a motorcycle?" Lacey asked.

"Dirt bikes first, then an old Triumph. Dad here helped me get it running. It was a passing obsession when I was a teenager. Then I discovered girls. Motorcycles don't have big back seats. Pink Cadillacs do."

"I nearly had heart failure every day when he was out riding those things," Nadine said. "I was so relieved when he switched his interests to girls. Some girls. Not all of them."

Lacey winked at Vic. "It was a lovely afternoon, Nadine. And now I have a much better picture of the artist and her work. The green silk in your painting wasn't a fluke, it was one of her signatures."

"Do you think it's related to that dress?" Danny asked.

"Call it a strong gut feeling."

"Universal synchronicity and gut feelings," Nadine said. We're onto something here."

"We have to confirm it's the same silk," Vic said.

"You read my mind," Lacey said.

"Darling, it's the big print-edition. I can read it with my eyes closed." Lacey punched him in the arm.

Nadine pointed the pink Caddy up Georgetown Pike to the little town of Great Falls and detoured to an ice cream shop. She parked the Caddy and made an announcement.

"I suggest we huddle over some mint chocolate chip or something."

Lacey had a chocolate cherry cone, while Vic went for cake batter. Nadine had peach, and Vic's dad opted for the mint chocolate chip, with sprinkles. They retreated to a table outside, beneath the shade of a maple tree.

"A fabric conservator could compare your fabric scraps with the painting to determine whether it's the same silk, the same weave, the same dye," Danny suggested.

"I know someone I can call," Lacey said.

"So you will need to borrow my little picture, after all," Nadine said, beaming.

"If you don't mind. As long as it wouldn't damage the painting," Lacey said.

"They could take a little sample from the back, where it's tacked into the frame," Danny suggested. "You'd never even see it. I never cared for it anyway."

"It's a lovely picture," Lacey opined. "Though I expect if I make it notorious, it might be more valuable."

"Danny, it's a nice painting," Nadine said. "And you know it.

But you take it, you two. Do whatever you need to do. You have a case to solve."

"You're sure?"

"I don't mind," Danny said. "It's just gathering dust." He winked at Lacey.

"Sean Daniel Donovan, that painting is dusted regularly and you know it," Nadine protested. "Don't you cast aspersions on my housekeeping."

"That's right," he acknowledged. "They come every two weeks like clockwork."

"More often around the holidays," Nadine agreed.

Danny chuckled. The elder Donovans seemed to be forever bantering with each other. For a moment, as Lacey gazed at them, forty years fell away and they looked to her just like newlyweds. Lacey looked at Vic, who just laughed.

"Pay no attention. They've been needling each other for as long as I've known them."

"No hurry bringing it back, either," Danny said, goading his wife.

"What have you got against that painting?" Nadine asked. "I like that painting!"

"Not the painting. That woman. Something wasn't right about her."

"Well, of course not. She was an artist."

Danny snorted. "I think your mother took pity on her, buying that thing."

"She had problems?" Vic asked his father.

"You know the type, Vic. They walk through our doors often enough."

"Did she really walk through your door?" Lacey asked. "I mean, as a client?"

"She's been dead so long, I guess I can talk about it. She was convinced her husband, her current and last husband anyway, was cheating on her."

"You never told me that," Nadine said.

"You never asked. And since she was a client, briefly, she had client confidentiality. But she's gone now, so it's all right, and this is just among family. Didn't take me long to figure out he *was* cheating on her. But she insisted he was trying to poison her too. He wasn't, not that I could ever establish. She had other delusions, such as physical complaints her doctor couldn't seem to confirm. He told her it was all in her head, and I finally decided he was right, she was crazy. That's a technical term," he said to Lacey.

"There's an irony," Lacey said. "If she was somehow being poisoned, it was probably by arsenic, and it was probably her own doing, because she was painting with Paris Green. She was almost certainly mixing pigments herself, like her hero, Cezanne. And if she dyed the silk herself too—"

"What did you say?" Vic looked up sharply.

"If she dyed the silk herself. She might have. Just supposing." Lacey took a big lick of chocolate ice cream in her mouth and closed her eyes. It was delicious. She gazed at Vic. "There's a connection somehow. There must have been more green silk."

"What makes you think she dyed the silk herself?" Vic asked.

"The shed where she mixed her paints," Lacey said. "She was a do-it-all-herself kind of woman. First of all, it's likely she had a quantity of Paris Green, maybe years old. You couldn't buy it off the shelf when she was painting. It wasn't even legal anymore, except maybe in pesticides. She certainly knew how to mix paint. There was paint splatter all over that shed. There was an old washtub in there too, with green stains on it. If she had a basic knowledge of chemistry—"

"You saw this on YouTube," Vic said accusingly.

She grinned at him. "I did see it on YouTube. It didn't look that hard. If you have the ingredients. The big question is, if she dyed the silk, did that silk wind up in Courtney Wallace's dress? And if so, how?"

"That's a lot of ifs." Vic knit his brow in concentration. His green eyes looked darker. "If that's the case, where's it been all these years?"

"Before we jump to any more incredible conclusions," Danny cut in, "you need to analyze the silk in the painting. See if it matches the pieces you have. If it doesn't, then all this speculation is leading us nowhere. Except to the counter for more ice cream."

"What's wrong, Lacey?" Nadine said. "Another headache?"

"Nadine, the whole thing is a headache. This silk. That silk. The dress. Courtney's death. Your painting. Someone throwing rocks. How could they all be connected? The whole thing is so improbable."

"But that's what I like best about it." Nadine's eyes sparkled.

Vic leaned over her. "Lacey, where clothes are involved, and where you're involved, I'm learning to simply go with it. It may be the wrong road, but we won't know until we go down it. Like they say: We may be lost, but we're making good time."

"And as long as we're going down the road together," Nadine added, "we might as well go full speed ahead."

"Your psychic friend could be right." Danny put a hand on Lacey's shoulder. "You'd be surprised how sometimes things work out. Secrets hidden for years rise to the surface. Maybe because the universe has a plan? Or maybe because people feel the need to confess. Sometimes the most unlikely pieces of a puzzle fall right into your lap. It's too early to discount this green silk thing as a red herring. And too early to tell the world how brilliant we are."

"Marie would say there is a higher purpose in all this," Lacey said, and Vic lifted one eyebrow.

"I'm not in the higher purpose business," Danny said, putting his other hand on Vic's shoulder. "I'm in the billable hours, work hard, stick to the facts, and do the right thing business. If positive things happen because we keep plodding along, trying to find the truth and do what's right, that's all to the good. In the meantime, you two, we're here to help you."

It was beginning to sound an awful lot like a family project. Lacey wasn't too sure how she felt about that yet. She'd traveled halfway across the country, to Washington, D.C., to build a career and escape her own family. Now she found herself in the middle of another family. She looked around at the happy Donovans, licking ice cream from their fingers and laughing at each other.

My new family?

Chapter 36

IT WAS DARK WHEN LACEY and Vic returned to her apartment. She missed being in her own place. After she picked up her car at his place, he insisted on following her home and staying with her. She didn't resist.

Vic's field operative tailing Peter Johnson reported by phone that "the target" had spent the entire afternoon in a Silver Spring sports bar, where he got drunk and complained loudly about "some no-talent bitch" trying to undermine him at his office. Vic's man in the field actually drove Johnson home, where the target collapsed in a beer-induced stupor and was still sleeping it off. Vic's guy was parked out in front of Johnson's townhouse. Vic had told his operative to keep close tabs on the target. *Couldn't get much closer than that.*

"No-talent bitch, huh? At least we know he's following the right Peter Johnson," she told Vic.

"Sounds like." Vic kissed her hard before setting up his laptop in her tiny office in the spare bedroom to review his field reports. She told him she'd be fine left to her own devices, as long as he wasn't far away for long.

Lacey knew she should go to bed early to prepare for Monday morning, but instead she poured herself a glass of Riesling and opened Aunt Mimi's trunk. It was one thing she'd missed over the weekend.

The trunk was a constant comfort to her. It was almost as if Mimi were there with her, whispering to her through the things she had saved in the huge steamer trunk. Mimi saved these things for herself, but in so doing she also saved them for her favorite great-niece. The trunk was Lacey's most prized possession, and she felt quite as rich as if she'd stumbled upon a pirate's treasure. Rather than gold doubloons, it held fabrics and patterns, some half-finished, some merely put into the trunk in that dream state where Mimi had a vision of the completed gown. But Mimi's attention span often wavered, and she went on to buy more fine cloth, a newer pattern, perhaps one of the Hollywood styles or a Vogue, all to Lacey's delight.

In addition to the dressmaking materials, Mimi had packed away old letters, photos, memorabilia, and magazines from the Thirties and Forties, which provided Lacey with hours of pleasure. There were choice copies of *Vogue*, *Mademoiselle*, and *Ladies' Home Journal*, as well as those amazing *LIFE* magazines from the war years, each issue a window into another era. What might have seemed superficial at the time had a poignancy now. During the war, Oldsmobile was making cannons instead of cars. The Singer Sewing Machine factories were retooled to produce artillery. Still, the ads promised that better days were ahead, and cars and sewing machines and appliances would all come down the line once again soon, when the war was over.

Lacey picked out a vintage *Mademoiselle*, "The Magazine for Smart Young Women," from late 1940. She didn't know what made her pick up this particular issue. She'd never opened this one before, and some things were simply tactile. This issue from before the war was printed on a much better grade of paper. Wartime magazines had tissue-thin pages, practically newsprint, which was now deteriorating, leaving small slivers of paper in their wake. But this prewar issue showed life in 1940 was still full of promise. And it had something even more interesting to show Lacey.

Flipping through the pages, she saw a familiar-looking black dress. She stopped, riveted by an article on stylish debutantes around the country. The universe, or an angel, or chance, supplied an answer to one of her questions.

Where had the Madame X dress come from?

Perhaps right here. It might be the very dress Lacey was looking at in *Mademoiselle*. The gown in the picture was worn by Miss Elizabeth "Betty" Lionsgate, of Richmond, Virginia. Ingrid Allendale had told Lacey she'd bought Courtney's gown at an estate sale in that very city. Lacey read on.

Betty's dress was one of her own "creations," she explained, and she was inspired by John Singer Sargent's *Portrait of Madame X*. "Making it was a lark," Betty told the magazine. "Of course, that painting was quite a scandal, because of that one strap dangling off her shoulder, before the artist repainted that little detail. But now this dress of mine is quite modern, don't you think? And I keep my straps up." Lacey stared at the picture for a long time.

Betty the debutante was photographed in color in much the same dramatic pose as the portrait, standing against a copper wall and resting her right hand upon a table, her left hand lifting up a swath of the skirt. Her skin was very pale, but Betty was not dark-haired like Madame X in the portrait. Thick auburn waves were pulled back from her face and fell down her back. Her complexion was clear and dewy, her profile softer, and instead of looking off into the distance like Madame X, Betty Lionsgate cast a mischievous sidelong glance at the camera, with the hint of a grin. She could have been posing for an ad for shampoo or Woodbury Facial Soap, instead of a fashion article.

The accompanying article quoted her on the dress. "I worked with Mother's dressmaker. Oh, she's a whiz with a needle. She used to work for Broadway stars in New York City. I was my idea to line it in white silk and cut out the fabric in the designs from a deck of cards—hearts, clubs, spades, and diamonds—so the lining shows through."

The brief bio note said that Betty Lionsgate was a "coed," a junior at the College of William and Mary in Williamsburg, Virginia, studying English, "with a minor in the opposite sex." Betty apparently was quite a live wire. She was roughly contemporaneous with Lacey's Aunt Mimi, another live wire. Lacey Googled the name Elizabeth Lionsgate, not expecting much. She found an obituary for an Elizabeth Lionsgate Howard of Richmond, Virginia, with a thumbnail biography.

In the blink of an eye, the vivacious young Betty of *Mademoiselle* had graduated from William and Mary and joined the WAVES during the war. A woman with an eye toward style would obviously, Lacey thought, pick the service with the best-looking uniform. The WAVES' Navy uniform was designed by the famous American designer Main Rousseau Bocher, better known as Mainbocher. It had enduring style. So, it seemed, did Betty.

Elizabeth Lionsgate later married a soldier named Howard, had children, and died in Richmond in her nineties, preceded in death by her husband. The obituary noted that although she'd had a long career in education, Betty's true joy was in "being a wife and mother."

Lacey wondered if there was an ancient newspaper rule about that. Were obituaries required to pull the wife-and-mother card, if possible, as if all other achievements ranked lower? She'd have to ask old Chester Bardwick, *The Eye*'s senior obit writer. Or maybe after Betty lived through the war, she was happy to take refuge in her family. She had, however, saved that dress of hers for decades. Part of her must have clung to the sparkling young woman *Mademoiselle* had profiled. The dress survived, practically unworn—until her family cleaned house after she died.

What would Betty Lionsgate Howard think of her black dress now?

Chapter 37

TO GREET THIS MONDAY MORNING, Lacey opted for easy comfort, navy slacks and a vintage navy gabardine jacket with pale blue piping and cuffs. The jacket required no blouse, but she added her favorite bra, her Red Bra of Courage. She wore a pair of teal sandals with kitten heels. Higher heels were out. She was still stiff from her roll down the riverbank two days before. Everything hurt.

This isn't fair, she thought with each step. *People in the movies bounce right back after taking a bullet. I'm a wreck after taking a single rock.*

Vic assured her everything would be okay. He followed her to D.C. and mentioned that Forrest Thunderbird, aka Turtledove, would be in the vicinity to keep a watch on her and make sure no rock throwers would come near. She parked her car in *The Eye*'s garage and rode the elevator up through the building. She gently lurched to her cubicle, her legs stiff and her hips a little sore from her bumpy ride down the hillside. Tucked under her arm, wrapped in brown paper, was Nadine's landscape by Jillian Hopewell, painted on green silk. In her head, a full agenda. In her tote bag, the 1940 copy of *Mademoiselle*.

Yesterday she had been running all day on adrenaline. Now she was dragging. All Lacey wanted was a cup of coffee, a couple of aspirin, and a clear head. And maybe a nap, but it was too early for a nap. She gently set her packages down and reached for the mug on her desk. She needed a cup of newsroom kitchenette coffee and she didn't even care how nauseating the brew might be.

A voice boomed behind her.

"Why, Lacey Smithsonian, what you been up to? You go ten rounds with someone last night? You're limping. Something I should know about?"

Detective Broadway Lamont popped his big head out of Felicity's cubicle. He had a doughnut in his hand, liberated from Felicity's latest groom's-cake concoction. For this masterpiece, she layered the doughnuts using a different type in every layer, creating a striped effect with multiple colors of frosting, blue, yellow, pink, and green. It was frightening.

"Good morning, Broadway. What are you doing here?"

"You're late."

She lifted her wrist to check the time. It was nine-thirty. "Long weekend. Let's just say I've already made up the time in extra hours."

Lamont was looking especially chipper this morning, in his pressed khakis and navy blazer over a bright green polo shirt. His grin looked particularly carnivorous.

"Hard at work? All weekend? You expect me to believe that?"

"Did you want to see me or the doughnut queen?" she inquired.

Felicity was nowhere in sight, but the doughnut cake had already been photographed for her column and left undefended, with a note on top: EAT ME!

He laughed, a deep, booming, unnerving sound. "Why not both?"

She waved her mug at him. "Coffee?"

"Don't mind if I do." He lumbered after her to the newsroom kitchen, taking the other clean FASHION *BITES* mug from her desk. She poured the remains of the carafe into his mug, then made a fresh pot.

"What's happening on homicide?"

"The usual. Bang, bang, shoot 'em up, you're dead. That sort of thing. But then I got a tip today. Anonymous. From a pay phone of all things, from a hotel that's retro enough to have a pay phone."

Lacey waited for the coffee pot to fill, and the other shoe to drop. When it was ready, she topped off the detective's cup and then hers.

"What was the tip?"

"Turns out you're not the only one who thinks Courtney Wallace was murdered."

"Really?" First she felt a tingle of excitement. Then she felt a chill. There was something that felt surreal about this revelation. Lamont was holding something back. "I never used that word in my stories. I never said it was murder."

"You suspected foul play, Smithsonian. You told me so yourself."

"Who called you?"

"Anonymous source, no name, female by the way, tried to use a fake English accent. Bad fake accent. Call came this morning, after your latest story hit the street." He pulled a folded copy of the LifeStyle section of *The Eye* from his jacket pocket. "This thing about the lining. The poison dye and all that." He spread out the section on the counter so she could be reminded of what she'd written. He pulled out his cell phone and held it up, as if demonstrating how he got the call.

Why is he drawing me a picture?

"Yeah, that thing. The lining. And—?"

"My anonymous tipster told me the killer is one—Lacey Smithsonian. Well, that would be *you*, wouldn't it?"

"What?!" she shouted. She shook her head as if she hadn't heard him correctly. "She told you *what*?"

He clicked a photo of her with his phone. "See? That's why I came over. I had to see the look on your face." He glanced at the photo on his phone and laughed with glee. "Priceless! Worth a thousand words. See what I'd have missed if I called and told you over the phone?"

"This is a terrible practical joke, Broadway."

"Maybe the caller thought so too, but I doubt it. She sounded serious. It's on tape. She says you're the killer. We have a habit of recording everything. Sounds better in court when you can play the tape."

"It's on tape?"

Several reporters appeared at the door of the kitchenette to investigate the scream. Lacey pushed past everyone and charged back toward her desk, Broadway Lamont on her heels, still laughing. She stopped in front of the small conference room. It had glass walls, but the big advantage over continuing this conversation at her cubicle was the door. She herded the big detective inside and slammed it behind them.

"Hey, I'd like another doughnut," he said to her rolled eyes. "I am a cop. I'm entitled."

"Not now!" Lacey couldn't worry about food at a time like this.

But who should magically appear outside the conference room but Felicity Pickles, with a small plate of doughnuts. She tapped on the glass. Lamont opened the door a crack.

Felicity handed him the plate. "Here, Detective. A little something to keep your strength up."

"Why, Ms. Felicity, you are a life saver," he said to her. "You will keep me apprised if you ever become free of Mr. Wiener Meyer, won't you?"

She giggled in response and waltzed off. Lacey gestured for Lamont to shut the door. He bogarted the plate and sat down.

"You know that's crazy, don't you?"

"I do." He leaned back in the chair, doughnut in one hand and coffee in the other. "But it rattled you. And I had to see it in person."

Her fellow reporters weren't quite crude enough to press their noses against the glass walls of the conference room, but there was a gathering of them taking place outside, with lots of chatting and staring, and doughnut munching. They'd be a poor excuse for reporters if they weren't curious. And hungry. Lacey turned her back. She didn't think any of them could read lips, but she wasn't taking any chances.

Her editor Mac Jones appeared at the door and marched right in without ceremony. He closed the blinds against the stares of the curious crowd outside. The door opened again and Tony entered.

"Not you, too!" Lacey complained. "Mac, get this story stealer out of here."

"Police reporter. You can't keep me out. What's up? Lacey? Mac? Broadway?"

Lacey sat at the table and rested her forehead on it. *Just to gather my thoughts.*

"It's all over the newsroom," Mac announced, "that you're a suspect in the demise of Courtney Wallace, which is supposed to be a freak accident. Somebody start talking. Lamont? Smithsonian?"

"That didn't take long, Jones," Lamont said to him. "I'm impressed." He offered the platter of doughnuts. Mac took one.

"We are a news organization, after all. Smithsonian, what's going on?"

"I have no idea. Ask the detective." She stared pointedly at Lamont and the others followed her gaze. "Ask him if I'm under arrest, while you're at it."

Lamont was unflustered. "I was just kind enough to report that I got an anonymous call fingering your fashion reporter here as the premeditated perpetrator of felony murder in the demise of Ms. Courtney Wallace. This troubles me, ladies and gentlemen."

"Now you're just messing with me, Broadway," Lacey said. "You don't believe that."

"This troubles me, not because Smithsonian's been called a suspect. I consider everyone a suspect, on principle. Though if she was the killer, it might deprive us all of her unique fashion insight. No, I am troubled, deeply troubled, that this nice little one-in-a-billion freak accident of ours, ready to be signed and sealed by the Medical Examiner of the District of Columbia, has been called into question.

Not just by one Lacey Smithsonian, with her clothing voodoo hoodoo. I get that. I mean she's got that murder jones in her bones. Nothing we can do about that. A wacky accident like this just gets her going, thinking 'How could this thing secretly be a murder?' But thinking that don't make it a murder. That's the way I like it. The less murder in this town, the better, that's what I think. But with this anonymous tipster, now I got to start thinking farther and wider. I got to start thinking murder."

"Do you know who called you?" Tony asked.

"Why, no. Tip came from a pay phone. Might be the last one left in D.C."

"Did your caller say how she managed it?" Tony asked. "Just wondering how Lacey pulled off a murder, what with her day job and her busy love life and all."

"Very funny, Trujillo," Lacey said. "Someone is accusing me of murder. And murdering someone I barely knew. And if you remember, the dress did it."

"What's wrong with you this morning, Smithsonian?" Mac said. "You have too much of a good time last night?"

"I'm sore and I'm stiff. Someone threw a rock at me Saturday. Above Great Falls. My guess is I was supposed to fall into the Potomac River and drown."

All eyes focused on her.

"Who did it?" Lamont asked.

"I don't know," she said, though she was beginning to have an idea. Was this Johnson's doing? Vic's man tailed him on Sunday, but not Saturday. Did he set someone up to call the police with that tip? That seemed like his style. *Sneaky.* She rubbed her shoulder and tried to stretch her arm out. It hurt. "Anyway, I didn't sleep well." Tony put his arm around her shoulder. She flinched. "Ouch. That hurts. Don't do that."

"You okay, Smithsonian?" Mac asked.

"Vic was with me. He cleaned it. You want to see my wound?"

"It cut you?" Lamont frowned. "Someone doesn't belong to the Lacey Smithsonian fan club. Someone took your article pretty seriously. Seriously enough to want to get you out of the way. So tell me about this assault. Walk me through it. Humor me."

Mac reached for another doughnut and sat down. Lacey counted off the basic facts on her fingers.

"One: I was at Riverbend Park Saturday afternoon, with Vic

Donovan. Two: Gregor Kepelov and Marie Largesse showed up."

Tony cut in. "She didn't have a vision, did she?" He pretended to faint.

"Don't mock me." Lacey continued. "Three: Marie had a vision and she was concerned for my safety. I am just reporting what happened. No snickering, please. Stuff a doughnut in it, Tony. And can somebody get me some aspirin, please?"

"What happened then?" Mac asked.

"Four: We took a walk through the woods. To see the bluebells. Five: Someone threw a big rock at me, from the woods up on the ridge. It hit me on the shoulder, hard, although the others think it was aimed for my head. We were on the trail below, next to the river. Six: I fell down the bank. Seven: Vic saved me from going in the drink. Eight: Vic and Gregor Kepelov gave chase. No luck. A car raced out of the parking lot, no plate numbers. Nine: We reported the incident to the park ranger. He suggested it was just kids. Ten: I have a headache and my shoulder hurts. That's it, no more fingers."

She left out viewing the painting at the gallery Friday, the visit to Jillian Hopewell's house on Sunday, and finding the possible origin of the dress in an old magazine. Those were not so much facts, she decided on the spur of the moment, as *leads.*

And if they're leads in this story, they're MY leads. Besides, I'm out of fingers.

There was a moment of silence. Tony grabbed a doughnut.

"Just why were you at this park?" Lamont asked. "Never been there myself."

"To see the bluebells. They're very pretty this time of year." She lifted her mug to sip her lousy coffee. It seemed to take a lot of effort. Her shoulder hurt.

"Just to see the bluebells?"

"It sounds pretty silly, I suppose."

"Not to me. I'm rather fond of the tulips," Tony said, with a hint of sarcasm. "I like to tiptoe through them."

"I don't care how it sounds," Lamont said. "This rock attack have anything to do with this murder someone wants to pin on you?"

"Search me," Lacey said. "You got the call. On tape. You go find your mystery caller."

"What are you getting at, Lamont?" Mac asked.

"Voodoo. Smithsonian's special brand of voodoo. Things that don't make sense make my head hurt."

"Yours too?" Lacey asked. "I'll split my aspirin with you. If I ever get any!"

Tony got up and rummaged around in the conference room cupboard for aspirin. He found a two-pack and tossed it to her.

Broadway Lamont looked disgruntled. He swallowed the last bite of doughnut. Lacey swallowed the aspirin and chased it with newsroom coffee. It was bracing.

"The rock-throwing incident didn't happen here in D.C., but it happened," Lamont said. "I got a caller dropping the dime on the fashion reporter. Someone's nervous that Smithsonian's getting too close to whatever it is, or whoever it is, and this Paris Green poison dress is looking more and more like murder. Why can't it be a simple shooting, a gang fight, a drive-by, a robbery gone bad? Nope, it's gotta be a damn baroque crazy-ass mystery. It does not make me happy. You got any suspects?"

"You want me to make a wild assumption without basing it on facts?" she asked. He didn't answer.

Mac asked, "Are you taking this anonymous call seriously, Detective?"

"I seem to remember being there at the Correspondents' Dinner with Smithsonian. It would take some kind of nerve to plan a twisted piece of killing with me right there as a witness. Nor did I see her slamming into the waiter who doused the suspect with the drinks. Smithsonian was as shocked as anyone when it happened. I know shock. I've been at this a while, folks. I listen to my gut. She felt something was up. That's her special voodoo. Then she goes off hunting for the origin of said dress and she found someone switched the lining out. Then she writes about it. Keeps at it. So if she's a killer, she's one crazy-ass murderer, thumbing her nose at a homicide detective. Besides all that, she's got a pretty good alibi for most of that night: Me."

"Sorry you came with me to the Correspondents' Dinner, Broadway?" Lacey asked.

"Hell no. It was a treat. You make it out of this alive, imagine the story I get to tell the boys at the office. I hope this whack job with the tip surfaces. We get calls all the time. People confessing to crimes they didn't commit. Cranks dropping a dime on some guy who crossed them in traffic. Big difference here? This crime ain't been labeled a crime. Maybe this person knows it's a murder and has inside information, personal information. Maybe this person just hates fashion. Or Smithsonian. At any rate, you're not in my crosshairs as a suspect. No more than the rest of the world, that is. On principle."

"So I'm in the clear?"

"If you call being attacked with a flying rock being in the clear," he said.

"This is ridiculous," Mac said. "It's the fashion beat, not the crime beat. Not the political beat. Not even the sports beat, which could always get someone in trouble."

"That's the word," Lamont agreed. "Smithsonian is a magnet for trouble."

"You took the words out of my mouth," Mac said.

There was a beat of silence. The detective got to his feet.

"Smithsonian. Stay well. Any more trouble, you call me. Any solid info, you call me. Any voodoo hunches, you call me."

Lacey saluted him as he left the conference room. Mac gestured for Lacey to stay. Trujillo made no move to go.

"I have to write a follow-up to the story," Lacey said.

"Another one? What's this one going to do?" Mac said. "Cause a showdown on the street at high noon?"

"Maybe I'll just type up my notes, until I have more."

"It's a plan."

"What about Peter Johnson, Mac? He's already tried to sabotage my work."

Mac breathed deeply. "He's on leave, as you know. I would have fired him, if I could. The Guild, you know. He's a jerk, but I don't think he could do this. Lamont says the caller was a woman. Trying to put on an accent."

"Johnson's not that creative," Trujillo said. "Does he even have any female friends he could coerce into a prank call? I don't think he has any female friends, period."

Lacey wasn't sure that made things any better. Johnson was the devil she knew. Now there were devils out there she didn't know.

"Listen, I have a few leads to follow. I have to get back to work."

"Dangerous leads?" Mac frowned.

"Just some calls. I think I found out where the dress came from. In the beginning. I have an old magazine article and a picture of the woman who probably had it made. If I'm right, it dates from just before the Second World War. It might round out the story."

"Work your leads. Aside from Johnson, you got any idea who might be naming you in this woman's death?"

"Not really. Courtney didn't have a lot of friends, but she had lots of enemies. Maybe I'm on that list now." On Friday Lacey ran into Zanna and Eric at the art show and slightly tipped her hand to Eve Farrand and Drake Rayburn. She was attacked by a rock on Saturday. Coincidence? "Thaddeus Granville hated her, but he seems to be okay with me, and I don't see him chasing after me in the woods with a rock like a caveman. On the other hand, he seems to know more about fashion than anyone else."

Mac reached for the last doughnut on the plate. "Long as it's on topic. By the way, you got a fashion column this week?"

"How about the high price of beauty, or something like that?"

"You got a knack. And you two, I've got other news. The galleys are in."

"The galleys? Are you talking about the book?"

"*Terror at Timberline?*" Trujillo asked.

"I have a set for each of you. I need them proofed ASAP. It's only two hundred and fifty pages. A walk in the park."

"Proofreading? Snooze." Trujillo stood up. "I hear the police beat calling me."

"Galleys are on my desk, with your names on them," Mac said. "Pick up a set. I need them back by the end of the week, no later. I mean it, Trujillo. This is *our* book I'm talking about here! If you don't want to help, then I guess you don't want your name on the cover."

"Aye, aye, captain. I'm on it. Lead on." Tony was right on Mac's heels as they left the conference room.

Lacey suspected Trujillo just wanted to make sure his section of the book was as *important* as hers.

Lacey Smithsonian's
FASHION *BITES*

The High Price of the Pursuit of Beauty

If every dress tells a story, what story would a poisoned dress tell? In the strange case of the Paris Green pigment, the story says: If you *dye,* you could *die.*

In folklore, myth, and history, the present of the pretty poison is a popular parable. Wicked witches are forever handing poisoned apples to Sleeping Beauties. Sixteenth-century French Queen Catherine de' Medici was said to have sent a pair of perfumed and poisoned gloves to a rival, who subsequently died. But then, Catherine (and wicked witches) didn't have modern weapons at her fingertips.

The pursuit of beauty through the ages—even today—is fraught with potential hazards we ignore at our peril. We like to say that dresses have *killer style.* We don't usually mean that literally. But countless women throughout the centuries have dallied unaware with dangerous modes of dressing. They have pushed the envelope to enhance their beauty and suffered the consequences, from tight-laced corsets that strangled them, to foot binding that crippled them, to belladonna that blinded them, to pretty green dyes that sickened and killed.

You might think all that is a thing of the past—but is it?

Are Fashion Hazards Lurking in Your Closet?

While your clothes may not contain traditional poison dyes (or then again, they might), they could be harboring other chemicals that can damage your health. Could your favorite blue jeans affect your human genes? Could your wrinkle-free clothes make your skin crawl?

Nonylphenol Ethoxylates (NPEs) are used as surfactants in clothing and can disrupt hormones and allegedly affect fertility. Phthalates are used in plastics as softeners, but they also appear in cosmetics and perfumes. They have been associated with endocrine disruption, leading to the development of breast cancer, obesity, and other adverse health effects. Formaldehyde, used both to preserve bodies and in "sizing" to keep clothes wrinkle-free, can irritate skin and cause allergic reactions. Yikes!

But the hazards don't stop there. Your feet can trip you up as well.

We don't bind our feet anymore. Or do we? You want to stand on your own two feet, but sometimes that's a little difficult with today's fashionable shoes. They are sometimes *cruel shoes*. They are often too high, too pointed, and too tight. They can squeeze the bones in your feet, causing pain and numbness, a condition known as Morton's neuroma. High heels can permanently tighten the Achilles tendon and cause hammertoes and bunions. There's more, but isn't that enough to make you pause before your next purchase of those delectable high-heeled stilettos? Yes, they look dangerously sexy, but your feet may really be the ones in danger.

You adore your flip-flops. You can buy them in any color or pattern, cover them in rhinestones, coordinate them with your pedicure, and wear them at the beach. They're so cute, so adorable, so easy to wear. They're great—if you want heel pain, plantar fasciitis, stubbed toes, sprained ankles, and stress fractures. That is, unless you are among the lucky minority of people who can't stand having something between their toes. We are the flip-flops immune, and we pass them by.

Corsets were once all the rage, and they are once again. I'm sure we've all heard about the hazards of corsets that previous generations of women wore to create those highly prized wasp-waist profiles and hourglass silhouettes. These whale-boned wonders could bruise internal organs, including the liver, spleen, and kidneys. They constricted the diaphragm, making it difficult to breathe, while creating that tradition of romantic *swooning* that previous centuries were so famous for. But that couldn't happen today, could it?

Hello, shapewear! That miracle of stretch! These skintight wetsuit-like undergarments can also strangle your insides, just like corsets, and cause great discomfort, as well as numbness in your legs. In some cases, they can even cause blood clots. Additionally, they are what is technically known as *silly looking*. An old-fashioned merry widow or long-line bra, in luscious lace, is much more attractive and easier to wear. But whatever shapewear style you prefer, be smart. Wear it sparingly, where and when it counts to perfect a certain look, not every hour of every day.

The eyes are the mirror of the soul. We want them to be big and beautiful. Belladonna, derived from deadly nightshade, was used by women during the Renaissance to dilate their eyes, giving them that sexy sixteenth-century come-hither look. Belladonna could also result in blindness, not to mention brain damage. While this herb has some modern medicinal applications as well, it can be deadly if misused.

Today, contact lenses are a godsend for both eyesight and beauty. However, if they are not used correctly, they can damage your vision, cause eye irritation, and infections. And that isn't very pretty, is it?

Fashion's fools follow every fad, whether good or bad. These fools are never the best dressed, because they don't listen to their instinct: the little voice inside that says, "That thing looks ridiculous on you! And it's killing me!" Listen to your inner voice. Be aware of what you wear and how it affects your health, as well as your style.

Don't be fashion's fool.

Chapter 38

THE WOMAN ON THE OTHER end of the phone, Lizzie Howard Ferguson, the granddaughter of Betty Lionsgate Howard, sounded a bit confused.

"Are you talking about Gran's funky old dresses?"

The woman lived in a small town in Oklahoma. She had cleaned up her grandmother's house in Richmond, Virginia, after she died. Ingrid Allendale helped Lacey track down the estate sales people there, and they led her to Lizzie Ferguson. Lacey conjured up a picture of a no-nonsense Midwesterner who had fallen far from her grandmother's southern debutante tree. That tree was probably a magnolia, Lacey reflected, which might not flourish in dusty Oklahoma.

"Yes." Lacey was primed to take notes, but she had no notes so far. This conversation wasn't promising. "A black gown with a white lining. It resembled the John Singer Sargent *Portrait of Madame X*."

"Is that a movie or something? Doesn't ring a bell. Let me think. Those dresses—they were beautiful, but so old. And tiny. Gran was tall and skinny. Who could wear them? I mean, I was born a size twelve. And I was never a dress-up kind of kid."

"Were there a lot of them?" Lacey asked.

"She held on to a half dozen or more. Real fancy stuff. Jackets, dresses. Sentimental value. I guess she had a different kind of life down there in the South. After she died, we moved all her things to a storage unit. My brother and I finally went back and cleaned her stuff out a few months ago. We got stuck with it. Took us a few years to get around to it. My mom was no good at cleaning up messes. She moved to Florida to kick up her heels. Too delicate for real work."

"And the clothes?"

"Consigned them to the estate sale ladies. That's where you got my number, right?"

"Right." Lacey sighed a little and thanked her.

"Tell me, you actually write about old dresses?" Lizzie Ferguson sounded a little amused. There was incredulity in her voice, too.

"Among other things. I'm a fashion reporter in Washington, D.C."

"Washington, D.C. My goodness. Takes all kinds, I guess. I

work in a medical lab. I wear scrubs most every day. We don't dress up much."

"I suppose not. I will be writing more about the Madame X dress. You realize that someone died in that dress?"

"Yes, I got that, that's pretty fascinating, but as you explained it, that wasn't Gran's fault. Sounds like it'll turn into an urban legend or something. It'll be all over the Web, I guess."

Lizzie Ferguson clearly wasn't going to lose any sleep over this story. Perhaps there were advantages to working in a lab, wearing scrubs, and not caring about clothes.

"You could look at it that way. I want to describe the history of the dress, and I'll include some information from the old *Mademoiselle* magazine article your grandmother was in."

"You actually have a copy of that. I heard about it. I never saw it. Don't read much. Don't have time."

Lacey played with her pen. "Do you like fashion?"

"Fashion." The woman on the other end of the phone laughed. "That would be Gran. Not me, and not my daughter. She just wears black. Dyed her hair blue. Sleeved her arms with tattoos, though I keep telling her that's just flirting with infection and hepatitis C. I try to keep my mouth shut about her looks. I'm just happy she washes her hair."

Alas, too many women settle for C&C: Clean and Comfortable.

"You're very understanding."

"I try. I named her Karen. She hates it. Now, she goes by LaVonya. LaVonya Galore. I have no idea what that's all about, but I just let it ride. My LaVonya is what she calls a 'neo-burlesque' artist. She's had two or three different stage names."

"Maybe she's just trying to find herself," Lacey suggested. "Wouldn't your daughter be interested in her great-grandmother's dresses?"

"I don't think so. She'd rather be bare naked on stage than get dressed up all formal. Kids these days, there's no call for fancy dresses and all that folderol. They just take up space. If I gave her those old dresses, they'd just end up in my basement. I'll tell her about your article. She can look it up online if she wants."

The debutante gene had not been passed down, apparently. Lacey ached to meet a little DNA from vivacious Betty Lionsgate, who joined the Navy and served in the war, but still cared about what she wore.

"Your daughter sounds like a free spirit."

"Is that what you call it? I thought it was called How to Irritate Your Mother. Well, I gotta go. You have a nice day."

"You too." Lacey clicked off and stared at her notebook. It was a blank page.

Fashion wasn't everyone's cup of tea. But that woman had no regard for her grandmother's treasured clothes, even though they were an essential part of her family history. The phone call just made Lacey sad. She thought about something as precious as Aunt Mimi's trunk being sold at a rummage sale, tossed carelessly in a storage unit, or worse, dumped in a landfill. Lacey thrummed her fingers on her desk. She decided she was too busy to worry about the demise of dress-up culture and the Decline of Western Civilization.

She searched for and found a number for a Gerhardt Hopewell in Sarasota, Florida. She called and left a message, explaining who she was and that she wanted information on his ex-wife, Jillian Hopewell. She hoped he was the right Hopewell. She didn't mention Courtney Wallace, or the silk lining, or the possible Paris Green connection. It would be better to explain those things in person, even if it was on the phone. He texted her back within minutes. He was out of town and couldn't speak with her until tomorrow.

Next on her list was Eric Park at Channel One News. He seemed happy enough to hear from her.

"Hey, Eric, any news on the video clip of Courtney? Is it going to surface?"

"No way. The suits here at the station are adamant about it not being released. And frankly, I've looked at it a couple of times and there's nothing much to see, I'm sorry to say. Unless you like watching Courtney in full meltdown mode."

"Darn. Nothing?"

"Not that I can see. I've really enjoyed your stories, though. Heard you had a chat with Eve on Friday?"

"News travels."

"She wouldn't talk about it though." He laughed. "Not that she ever tells me anything."

"It was off the record. And really there was nothing much to talk about. By the way, did you and Zanna or Eve happen to take a trip up to a vintage store in Baltimore last Tuesday, after Courtney's funeral service?"

"Not me. After that, I was editing footage all day. No idea where Zanna went afterwards. And Eve was in and out. Why?"

"Oh, someone I know saw a couple of reporters up there. I just thought it might have been you guys. Anyway, I saw Eve on Friday, just before I saw you and Zanna at the gallery. On Saturday, someone threw a big rock at me in Riverbend Park. That was my big weekend."

"You're kidding! Somebody attacked you? I don't believe it. Are you okay? You sound okay, I hope you are."

"I'm good. Eric, what I want to ask you is absolutely not for release. To anyone."

"Not even to Eve?"

"Not to anybody. Just between us."

"You don't want me to tell anyone? Not fair." He sounded amused. "This is TV. We tell people stuff."

"I know. But I really need to see your footage of the waiter running into Courtney. I know you've watched it, but maybe fresh eyes will catch something new."

She was taking a chance, asking for his help. Eric couldn't have pushed the waiter, he was filming Courtney when it happened. But that didn't mean he couldn't be in league with the person who did.

"I had to watch it. I'm only human and human means curious. But there's not much in it but Courtney. Courtney and a bit of the waiter. Besides, it's Channel One footage. I couldn't just walk you into the editing room over here. People would talk."

"Come on, Eric. It's worth a try. Please. There must be a way."

He paused. "You know, sometimes the strangest things show up on YouTube. We've all been waiting to see it happen with this clip. Who knows if it's even possible. But maybe today it will magically appear. If it does turn up there, I promise it's not going to tell you much."

"It could turn up on YouTube?"

"The whole clip. Unedited. Unauthorized. I'm just saying it could happen. You know Washington. It leaks like a sieve."

"That it does. So my roof could be leaky today?"

"I'd say it's cloudy with a chance of leaks. Pack an umbrella."

"I'll be hoping for rain."

"After lunch would be good. You might look for a YouTube channel with the words 'leaky roof' in the name. Nothing else."

"Got it. Thanks, Eric."

"If something good happens, I mean good as in *news*, I want an on-air interview."

"With you? Not Eve?"

"No Eve. Who says I don't deserve a shot on camera, instead of behind it?"

Everyone in this town has ambitions.

"Okay. Ground rules: If something newsworthy comes from anything I might or might not find on YouTube today, I talk on camera to you," Lacey said. "And only you. And only after I release my story. But watch out, Eve might have a fit."

"Eve is temperamental. I wouldn't let it bother you."

After clicking off with Eric and writing up her column and some fashion news briefs about a fashion show and a new collection at a boutique, Lacey went to lunch at one of her favorite secret lunch spots. She was careful to avoid any place where she might run into Brooke, Damon, Broadway Lamont, or anyone from *The Eye*. It was a tiny respite.

Back in the office after lunch, she contacted a fiber forensics expert, Rebecca Paulson, who used to work at the Smithsonian Institution and now was a freelance consultant and writing a book about Colonial dress. They had spoken on the phone once before, for an article Lacey wrote on early American textiles of the Colonial era. They'd never met in person, but this time, Lacey had something to deliver face to face.

Paulson agreed to a quick meeting at a coffee shop on P Street near Dupont Circle, about six blocks away. Although it was hot and steamy, Lacey was glad to get outside again, and she had just enough time to walk. She wanted to limber up her sore muscles. She grabbed her purse and the painting and waved good-bye to Mac as she dashed past his office door.

Halfway to Dupont Circle on Connecticut Avenue, she stopped suddenly and looked around. She felt as if she were being watched. She saw nothing, other than sidewalks full of her fellow Washingtonians.

You're being dramatic, she told herself. *You don't have time for that*. She knew Vic had Turtledove watching her. She didn't see him, or feel his comforting presence. That was probably a good thing, she decided. If she didn't spot him, no one else would.

Lacey arrived first at the coffee shop and ordered an iced decaf mocha. She grabbed the only available table. It was in the window, which gave her a view of P Street.

Rebecca Paulson breezed in the door as Lacey sat down. She bought a large bottle of water and strode over to Lacey's table. In person, Paulson was a trim woman on the tall side, with glossy brown hair and round tortoiseshell glasses that gave her a sort of whimsical intellectual air, like a scholarly schoolgirl. A queen of Geek Chic. She wore a white blouse, gray skirt, and clogs, perfectly suited to lab work. *And yet much better than scrubs.* Paulson had a brisk but friendly manner.

"Hello, Lacey? I recognized you from your column. Thanks for calling me again."

"My pleasure." The recognition was not really a pleasure. Since Mac had insisted on putting a photo on her column, random people now squinted at her, wondering how they knew her. They knew they'd seen her somewhere, but couldn't place her. It could be awkward. "Have a seat. It's so nice to meet you in person."

"Me too. I read your columns all the time, they make me laugh."

"Glad to hear it. That's usually what I'm going for."

"You said you wanted a fabric comparison?"

"If it's possible."

"It's possible. What do you want compared?"

Lacey pulled the painting from her tote and one of the green silk scraps she received from Lola Gallegos. She unwrapped a corner of the painting to show Paulson the green silk it was painted on.

"You can take it out of the frame, if you need to. There may be some extra fabric tucked up in the back."

"Probably won't be necessary," Paulson said. "And you want to find out what, exactly?"

"To see if they're a match or not. This silk scrap and the silk in the painting." Lacey didn't provide any context or back story. She didn't want to influence her analysis by suggesting they were connected. "And anything you can tell me about the samples' ages or origins, or anything unusual about them. That would be of interest too."

"Can do. I'll put them under the microscope. After I complete my examination, maybe you can tell me what it's all about." Rebecca smiled and stood up, tucking the painting under her arm and the silk scrap in her bag.

"Do you know how long it will take?"

"I'll call you as soon as I finish."

"I appreciate it."

"Is this life or death?"

Interesting way to put it. "It could be," Lacey said.

Rebecca nodded. "No problem. It usually is in D.C." She took a swig of her water, screwed the cap back on, and gathered her things. Every movement was efficient. She said goodbye and walked swiftly out the door and up the street. After her whirlwind meeting, Lacey was in no hurry to get back to the newsroom. She sipped her mocha, savoring the chocolate in it.

Turtledove materialized next to her. He had an apple and an iced tea in hand. Lacey was surprised, but with someone throwing rocks at her, she didn't really mind having a bodyguard.

"I didn't even see you," she said.

"That's kind of the point." He grinned at her and bumped her uninjured shoulder gently with one big fist. "My specialty."

"Guess it is. Did you notice anything?"

"The usual midday Dupont Circle crowd. Lots of Washington types. Some theatre folks."

Turtledove was very large and very muscular, but at the same time, graceful. He was a beautiful blend of multiple ethnicities and he set many hearts aflutter with his dark soulful eyes and brilliant smile. He was one of Lacey's favorite people, even though she knew very little about him. Except that he played a mean jazz trumpet and he was a good man to have around in a crisis. She trusted him.

"We're close to a lot of the smaller theatres. *The Eye*'s theatre critic lives just around the corner."

"Tamsin. Interesting lady. Did you see the latest on DeadFed?" Turtledove was a wonderful guy, except for being a faithful follower of Conspiracy Clearinghouse. "I think you'll be interested."

"Oh no. Now what?"

He showed her his phone.

CRIME OF FASHION BEAT HEATS UP!
MURDER SLANDER HITS FASHION SLEUTH SMITHSONIAN
By Damon Newhouse

Is fashion reporter Lacey Smithsonian too close to the truth about murdered Channel One personality Courtney Wallace?

An anonymous tipster to Conspiracy Clearinghouse has accused Smithsonian of being complicit in Wallace's death. Responding to our query, D.C. homicide detective Broadway Lamont attributed the claim to a crank. "Any investigation is subject to crackpots with crazy accusations. This appears to be one of them," he told this reporter. The Clearinghouse agrees.

This reporter has learned from confidential police sources that the unknown tipster is being investigated as a person of interest in the Wallace case. Wallace's death was initially ruled an accident, but is now thought to have been the fruit of a lethal conspiracy reaching deep into the hidden world of Washington media...

Apparently the woman who called Broadway Lamont with her accusation against Lacey had also contacted Damon Newhouse. Lacey handed back his phone with a sigh.

"Damon's on your side," Turtledove said. "He does get a little carried away sometimes."

Lacey emitted a small strangled scream. *And he weaseled a quote out of Broadway Lamont?*

In light of this story, Lacey thought it was odd she hadn't heard from Brooke. Even as the thought occurred to her, her phone jingled. It was a text from Brooke. She was on her way to a hearing and would "debrief" Lacey later.

"Swell. He's on my side. I'm thrilled. He should have let it drop. He just rose to the bait of this 'anonymous tipster.' Damon's being used."

"Damon's just shaking the tree of truth. The truth will set you free."

"And sometimes the truth will get you killed," she replied.

"That's why I'm here. To see that doesn't happen."

She trusted Turtledove with her life, but now it felt even more like she had a target on her back. Or on her shoulder. Lacey phoned Mac and told him she was knocking off for the day. Turtledove escorted her to *The Eye*'s parking garage and then followed her home.

On her blue velvet sofa, Lacey checked YouTube again on her laptop and found the leaked clip of Courtney and the champagne shower had finally surfaced. *Thank you, Eric!* She called Vic. He was in his Jeep, but he promised to watch it ASAP. Lacey watched the clip to the end, fascinated. She played it again, and again.

Eric's camera began in an extreme close-up on Courtney's face, then pulled back to frame her full height. Then back in tight again, but on her back. Courtney was dodging through the crowd and Eric was obviously hustling to keep up. She was trying to flag down a fleeing celebrity for an interview when a sliver of waiter Will Zephron came barely into the frame, his tray balanced on one hand. Suddenly, he lurched forward and his white-shirted arm and the tray of champagne flutes flew straight up. The tray tilted forward and dumped its contents, catching Courtney full in the face and down the chest. A dozen or more full glasses hit the broadcaster, soaking her face, hair, and dress. A few drops even landed on the camera lens. Lacey dialed the clip back and watched it again.

Courtney's dripping face morphed from stunned surprise into a grimace of shock and horror. She screamed and cursed, while Zephron staggered against another guest, trying to catch his balance. He seemed as stunned and outraged as she was, perhaps even more dramatically. His mouth and eyes were wide open, yelling "No!"

Courtney spun around, shaking her wet hair and yelling obscenities. She looked right into Eric's lens and froze. Realizing this was all being caught on camera, she pulled her shoulders back, fought to regain her composure, wiped her hair out of her face, and smiled for the camera.

"Well, folks, just a slip, a trip, and a fall. This story is all wet. But I'll be back with fresh updates throughout the evening as the President addresses the media. Reporting live from the White House Correspondents' Dinner, for Channel One News, I'm Courtney Wallace."

Lacey combed every frame for a glimpse of someone, anyone, giving Will Zephron that hard shove in his back and arm that he remembered feeling. His arm, tray, and face were in a few frames, but not his back. The scene was chaotic as the crowd parted around Courtney, fleeing the flying champagne and the embarrassment, the bustling waiters cleaning up the mess. But the camera stayed on Courtney. Most of it was filled with Courtney screaming expletives, as Eric promised. There was nothing suggestive that Lacey could see—except a flash of muddy yellow-colored cloth in the corner of one frame. Then it was gone.

She was about to play it again when Vic arrived with a bottle of wine. He kissed her hello and headed to her tiny kitchen to check out her larder. The cupboard was as bare as Old Mother Hubbard's, as usual. The cheese was all gone. There was popcorn.

"Wine and popcorn for dinner again, Lacey?"

"It's been weeks since I had popcorn. Festive and nutritious. Want some?"

"I'll phone for pizza. Extra pepperoni?" He settled down on the sofa by her side. Lacey flipped her laptop open again.

"Want to watch a movie with dinner? This is my favorite movie of the day."

"You're watching it again?" Vic inquired, while rubbing her neck and shoulder where it was sore. Lacey leaned back into him.

"Just one more time." As bodyguards went, he was lots more fun than Turtledove.

"Are you sure?" His hands played a magic flute on her spine.

"Never mind. I'll watch it again tomorrow."

When Brooke called, Lacey let the call go to voicemail.

Chapter 39

"HEY, LACEY, DID YOU SEE YouTube?" Harlan Wiedemeyer said, the first thing Tuesday morning. "The Courtney Wallace Channel One News video was leaked. Kind of like the champagne that did her in."

"You're stretching the metaphor," Lacey said. *If Wiedemeyer's seen it, everyone else has too.*

"If there's a metaphor to be stretched, I'm the man to stretch it."

"The champagne didn't act alone."

He laughed. "True."

Except for Wiedemeyer hanging around the LifeStyle section to see what new kind of groom's cake Felicity would come up with, it was a quiet morning. Lacey wore a sleeveless red cotton dress with a hint of sailor trim. The skirt fell below her knees, covering most of the bruises from her fall over the weekend, and she had her vintage white bolero jacket trimmed in red to put on when the air conditioner blasted her desk.

Felicity was away from her cubicle. Lacey had a fresh cup of decent coffee from the bakery and a protein bar to munch. Wiedemeyer had a Krispy Kreme doughnut.

So far, there wasn't much fallout from the DeadFed piece, except her mother had called late last night wanting to know what kind of nonsense Lacey was up to this time. Lacey averted disaster, and a possible trip by her mother to D.C., by blaming Damon for blowing it all out of proportion. She assured her mother that the nice homicide detective, Broadway Lamont, knew she was innocent and was taking care of everything. Lacey was waiting for fallout from the leaked clip on YouTube. Channel One was saying nothing, so far. They must have expected someone over there to leak it sooner or later.

Wiedemeyer wandered off to look for his lady love, and she watched the YouTube video again. Elizabeth Lionsgate's gown was truly lovely and Courtney wore it well, when she wasn't being an obnoxious broadcast diva. The camera caught a glimpse of her shoes, which Lacey hadn't really noticed before. They were expensive, black suede with tall silver stiletto heels.

Pretty, Lacey thought. *Awfully high, though, if you're going to be on your feet covering an event all evening.* She was surprised

Courtney had been able to stay on her feet through the champagne attack.

And then, Lacey saw that flash of muddy yellow fabric again. The fabric may have had nothing to do with pushing the waiter into Courtney. Or perhaps everything. But Lacey thought she recognized it. Zanna Nelson was wearing a mustard-colored dress when Lacey found the two of them in the ladies' room after the champagne shower. Was it the same dress? If Zanna had selected something black, like the majority of the media and their guests, she would have blended right in. That mustard color was memorable in an unattractive way. But it didn't prove that Zanna sabotaged Courtney, only that she was somewhere nearby. Nor did the rest of the pieces fit together. It was a jigsaw puzzle. A suggestive jigsaw.

She watched the video one more time, trying to catch a glimpse of more than a mustard dress. Nothing.

Zanna was beautiful but bland, one of those people who slipped under the radar. Lacey thought about what Eric Park had told her about the night of Zanna's meltdown, years ago. The fierce ambition that butted up against the reality that Courtney was fate's favored one, and not Zanna. Jealousy, envy, resentment, and a misplaced sense of entitlement all played a role. The would-be television news star lacked the magical alchemy to be on television. Pretty though she was, she seemed to have faded into the background of her own career. But underneath, she seethed.

Lacey compared Zanna's envy with the corrosive jealousy she felt radiating from Peter Johnson. She glanced around the newsroom, relieved he wasn't there. He was still on a forced leave of absence. Unfortunately, he was scheduled to return. Lacey had little hope she would see a changed man. Unless it was for the worse, after ten days of booze and resentment.

Had Zanna changed? Did anyone ever really change? Lacey returned to her other theory: Courtney's troubles started last year. Did Zanna have a hand in it? Did Eve Farrand, or even Eric Park? They were all close to Courtney, all ambitious, all old friends or coworkers who had a shared history, and shared animosities.

What about Drake Rayburn? Did he have a motive? Was he 'hooking up' with Eve to get back at Courtney? He'd seemed easily rattled at Martin's Tavern, and Drake and Eve were at the Correspondents' Dinner, but they weren't visible in Eric Park's clip of the champagne incident. Somebody wearing a muddy yellow dress *was*. It had to be Zanna. Lacey saw her with Courtney just minutes later, in the ladies' room.

Nothing Lacey knew of linked Zanna, or any of them, to the Paris Green lining. They hadn't shown any particular interest in fashion, or history. Or chemistry. Would Zanna have any knowledge about anything as obscure as Paris Green dye? For that matter, none of these people had any apparent connection to the one person Lacey suspected of having been a local source of that pigment, Jillian Hopewell.

Lacey's phone rang. It was textile expert Rebecca Paulson.

"Thanks for getting back to me so quickly," Lacey said.

"No problem. I had some time and I was curious," Rebecca said.

"What did you find?" She was holding her breath.

"The two silks are entirely consistent with having originated from the same source at the same time. I'm sorry that I can't say one hundred percent that they are from the same exact silk. But unless there was only one source in the world, this is the closest I can come. And both are consistent with heavy dress-grade silk from the mid-twentieth century."

"What's your best guess?"

"Guess? I don't guess. However, two pieces of silk, same weave, same fiber properties, both dyed with a copper acetoarsenite compound known as Paris Green, the composition of which also matches? I'd be stunned if they weren't from the same material and the same dye lot, though they could have both been dyed at a later date than they were woven. And interestingly enough, the paint pigments in the painting also contain various shades of the same Paris Green."

"You can tell that?"

"Of course. Microscopic analysis of the crystalline structure and particle size. Easy-peasy, as they say."

Easy for you to say. "So they are connected."

"This is, I take it, the 'Lethal Black Dress' you wrote about, the one with the Paris Green lining?"

"Yes, I'm still working on it. I've found out where the dress originated, and where the lining came from, and how they came together. But not the who or why. If I find out, it will be on the front page." She hoped it would be, anyway.

"It sounds intriguing. Foul play suspected?"

"Very possibly. May I use your name and your fabric analysis?"

"I'd be crushed if you didn't," Paulson said. "We geeky lab rats don't get much in the way of publicity."

಄

"Smithsonian." A heavy manila envelope landed on her desk. Mac stood by, waiting for her to turn her head away from the screen.

"What is that?" She was afraid she knew.

"Galleys. Hand delivered. *Terror at Timberline.*"

She groaned. *More like Terror on Deadline.*

"Ah, yes, the galleys. You really have to do something about the title, Mac."

"The title is what it is. Read it and get it back to me."

"When is it due?"

"ASAP."

"I should have known."

"Read all of it, yours and mine and Tony's sections. Read it like a book, not a punishment. And proofread it too. The sooner we all get it read, the sooner it will be in print."

She realized this would be the first time she'd be reading his and Tony's versions of what happened in and around Sagebrush, Colorado, this past February. She was a little curious, in spite of herself.

"And ASAP means?"

"Friday."

"Friday?" *Like I don't have enough to do.* "Can I take this home?"

"I'd rather you didn't," Mac said. "If you read it here, it won't get lost. Won't get any blood on the pages."

"That's what you say. But this is a newsroom, for pity's sake. Can you guarantee I'll have peace and quiet and time to read this?"

He glared at her. "You're a reporter. Multitask."

"Tell you what, I'll stay late every evening this week and read it when it's quiet. I'll expect comp time. Two full days. Deal?"

"I don't think Claudia will have a problem with that. She's just as excited about this book as we are. And we *are* excited, aren't we?"

Lacey nodded in resignation.

"We're all aquiver with excitement, Mac."

Writing a book is hard, she thought.

Chapter 40

LACEY MET LATOYA AT THE Greek place around the corner for a quick bite after work. She didn't want to take too long. She had to get back to the galleys.

"Hey, girlfriend," LaToya said as they sat down. "Heard you had a visit from Detective Broadway Lamont recently."

"He came to see me. Someone accused me of murder."

"Oh please, I already heard all about that. You ain't no murderer. Get to the important parts. How did that big handsome man look? Did he ask about me?"

Their gabfest was mostly about LaToya's romantic chances with Broadway Lamont. It suited Lacey. She didn't have to keep up her end of the conversation, except with an occasional comment and nod. She encouraged LaToya to keep the ardor turned on low. Broadway struck her as the type who'd rather do the pursuing than be pursued.

Turtledove was staying in the background, but Lacey was aware of his presence. He was another big guy who didn't want to get too close to LaToya. She had once expressed an interest in the tall, dark, and handsome Turtledove and probably would again. It was funny how big, tough guys could be afraid of women.

Help, help, she might attack me with a love bomb! As far as Lacey was concerned, they were big babies. Part of the problem was there were far too many attractive, smart, capable women in D.C. The few comparable men simply had their pick. It was too easy for them.

As LaToya chattered on about men, men, and more men, Lacey wondered about her phantom rock thrower. Reporters shouldn't need hired muscle trailing them. Nothing had happened to her since the Riverbend incident. Maybe it really was just a couple of kids, as the park rangers had said.

❧

When Lacey returned to *The Eye*, the newsroom was relatively quiet. Most of the newspaper had been put to bed. In the early hours of the morning, the printing plant would be humming, churning out the morning print edition, but that was off-site in suburban Maryland. *The Eye* would fully awaken at dawn when the first reporters started arriving, the ones with hard news beats and early deadlines. There were few perks to Lacey's fashion beat, but a more flexible schedule was one of them.

Mac was already home with Kim and the girls. Most of the reporters had filed their stories and were gone. The couple of reporters on night watch duties held court in the break room, on the other side of the floor. Lacey didn't see them. Nobody was left in the LifeStyle area. The cleaning crews were finished vacuuming and emptying wastebaskets. In her section of the newsroom, most of the bright overhead lights were turned off. A few desk lamps had been left on.

A light was on in Felicity's cubicle, though she was nowhere to be seen. Left behind, practically glowing in the lamplight, was some sort of pink strawberry cake confection, which Felicity had named in her column a "Pink Sky Angel Food Cloud Cake." Lacey thought that was too many words, too much pink, and certainly too much sugar. No doubt it figured prominently in the food editor's wedding plans. It was half eaten, with the food editor's signature note: EAT ME!

The seductive pink monument to excess awaited more worshipers. After debauching the day staff with fattening muffins and cookies and glazed doughnut groom's cakes, Felicity was now after the night crew.

What is her ultimate plan? Lacey wondered. *World domination?*

Across the floor, a few late-shift editors were working in their offices, down a hallway that couldn't be seen from the newsroom. Their doors were shut. They weren't bothering anyone. They were waiting on news from overlong Congressional hearings and a review of a new play. It was unusual that press night for a play was so early in the week, but sometimes that happened. It was bound to irritate the local critics. Tamsin Kerr would be one of those most irritated.

Lacey's cell phone rang. It echoed in the empty newsroom and startled her. The number told her it was Vic, checking in with her.

"You okay?"

"I'm fine," she said. "Turtledove has nothing to do tonight."

"Just the way I like it. He's watching the building, moving around. It's a nice night to hang out in Farragut Square."

"The guard at the front desk knows to let him in if he gets bored. You could probably just let him go home. I am perfectly safe."

"Famous last words."

"I love you too."

"I'll pick you up around eleven."

"See you soon."

She set her phone on her desk. Lacey hoped Gerhardt Hopewell would call her back. Did he know more about the silk? How much was left and where did it end up? How did it wind up in the fatal dress? There was a feeling in the air of things undone, of events yet to happen. She had pulled a lot of threads, but she hadn't been able to weave them all together yet. She wanted to write the final Lethal Black Dress story. Not rehash the past with *Terror at Timberline.*

Lacey sat down and turned on her desk light against the gloom. She pulled the galleys out of the envelope. It carried a triple byline: Douglas MacArthur Jones, Lacey Smithsonian, and Anthony Trujillo. All three parts of the story converged in a cold cabin in Colorado. Leaning back, she propped her feet up on the bottom file drawer. As she read, she found she was turning the pages as fast as she could. A paragraph of Mac's popped out at her.

It was February on Colorado's Western Slope. The air carried a bone-biting cold, despite the bright blue skies. A wild pony appeared on the ridge overlooking an old cabin, a cowboy camp left over from the days of cattle drives. It might have been a magical scene, if what was waiting in the cabin wasn't a nightmare.

Could be worse. She flipped to Tony's section, which detailed the various victims' disappearances and the law enforcement efforts to connect them and solve the case. His account was based on the facts and the police department's and sheriff's accounts.

The first woman disappeared one night in the spring. Her family was not overly concerned. She was known as a party girl. She would eventually come home. And she did, eventually. In a body bag.

Could be better. Lacey read on, taking just one break to make a fresh pot of hot decaf coffee. She returned to the sound of her desk phone ringing. Gerhardt Hopewell had finally called back. She checked the time. It was ten-fifteen.

"I was afraid this would be too late to call," he said. "I have a poker game on Tuesday nights, you see. Bunch of old geezers, like me. At least we're the early-to-bed types."

"No, it's fine. I'm still at the office. Thanks for getting back to me."

"What can I do for you?"

"I have a few questions about Jillian Hopewell."

"Jillian? My goodness. It's been years. First, some art gallery calls me about her. And now you. Is this about that showing they had of her paintings?"

"In a way. I wanted to ask about her paintings on silk. The green silk."

"Those." He was quiet for a moment. "I remember those."

"Did she dye the fabric herself? I'm asking because that dye was no longer commercially available. And it was known to be toxic as far back as the mid nineteenth century."

"Tell that to Jillian. I tried. It just made her more eager to do it herself. She mixed the dyes and the paint herself, out in that damn shed of hers. She was obsessed with it, obsessed with Cezanne, obsessed with doing everything the way he did it a hundred years ago. It didn't matter if it was obsolete or if it damaged her. She was all about suffering for her art."

"Was there a lot of it? The silk? Yards of it?"

"Not just yards. Bolts of it."

"All Paris Green?"

"Most of it, anyway. She made a big batch of the green stuff. Probably way too much. Eventually Jillian got tired of the silk and went back to canvas."

"Sounds like there might have been a lot of green silk left over."

"There was. As far as I know. We were splitting up at that point. I tried not to comment on her excesses. What is this all about?"

Lacey filled him in briefly on Courtney Wallace's death and the Madame X dress with the Paris Green lining. "The expert opinion is that the dress lining material was likely to have come from the same source as the silk in one of her paintings."

"Dear God."

"I'm sorry to upset you."

"Don't worry. I'm getting old, but the shock won't kill me. I always wondered if the dye and that paint and everything affected Jillian in some basic way. Like the Mad Hatter. In the head, you know. She was always fragile physically, but as time went on she increasingly made no sense. Painting for hours and days on end, as if it would save her soul or something. Holing up in that little shed of hers, mixing up God knows what kind of toxic mess. She talked of immortality. She should have been worried about her own mortality. By the time we split up I didn't know her anymore."

"She was a good painter," Lacey said.

"But not a great one. Jillian could never accept that. How did you know about the silk painting? I thought the show was just her canvases. All they wanted from me was a little background for the brochure, where she liked to paint, her artistic influences, things like that."

"The show was just the canvases, but I've seen a couple of the Riverbend landscapes elsewhere, on that beautiful green silk."

"And now you tell me a woman is dead. But how could it be Jillian's silk? It was so many years ago, and I don't even know what happened to it. We were divorced when she died. She was in bad shape. Sick, unhappy, no money to speak of. I let her stay in the house. I always thought it was too small for the two of us, especially as she insisted on keeping her studio there. Paints, brushes, easels, canvases everywhere, paint all over the place. I could barely turn around in it."

"Do you have a guess what might have happened to the silk?" Lacey prompted.

"The trash, I would have thought, but it could have gone to her family. I sold the house, but they took care of things when she died. Apparently not very well, from what you told me. But I was done, burned out. I washed my hands of her and her things."

"Her family." Lacey's antennae went up. "Where are they? What was their name? All I could find on the web for her was Hopewell, your name."

"Jillian had a lot of names, a lot of husbands. No children, though. I was the last one of four husbands. You would think I could take a hint, but no. I had to find out the devil behind the angel mask." He took a deep breath. "You ready? Her full married name was Jillian Susanna Nelson Brighton Holstein McIntyre Hopewell."

"Nelson was her family name? Jillian Susanna Nelson?" Lacey's scalp tingled. "Was she related to a Zanna Nelson?"

"Who is that?"

"A television reporter here in Washington, D.C. Late twenties."

"I wouldn't know. Jillian's family lived in Washington at one time. I only met her parents, and they're long dead. But Nelson is a common name. Late twenties, you say? This Zanna Nelson would have been a baby when Jillian died. Might be a niece or something."

"Yes, you're right." Lacey tried to sound calm, but she was agitated. She stood up at her desk and paced. She thought she heard a sound. Perhaps the editors down the hall were stirring.

"One thing about Jillian," Gerhardt Hopewell went on. "When she was good, she was very, very good—"

"—And when she was bad, she was horrid?" Lacey completed the couplet for him. He laughed. She thanked Hopewell, promised to let him know how the story turned out, and hung up.

And when she was bad she was horrid. *Just like Zanna Nelson?*

The sound in the hall came closer. Someone was coming down the hallway toward her cubicle. Whoever it was, she was clomping her way nearer in a pair of high-heeled shoes that were at least a size too large for her. They thumped on the carpet, slapping their soles against the floor.

Where the illuminated hallway met the darkened newsroom, Lacey saw the silhouette of a woman. The woman stepped into a pool of lamplight by the door.

"Hello, Zanna."

Chapter 41

"HELLO, LACEY SMITHSONIAN, FASHION REPORTER. Fashion reporter on a second-rate newspaper. Working late? Not a very important job, is it? Not like being on TV."

"Second-rate?" Lacey asked. "Most people think *The Eye* is third-rate." Zanna didn't laugh. "What do you want, Zanna? It's a little late for an interview."

Zanna stepped in, closer to the light. She stopped right across the desk from Lacey. They stood looking at each other. Zanna's skin looked flushed. Her hazel eyes were glazed; they gleamed in the half light. She was wearing a length of the Paris Green silk wrapped around her throat like a long scarf.

"Not too late for a fashion reporter though, is it? Or maybe it is too late."

"How did you get in?" Lacey asked. "There's a guard at the front desk. She would have announced you. I would have gone down to sign you in."

After I called the police. And Vic. And Turtledove.

"If I was stupid enough to go through the front door." Zanna's cupid's bow of a mouth pursed into a smirk. "But I'm not stupid. Not like a pathetic, stupid, fashion reporter."

This is going well. Has she been drinking? Lacey didn't smell alcohol. Still, something was very off in Zanna's manner. *Is she high on something? Is it the Paris Green?*

"I came in through the garage. You'd be surprised how men will open a locked door for you and hold it to let you into the elevator, when you bat your eyelashes and say you forgot your key card. I just waited for the right stupid man to come along."

Zanna sounded very proud of her accomplishment. She lurched unsteadily on the unfamiliar five-inch heels. They didn't fit. Not her feet or her style.

"Why did you come here tonight, Zanna?"

"To talk to you, Ms. Fashion Reporter. I have something to show you. I have to explain something to you that you are too stupid to understand."

That figures. I don't have enough editors telling me where I've gone wrong.

"I'm sure you're right. You're the smart one," Lacey said. "So tell me."

"That's right, I am the smart one. Courtney was stupid. She thought she was going to save her career by being a fashion reporter. What a ridiculous idea! Fashion reporters are *stupid.*"

"I've had my share of stupid moments," Lacey agreed. *This might be one of them.*

"I'm glad you agree." Zanna giggled. The odd sound echoed in the empty newsroom.

Certainly someone will come back to the newsroom any minute now. Right?

Lacey's attention was drawn back to the too-big shoes. Black suede with shiny silver spike heels that flashed in the lamplight. Expensive and tall. Lacey had seen them in the YouTube video, worn by another woman. A dead woman. They looked dangerous. Were they dance shoes, tango shoes?

Lacey wasn't interested in a tango or a tangle with this woman. She wanted Zanna gone. She wanted to call for help. She wanted the cavalry. She started to reach slowly for her cell phone on her desk. It was closer than her desk phone, but still out of reach.

"Aren't you afraid you'll fall in those shoes?" she asked.

"I don't know what you're talking about. These are fabulous shoes." Zanna tottered even as she said it.

"But they aren't your shoes, are they, Zanna? Those are Courtney's shoes. She wore them to the White House Correspondents' Dinner. That's where I've seen them before. On her feet."

"You noticed her shoes? I suppose that's the kind of thing a stupid fashion reporter would notice. She had big feet, the bitch. Well, they aren't Courtney's anymore. These are my shoes now. In fact, I came to show them to you. Do you like them?"

"Did you steal them? So you could walk a mile in Courtney's shoes?"

"She deserved it. She took my career. All I took was her lousy shoes!"

"And her life?" Zanna giggled again, and that told Lacey everything she needed to know. "Courtney was your friend."

"Friend? I hated Courtney. She was always so lucky. So perfect. So blond. It didn't matter how stupid she was, with that blond hair."

We agree on one thing. "Eric says it wasn't luck. He says she had whatever magic it took to look good on television."

"Eric doesn't know anything. He's just a cameraman."

"Wasn't it enough that you helped plant the story that got her kicked off the investigative team?"

"You figured that out? Good guess. I'm pretty smart, huh? Well, it was in a good cause. That senator and that Thaddeus Granville person are lousy cheating bastards. You couldn't have known it was me, because I was so slick. Courtney didn't even know she was getting the information from me." A small vein in Zanna's forehead started to throb. Her face colored. Her voice climbed higher and then cracked. It wouldn't sound good on television. "I nearly brought down a stupid senator. I brought down an empty-headed blonde."

"Good work, outsmarting all the stupid people. I suppose it was an anonymous call? Like the one you made about me?"

"Keep guessing."

"I'm tired of guessing, Zanna. It's time to go home. Let's call security and get you a ride somewhere safe." Lacey leaned forward for her phone and Zanna pushed her back, hard, with both hands.

"You don't know how I did it! You're not smart enough to know that. I'm smarter than you are. Can't you see that? I belong to Mensa, did you know that?"

I'm sure this is a proud moment for all Mensans everywhere.

Lacey told herself to stay calm. She eyed her phone, now as far out of reach as her desk phone.

"You're not a member of Mensa, are you?" Zanna sneered.

"Just the Newspaper Guild." *And what has it done for me lately?*

"I'm in SAG-AFTRA. That proves I'm smarter than you are."

"You proved you were smarter than Courtney too, didn't you?"

"I merely wanted the world to see she was a bad reporter," Zanna shouted. "Courtney didn't belong in television. She took the job I should have had. I should be on camera every night, not her."

On camera. It was true, and sad, that only a certain kind of face seemed to work in broadcast news. Zanna's face was symmetrical, well proportioned, traditionally beautiful, but on camera it seemed smaller, blank and lifeless, even forgettable. In contrast, Courtney's carved cheekbones, shark-like smile, and pushy personality had always been striking and memorable on camera.

Lacey was seeing a glimpse of the Zanna that Eric Park had seen on a night long ago, hysterical because she wasn't invited to a journalism-insider party. In Zanna's face, Lacey could also see Peter Johnson. Jealousy beyond reason. Pure and simple and scary. And maybe something more. *Some people once used small doses of arsenic as a drug, a stimulant. Is she flying on an arsenic high?*

"She was stupid and you're stupid too." Zanna was getting louder. Lacey thought she should encourage that.

"Speak up, Zanna, I can't hear you. Perhaps I'm not the smartest person in this room, but I did figure out how Courtney's dress ended up with a poisoned lining."

"If you were so smart, you would think about what she took from me. She stole from *me*. My job, my life, my career."

"Is that why you killed her?"

"Don't you know? It wasn't murder. It was a freak, one-in-a-million accident," Zanna said. "That's what everybody says. That's what the cops say."

"Until you threw a rock at me in Riverbend Park. And then told the police I had something to do with her death. It all backfired, Zanna. Don't you realize? I went to the Correspondents' Dinner with a Metropolitan Police Department homicide detective! He was with me when you slammed into that waiter. It's on Eric's video clip. No one else was wearing that particular mustard color. Just you."

Zanna wobbled on her sky-high heels. "You got him to leak that stupid clip, didn't you? It doesn't prove anything. You think you know everything? Well, you don't," she screamed.

That should wake up the homeless people in Farragut Square, Lacey thought. Where the hell were the night-shift editors? Were they deaf? Why didn't they come out and see what was going on? Lacey's desk phone rang and both women jumped.

"Don't answer that!" Zanna shouted. Lacey reached for it. Zanna grabbed the phone and ripped the cord out.

Great. Just keep her talking.

"The silk belonged to your late aunt, Jillian Hopewell. The artist. She was your aunt, right? You even covered her show at the gallery. Did you tell your viewers you used your aunt's poisoned silk to commit a murder?"

"No! No one knows she was my aunt. How do you know that? How did you find out about the silk?" Zanna's lower lip trembled. "I know. You guessed. Like everything else you guessed at. It was the perfect murder. No one could have known. No one knew that silk was dangerous."

"Except me." *Stupid fashion reporter here.*

"Shut up."

"Tell me about the silk," Lacey said, retreating toward another cubicle. There were desk phones all over the newsroom, she just had to reach one, with enough time to dial 911.

"I brought some of it for you. It's a present for your neck. That's why I came, Lacey." Zanna unwound the green silk from around her throat and held it up to the light. Lacey approached, in spite of herself. "I heard all about it when I was a little kid. My poor tragic aunt, the crazy artist. It was the paints and dyes she used that killed her. We all knew that. That stuff was in my parents' basement for years. Poor dead Aunt Jillian was proof it could kill. Here, take it, it's for you."

She reached out to Lacey, as if to drape it around her shoulders like a scarf. *Like a noose.* Lacey saw the beautiful green silk coming for her and took a step back.

"It belongs with you. You're the killer and that was your weapon. You keep it."

Lacey heard a quiet cough. Someone else was in the newsroom, somewhere. Perhaps just coming through the doorway. Zanna snapped the silk taut like a garrote. Lacey couldn't take her eyes off of it.

"I have more. I knew someday it would come in handy. For instance: When I wanted to get rid of the woman who stole my life!" She wrapped it around her hands, playing with it, almost like a cat's cradle.

"Courtney. How did you get her to take the fabric?"

Zanna smiled. "So easy. If you're a moron like Courtney. I told her the old lining had to be replaced, but a new lining could be even better. Prettier. Green to match her eyes. I told her she had such pretty green eyes, and she just lapped it up. Doesn't that make you want to vomit? I told her I could help her. I had some vintage silk that might work." Zanna laughed again, longer this time and louder. "I even found her the Madame X dress with the ripped lining. I showed it to her online and made her think it was her idea to run out and buy it. Courtney was like a magpie with something shiny."

"You handed it to her like a perfect red apple from a witch."

"But Courtney was the witch. Don't you see that?"

Lacey's cell phone jingled on her desk. Probably Vic or Turtledove. It was still too far away to make a lunge for it, with that green garrote waiting for her. Zanna looked at the phone and smiled. She shook her head *no* and waggled a finger. She slid the phone farther away on the desk. It stopped ringing.

Zanna didn't see Lacey's hand slowly reaching for her big red ceramic FASHION *BITES* mug. She rested her hand near it, keeping the desk between them. She hoped her fresh coffee was still hot. Lacey cheered herself with the thought that whoever had slipped into the newsroom might be calling for help right now.

Zanna fell silent. She must have been thinking the same thing. She locked eyes with Lacey.

Without dropping her eyes, Zanna lifted one foot behind her and grabbed one stiletto-heeled shoe. Then she kicked off the other one. She hefted the shoe in her hand. The silver spike heel looked like a silver dagger. She raised it high and pointed it right at Lacey. The silk fluttered out of her hands and fell over the phone on Lacey's desk.

"I think this adds a nice symmetry, don't you think," Zanna said. "Courtney died by the dress. You'll die by this stiletto. You are just dirt under my feet, both of you."

Wiedemeyer's words about the notorious spike-heel murder story he was writing earlier came back to Lacey: "*Poor bastard didn't have a chance… Pithed like a frog in a tenth-grade science class.*"

"I get the symbolism," Lacey said, backing up a little. "Live by the shoe, die by the shoe."

"Would you shut your mouth?! You think you're funny? You're not! You're going to die! You think that's funny?"

"Not really." Lacey was mad. She was tired of listening to this woman. And even though she knew she should have kept quiet, she just couldn't. She leaned forward on her desk, still eye to eye with Zanna. She reached for her phone, hidden under the silk. "You'll never fill Courtney's shoes. Don't you know that? She was the real deal, a blond TV diva. Zanna Nelson is just an imposter!"

Her right hand finally found her cell phone, a lump under the silk, just as it jingled again. Zanna growled and swung the stiletto down at Lacey's hand. The heel impaled the silk and the phone beneath it, the spike sliding right between her fingers, nailing the phone to the desk with a crunch. It went silent. Lacey jumped back before Zanna could swing again and nail her hand to the desk. She grabbed for her coffee mug instead of her phone.

"Don't move," Zanna commanded, but Lacey was not in the mood for taking orders. Zanna lunged toward her over the desk, stiletto heel raised high. Lacey threw semi-hot coffee in the woman's face and followed it with a backhanded mug to the side of her head. It was a glancing blow. Zanna grunted and went down, but she bobbed back up like an inflatable punching bag.

Lacey vaulted over her desk at Zanna, taking her mug with her. Later, she would wonder why she had never achieved such a gymnastic feat in high school as vaulting over a desk. But then, her teachers weren't killers, just mean. This was a different situation. She swung the mug at the other side of Zanna's head and just missed as the woman twisted away and fell again. Lacey heard another cough somewhere in the half light of the newsroom.

"Who's out there? I hear you coughing!" Lacey called to the office at large. Zanna scrambled to her feet, staggering and making guttural noises.

"It's Tamsin Kerr, Lacey. Quite a show, I must say."

"For God's sake, call the police, Tamsin! Call the guard desk! Call somebody!"

"Right. Sorry, I was doing that, but I became rather riveted by the action. Taking notes, actually."

"Notes? On what? What are you waiting for?"

"Well, my cue, of course."

"This is it! Go! Call!"

Zanna was on her feet again and charging. Lacey retreated behind her desk. In a fury Zanna swept everything off the desktop, notebooks and newspapers, pens and markers, phonebooks and framed photos, and the galleys of *Terror at Timberline*. Lacey dodged out of the way of flying debris, slipping into the gap between the cubicles, hers and Felicity's. Zanna circled, swinging her stiletto heel like a scythe. Her eye was caught by the sight of the pink angel food cloud cake on Felicity's desk, still waiting to be consumed.

Such was the strange power of Felicity's rosy pink confection, Zanna stopped for a split second to contemplate the cake. She raised her empty hand toward the tower of pink icing. Lacey watched, fascinated. Was she going to stop in mid attack to eat a piece of cake? No. She plunged her fist into the middle of Felicity's half-eaten dessert, grabbed a gooey pink hunk of angel food cake and lobbed it at Lacey's face. Lacey ducked, but it landed with a splat in her hair and hung there. Zanna found this amusing.

Lacey wiped a sticky glob of cake and icing out of her hair and threw it back at Zanna. It caught her full in the face. Zanna gasped and staggered backwards. Lacey took another handful of cake and smashed it into Zanna's face and hair. Someone started to laugh in the background. Zanna was not nearly so amused now. She wiped pink icing from her eyes, bared her teeth, and lunged at Lacey with her stiletto heel.

Lacey sidestepped her lunge. Zanna slashed wildly with the heel and managed to graze Lacey's left upper arm. It drew blood, it hurt like hell, and it ripped the sleeve of her vintage white bolero. Lacey looked down at her torn sleeve, aghast.

"Oh no, you don't! I like this jacket!" She body-slammed Zanna as hard as she could. Her mug tumbled to the floor, but she leaned sideways and picked it up, curling her fist around the handle. Zanna slammed her back, Lacey grabbed Zanna's hair, and they staggered together. The struggling women swept the pink cake off Felicity's desk and rolled onto the floor with it, grappling like mud wrestlers in the smashed cake and icing. Lacey lost her grip on the mug again.

She managed to knock the black-and-silver shoe out of Zanna's grip with one foot, another ninja move she'd never dreamed of in high school. After a split-second decision *not* to grab the shoe and crack Zanna's skull open with it, Lacey kicked it under a desk. She slapped Zanna hard across the face and stood back, panting.

Zanna seemed to be speaking a foreign language. There were only gasps and nonsense syllables. She pulled herself up onto her hands and knees and panted for air. Lacey backed away from her on the sticky floor to catch her own breath. In the background, Tamsin could be heard raising her voice, talking excitedly to someone on the phone.

"No, I told you, I can't stay on the line any longer! I have to watch this. I have a review to write. No. I am on deadline. Well, you can tell that to Detective Broadway Lamont. Yes, that's what I said. He's in Homicide. Lamont is who we usually deal with for this sort of thing. Tell him to come to the offices of *The Eye Street Observer*. Right away. And send an ambulance too. *Eye Street Observer*. What? Seriously?" Tamsin sighed loudly, dramatically. "Good. God. Obviously, it's on Eye Street, you imbecile. At Farragut Square. Yes, it's a newspaper, and if you don't arrive before blood is spilled, there will be a huge, outraged story in tomorrow morning's paper about your department's woeful failures in emergency response and customer service."

There was a pause, and then Tamsin continued. "That is correct.

I guarantee it. Have you heard the saying: Never argue with people who buy ink by the barrel?" There was another pause. "Yes, that's a real saying! Look it up when you learn to read. Right. Assault. Battery. Whatever you call it. Murder in progress. Make that attempted murder. Oh, this is ridiculous, just get somebody with a gun and a badge over here! I want to hear sirens screaming in two seconds! I am putting this phone down right *now*."

Lacey scrambled to her feet and picked up the now-empty coffee mug. It was her favorite FASHION *BITES* mug. She didn't want it to get broken. She gazed around at the damage. The newsroom was a disaster. She scanned the debris for the green silk, thinking she could use it to tie Zanna up until somebody arrived with handcuffs.

Zanna seemed to be coming back to her senses. She dragged herself to her feet, shaking her head, and suddenly lurched toward Lacey, her empty hands outstretched like claws. She raked her fingernails across Lacey's cheek. Lacey felt the sting of her nails as they drew blood. Blood dripped down her face.

"Your face is a mess, fashion reporter." Zanna stretched out her claws again. "Wanna turn the other cheek? A matching scar, that's what you need. Besides, who cares what a *print* reporter looks like?"

Lacey wiped her face and looked at her bloodstained hand.

"You broadcast bitch. I will take you down."

Zanna lunged again, slashing at the air with her nails. Lacey dodged. She narrowed her eyes and took a deep breath. She gripped the mug's handle in her right hand. Lacey had never played baseball, or even softball, except when a high school gym teacher was making her go through the motions, but now she assumed the pitcher's position. She drew back her right arm. She aimed and swung, followed through with good form, mug still in hand like an extended fist, and released her missile.

FASHION *BITES* connected with the side of Zanna's head with a loud hollow *smack*. Her eyes went wide and rolled back in her head. She opened her mouth to scream, but no sound came out. She crumpled to the floor in a heap.

It was quiet in the newsroom.

Lacey stood still, feeling her heart beat hard and fast against her chest wall. She tried to catch her breath, while watching to make sure Zanna didn't rise again. She picked up her mug. The handle was broken, but her shaking hand was ready to pitch again, if need be.

"Is she dead?" Tamsin Kerr crept closer, notebook in hand,

curious to see whether there would be a curtain call.

"I don't think so. She's breathing."

"Well done. This isn't the kind of thing I often see on stage. Would have improved tonight's show."

"Stage fighting is choreographed with a little more precision," Lacey agreed, still panting.

"But much less passion," Tamsin said. "The raw, ragged emotions on display here tonight were very compelling to experience live. I probably wouldn't have believed it in the theatre. I might have thought it was too artfully contrived to be quite real. But in real life, it was, well, very realistic. Most notably discharged, Lacey. By the way, you're bleeding. A little."

Lacey wiped her cheek again and smeared the blood. It stung. She heard the noise of more people heading their way. The late-shift editors finally ambled into the newsroom from across the hall, coffee cups in hand, wondering what on earth was going on. Sirens and police cars could be heard racing toward *The Eye*. The sound of feet pounding down the corridor in their direction grew louder. Lacey looked up.

Vic and Turtledove were running through the door toward her. Vic reached for his handcuffs, while Turtledove flipped Zanna face-down like a rag doll. Vic cuffed her to the infamous Mariah Death Chair. Zanna was semi-conscious again, but she seemed dazed and began to cry. Turtledove squatted by her silently. Vic ignored her and reached for Lacey.

"My God, Lacey." Vic held her tight, then pulled her into the light and gently stroked her face. "Did she do that? Are you okay?"

"My arm is killing me. And my face hurts." She held on to him as tight as she could with one good arm. "She smashed my phone. And I broke my favorite mug. Other than that—"

"You don't understand," Zanna sobbed. "She tried to kill me. With the deadly silk. Just like she killed Courtney Wallace. It's not me! It's her!"

"Shut up, lady." Turtledove looked disgusted that he'd missed the intruder. "How'd this piece of trash get in, anyway? I never took my eyes off this building. I watched every door and window. And why didn't you answer the phone, Lacey?"

"The garage," she said. "The door down there is locked, but she flirted her way in. According to her. And I tried to get the phone, but, well, things happened."

Detective Lamont thundered down the hall, making the floor shake. Lacey could hear him coming the moment he got off the elevator. He was followed by a mob of uniformed cops and emergency personnel. Lamont stopped short to take a long look at Lacey, the fight scene, and Zanna Nelson. He stared sadly at the layer of pink cake crumbs and icing and papers and desk detritus covering the floor. *Terror at Timberline* was scattered everywhere. He eyed Zanna Nelson, shackled to the Death Chair, sobbing and wailing and kicking her feet.

"Damn. I'm afraid this one's got psychiatric hold written all over her," he said.

SMITHSONIAN HOOKS BROADCASTER KILLER
DRAMATIC SHOWDOWN AT EYE STREET OBSERVER
By Tamsin Kerr, Observer Theatre Critic and Staff Writer

A new play opened on Fourteenth Street Tuesday night, but despite its attempt at shocking the audience, it could not hold a candle to the theatrical extravaganza witnessed by this critic at *The Eye Street Observer,* where in a late-night command performance fashion reporter Lacey Smithsonian captured the alleged killer of television personality Courtney Wallace.

Upon returning to *The Eye* to pen a review of the new show, *The Brain-Dead Monkey,* this critic happened upon the confrontation between Smithsonian and the suspect already in progress in the newsroom, around Smithsonian's work cubicle.

Zanna Nelson, an on-air employee of Channel One News, was arrested after the curtain by Metropolitan Police Detective Broadway Lamont, who responded to this critic's report of an ongoing disturbance and assault at the newspaper.

Nelson is expected to be arraigned tomorrow. The charges will include, but may not be limited to, murder, attempted murder, assault, battery, stalking, trespass, and vandalism, according to Detective Lamont. Overacting might be plausibly added to these charges.

Act One: Drama Links Green Silk With Murder
Smithsonian was the first investigator to connect the suspicious death of broadcaster Courtney Wallace to the toxic silk lining of the dress she wore to the White House Correspondents' Dinner, where Wallace collapsed and later died at George Washington University Hospital. Although a Metropolitan Police spokesman called Wallace's death an apparent accident, Smithsonian redoubled her investigation, based on her professional insight into the role of clothing in human behavior. Apparently alarmed by the accuracy of her subsequent news coverage in *The Eye Street Observer*, Nelson set her sights on silencing the fashion writer.

When an angry Nelson gained unauthorized access to the newspaper offices late Tuesday evening, Smithsonian first tried to talk the agitated suspect down. However, the more calm and reasonable the fashion reporter was, the more agitated Nelson became.

The suspect admitted that she knew the silk was toxic and that she supplied it to Wallace for her use in the dress with deliberate malicious intent, her motive pathological jealousy and envy, and further, that she now intended to murder Smithsonian. Her motivation for this attempted murder remains, to this reviewer, unsatisfying, as in so much current drama. Discovering plausible motivations for obviously deranged characters is a dramatic conundrum which has challenged playwrights from Shakespeare to Tennessee Williams, and beyond.

Nelson at times appeared incoherent and babbling. It is still unclear whether she was ill, insane, under the influence of drugs or chemicals, or giving an eccentric but undeniably powerful performance. This critic is inclined to credit her work with the terrifying intensity of madness or intoxication or both, while leaving the question of performance-enhancing drugs to the D.C. Crime Lab's toxicology section. Nelson spat her dialogue at Smithsonian in a style worthy of a young Meryl Streep, catching her breath raggedly and lurching from one bizarre rant to the next, which soon escalated into violence.

Act Two: Stiletto Meets Mug in Hand-to-Heel Combat

Nelson struck the first blow in the ensuing physical combat, attempting to strangle Smithsonian with a length of the poisoned silk. Smithsonian fought back valiantly, while this critic called the police and was detained on the phone for several minutes by an incredulous 911 dispatcher. It was riveting when Smithsonian leapt over her desk to press her counterattack. Nelson escalated her assault, even resorting to the antiquated dramatic trope of a food fight. Still, this tired bit of seriocomic stage business appeared fresh and compelling under the circumstances.

Nelson appeared to have gained the upper hand, wielding as her weapon a black-and-silver stiletto-heeled shoe with a sharp spike heel. The shoe was one of a pair worn by Courtney Wallace on the night of her death and was allegedly removed from her body by Nelson, presumably as a souvenir.

However, in self-defense Smithsonian launched a heavy ceramic mug (a promotional item available from *The Eye Street Observer*'s Web site) emblazoned with the title of her popular LifeStyle section column, FASHION *BITES*. The mug found its mark. And bite it did. FASHION *BITES* connected with her attacker's head, rendering the suspect unconscious and concluding the combat interlude of the drama. In the denouement, help soon arrived in the form of the Metropolitan Police, paramedics, and concerned citizens.

In the leading role, playing herself, Smithsonian delivered an exemplary performance as an investigative journalist under attack simply for pursuing the truth. Tentative at first, her characterization gained gravitas and authority as she rose to the challenge of creatively defending herself against a murderous assault by a madwoman.

At curtain, the entire cast had given their all and no curtain call was expected. This critic can confidently recommend this two-woman show as one of the most dramatic performances she has witnessed in Washington, but the production will not be held over for an extended run. This was, it is to be hoped, a once-in-a-lifetime event.

Kerr's Stars

The Eye Street Observer, untitled special performance: One night only.

Rating: Five Stars

The Brain-Dead Monkey at Thesaurus Theatre: Go only if you are the eponymous monkey or have excess brain cells you are willing to impair.

Rating: One and a Half Stars*
(*One-half star awarded for an unexpectedly amusing performance by the monkey.)

Chapter 42

LACEY SMITHSONIAN'S CAPTURE OF ZANNA Nelson was prominently played in the newspaper and its online edition for the rest of the week. It created a one-week's media sensation in Washington, bookended by a Presidential gaffe and a Mideast crisis.

Mac Jones was still trying to find out who allowed the theatre critic Tamsin Kerr to write a front-page "review" about the confrontation for the Wednesday early edition. None of the night editors or staff would admit to having seen it, edited it, or approved it. And yet there it was, big and bold, above the fold. Along with a photograph of Zanna Nelson in handcuffs, Lacey Smithsonian being attended by paramedics, and Broadway Lamont looking sternly about the debris-strewn newsroom.

"We write the news. We don't critique it," Mac muttered to anyone within earshot.

"I don't know, Mac," Tony said. "I would have paid to see that performance. And it got a great review."

Mac buried his face in his hands. "This is a newspaper. It's supposed to be the facts."

Tamsin Kerr was unapologetic. "It is the facts, Jones," she said. "And something more. My unique interpretation of the action and its meaning in a context our readers can appreciate: Entertainment. Comedy. Drama. Spectacle."

"Spectacle is about the right word for it. Circus is another. Who on earth, Kerr, or on this newspaper," Mac demanded, "told you that you could do this story the way you did it?"

"Who can say, Jones? Memory fails. It was a beehive of journalistic activity here last night after Smithsonian's encounter with Nelson. You should have seen it, you'd be proud. The Production Department was in an uproar. Somebody down there was tearing apart the whole front page and remaking it around the attack at *The Eye*. Somebody said we needed to kill the *Brain-Dead Monkey* review for space. A mercy killing, if you ask me. Somebody suggested that, because I was an eyewitness, why not write what I saw, to tell our own story and scoop our competition. Why not, indeed? I caught the fever and flavor of the moment and communicated that to our readers in my own inimitable style," she told Mac.

"You're not a news reporter."

"No. I'm better than that. I am a critic. That is my job, Jones. I gave *The Eye*'s dramatic confrontation five stars, by the way. I never give five stars. Think about *that*." She stalked out of the newsroom, majestically as usual.

Mac stood there scratching his head and fuming. "Critics! Spare me from critics."

Lacey was fascinated (and slightly appalled) by Tamsin's take on her confrontation with Zanna. She was glad it appeared in *The Eye* first and scooped all the other media in town. It hit the wires and was picked up in print and online around the country and around the world, usually in some section resembling "News of the Weird." Proving yet again, Lacey told Harlan Wiedemeyer, that every news organization in the world had some poor bastard working a beat just like his Death and Dismemberment beat. He shrugged: It went without saying.

Lacey's feature article explaining the origin of the dress, its journey to becoming a weapon in Zanna Nelson's hands, and the aftermath of Courtney's death, appeared the following day. The two-page spread featured a wealth of interviews and photographs, including the vintage *Mademoiselle* picture of debutante Betty Lionsgate in the stunning black gown with its original white lining, and Hansen's best shot of Courtney in the Madame X dress with the deadly green lining at the White House Correspondents' Dinner. There were also pictures of the silk scraps next to Nadine's painting on green silk and the postcard from Jillian Hopewell's art show at the gallery in Old Town.

A sidebar on the fate of Hopewell's paintings that were shown at the Old Town exhibit was also added to the mix for the later edition. While most of Hopewell's works were painted on canvas, those too were strongly suspected of containing Paris Green pigment in her self-mixed paint. They had all been purchased. *The Eye* was attempting to contact the buyers, but not all of them had been tracked down yet. One of the known buyers, who was happy to speak with Lacey, was a former KGB spy turned adventurer and soldier of fortune, Gregor Kepelov. He was now on the trail of one of the silk paintings himself. Acting, he said, on behalf of a major museum with an interest in crime. Big Mike, Nadine told Lacey, was hanging onto his painting in the hope of the price going higher.

Felicity was in mourning. She mourned the senseless loss of

cake, her Pink Sky Angel Food Cloud Cake.

Lacey kept her promise to Eric Park and gave him an on-air interview for Channel One News after *The Eye* broke its story. It was the least she could do for him for leaking the clip, and it was well received, raising his profile at the station. Channel One News tried to treat the story as if its own reporters had broken it in partnership with Smithsonian. However, it took some dancing on their part to finesse what they said about Zanna Nelson. The station first described her as a "part-time, swing-shift employee." They then corrected that description to "former short-term employee."

As for Zanna Nelson, she was locked up on a psychiatric hold pending her eventual transfer to jail and trial for murder and other charges. While Nelson cooled her heels in the mental ward, *The Eye*'s health editor produced a lengthy article on the potentially corrosive effects of envy in the workplace, particularly in a place like the District of Columbia where the hard-charging workaholic lifestyle reigned, and where mental illness could masquerade under any number of guises. Until it was too late.

Not to be outdone, Channel One produced an on-air feature with a psychiatrist about the warning signs of imminent workplace violence. They said there were no red flags in Zanna Nelson's work history, but they used her breakdown and alleged crimes as a cautionary tale. Lacey wasn't sure whether this feature was a naked grab for viewers' eyeballs, exploiting the news hook of their "family tragedy," or genuine guilt that this had happened in their own corrosively toxic workplace. *Probably all of the above.*

Damon Newhouse lauded Smithsonian's counterattack, and he also reported on DeadFed that Zanna Nelson was thought to be a tool of a larger conspiracy to infiltrate the television news with mind-controlled killer zombies. He named several other well-known Washington on-air personalities as suspected zombies and promised to blow the lid off this story in future articles.

Lacey hoped Nelson would just plead guilty, so everyone could avoid endless courtroom proceedings and lawyerly shenanigans. Brooke retorted that "lawyerly shenanigans" were her stock in trade, and in fact a high art. Nelson's public defender was giving no hints about her strategy, but an insanity defense was considered possible.

Detective Broadway Lamont promised Lacey, when she was feeling up to it, that he would personally escort her to the medical examiner's office to visit the by-now infamous Madame X dress, still locked up in a secure evidence room. The dress might be released back to the family eventually—or not, now that it was evidence in a murder case. But Lacey would be allowed to view it, as long as she promised not to touch anything, or wreck anything, or tune in to any "fashion voodoo." Lacey agreed. Courtney's dress probably wouldn't tell her anything she didn't already know, she realized, but perhaps it would set her mind at rest. And it would let her see the end of the story.

"I told you not to get blood on those galleys," Mac said to Lacey late Wednesday.

"There's just a little. Sorry."

"Guess I didn't mention not getting dirt and cake and pink frosting on them either," he said.

"You didn't. And it was in a good cause."

"It's always in a good cause with you."

He dropped a fresh print of the *Terror at Timberline* galleys on Lacey's desk. He informed her that, attack or no attack, he still needed it read and returned by Friday. Lacey informed him Friday was good for her, but it would have to be some other future Friday, because she was not working late nights alone in *The Eye*'s newsroom ever again. Mac just snorted and stomped away.

By the end of the week, Lacey was finally sleeping well at night again and the scratches on her shoulders and face were healing. She wasn't thinking very much about the Lethal Black Dress, or Paris Green, or Zanna Nelson. She dwelled on the aftermath—the sweet aftermath—with Vic.

გ

And yet for Vic, the immediate aftermath, that very night, had been bittersweet. He was glad Lacey was safe, but he felt terrible that he hadn't made it there in time to prevent the fight. He was a block or two from *The Eye* when Turtledove called to report that Lacey wasn't answering either her desk phone or her cell. Vic arrived just as Turtledove entered the lobby and they charged upstairs together. Turtledove was also feeling remorseful about not checking the parking garage entrance, which he, and everyone at *The Eye*, thought was secure. Though he admitted he might not have suspected quiet, pretty Zanna was a potential assailant. No one else had either.

Lacey had tried to reassure both of them that night, after the fight, after the uniformed cops took their statements and departed with their suspect in custody, leaving them in the wreckage of the newsroom with Broadway Lamont and the crime scene techs.

"I really only suspected her tonight, myself. Right before she showed up here."

"Looks like you beat her up pretty good," Turtledove said. "Without us." He looked pretty miserable himself.

"But who's going to look better in the morning?" Lacey knew she bruised easily, but she wasn't sure Zanna would even carry a mark. *Maybe a lump on her head where I mugged her.*

Vic wiped her scratched face with something that stung from the office first aid kit. The paramedics had already bandaged her arm.

"That woman isn't your typical killer," he said. "She wasn't even on my radar."

"Ouch. No, she isn't typical. She killed one woman with a dress. She tried to kill me with a rock. And a shoe."

A shoe, Lacey noticed, that was just then being bagged for evidence, along with its mate and a tattered scarf of green silk. And her shattered cell phone. Lamont also instructed the tech to bag as evidence her favorite FASHION *BITES* mug. In two bags. The handle was broken.

"Shame," Lamont said. "That's my favorite mug to use when I visit over here."

"Will I get it back?"

"Get it back?" He just laughed.

Lacey made a mental note to have Mac order several more of her special mugs. Maybe she'd surprise Lamont with a new one. That would give the other homicide guys at his office something to talk about. Especially if she had them made in hot pink.

She pulled a mirror from her desk drawer and inspected the damage. There were three long bloody streaks across her cheek. She shuddered.

After Lacey was photographed from several angles for yet more evidence, Vic gently applied sterile surgical strips to her wounds. "I have to tell you, sweetheart, I'm very proud of you. You have a wicked pitch. Knocked her right out."

"As long as I have the power of Fashion Bites in my fist."

"Darling, I know this isn't the most romantic time and place for this. I'm sorry." He pulled a small velvet box from his pocket. "Seems like we haven't had too many quiet moments lately. But before anything else happens I want you to have this, if you'll still have me."

He offered the box to her. She opened it and caught her breath. Her engagement ring rested there, clean and sparkling and freshly resized. It looked much larger than she remembered it, with the substantial Donovan family diamond nestled in the gold filigree.

"Oh, Vic. It's beautiful. Oh my God."

"Will you marry me? Please." He slipped it on her finger and bent down on one knee. The diamond looked huge.

Lacey blinked back tears. She didn't know if she was laughing or crying. "Of course I'll marry you. I already said yes! Don't you remember?" She was laughing now, and he was too.

He had first proposed to her under a hail of bullets. Giving her the ring in the aftermath of this brush with death was not just fitting, it was perfect.

The ring looked right and felt right. It was unique. As unexpected as their love story. She leaned into him and kissed him hard, barely noticing that "Long Lens" Hansen had somehow materialized out of the gloom and was taking their photograph.

"I'm sorry about the surroundings," Vic said. "I was planning something a little, well, grander."

"But Vic, what could be grander? You and me at *The Eye* in the middle of the night? With cops bagging evidence, *Terror at Timberline* all over the floor, pink cake crumbs everywhere, icing stuck in my hair, and surgical tape on my face? Sweetheart, I wouldn't have it any other way."

About the author

ELLEN BYERRUM is a novelist, a playwright, a reporter, a former Washington, D.C., journalist, and a graduate of private investigator school in Virginia. Her Crime of Fashion mystery series stars a savvy, stylish female sleuth named Lacey Smithsonian. Lacey is a reluctant fashion reporter in Washington D.C., which she lovingly refers to as "The City Fashion Forgot."

Lacey longs to be taken seriously as a "hard news" reporter. But her nose for nuance, her eye for a great story, and her untamable talent for getting into trouble make her the perfect newshound for her newspaper's underappreciated Crime of Fashion beat. Her "ExtraFashionary Perception," her finely honed sense for what we tell the world through the way we dress, helps her solve crimes where others are clueless. In her vintage suits and killer heels, Lacey trips over fatal fashion clues, fabulous shoes, dangerous women, drop-dead men, and the occasional corpse (well-dressed or otherwise).

Fashion sleuth Lacey Smithsonian and her creator Ellen Byerrum have much personal history in common: a fondly remembered balcony view of the Potomac River, a love for vintage clothes, and a humorous viewpoint on life, love, mystery, and fashion.

And a window seat on the wild and wacky world of Our Nation's Capital. Follow Ellen Byerrum on the Web at **ellenbyerrum.com**.

Also by Ellen Byerrum

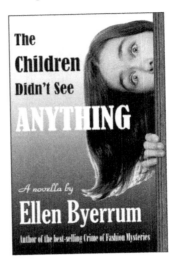

The Children Didn't See Anything

MEET INQUISITIVE EVANGELINE, one-half of the precocious twelve-year-old Bresette twins. It's just another summer vacation for them, swimming, squabbling, and coping with their lawyer parents—until a woman dies at their grandparents' country club. Evangeline notices the corpse is missing a pair of diamond earrings. Her twin brother, Raphael, would rather leave the worrying (and asking nosy questions) to the grown-ups, who assume the children didn't see anything and haven't got a clue. But Evangeline does have a clue—and *curiosity*.

This engaging preteen detective uses her wits (and her Barbie Doll Crime Scene Reconstruction Team) to puzzle out the mystery of the missing earrings and a death no one else believes is suspicious. Her search for justice proves far more dangerous than she suspected.

Written by the author of the best-selling Crime of Fashion Mysteries, this novella will charm middle grade and older readers. **The Children Didn't See Anything** is available now from Amazon in a Kindle Edition and is coming soon to Amazon as a trade paperback.

CPSIA information can be obtained at www.ICGtesting.com
Printed in the USA
LVOW04s2123260415

436196LV00012B/98/P